BASIL AND OREGANO™

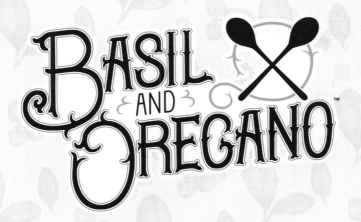

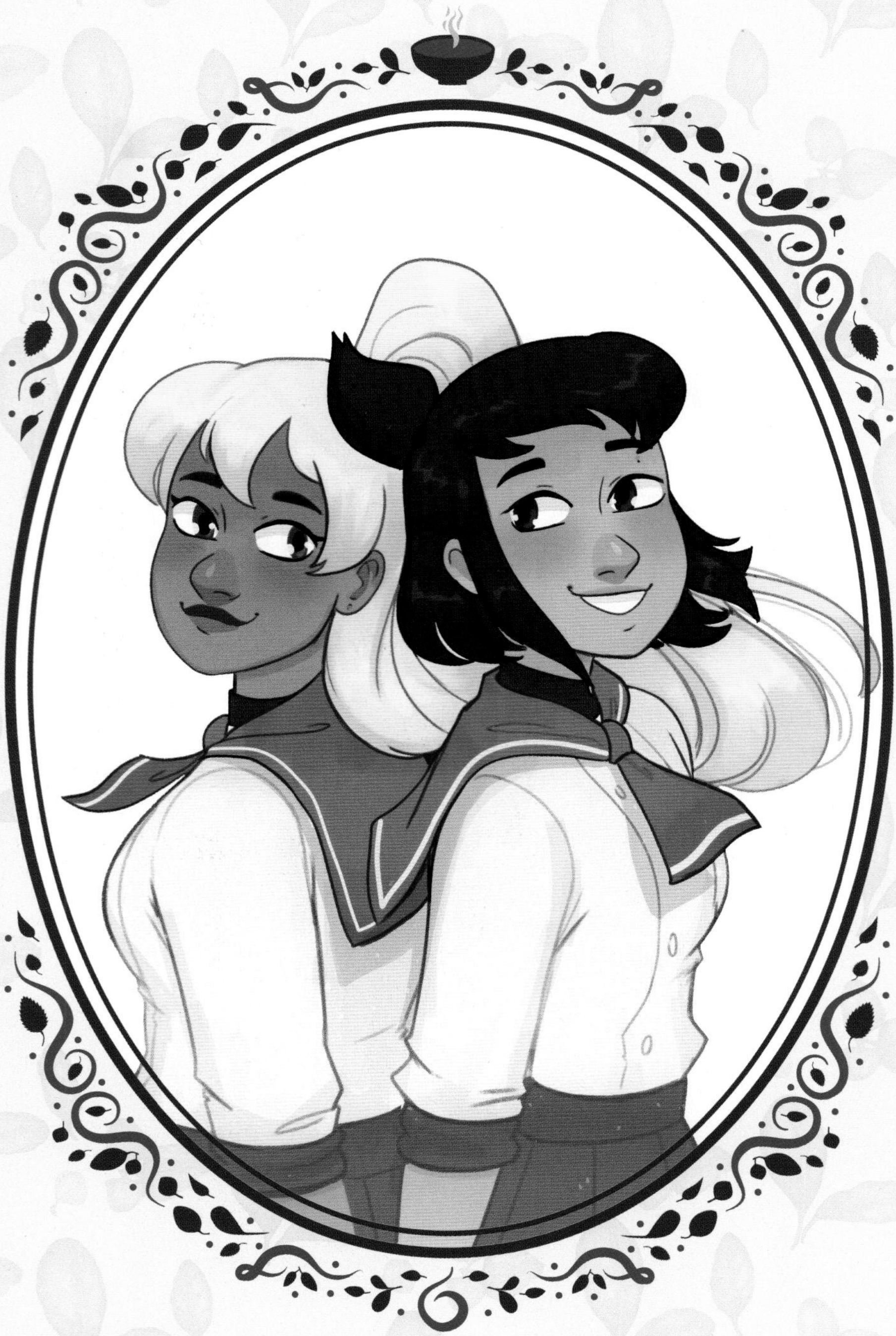

BASIL AND OREGANO™

Written and Drawn by
MELISSA CAPRIGLIONE

Letters and Flat Colors by
SARA TODD

Cover by
MELISSA CAPRIGLIONE

Muslim Sensitivity Reader:
FADWA (WORDWONDERS)

Dark Horse Books

President and Publisher **Mike Richardson**

Editor **Brett Israel**

Assistant Editor **Sanjay Dharawat**

Designer **Anita Magaña**

Digital Art Technician **Samantha Hummer**

Neil Hankerson, Executive Vice President • Tom Weddle, Chief Financial Officer • Dale LaFountain, Chief Information Officer • Tim Wiesch, Vice President of Licensing • Matt Parkinson, Vice President of Marketing • Vanessa Todd-Holmes, Vice President of Production and Scheduling • Mark Bernardi, Vice President of Book Trade and Digital Sales • Randy Lahrman, Vice President of Product Development and Sales • Ken Lizzi, General Counsel • Dave Marshall, Editor in Chief • Davey Estrada, Editorial Director • Chris Warner, Senior Books Editor • Cary Grazzini, Director of Specialty Projects • Lia Ribacchi, Art Director • Matt Dryer, Director of Digital Art and Prepress • Michael Gombos, Senior Director of Licensed Publications • Kari Yadro, Director of Custom Programs • Kari Torson, Director of International Licensing • Christina Niece, Director of Scheduling

Published by Dark Horse Books
A division of Dark Horse Comics LLC
10956 SE Main Street
Milwaukie, OR 97222

DarkHorse.com
To find a comics shop in your area,
visit comicshoplocator.com

First edition: May 2023
Trade Paperback ISBN 978-1-50672-870-4
Ebook ISBN 978-1-50672-871-1
10 9 8 7 6 5 4 3 2 1
Printed in China

Names: Capriglione, Melissa, author, artist.
Title: Basil and Oregano / created by Melissa Capriglione.
Description: First edition. | Milwaukie, OR : Dark Horse Books, 2023. | Audience: Ages 12+ | Summary: Basil Eyres and Arabella Oregano are both students of cooking with magic at Porta Bella Magiculinary Academy, and although the two are instantly smitten with each other, Arabella has a secret with the potential to throw Basil's future aspirations into jeopardy.
Identifiers: LCCN 2022001579 | ISBN 9781506728704 (trade paperback) | ISBN 9781506728711 (ebook)
Subjects: CYAC: Graphic novels. | Schools--Fiction. | Love--Fiction. | Cooking--Fiction. | Magic--Fiction. | Secrets--Fiction. | LCGFT: Coming-of-age comics. | Romance comics. | Graphic novels.
Classification: LCC PZ7.7.C365 Bas 2023 | DDC 741.5/973--dc23/eng/20220204
LC record available at https://lccn.loc.gov/2022001579

MIX
Paper from responsible sources
FSC® C109093

to sara

the basil to my oregano

Chapter
ONE

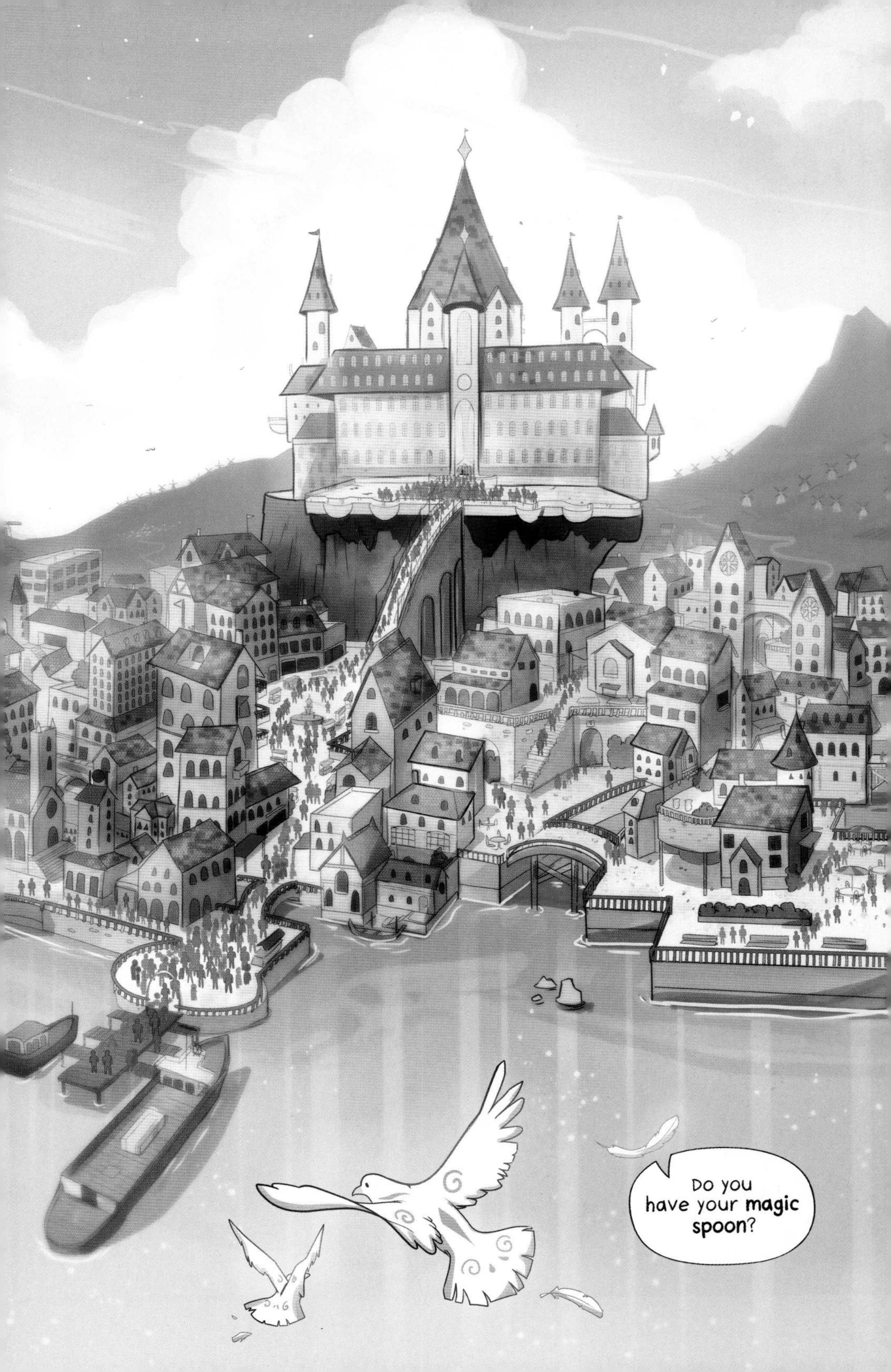
Do you have your **magic** spoon?

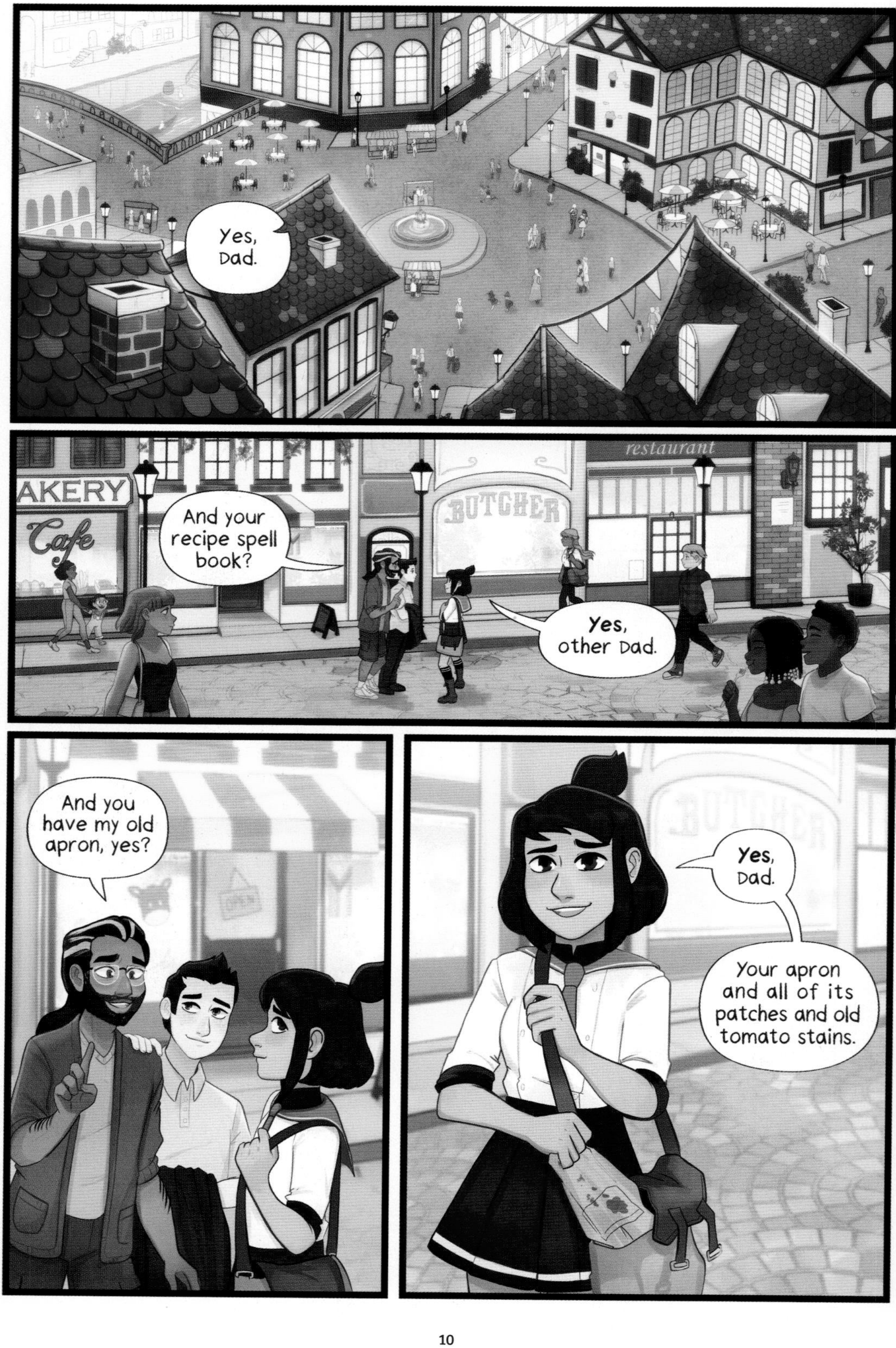
Yes, Dad.
AKERY
Cafe
BUTCHER
restaurant
And your recipe spell book?
Yes, other Dad.
And you have my old apron, yes?
OPEN
BUTCHER
Yes, Dad.
Your apron and all of its patches and old tomato stains.

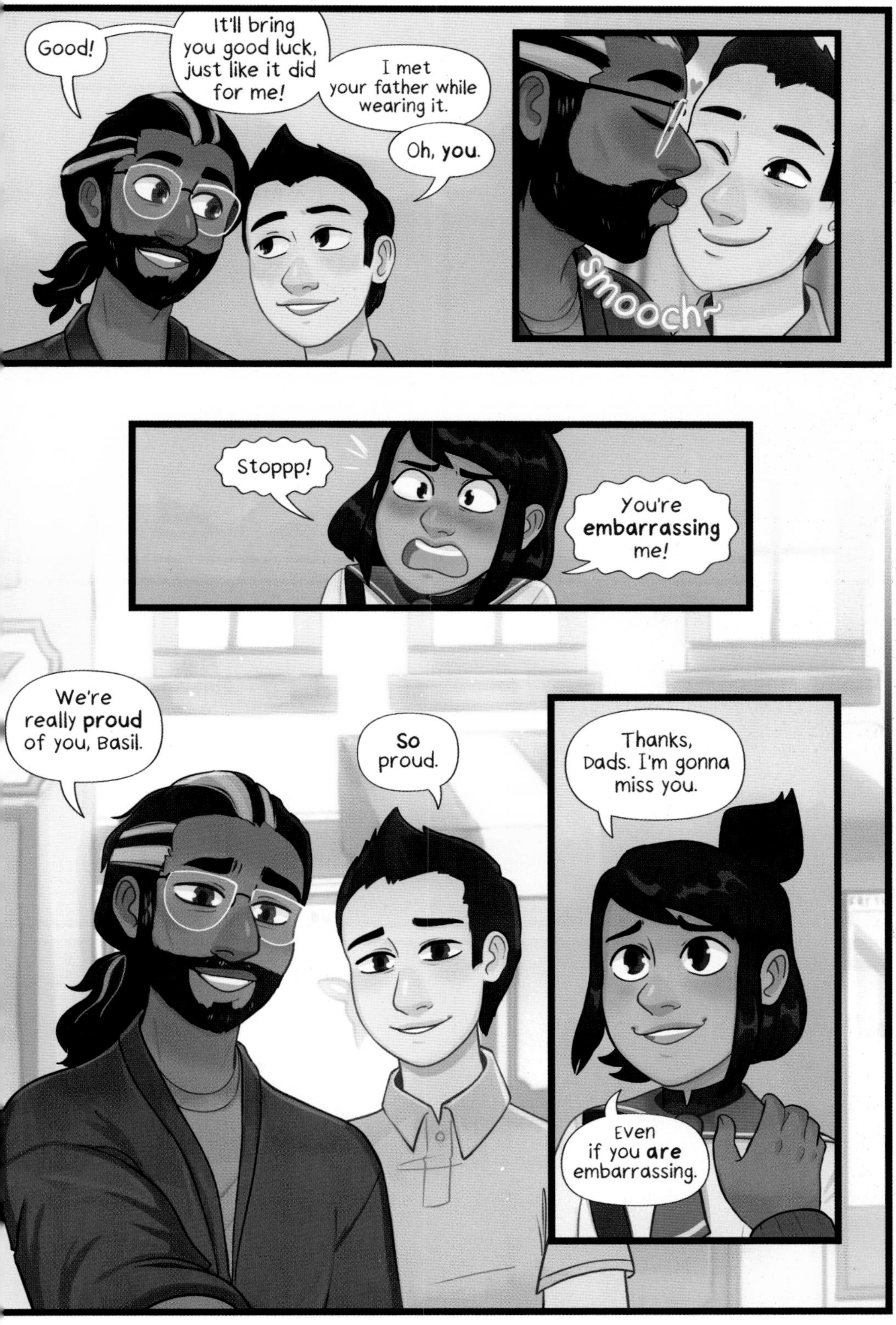
Good!
It'll bring you good luck, just like it did for me!
I met your father while wearing it.
Oh, you.
smooch~
Stoppp!
You're embarrassing me!
We're really proud of you, Basil.
So proud.
Thanks, Dads. I'm gonna miss you.
Even if you are embarrassing.

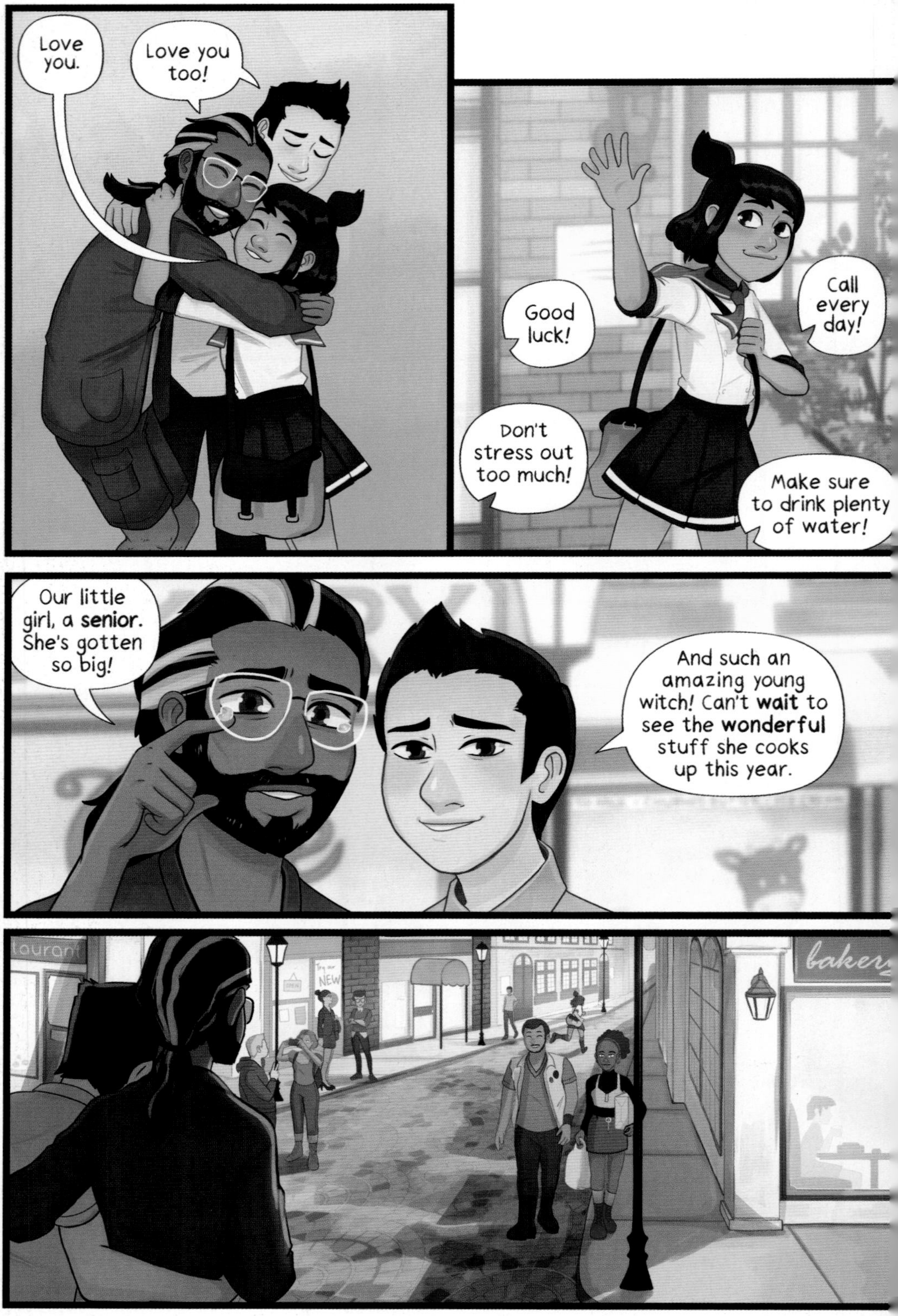
Love you.
Love you too!
Good luck!
Call every day!
Don't stress out too much!
Make sure to drink plenty of water!
Our little girl, a **senior**. She's gotten so big!
And such an amazing young witch! Can't **wait** to see the **wonderful** stuff she cooks up this year.
bakery

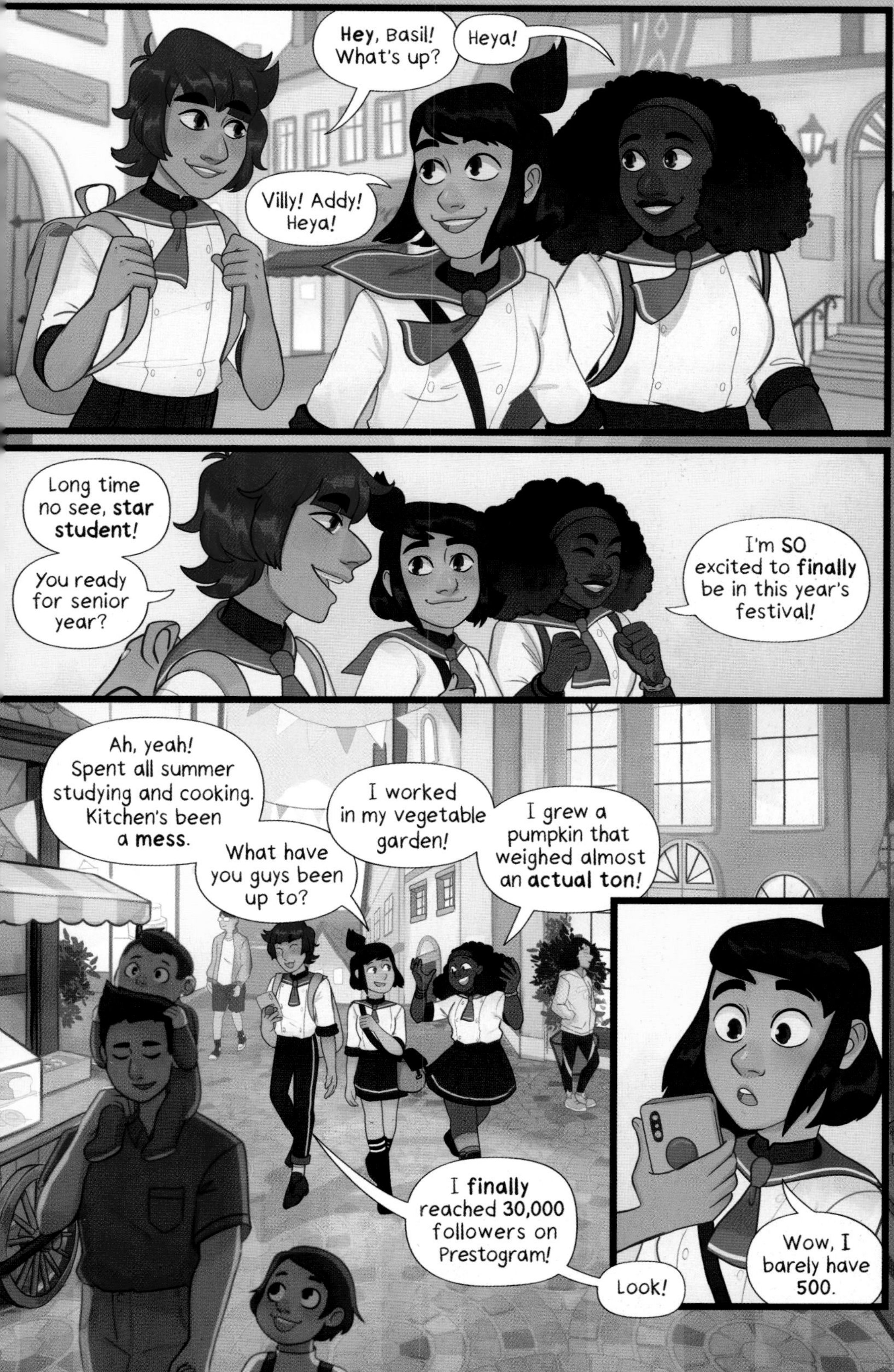
Hey, Basil! What's up?
Heya!
Villy! Addy! Heya!
Long time no see, star student!
You ready for senior year?
I'm SO excited to finally be in this year's festival!
Ah, yeah! Spent all summer studying and cooking. Kitchen's been a mess.
What have you guys been up to?
I worked in my vegetable garden!
I grew a pumpkin that weighed almost an actual ton!
I finally reached 30,000 followers on Prestogram!
Look!
Wow, I barely have 500.

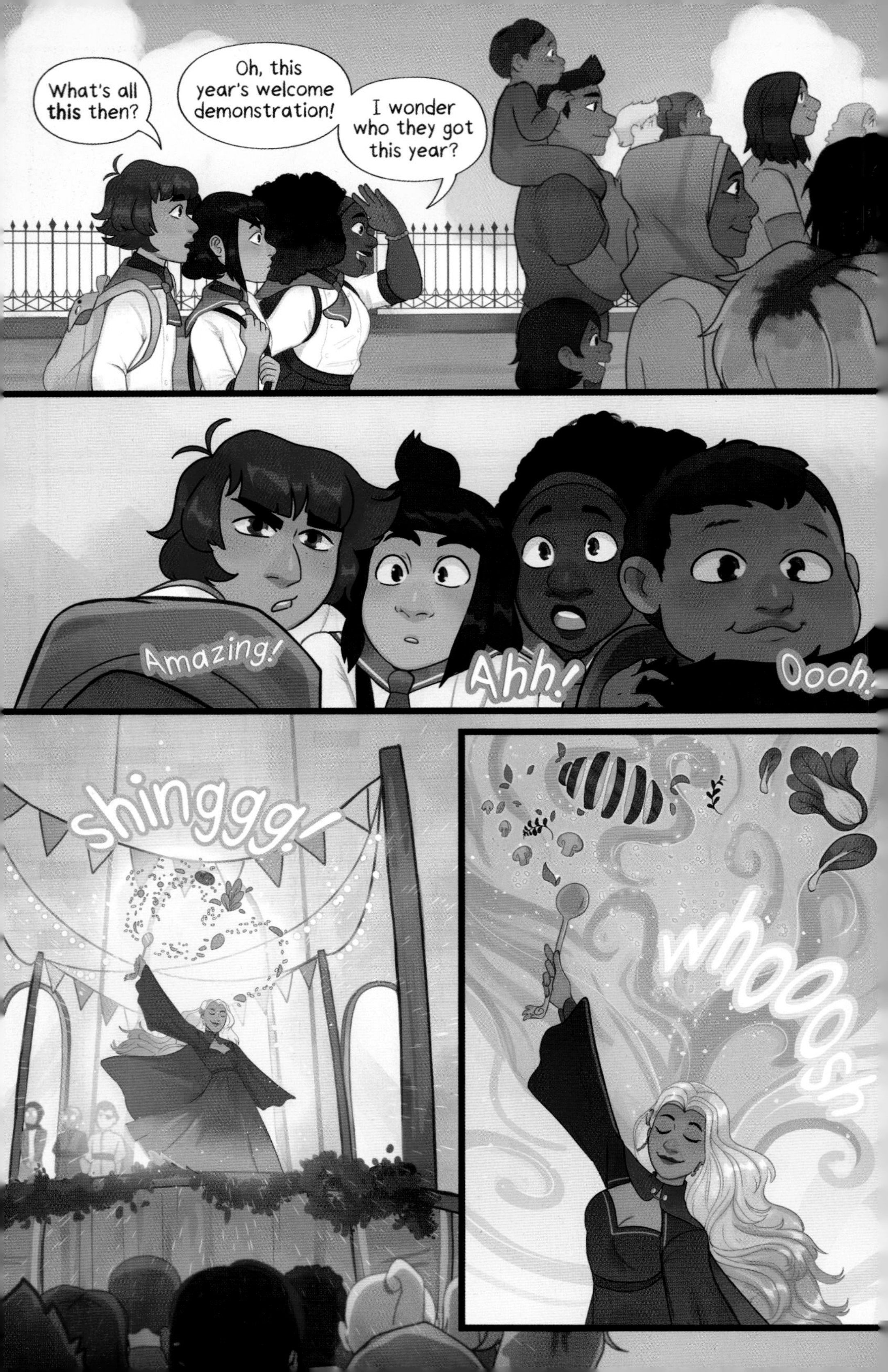
What's all **this** then?
Oh, this year's welcome demonstration!
I wonder who they got this year?
Amazing!
Ahh!
Oooh.
shinggg!
whooosh

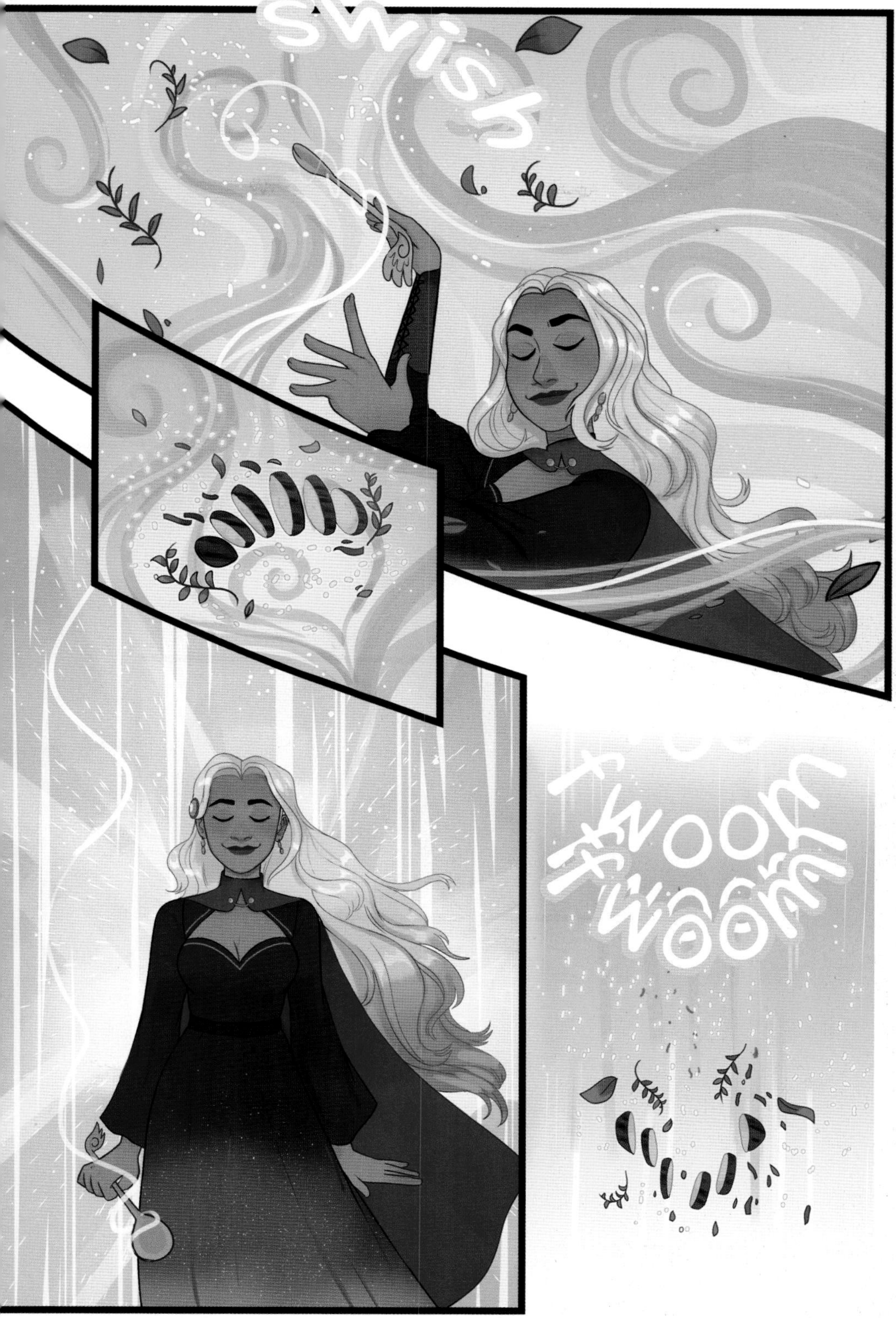
swish
fwoom
fwoom

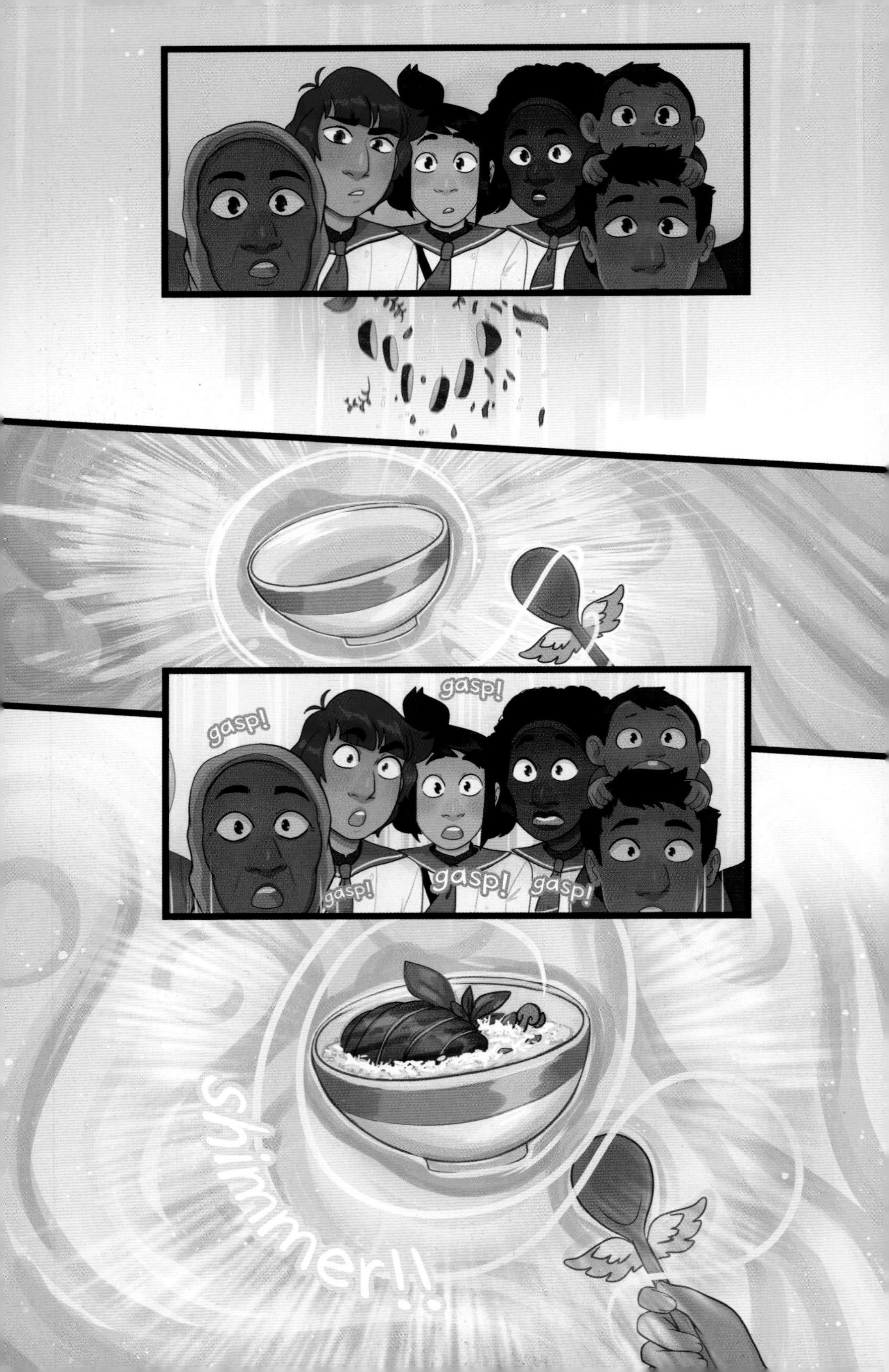
gasp!
gasp!
gasp!
gasp!
gasp!
shimmer!!

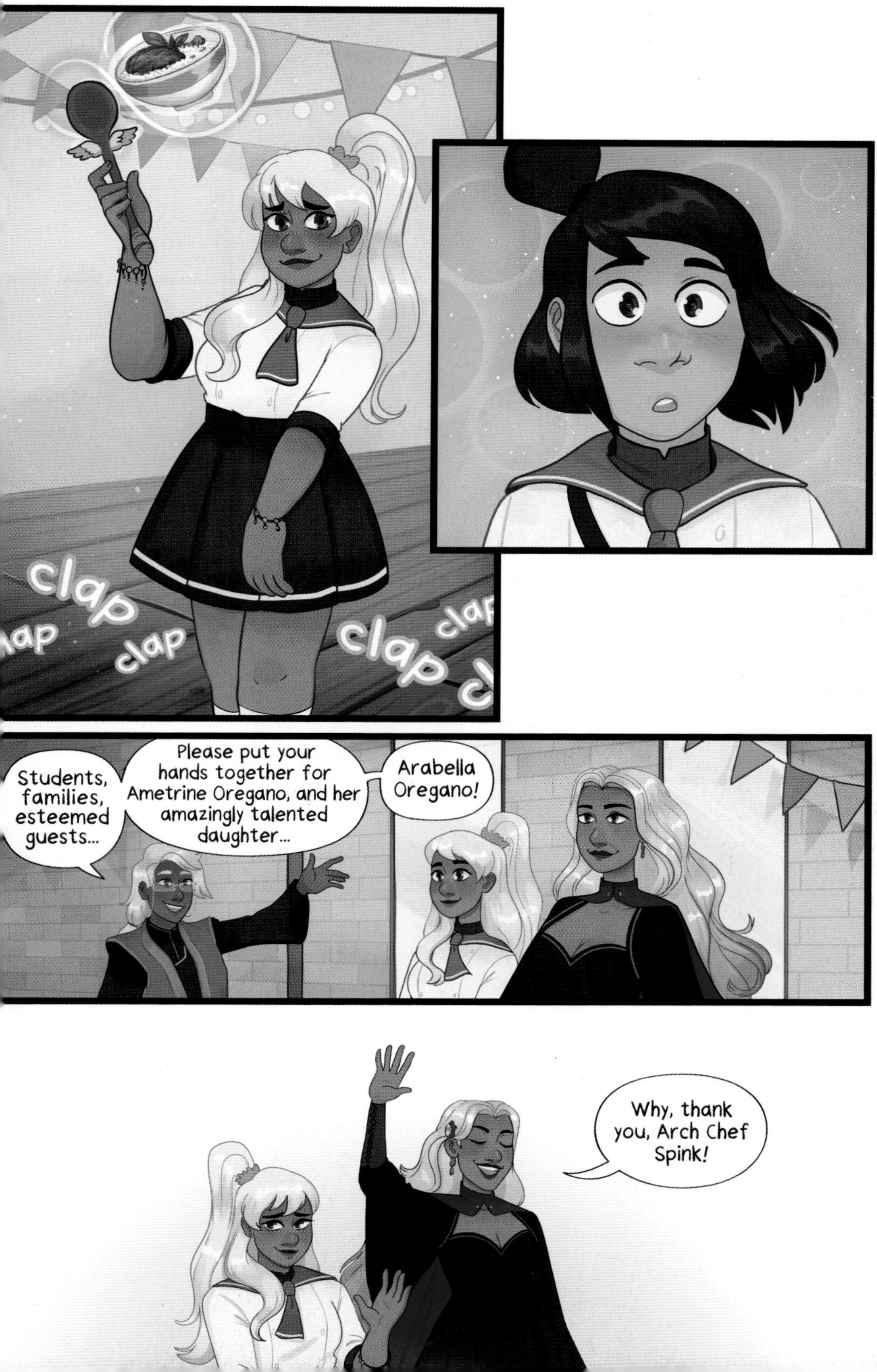
clap
clap
clap
clap
clap
Students, families, esteemed guests...
Please put your hands together for Ametrine Oregano, and her amazingly talented daughter...
Arabella Oregano!
Why, thank you, Arch Chef Spink!

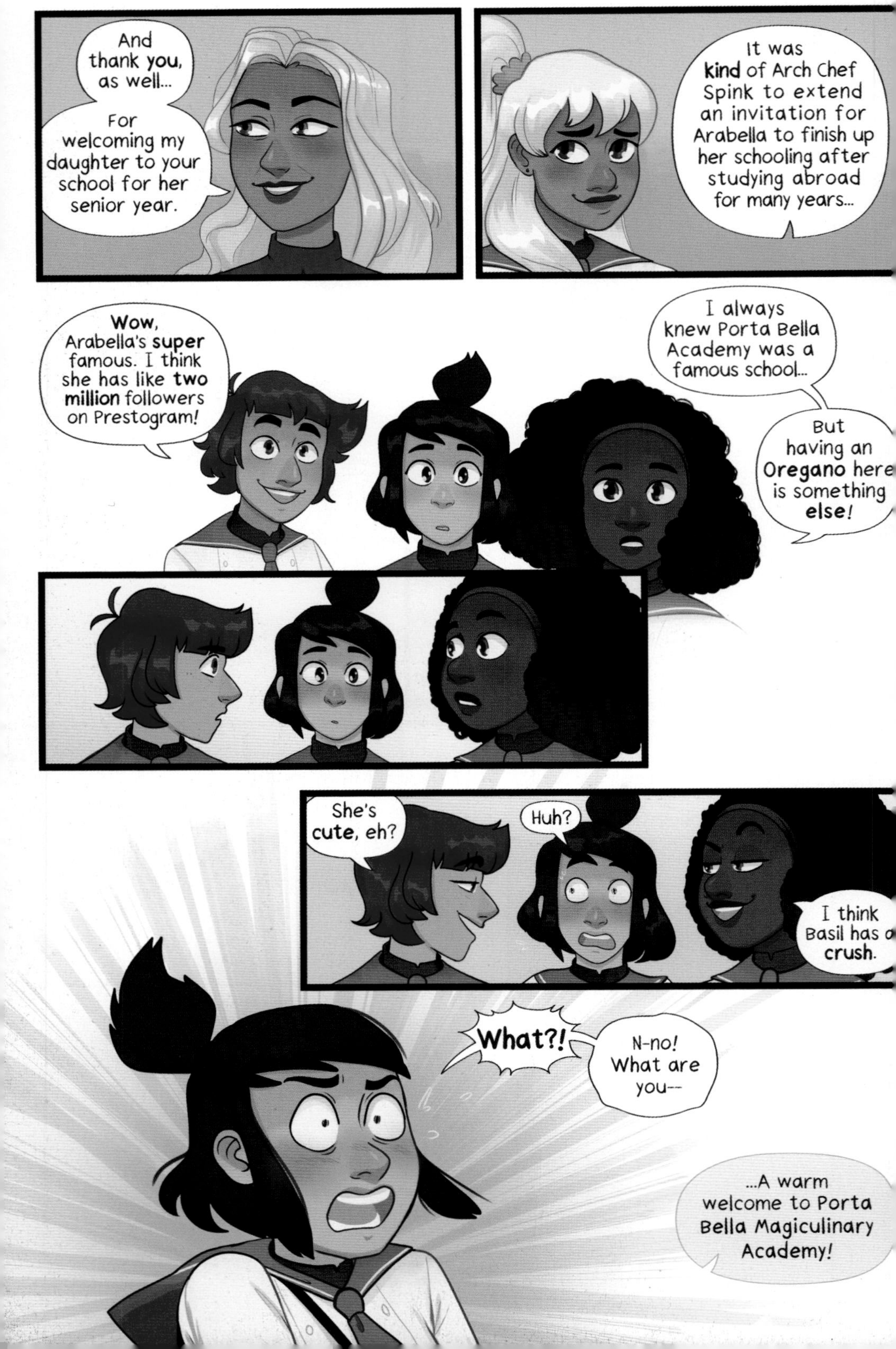
And thank **you**, as well...
For welcoming my daughter to your school for her senior year.
It was **kind** of Arch Chef Spink to extend an invitation for Arabella to finish up her schooling after studying abroad for many years...
Wow, Arabella's **super** famous. I think she has like **two million** followers on Prestogram!
I always knew Porta Bella Academy was a famous school...
But having an **Oregano** here is something **else**!
She's **cute**, eh?
Huh?
I think Basil has a **crush**.
What?!
N-no! What are you--
...A warm welcome to Porta Bella Magiculinary Academy!

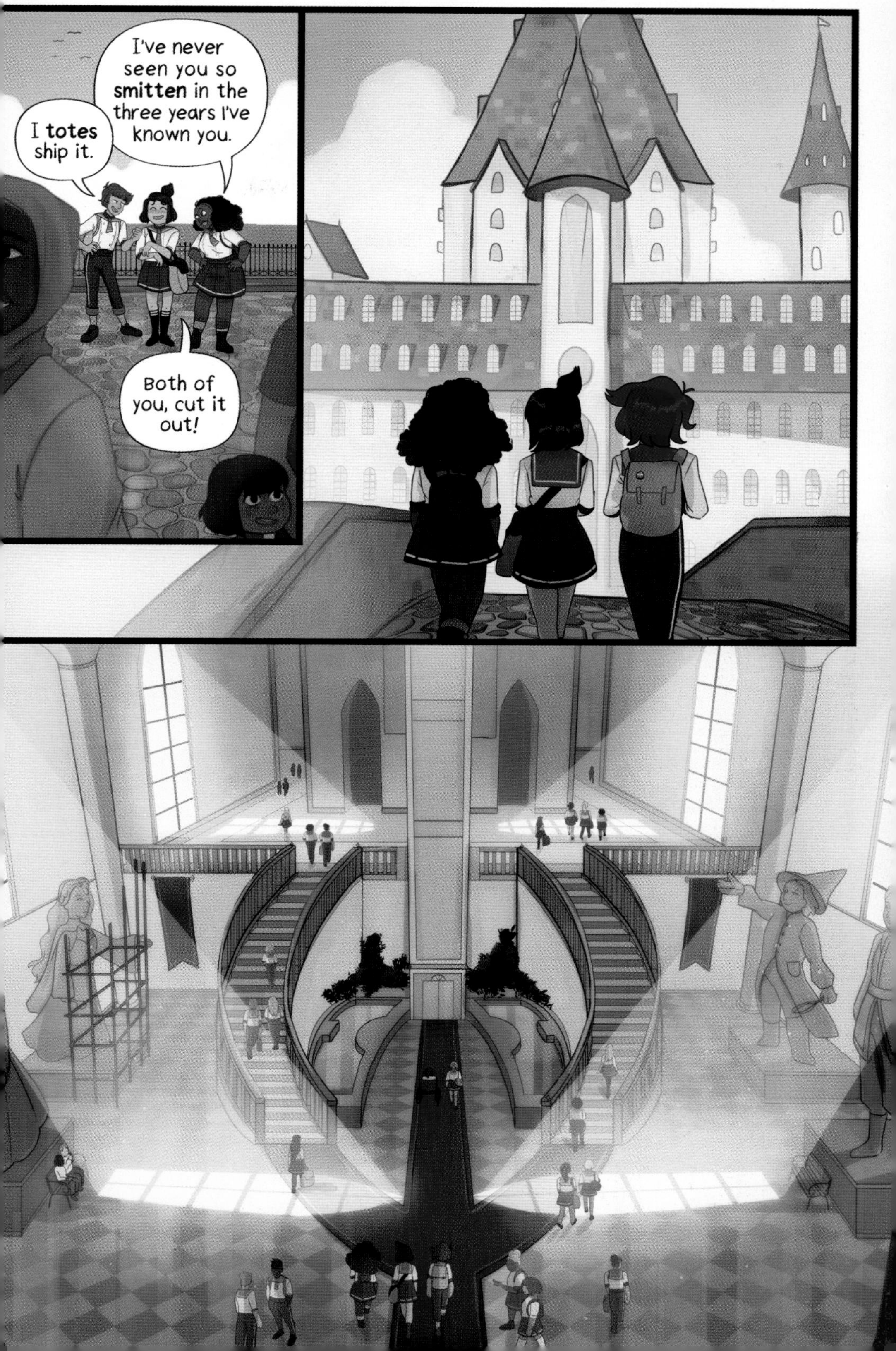
I've never seen you so **smitten** in the three years I've known you.
I **totes** ship it.
Both of you, cut it out!

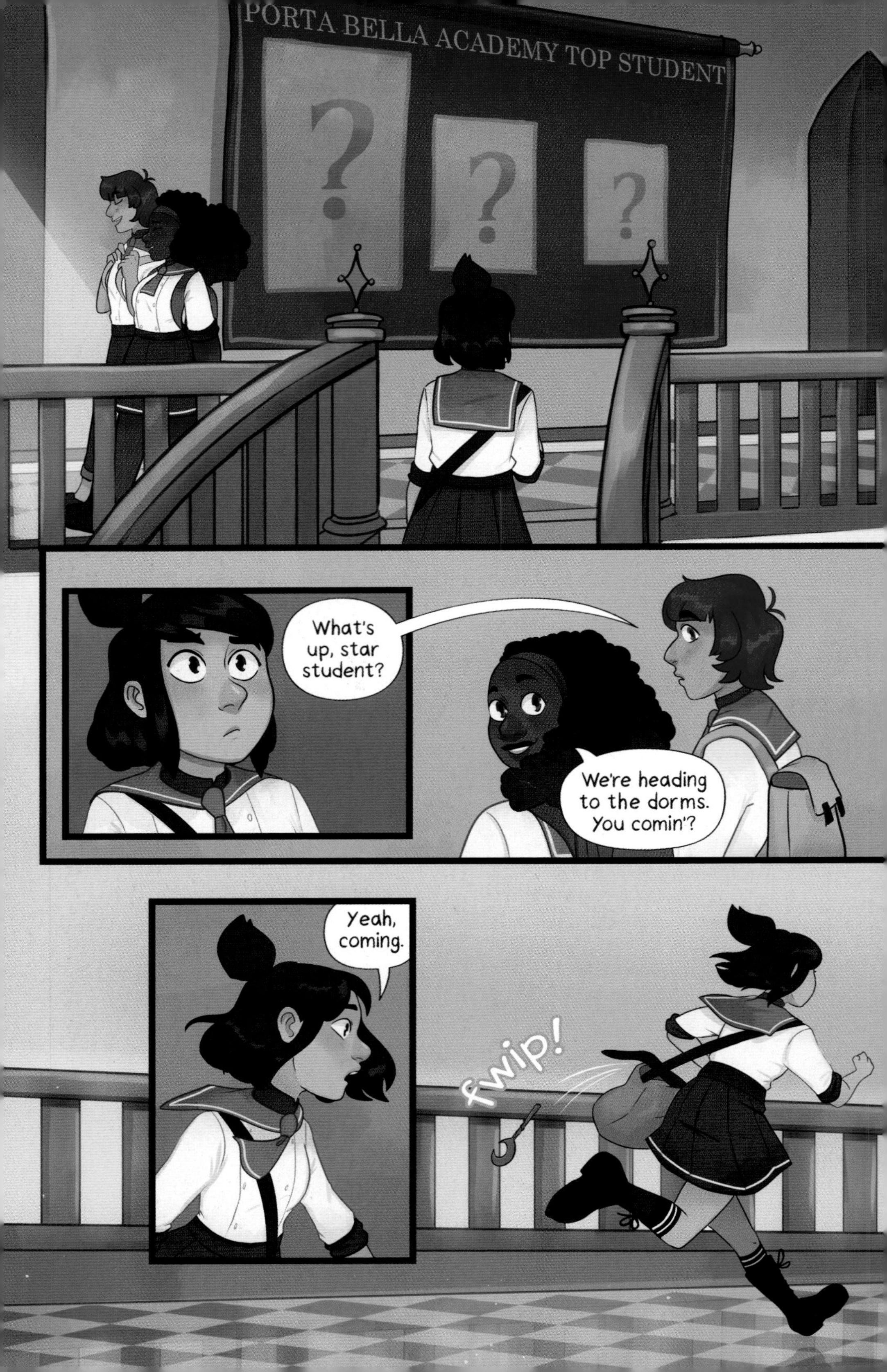
PORTA BELLA ACADEMY TOP STUDENT
What's up, star student?
We're heading to the dorms. You comin'?
Yeah, coming.
fwip!

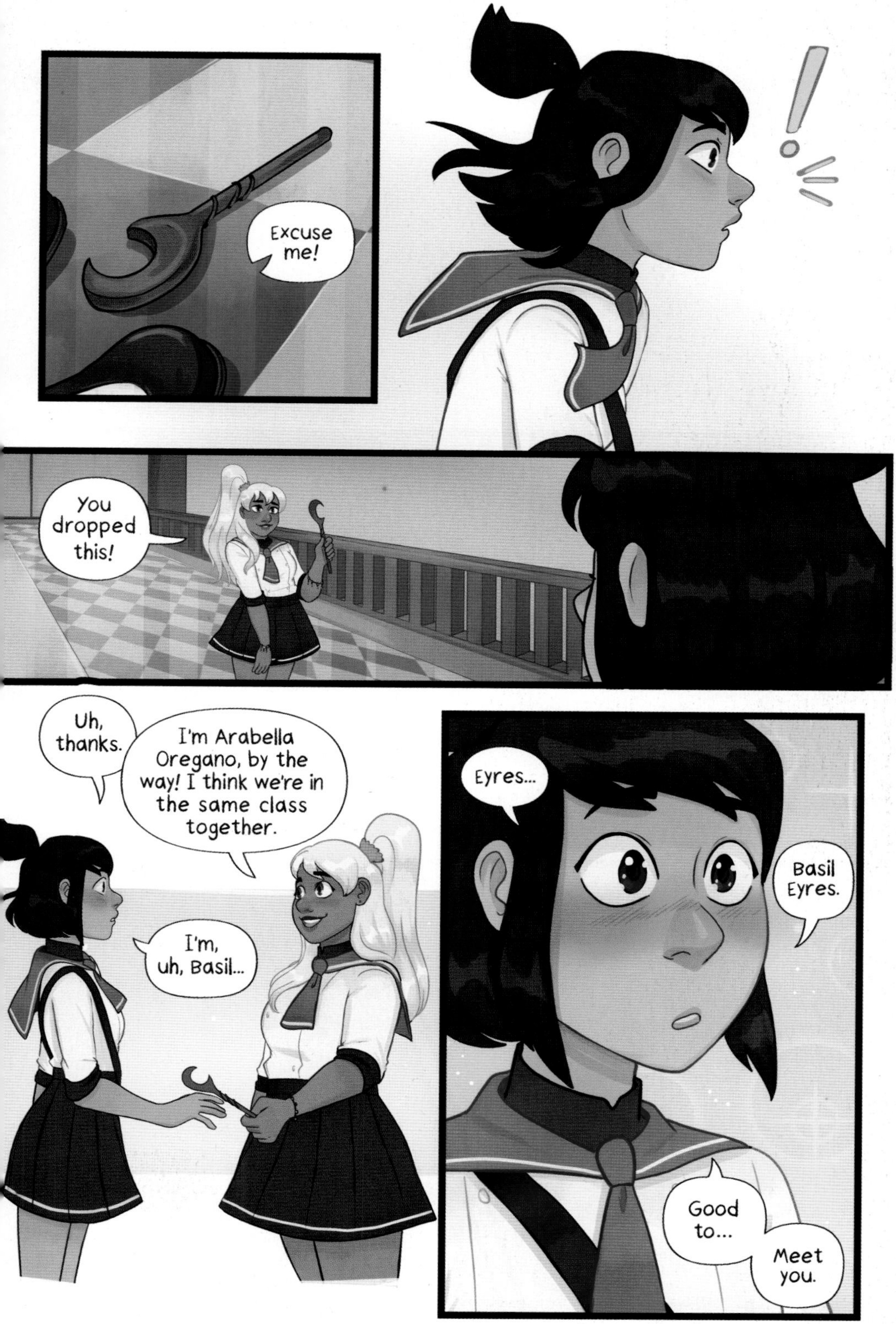

Excuse me!
!
You dropped this!
Uh, thanks.
I'm Arabella Oregano, by the way! I think we're in the same class together.
I'm, uh, Basil...
Eyres...
Basil Eyres.
Good to...
Meet you.

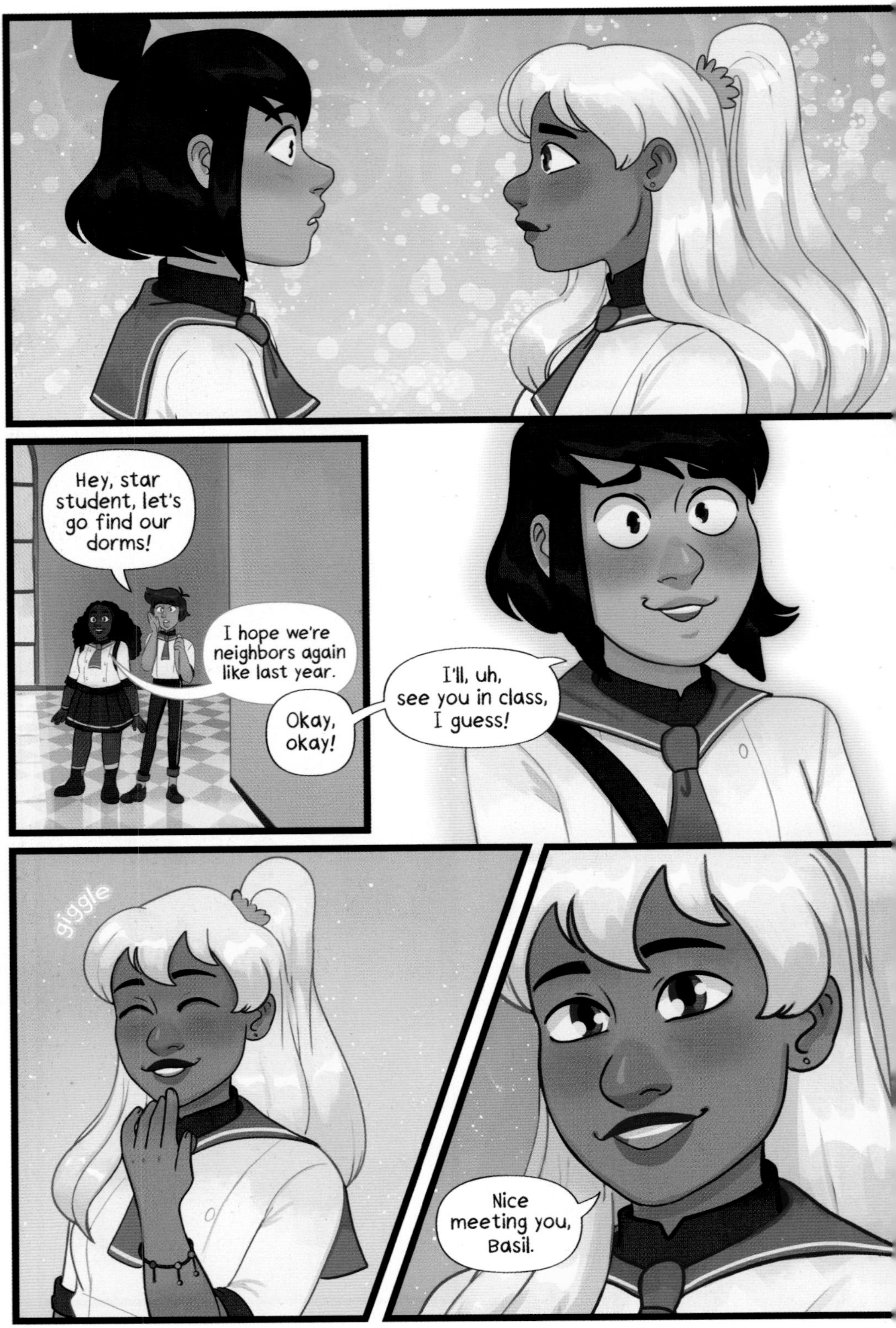
Hey, star student, let's go find our dorms!
I hope we're neighbors again like last year.
Okay, okay!
I'll, uh, see you in class, I guess!
giggle
Nice meeting you, Basil.

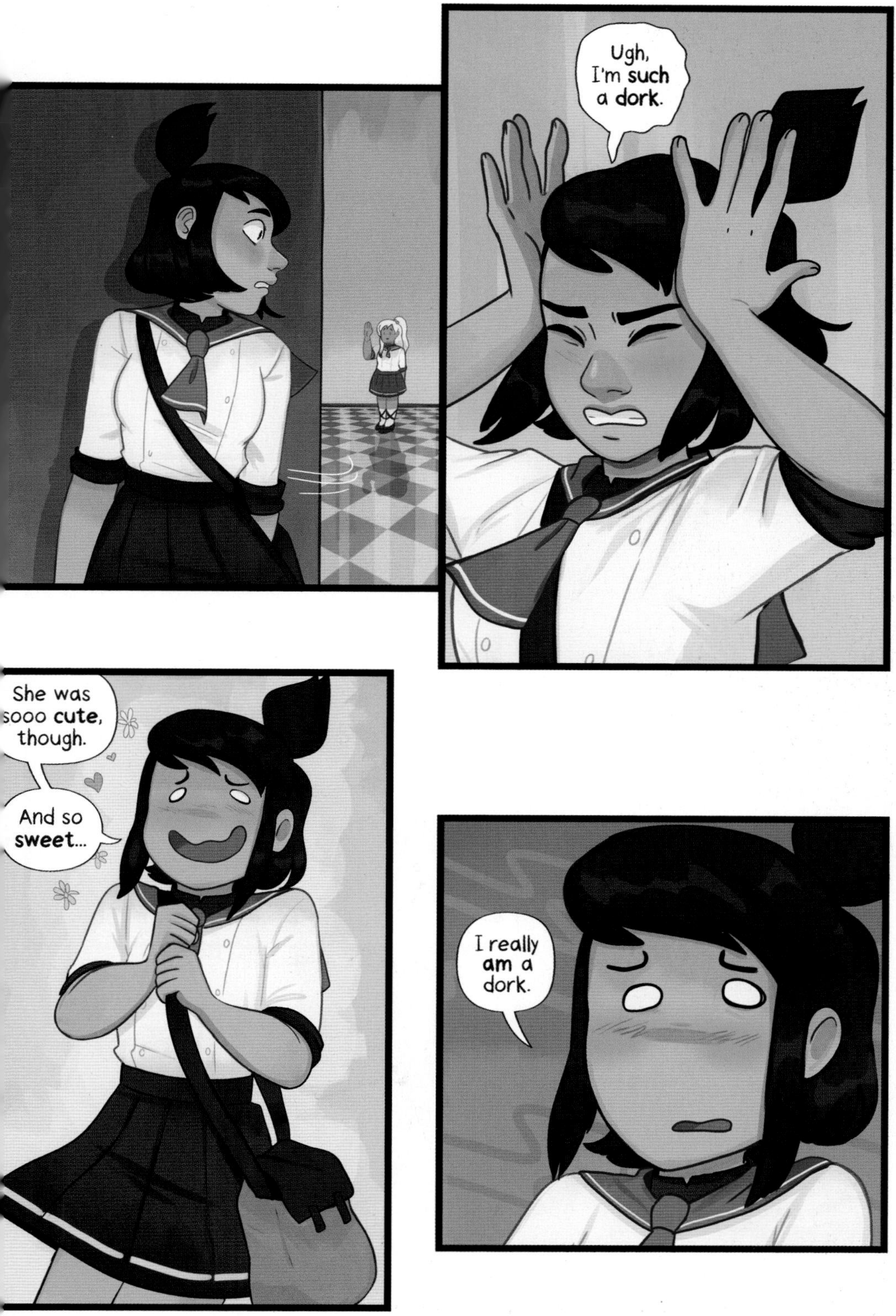
Ugh, I'm such a dork.
She was sooo cute, though.
And so sweet...
I really am a dork.

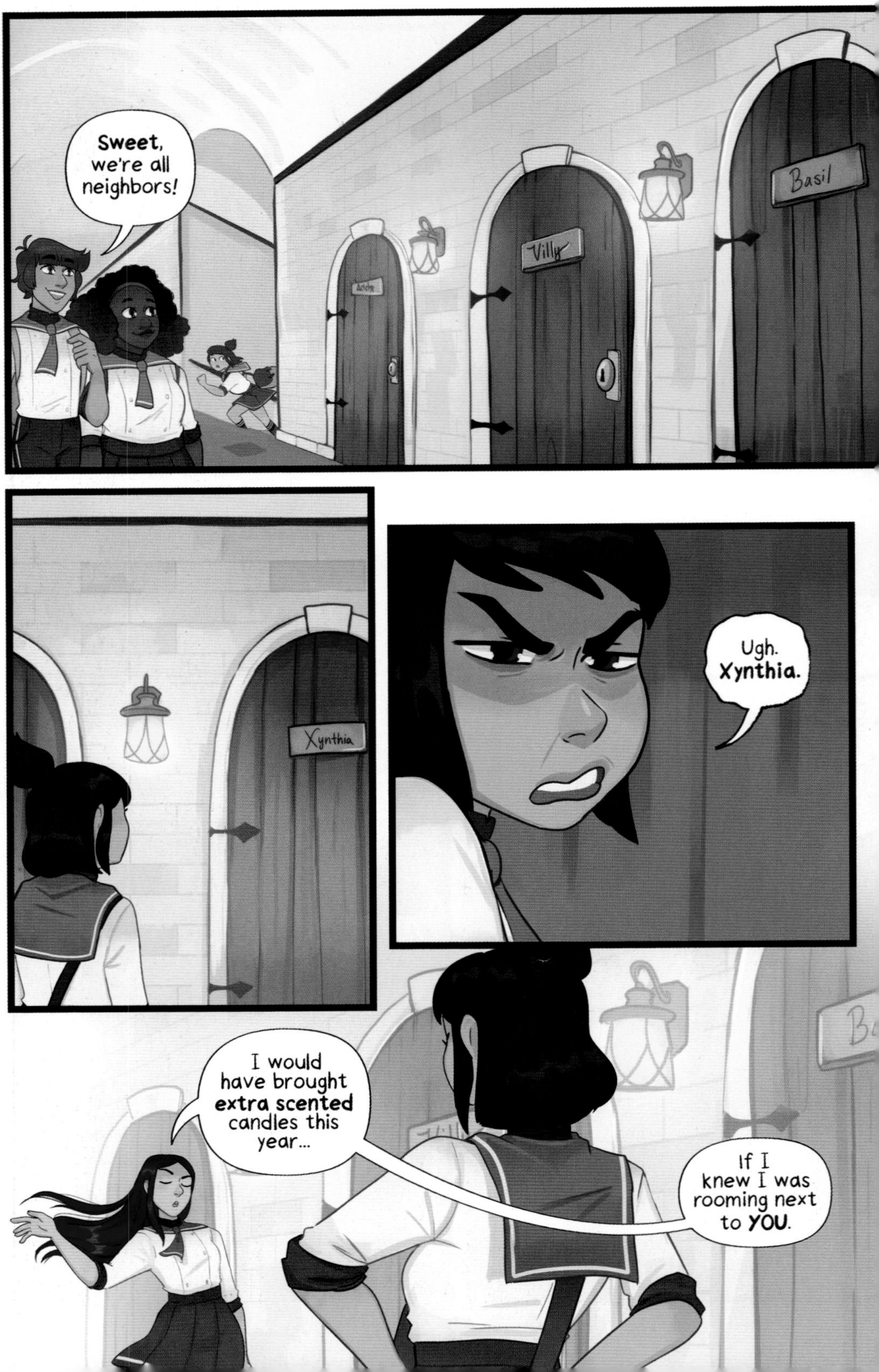

Sweet, we're all neighbors!
Villy
Basil
Xynthia
Ugh. **Xynthia.**
I would have brought **extra scented** candles this year...
If I knew I was rooming next to **YOU**.

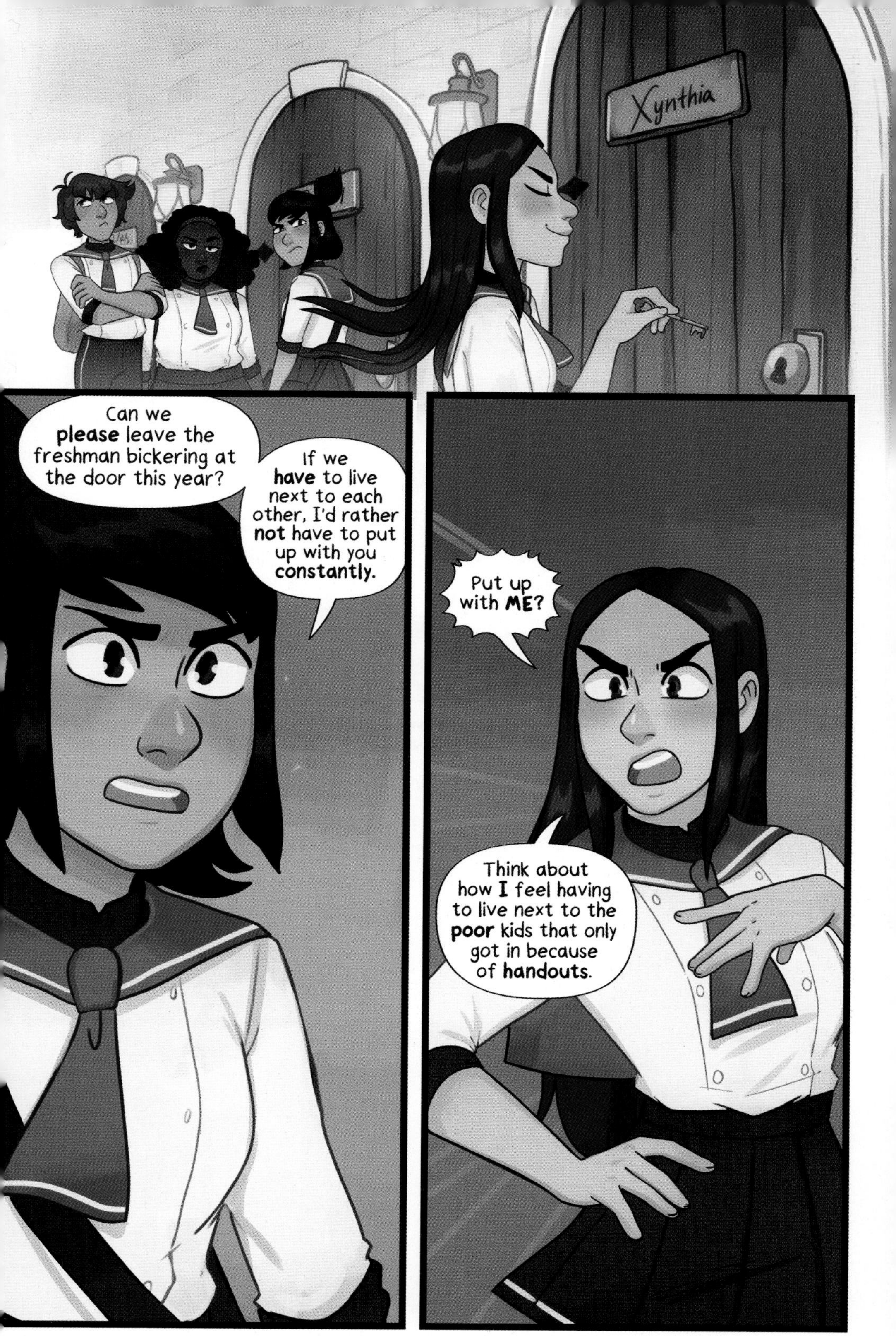
Xynthia
Can we please leave the freshman bickering at the door this year?
If we have to live next to each other, I'd rather not have to put up with you constantly.
Put up with ME?
Think about how I feel having to live next to the poor kids that only got in because of handouts.

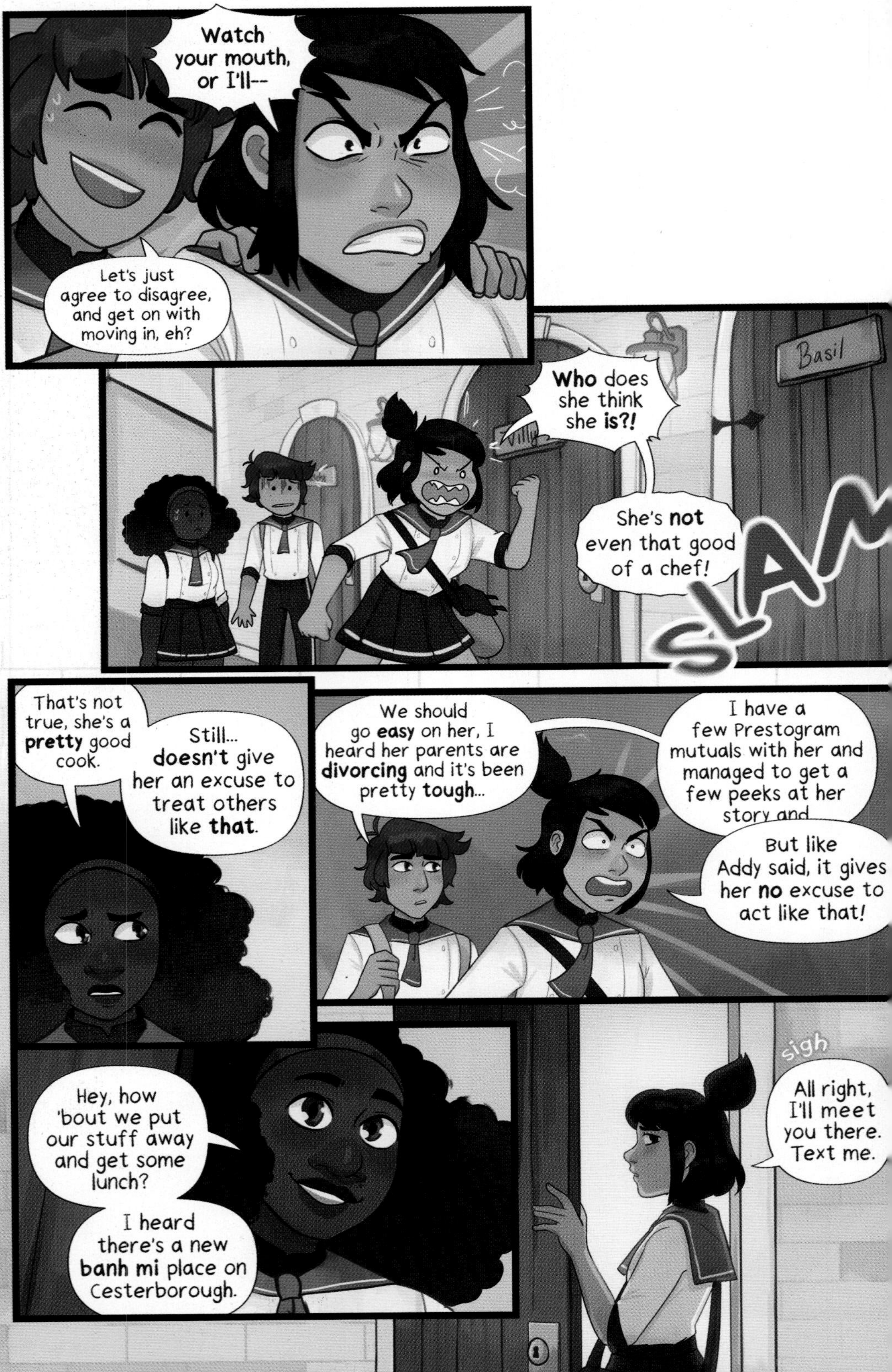

Watch your mouth, or I'll--
Let's just agree to disagree, and get on with moving in, eh?
Basil
Who does she think she is?!
She's not even that good of a chef!
SLAM
That's not true, she's a pretty good cook.
Still... doesn't give her an excuse to treat others like that.
We should go easy on her, I heard her parents are divorcing and it's been pretty tough...
I have a few Prestogram mutuals with her and managed to get a few peeks at her story and
But like Addy said, it gives her no excuse to act like that!
Hey, how 'bout we put our stuff away and get some lunch?
I heard there's a new banh mi place on Cesterborough.
sigh
All right, I'll meet you there. Text me.

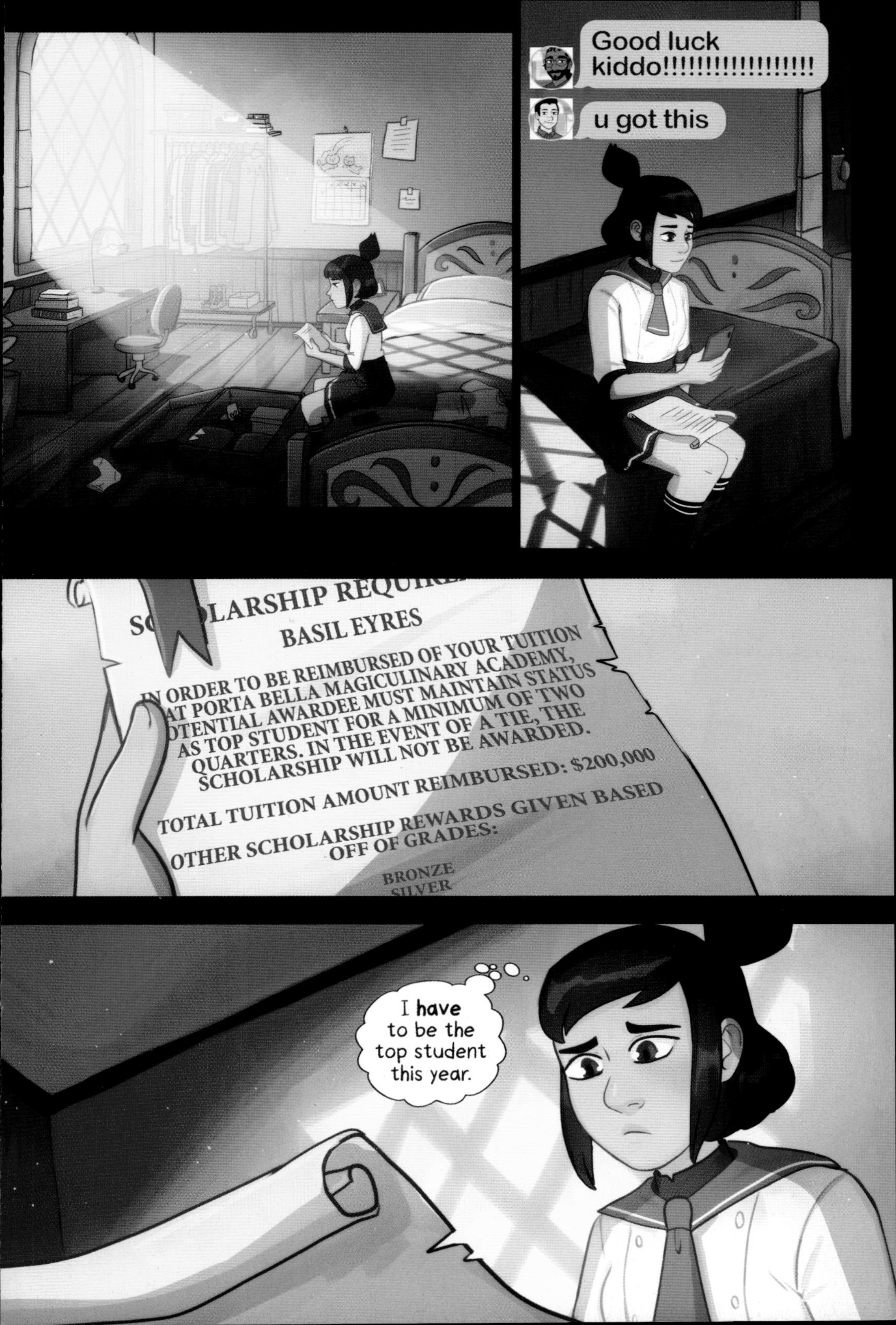
Good luck kiddo!!!!!!!!!!!!!!!!!!!
u got this
SCHOLARSHIP REQUI
BASIL EYRES
IN ORDER TO BE REIMBURSED OF YOUR TUITION AT PORTA BELLA MAGICULINARY ACADEMY, POTENTIAL AWARDEE MUST MAINTAIN STATUS AS TOP STUDENT FOR A MINIMUM OF TWO QUARTERS. IN THE EVENT OF A TIE, THE SCHOLARSHIP WILL NOT BE AWARDED.
TOTAL TUITION AMOUNT REIMBURSED: $200,000
OTHER SCHOLARSHIP REWARDS GIVEN BASED OFF OF GRADES:
BRONZE
I have to be the top student this year.

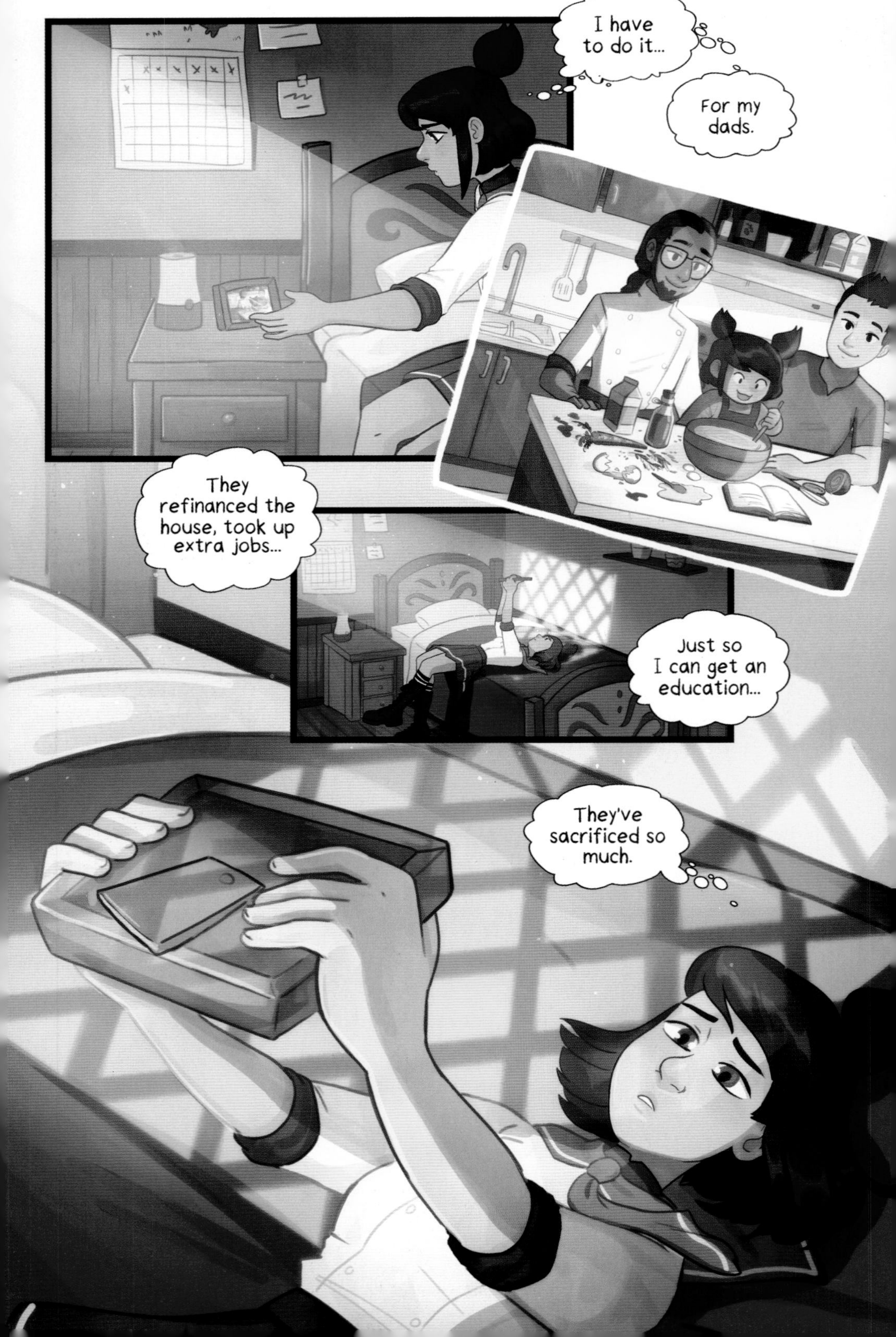

I have to do it...
For my dads.
They refinanced the house, took up extra jobs...
Just so I can get an education...
They've sacrificed so much.

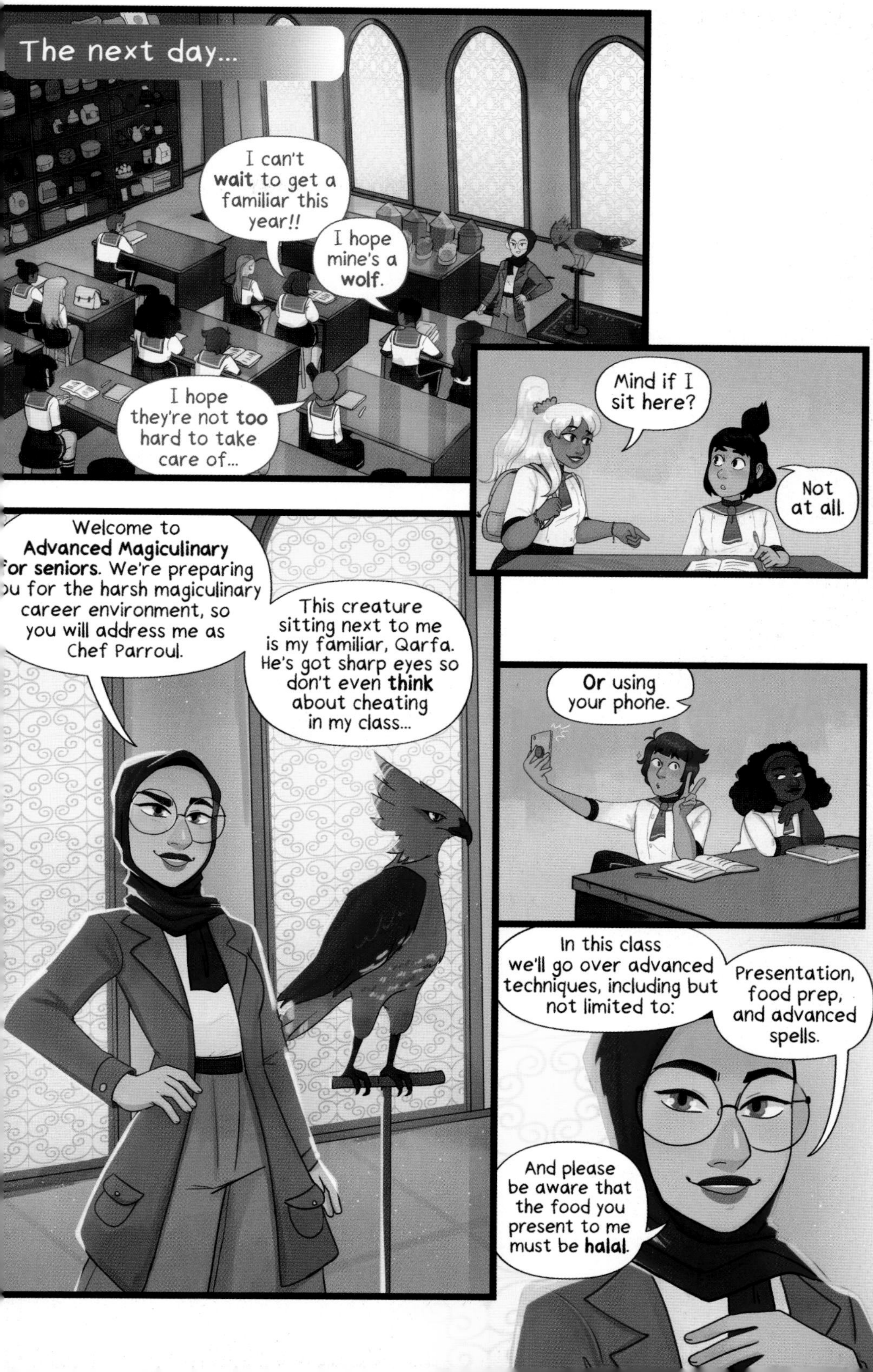

The next day...
I can't **wait** to get a familiar this year!!
I hope mine's a **wolf**.
I hope they're not **too** hard to take care of...
Mind if I sit here?
Not at all.
Welcome to **Advanced Magiculinary for seniors**. We're preparing you for the harsh magiculinary career environment, so you will address me as Chef Parroul.
This creature sitting next to me is my familiar, Qarfa. He's got sharp eyes so don't even **think** about cheating in my class...
Or using your phone.
In this class we'll go over advanced techniques, including but not limited to:
Presentation, food prep, and advanced spells.
And please be aware that the food you present to me must be **halal**.

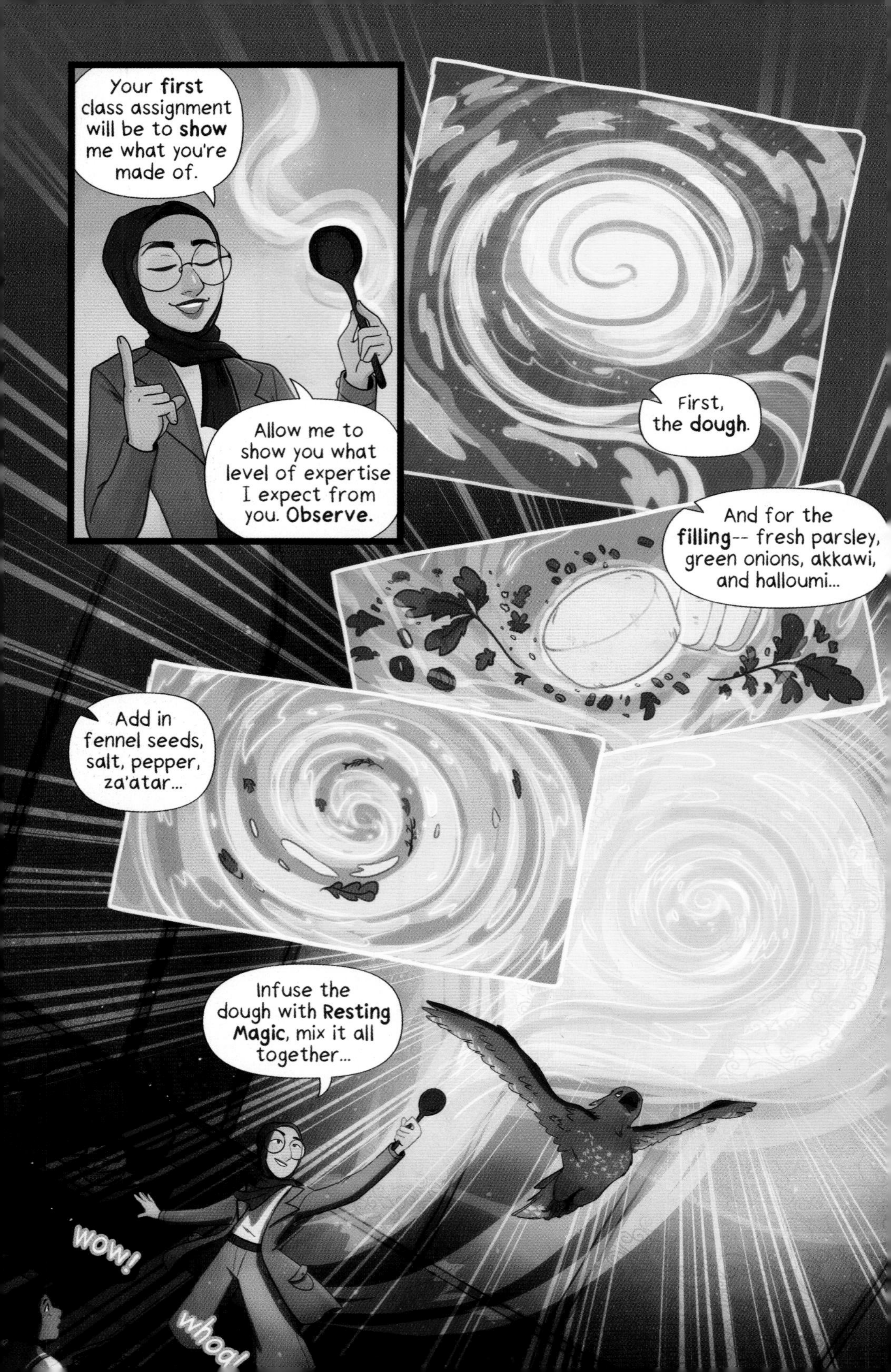
Your **first** class assignment will be to **show** me what you're made of.
Allow me to show you what level of expertise I expect from you. **Observe.**
First, the **dough**.
And for the **filling**-- fresh parsley, green onions, akkawi, and halloumi...
Add in fennel seeds, salt, pepper, za'atar...
Infuse the dough with **Resting Magic**, mix it all together...
WOW!
whoa!

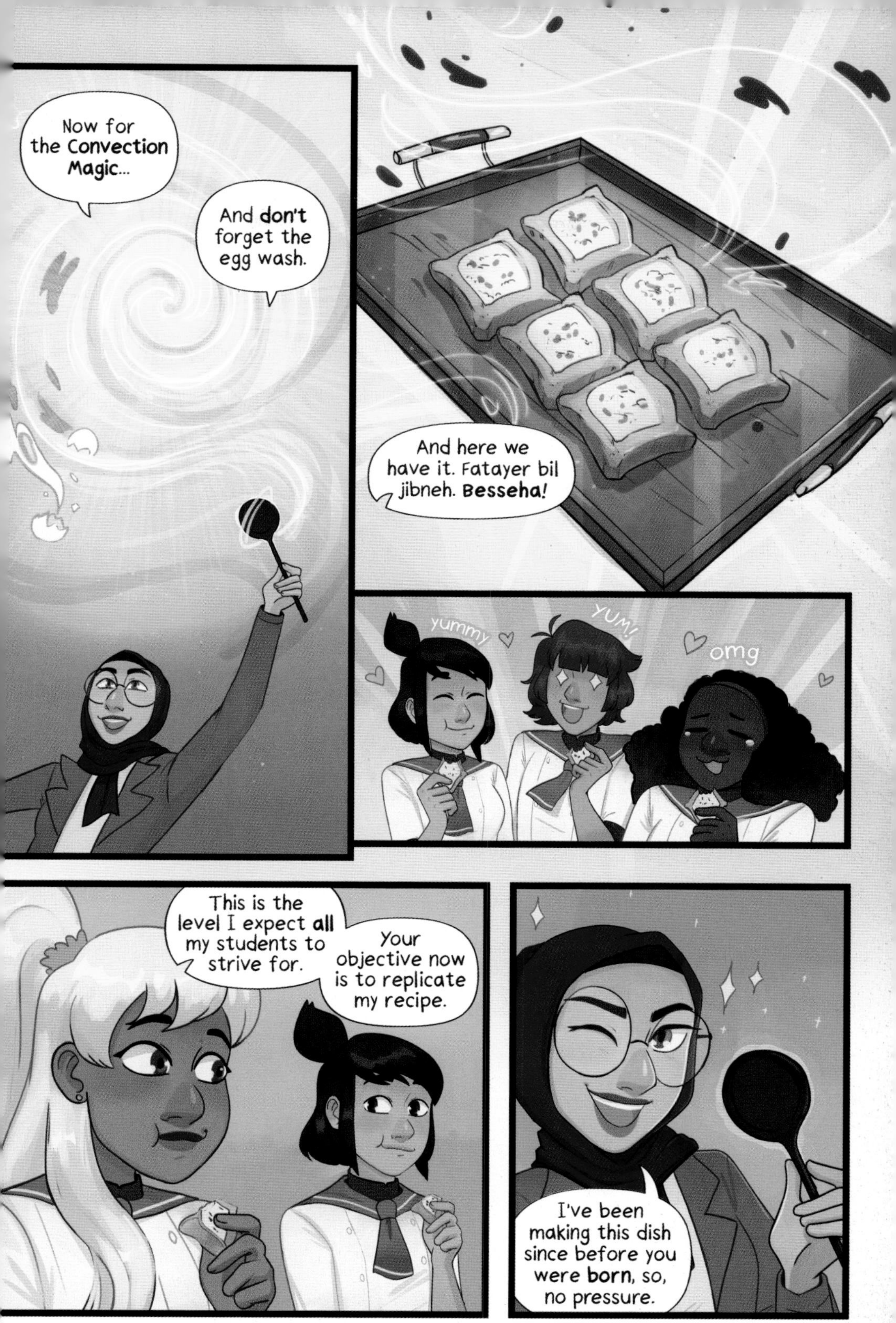
Now for the Convection Magic...
And don't forget the egg wash.
And here we have it. Fatayer bil jibneh. Besseha!
yummy
YUM!
omg
This is the level I expect all my students to strive for.
Your objective now is to replicate my recipe.
I've been making this dish since before you were born, so, no pressure.

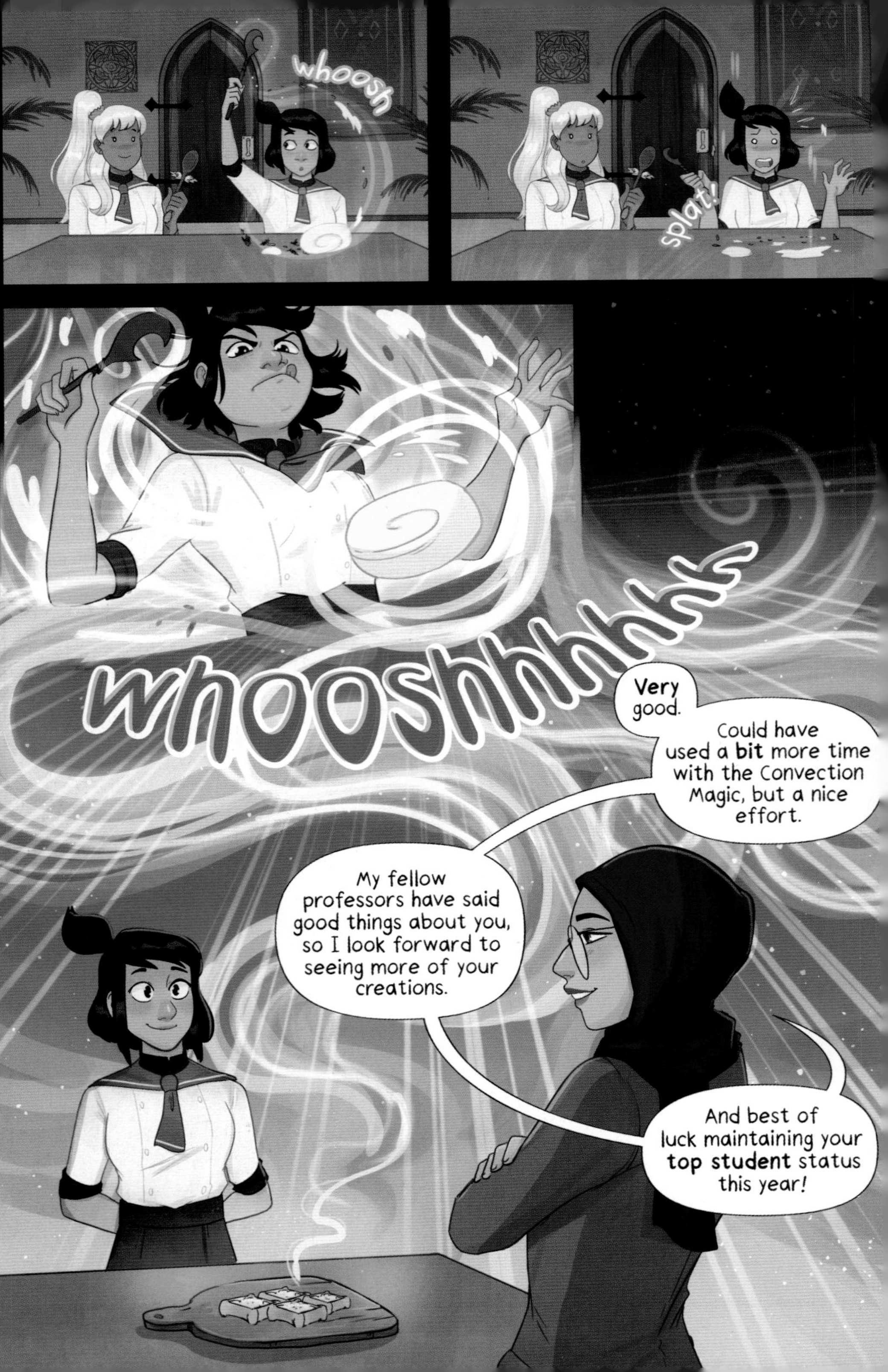
whoosh
splat!
whooshhhhht
Very good.
Could have used a bit more time with the Convection Magic, but a nice effort.
My fellow professors have said good things about you, so I look forward to seeing more of your creations.
And best of luck maintaining your top student status this year!

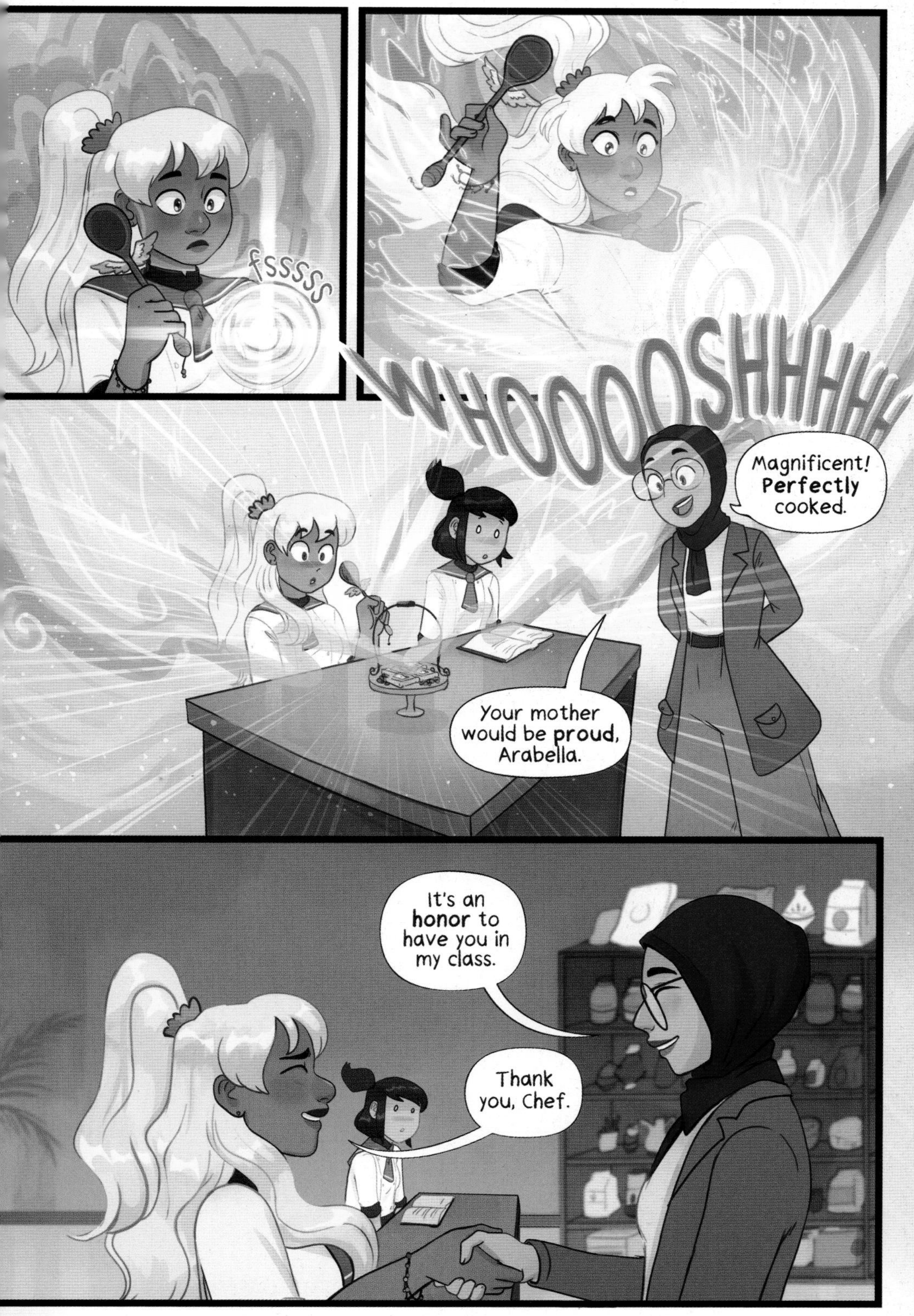
fsssss
WHOOOOSHHHHH
Magnificent! Perfectly cooked.
Your mother would be proud, Arabella.
It's an honor to have you in my class.
Thank you, Chef.

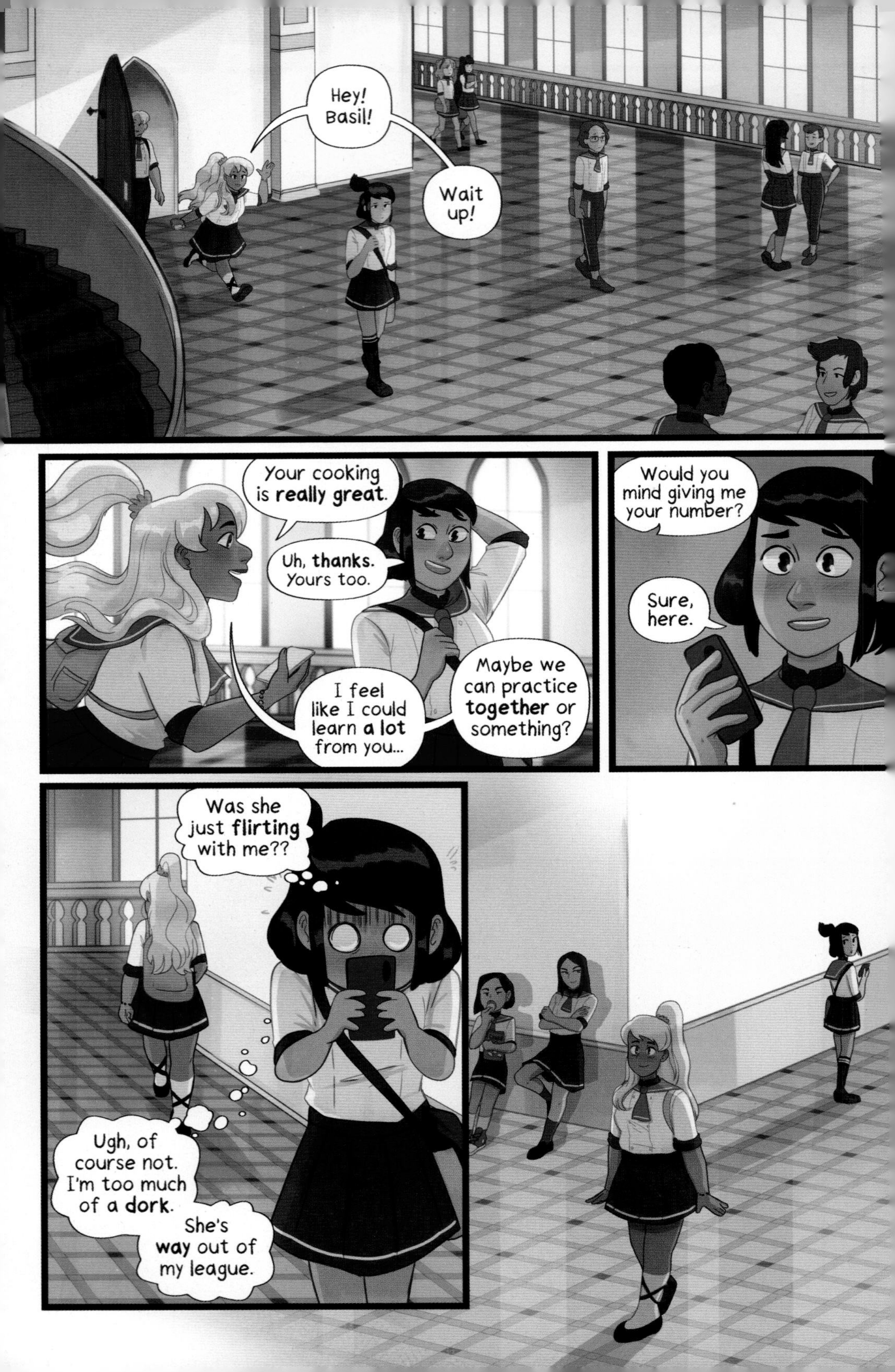
Hey! Basil!
Wait up!
Your cooking is **really great**.
Uh, **thanks.** Yours too.
I feel like I could learn **a lot** from you...
Maybe we can practice **together** or something?
Would you mind giving me your number?
Sure, here.
Was she just **flirting** with me??
Ugh, of course not. I'm too much of a **dork**.
She's **way** out of my league.

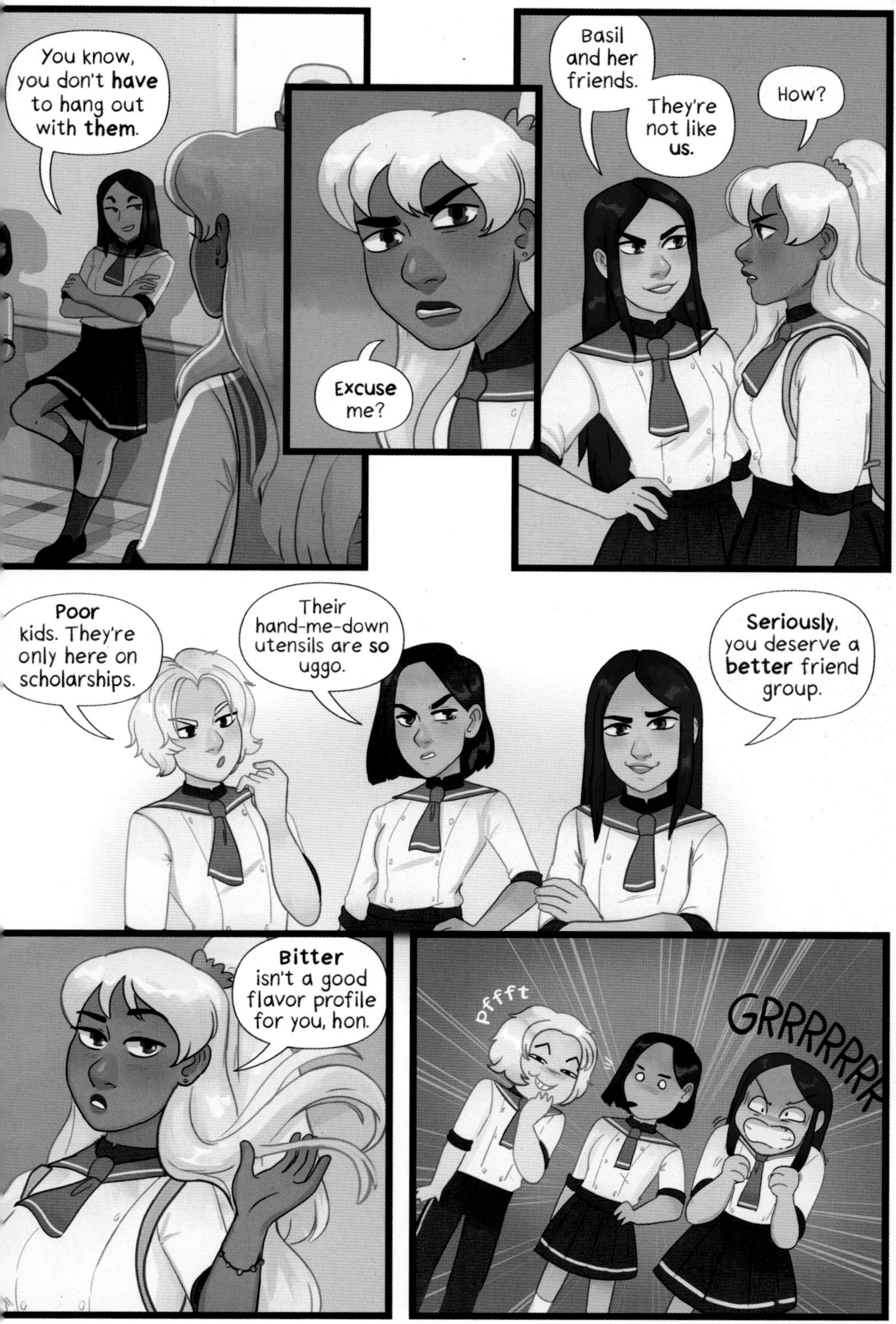

You know, you don't **have** to hang out with **them**.
Excuse me?
Basil and her friends.
They're not like **us**.
How?
Poor kids. They're only here on scholarships.
Their hand-me-down utensils are **so** uggo.
Seriously, you deserve a **better** friend group.
Bitter isn't a good flavor profile for you, hon.
pffft
GRRRRRRR

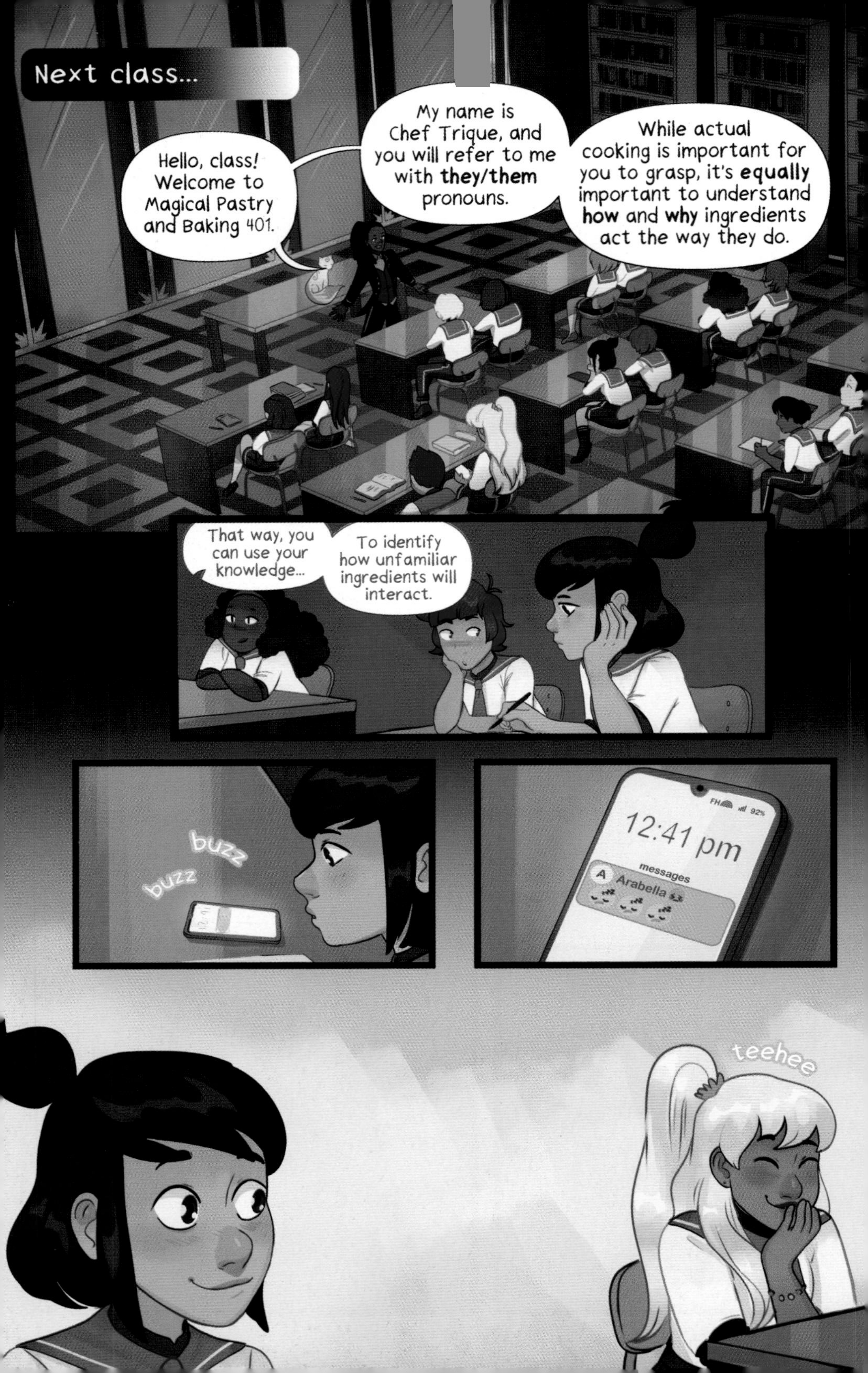
Next class...
Hello, class! Welcome to Magical Pastry and Baking 401.
My name is Chef Trique, and you will refer to me with **they/them** pronouns.
While actual cooking is important for you to grasp, it's **equally** important to understand **how** and **why** ingredients act the way they do.
That way, you can use your knowledge...
To identify how unfamiliar ingredients will interact.
buzz
buzz
12:41 pm
messages
Arabella
teehee

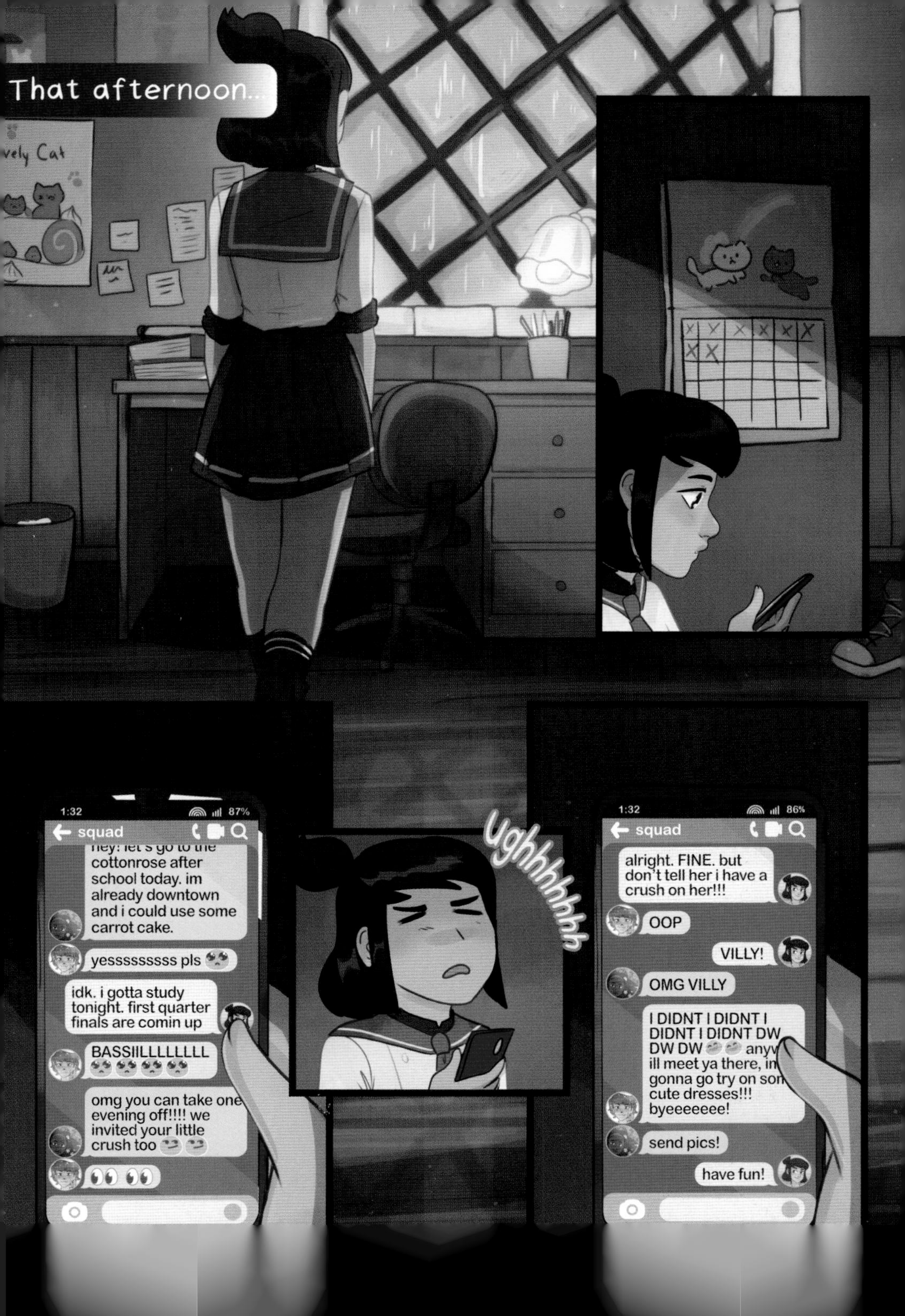
That afternoon...
1:32 87%
squad
cottonrose after school today. im already downtown and i could use some carrot cake.
yessssssssss pls
idk. i gotta study tonight. first quarter finals are comin up
BASSIILLLLLLLL
omg you can take one evening off!!!! we invited your little crush too
Ughhhhhhhh
1:32 86%
squad
alright. FINE. but don't tell her i have a crush on her!!!
OOP
VILLY!
OMG VILLY
I DIDNT I DIDNT I DIDNT I DIDNT DW DW DW anyw
ill meet ya there, im gonna go try on som cute dresses!!! byeeeeeee!
send pics!
have fun!

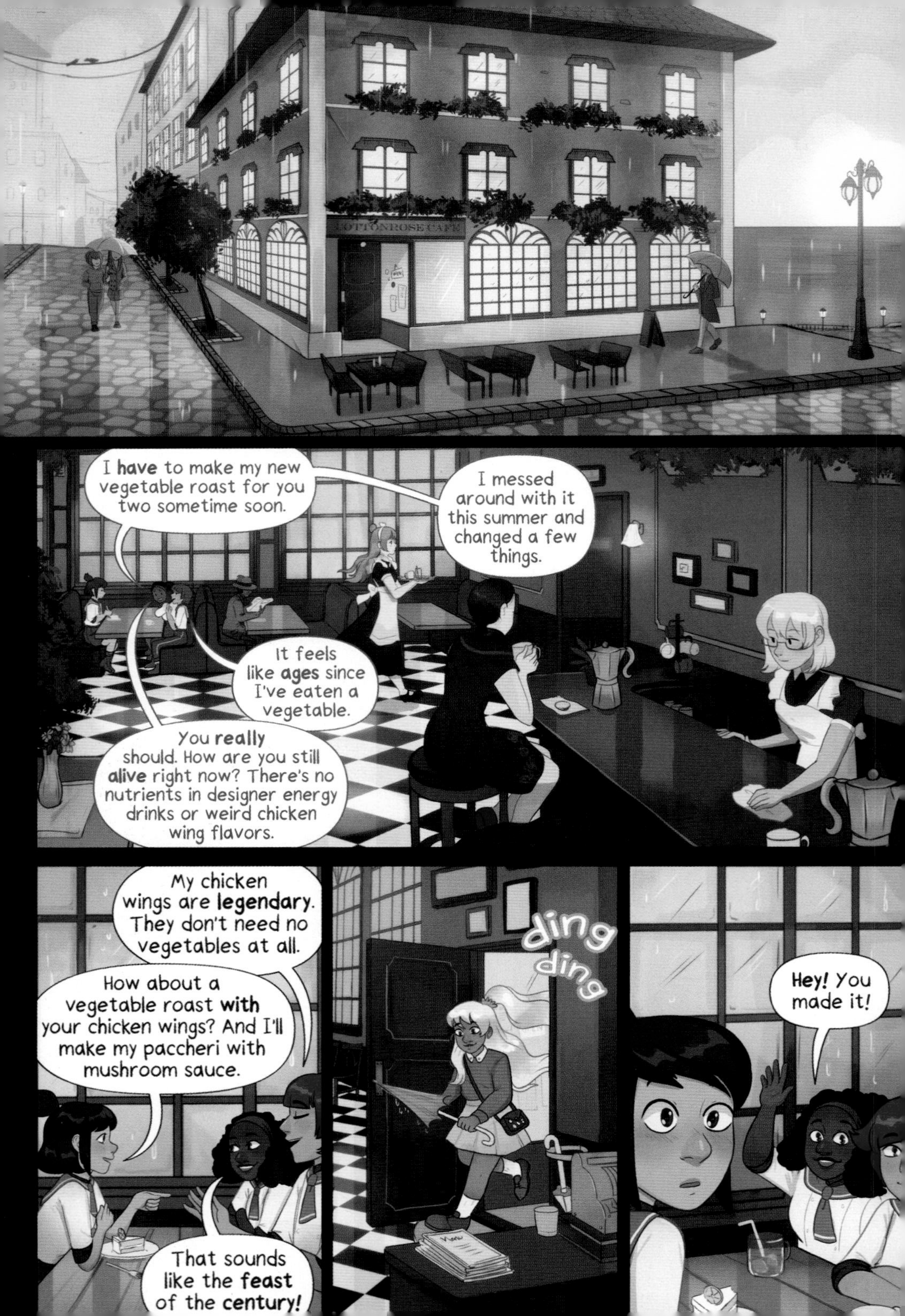

I **have** to make my new vegetable roast for you two sometime soon.
I messed around with it this summer and changed a few things.
It feels like **ages** since I've eaten a vegetable.
You **really** should. How are you still **alive** right now? There's no nutrients in designer energy drinks or weird chicken wing flavors.
My chicken wings are **legendary**. They don't need no vegetables at all.
How about a vegetable roast **with** your chicken wings? And I'll make my paccheri with mushroom sauce.
That sounds like the **feast** of the **century**!
ding ding
Hey! You made it!

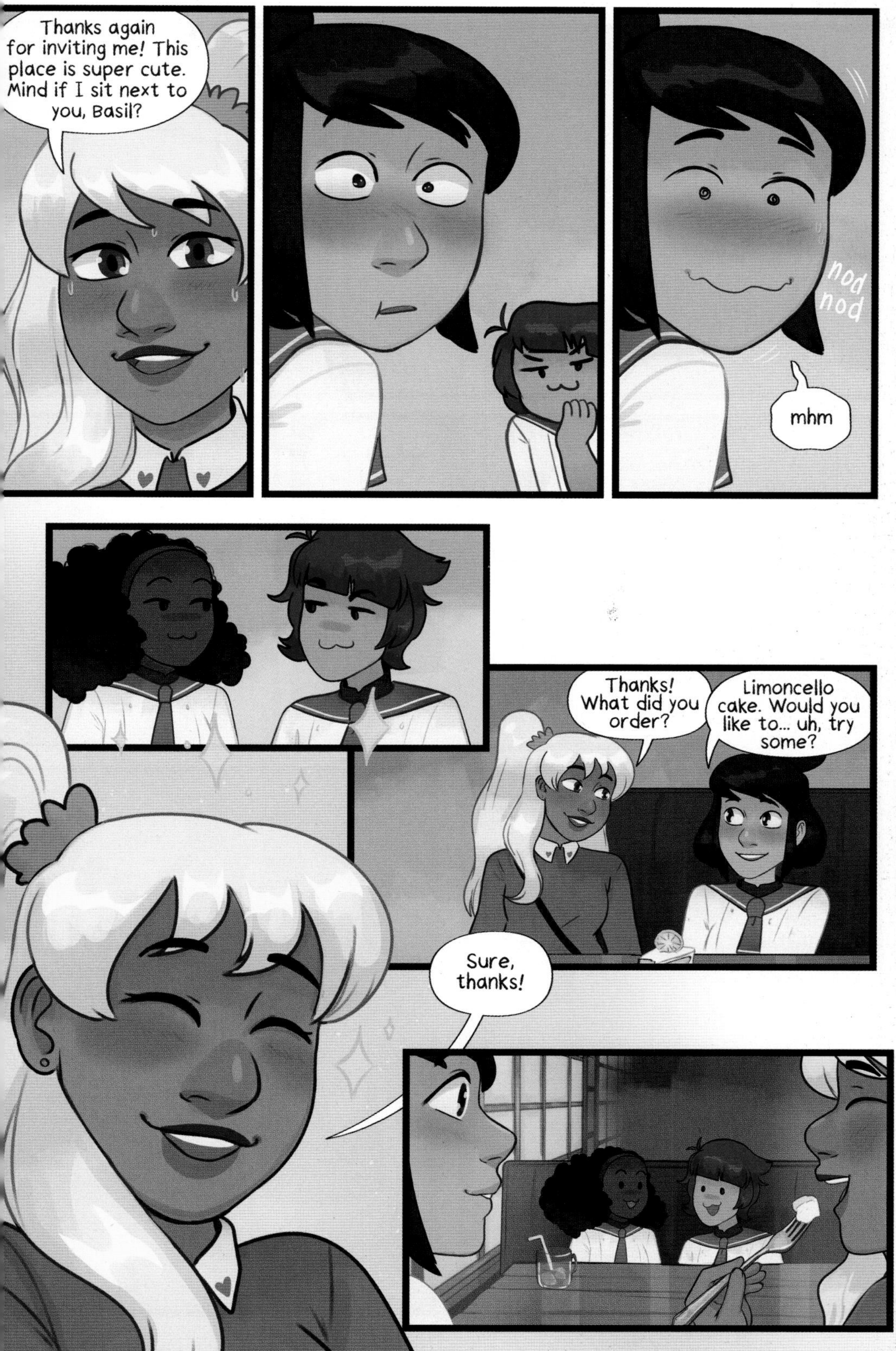

Thanks again for inviting me! This place is super cute. Mind if I sit next to you, Basil?
nod nod
mhm
Thanks! What did you order?
Limoncello cake. Would you like to... uh, try some?
Sure, thanks!

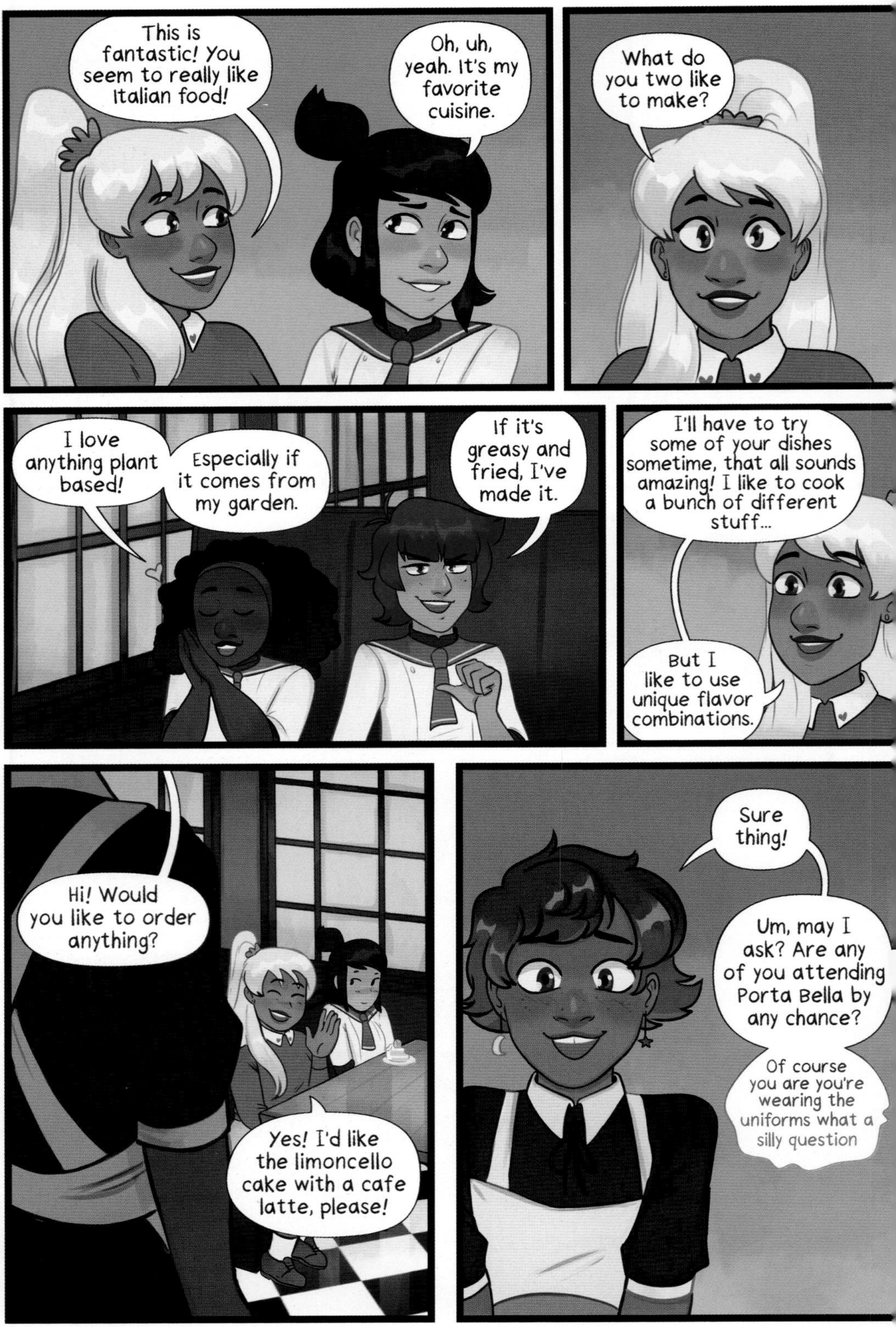
This is fantastic! You seem to really like Italian food!
Oh, uh, yeah. It's my favorite cuisine.
What do you two like to make?
I love anything plant based!
Especially if it comes from my garden.
If it's greasy and fried, I've made it.
I'll have to try some of your dishes sometime, that all sounds amazing! I like to cook a bunch of different stuff...
But I like to use unique flavor combinations.
Hi! Would you like to order anything?
Yes! I'd like the limoncello cake with a cafe latte, please!
Sure thing!
Um, may I ask? Are any of you attending Porta Bella by any chance?
Of course you are you're wearing the uniforms what a silly question

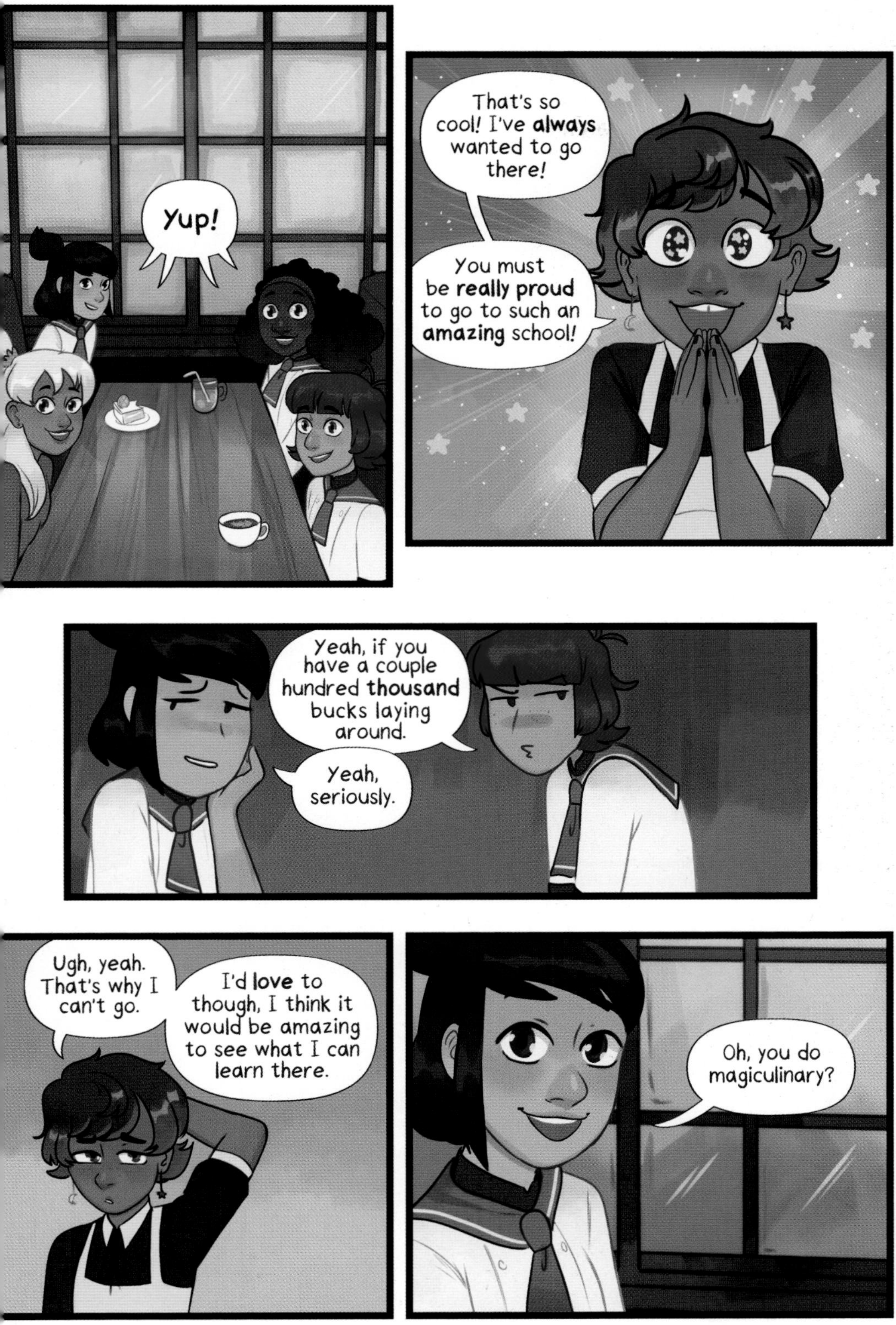
Yup!
That's so cool! I've **always** wanted to go there!
You must be **really proud** to go to such an **amazing** school!
Yeah, if you have a couple hundred **thousand** bucks laying around.
Yeah, seriously.
Ugh, yeah. That's why I can't go.
I'd **love** to though, I think it would be amazing to see what I can learn there.
Oh, you do magiculinary?

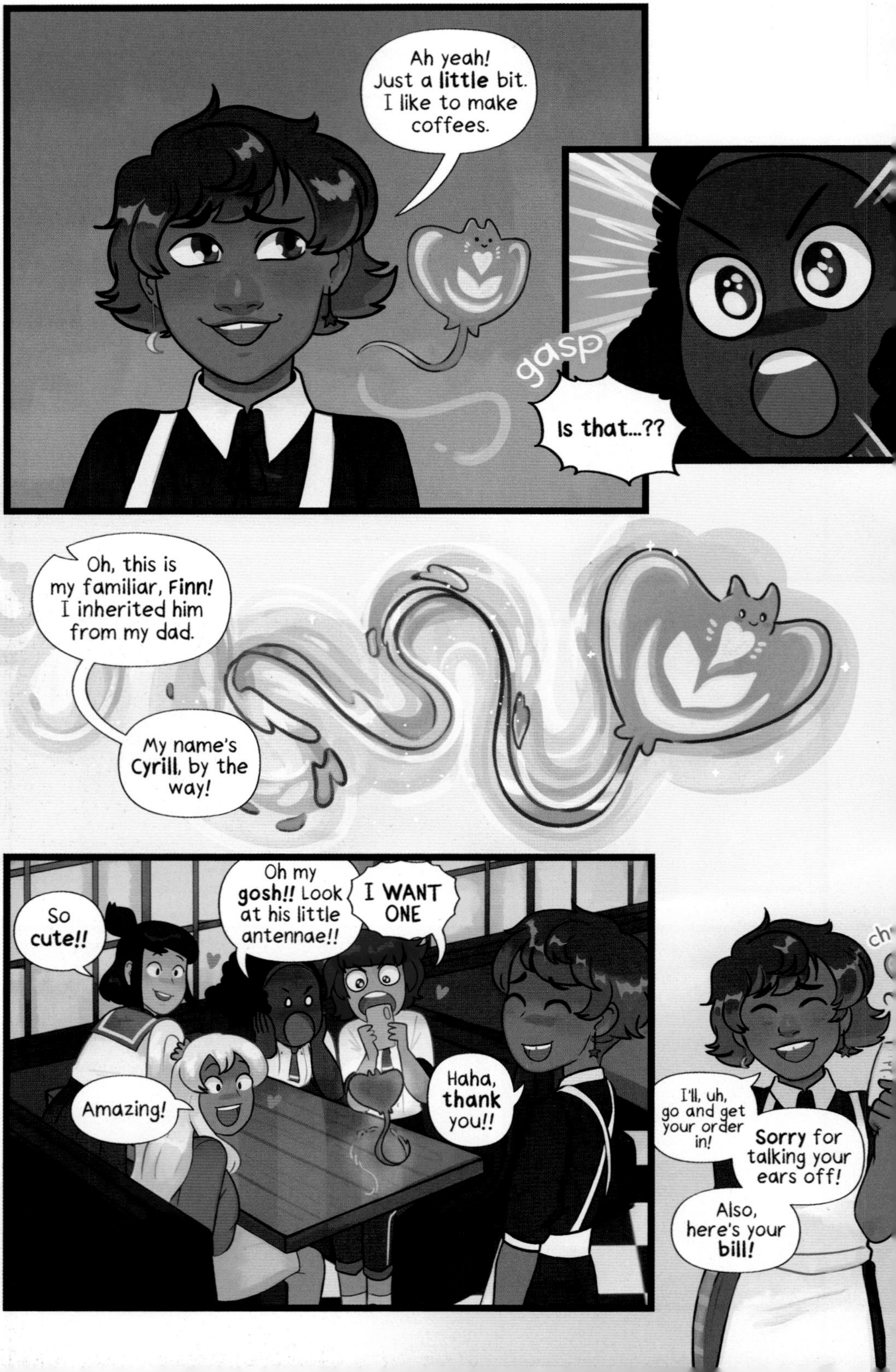

Ah yeah! Just a **little** bit. I like to make coffees.
gasp
Is that...??
Oh, this is my familiar, **Finn!** I inherited him from my dad.
My name's **Cyrill**, by the way!
So **cute!!**
Oh my **gosh!!** Look at his little antennae!!
I WANT ONE
Amazing!
Haha, **thank** you!!
I'll, uh, go and get your order in!
Sorry for talking your ears off!
Also, here's your **bill!**

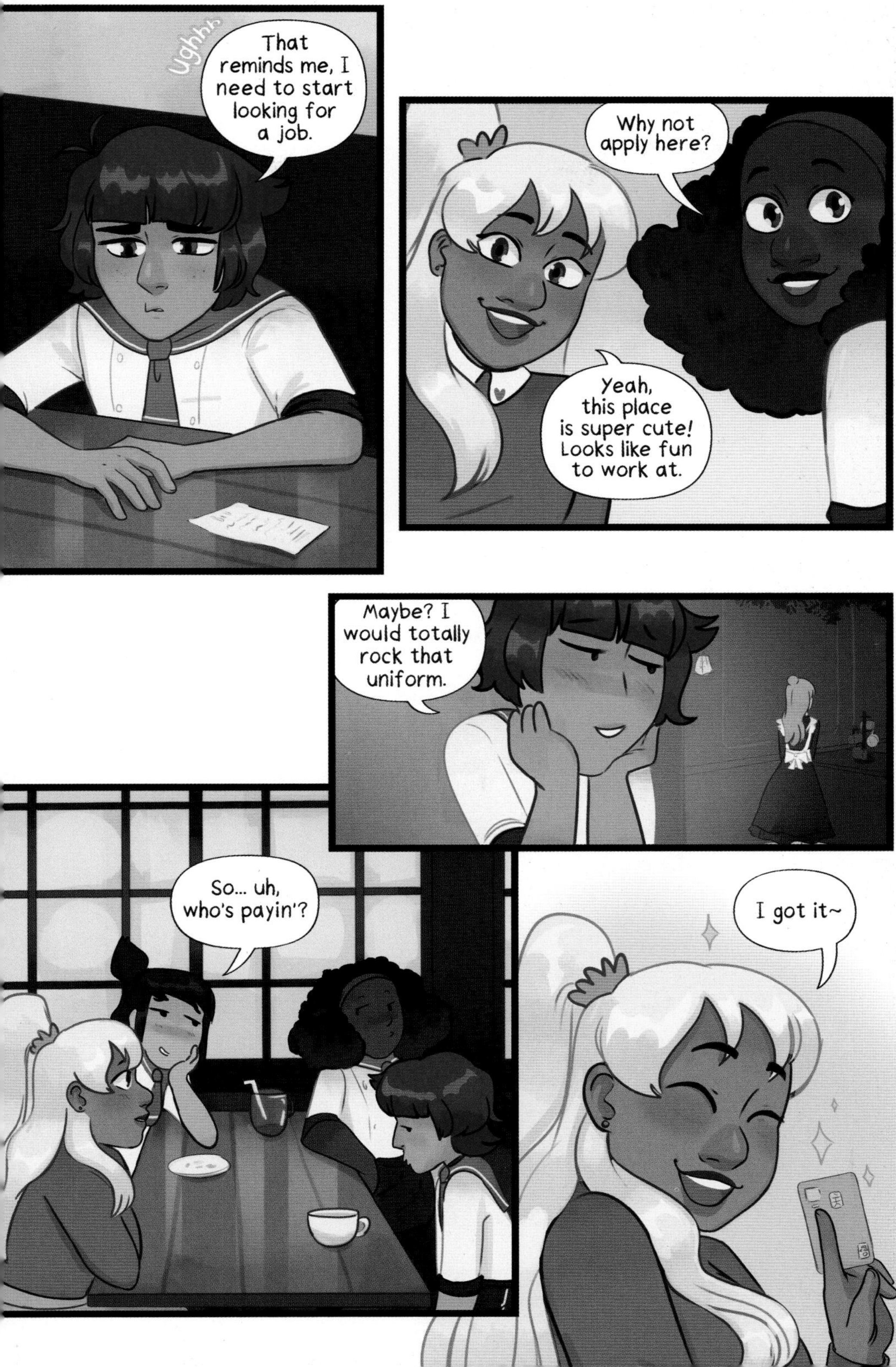
Ughhh
That reminds me, I need to start looking for a job.
Why not apply here?
Yeah, this place is super cute! Looks like fun to work at.
Maybe? I would totally rock that uniform.
So... uh, who's payin'?
I got it~

Chapter
TWO

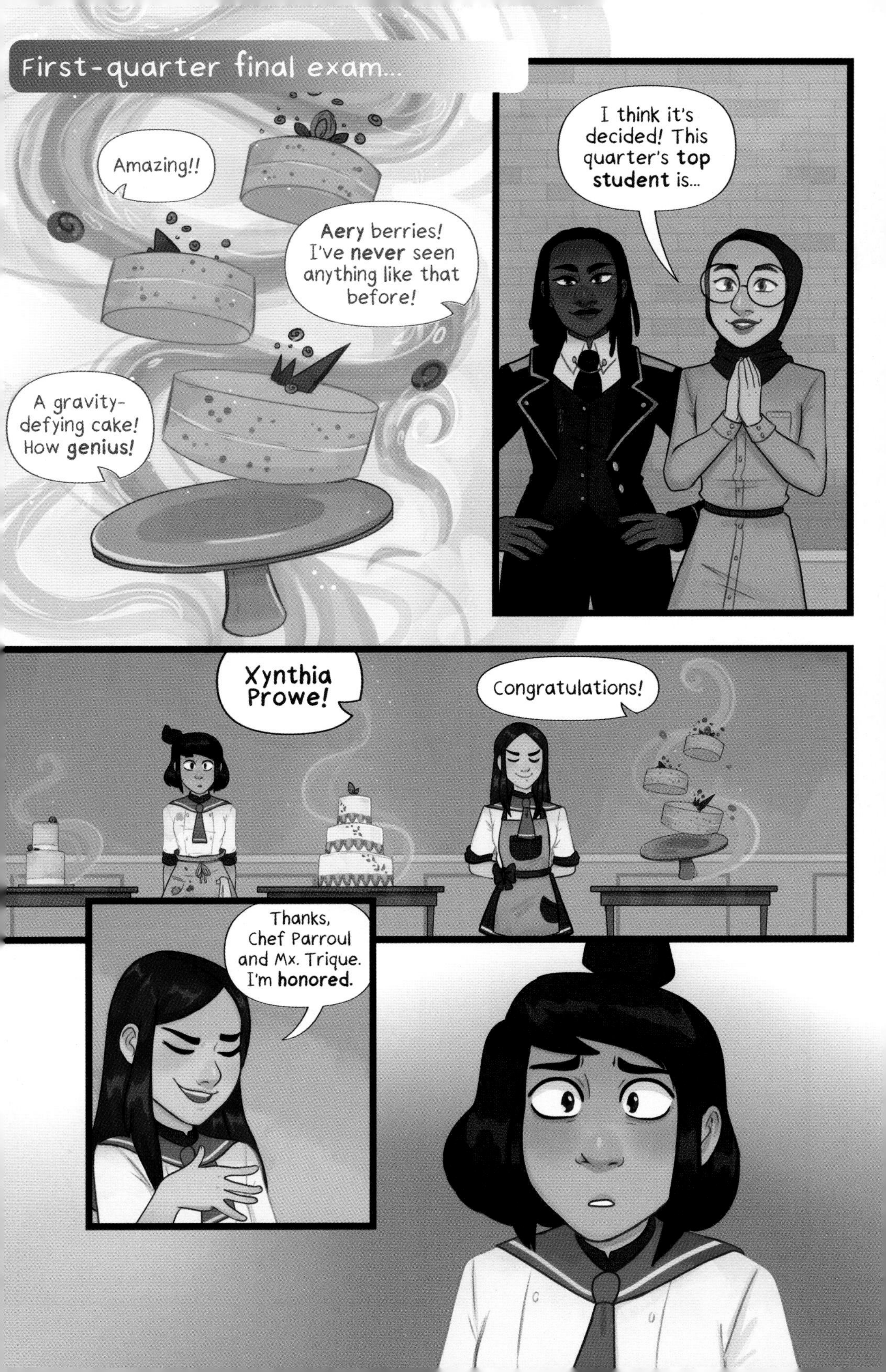
First-quarter final exam...
Amazing!!
Aery berries! I've never seen anything like that before!
A gravity-defying cake! How genius!
I think it's decided! This quarter's top student is...
Xynthia Prowe!
Congratulations!
Thanks, Chef Parroul and Mx. Trique. I'm honored.

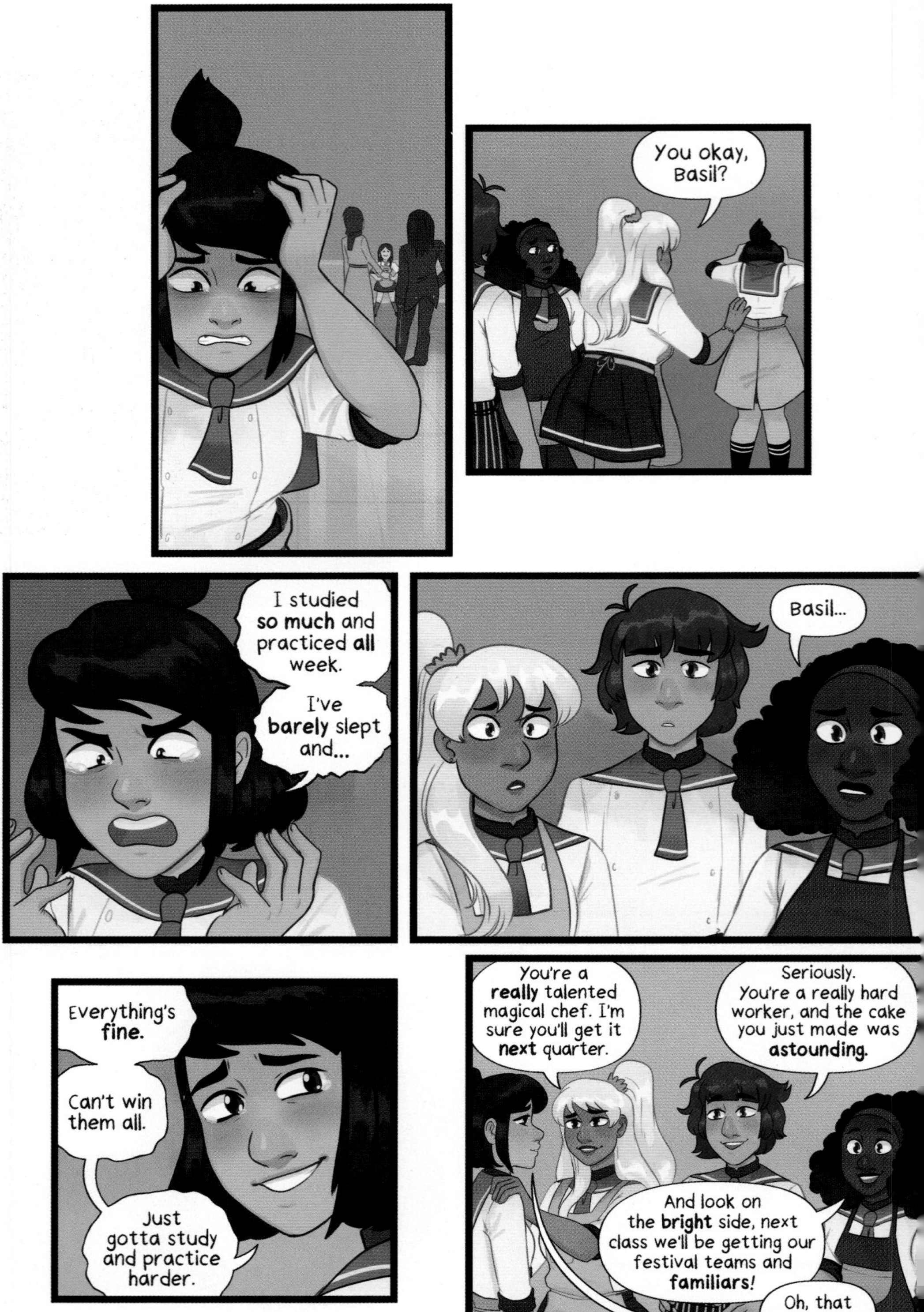
You okay, Basil?
I studied so much and practiced all week.
I've barely slept and...
Basil...
Everything's fine.
Can't win them all.
Just gotta study and practice harder.
You're a really talented magical chef. I'm sure you'll get it next quarter.
Seriously. You're a really hard worker, and the cake you just made was astounding.
And look on the bright side, next class we'll be getting our festival teams and familiars!
Oh, that is exciting!

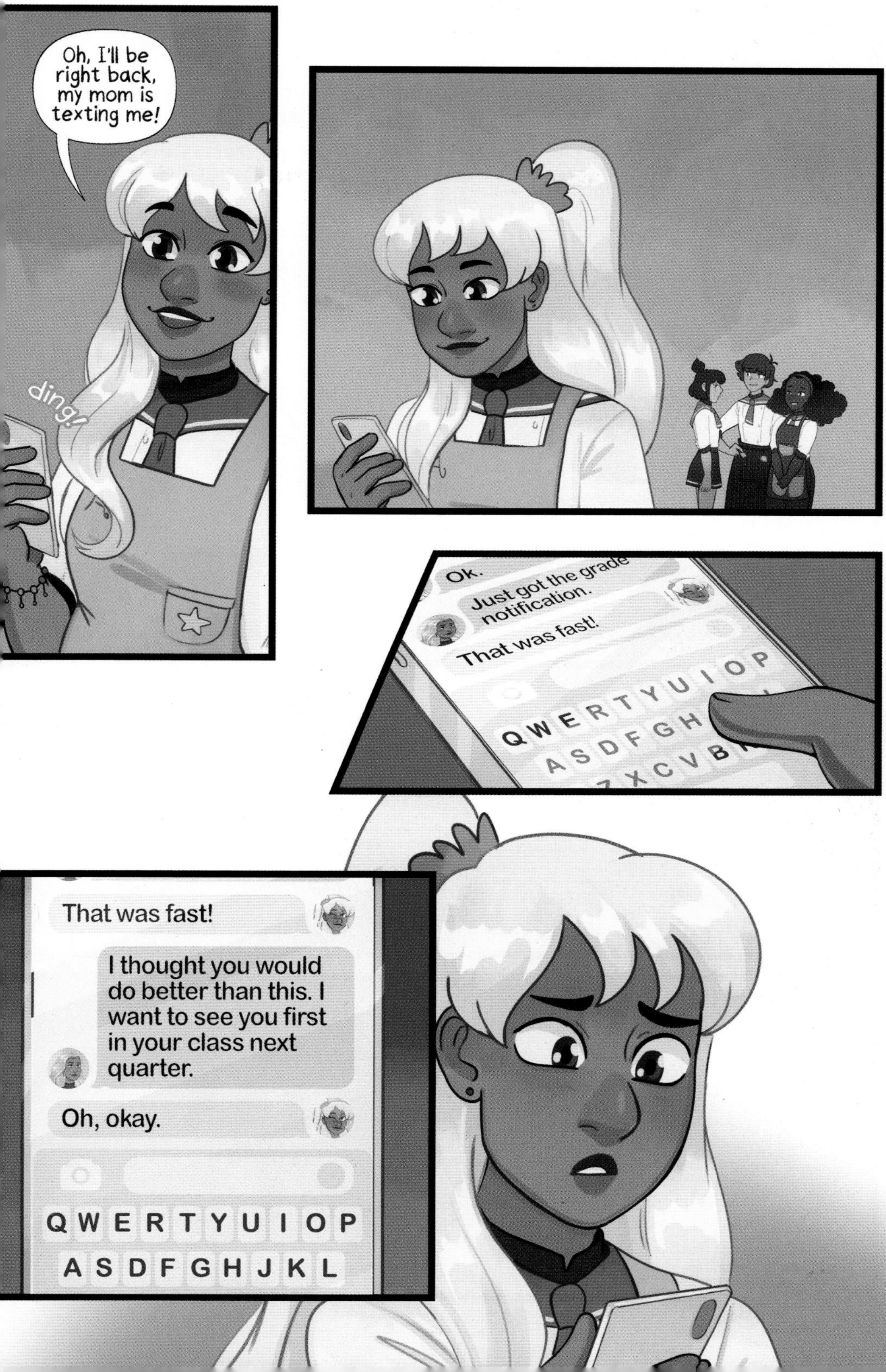
Oh, I'll be right back, my mom is texting me!
ding!
Ok.
Just got the grade notification.
That was fast!
QWERTYUIOP
ASDFGH
That was fast!
I thought you would do better than this. I want to see you first in your class next quarter.
Oh, okay.
QWERTYUIOP
ASDFGHJKL

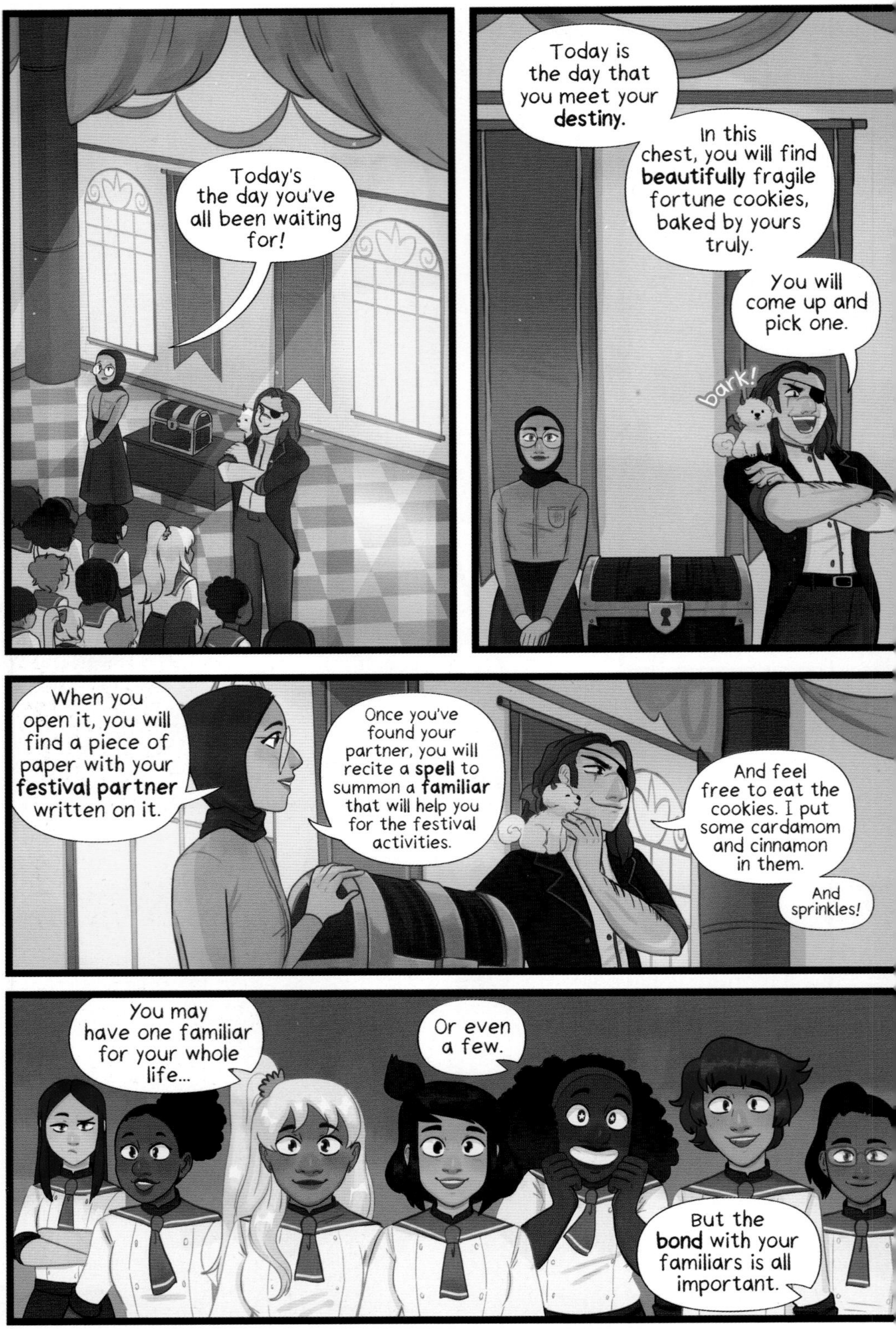
Today's the day you've all been waiting for!
Today is the day that you meet your **destiny.**
In this chest, you will find **beautifully** fragile fortune cookies, baked by yours truly.
You will come up and pick one.
bark!
When you open it, you will find a piece of paper with your **festival partner** written on it.
Once you've found your partner, you will recite a **spell** to summon a **familiar** that will help you for the festival activities.
And feel free to eat the cookies. I put some cardamom and cinnamon in them.
And sprinkles!
You may have one familiar for your whole life...
Or even a few.
But the **bond** with your familiars is all important.

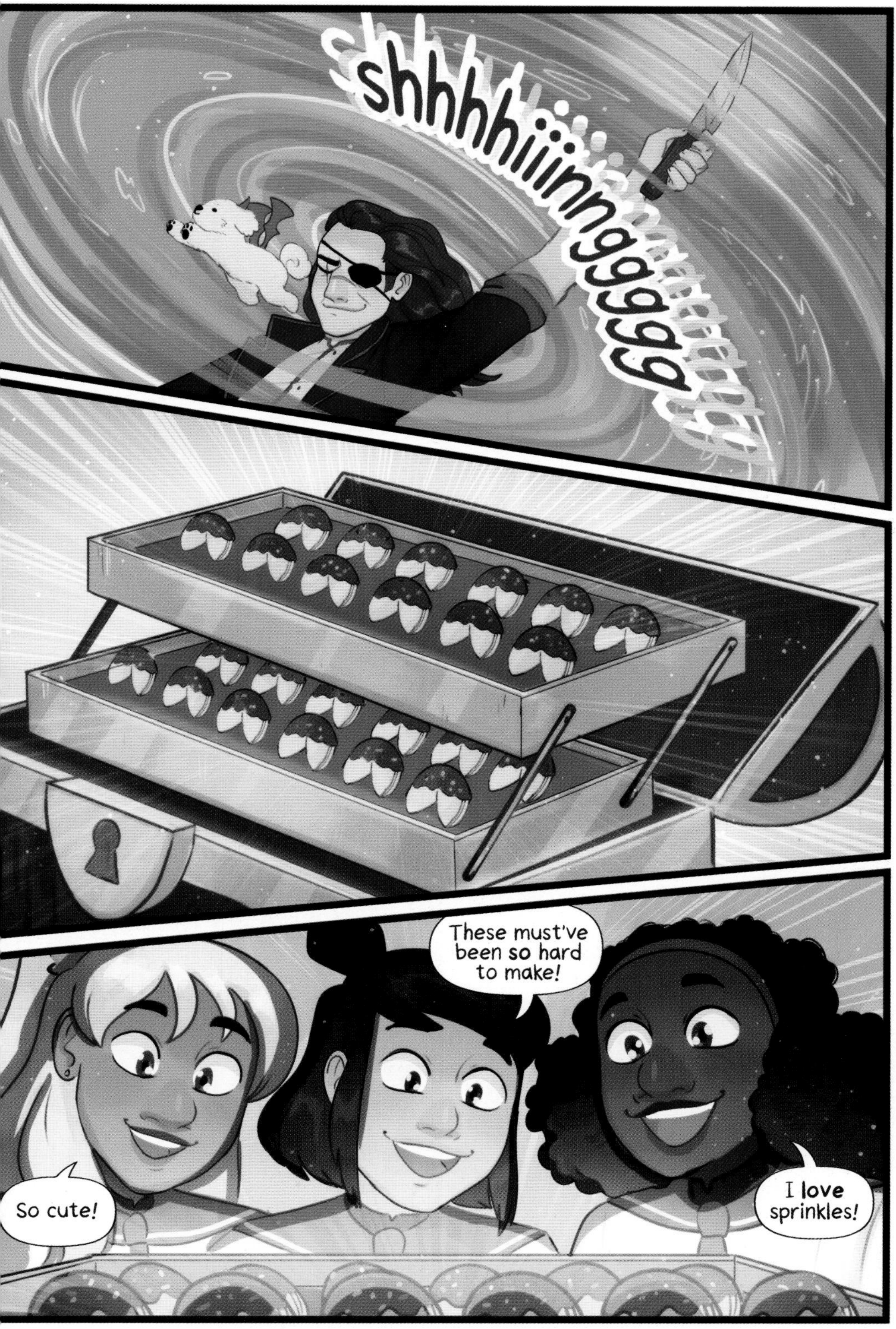
shhhiiinngggg
These must've been so hard to make!
So cute!
I love sprinkles!

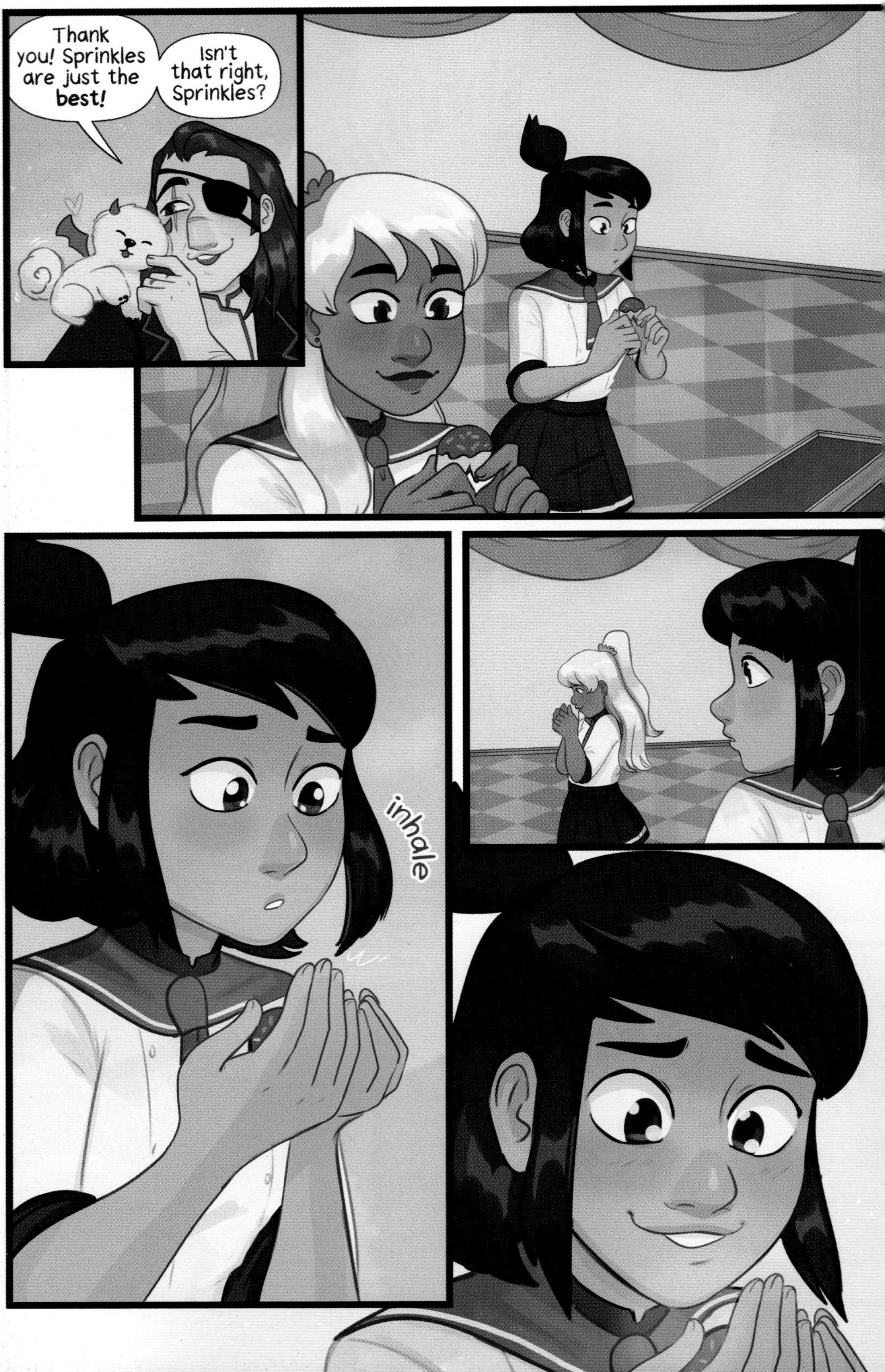
Thank you! Sprinkles are just the **best!**
Isn't that right, Sprinkles?
inhale

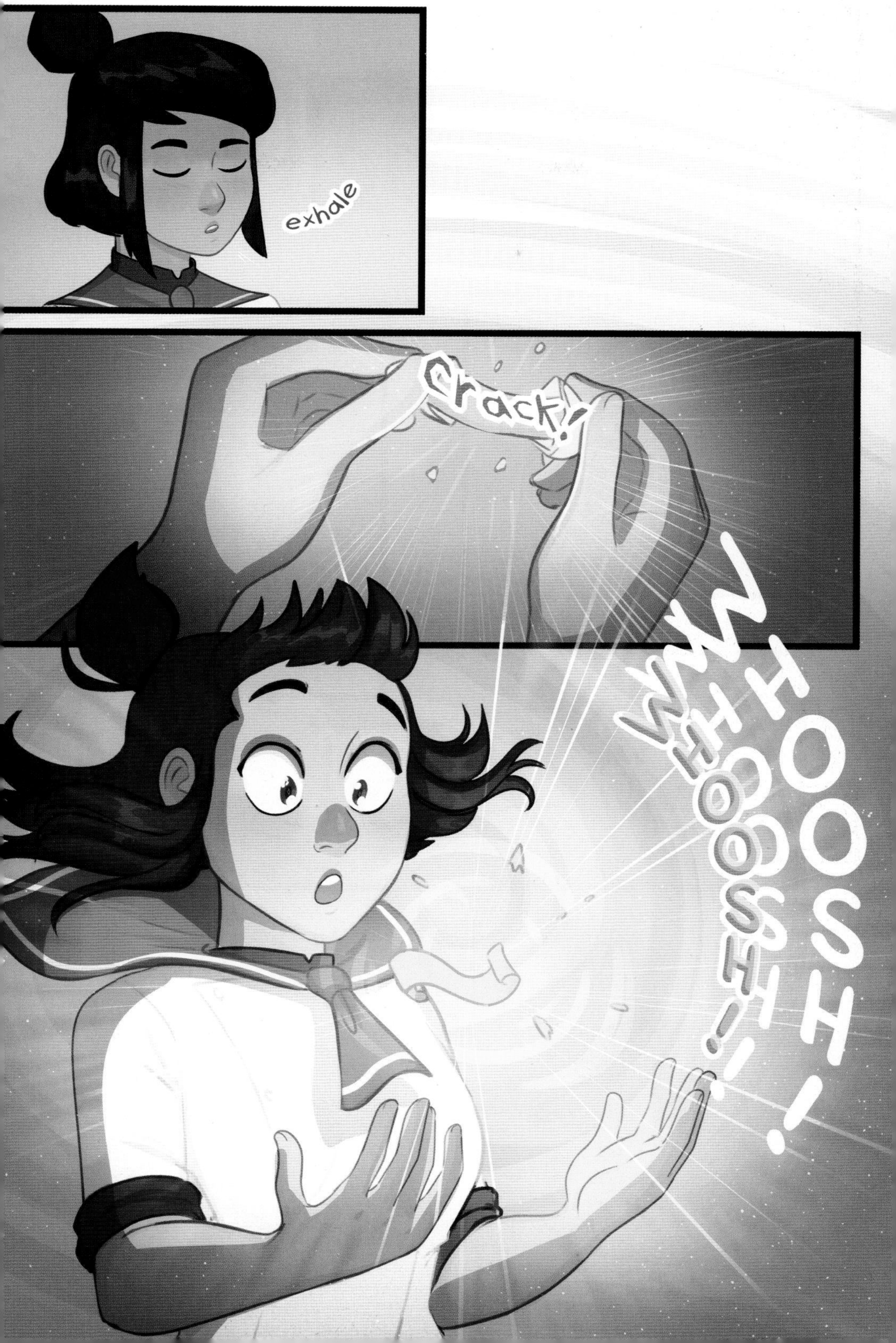
exhale
Crack!
WHOOOSH!
WHOOOSH!!

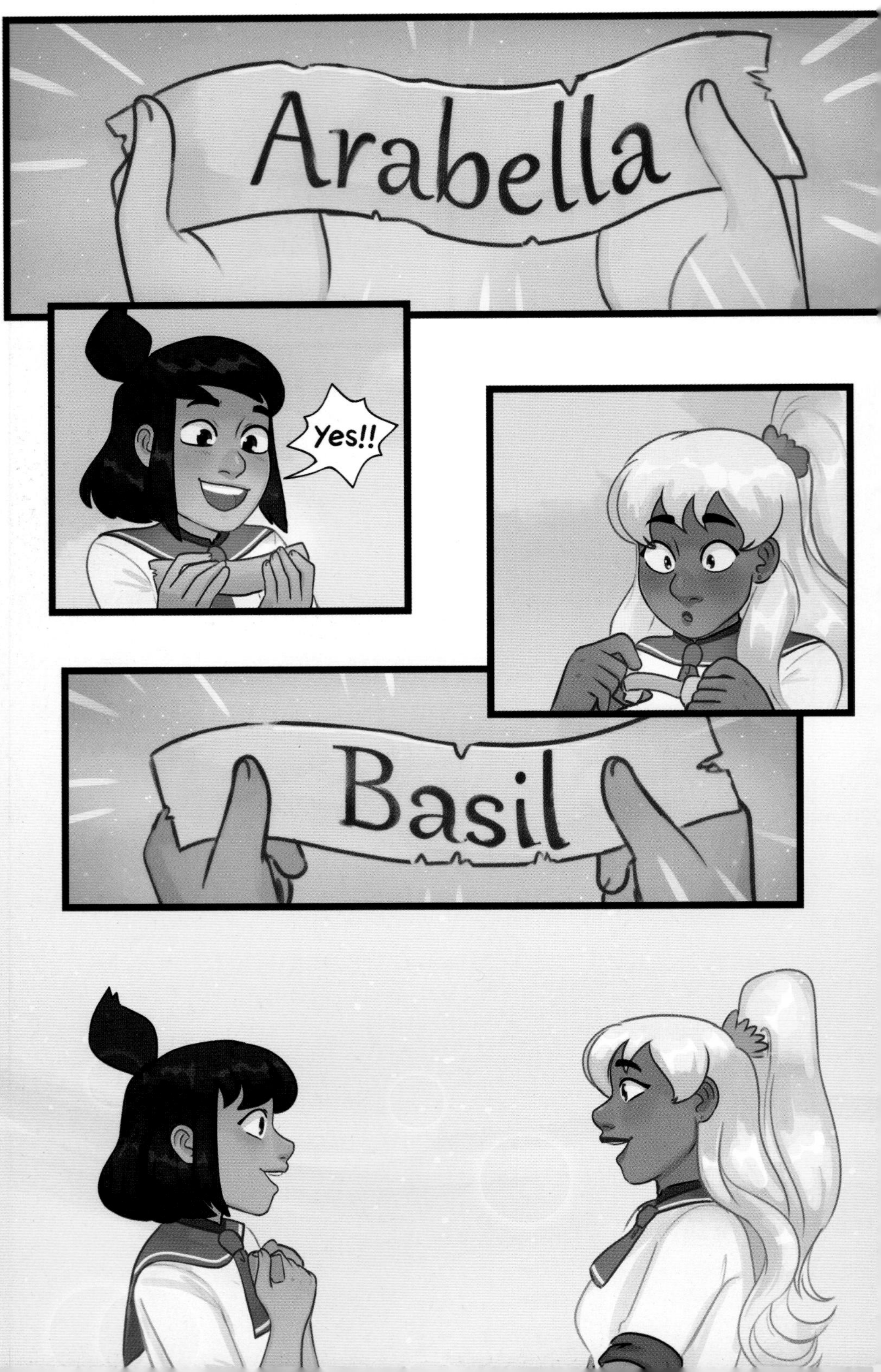
Arabella
Yes!!
Basil

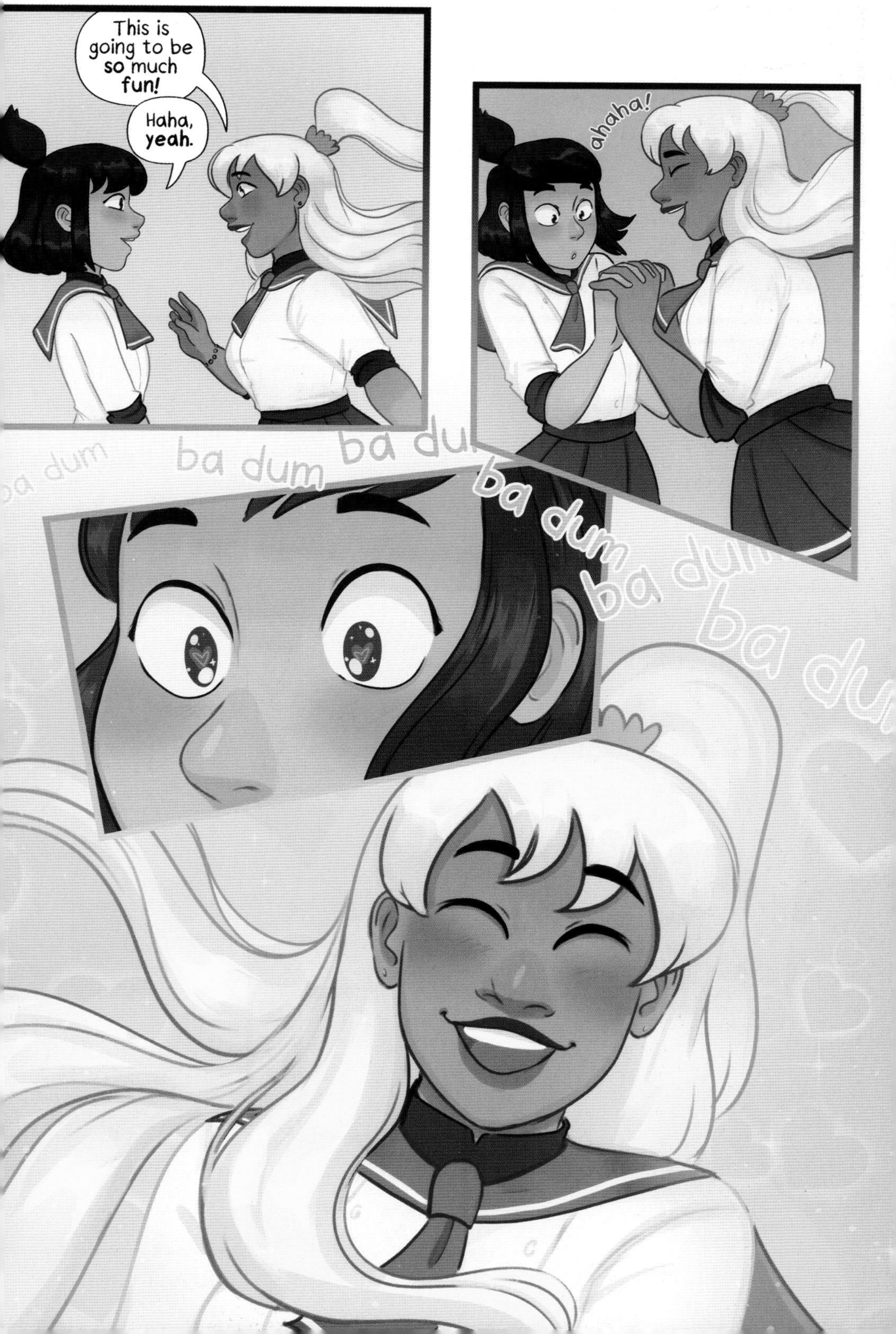
This is going to be so much fun!
Haha, yeah.
ahaha!
ba dum
ba dum
ba du
ba dum
ba du
ba du

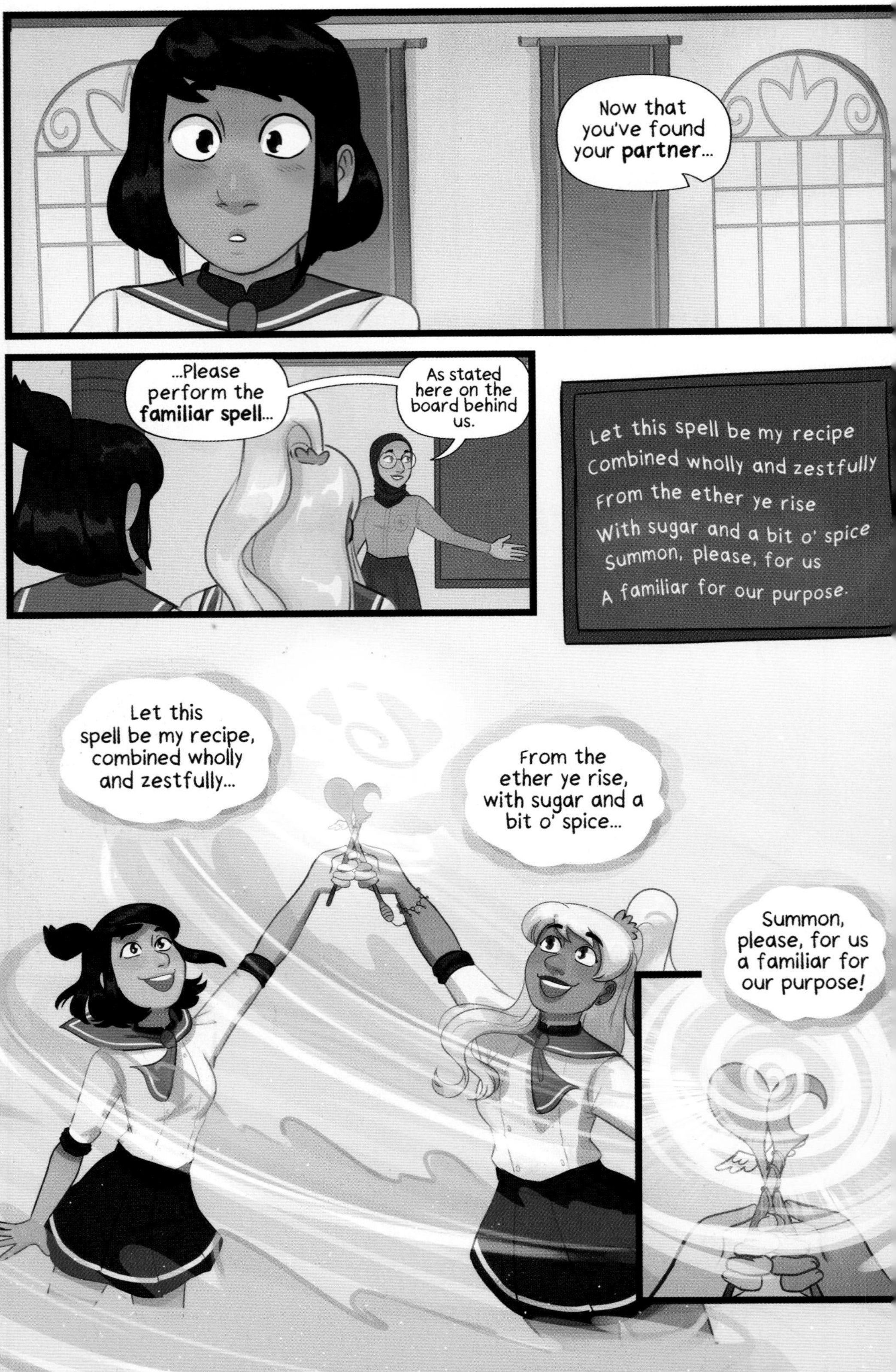
Now that you've found your **partner**...
...Please perform the **familiar spell**...
As stated here on the board behind us.
Let this spell be my recipe
Combined wholly and zestfully
From the ether ye rise
With sugar and a bit o' spice
Summon, please, for us
A familiar for our purpose.
Let this spell be my recipe, combined wholly and zestfully...
From the ether ye rise, with sugar and a bit o' spice...
Summon, please, for us a familiar for our purpose!

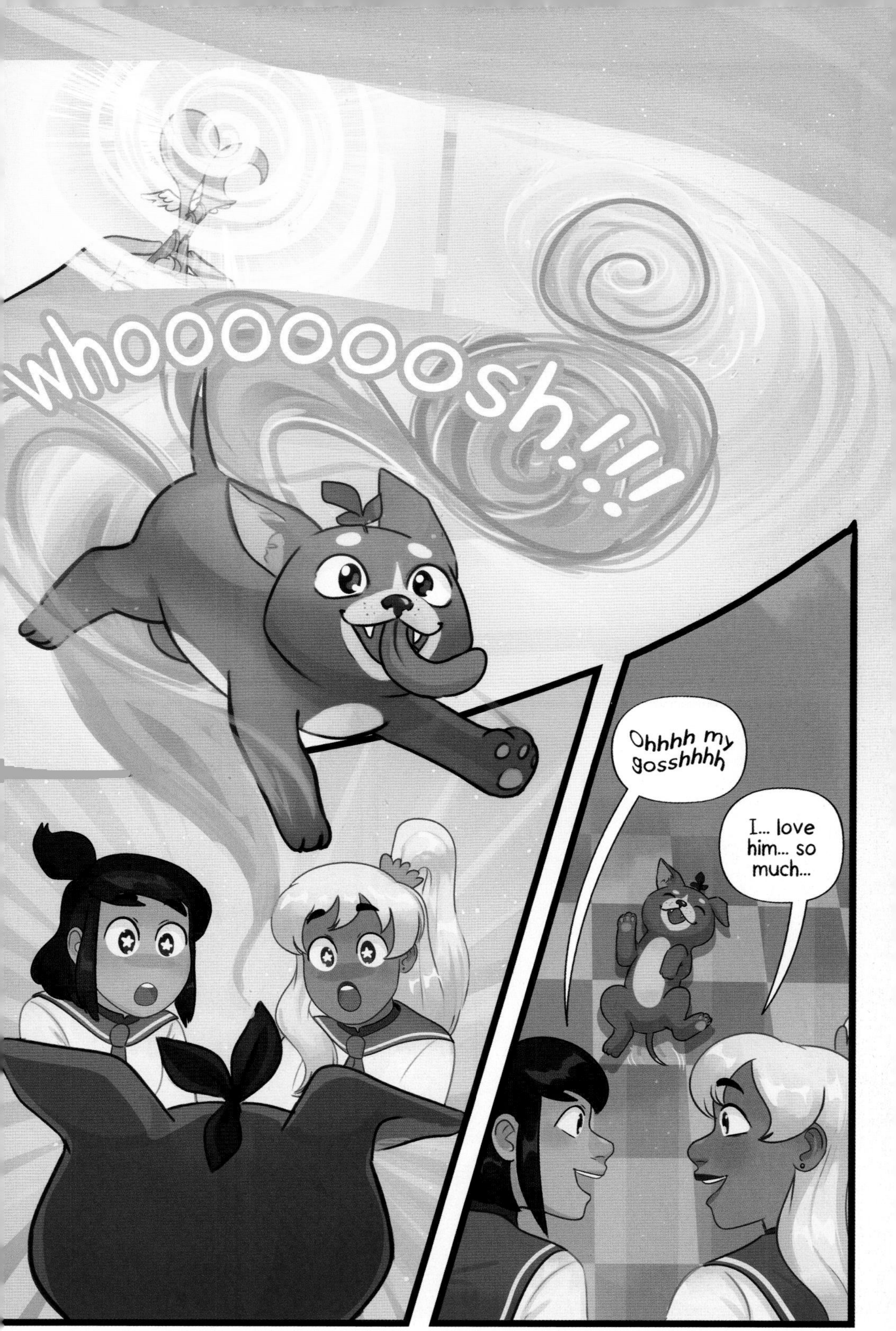
WHOOOOOOSH!!!
Ohhhh my gosshhhh
I... love him... so much...

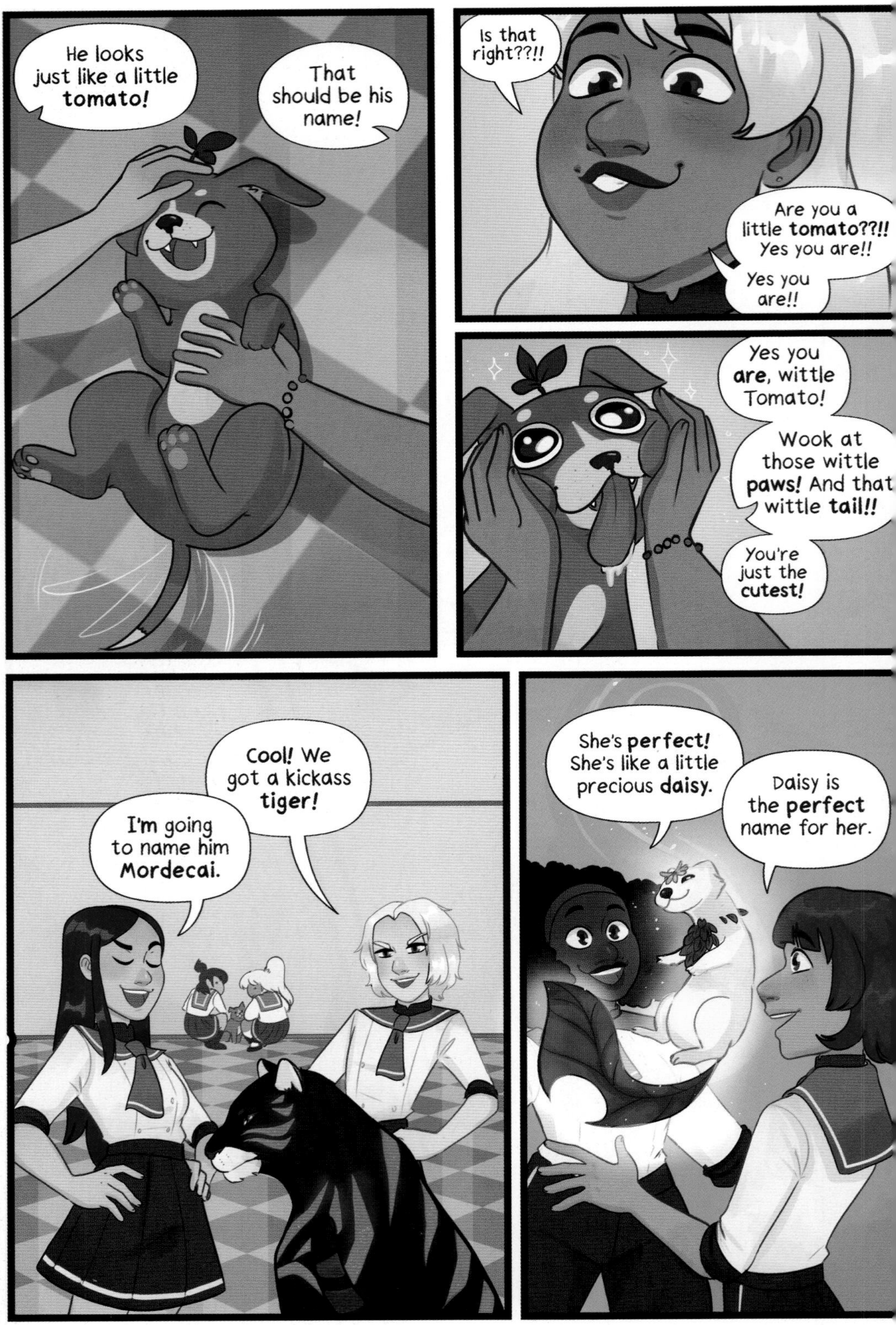
He looks just like a little **tomato!**
That should be his name!
Is that right??!!
Are you a little **tomato??!!** Yes you are!!
Yes you are!!
Yes you **are**, wittle Tomato!
Wook at those wittle **paws!** And that wittle **tail!!**
You're just the **cutest!**
Cool! We got a kickass **tiger!**
I'm going to name him **Mordecai.**
She's **perfect!** She's like a little precious **daisy.**
Daisy is the **perfect** name for her.

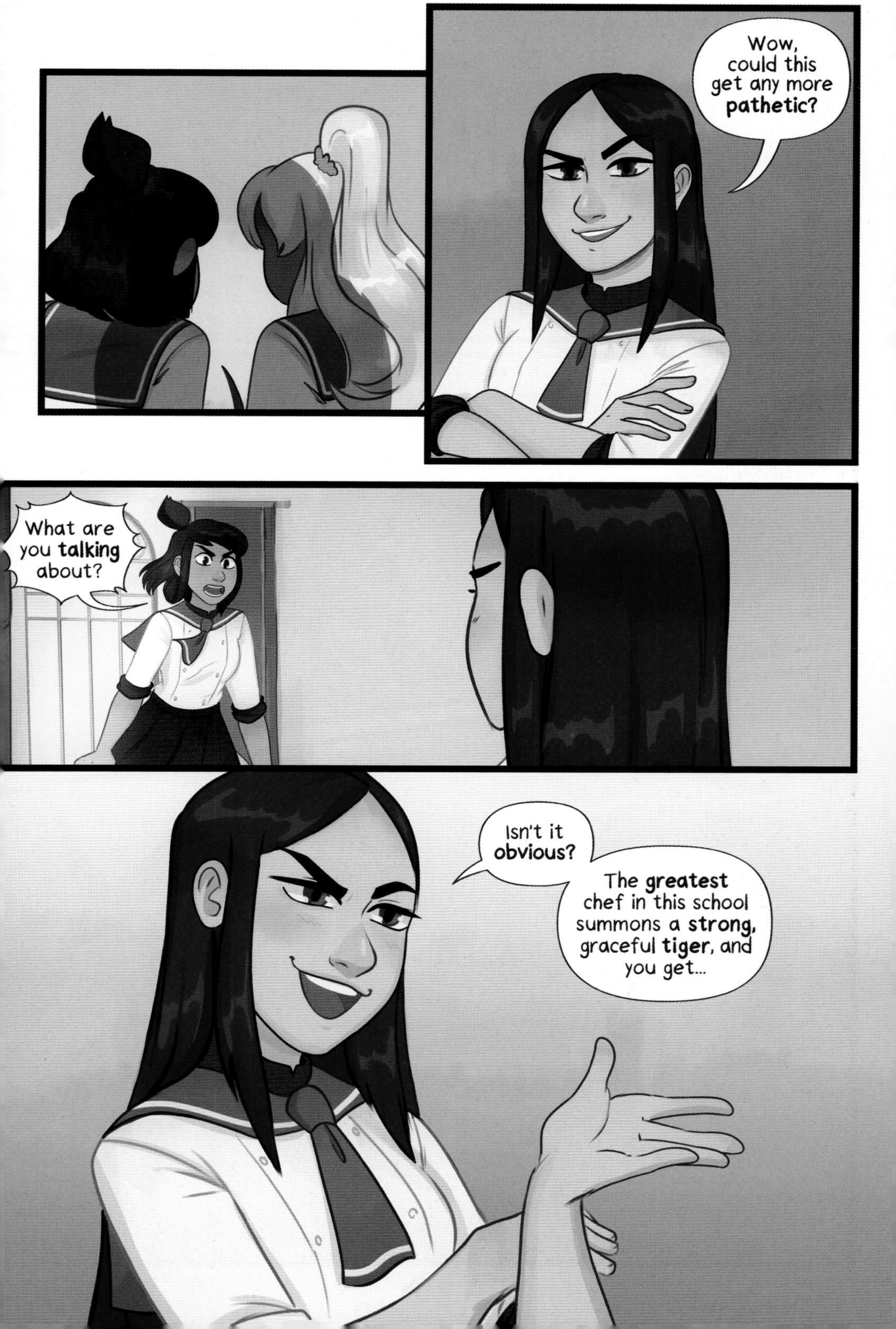
Wow, could this get any more **pathetic?**
What are you **talking** about?
Isn't it **obvious?**
The **greatest** chef in this school summons a **strong,** graceful **tiger**, and you get...

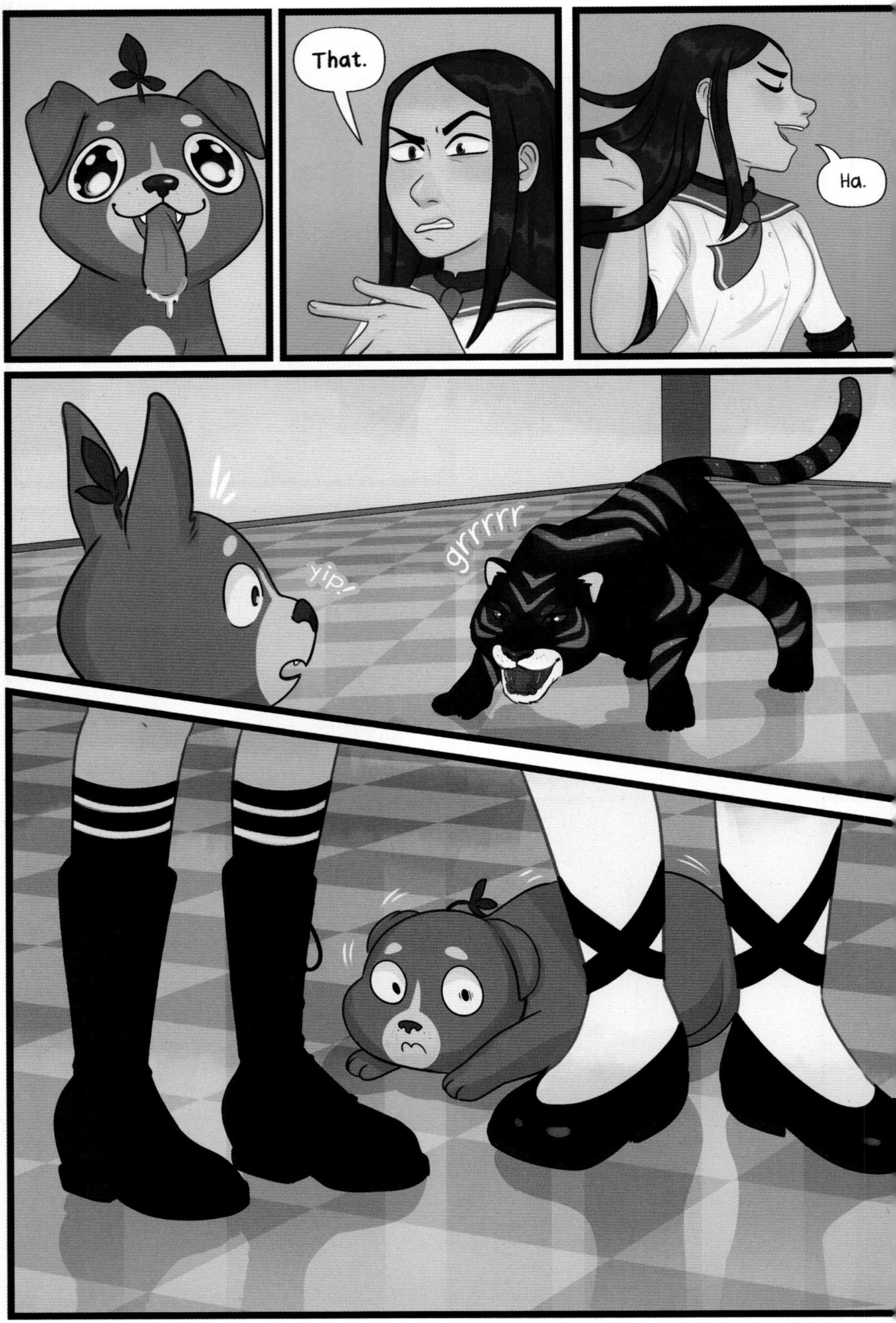
That.
Ha.
grrrrr
yip!

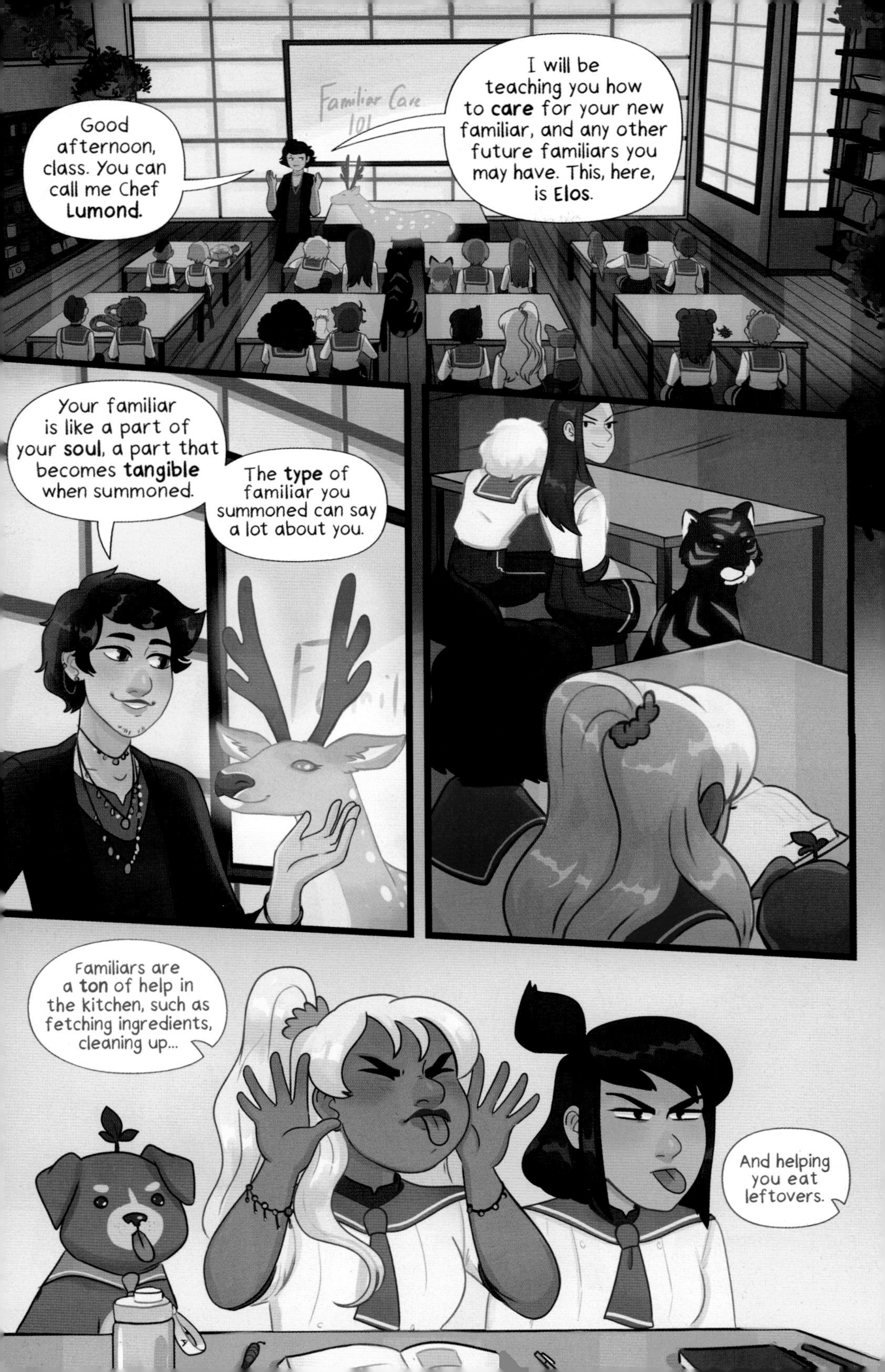
Familiar Care 101
Good afternoon, class. You can call me Chef **Lumond.**
I will be teaching you how to **care** for your new familiar, and any other future familiars you may have. This, here, is **Elos.**
Your familiar is like a part of your **soul**, a part that becomes **tangible** when summoned.
The **type** of familiar you summoned can say a lot about you.
Familiars are a **ton** of help in the kitchen, such as fetching ingredients, cleaning up...
And helping you eat leftovers.

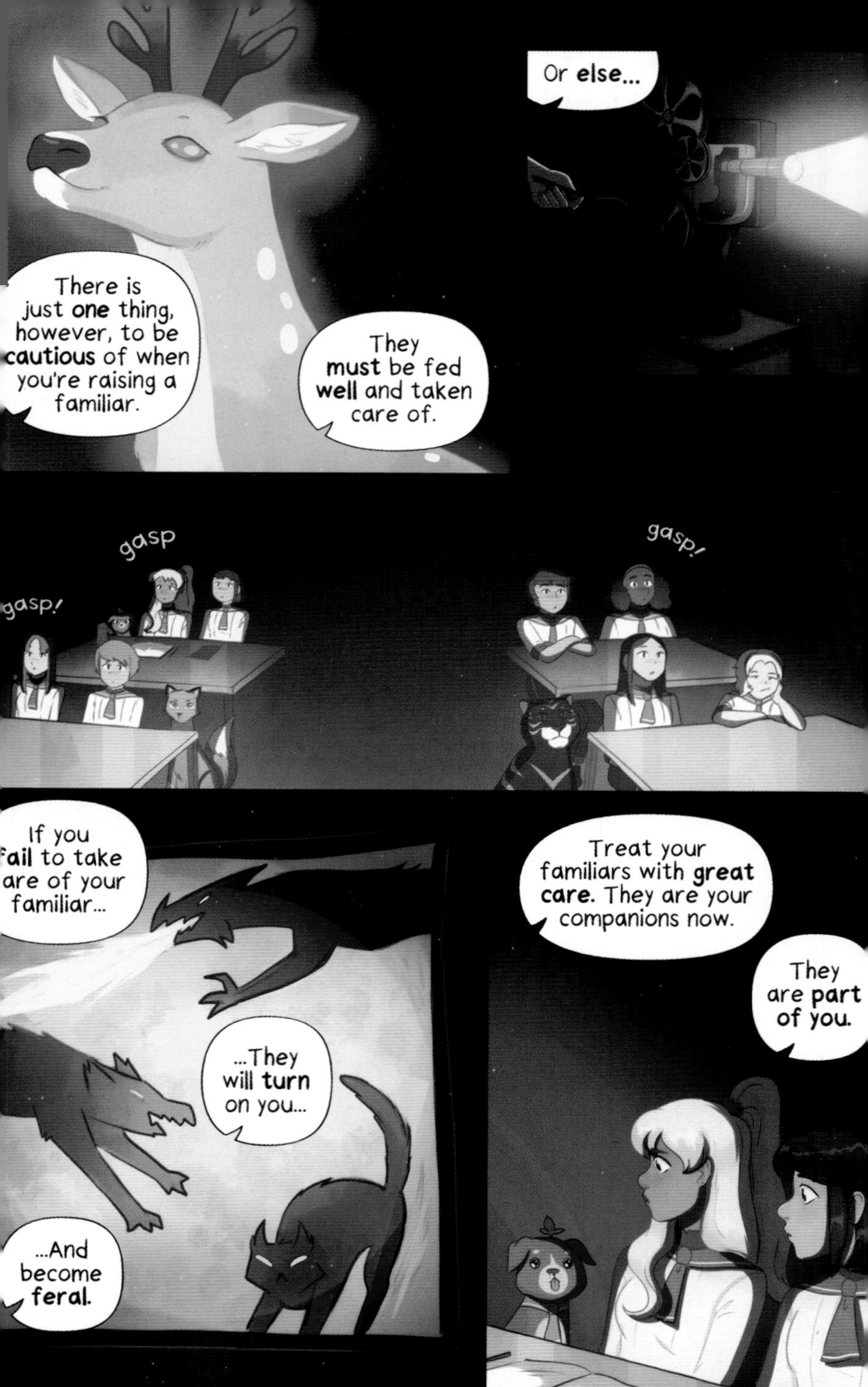

There is just one thing, however, to be cautious of when you're raising a familiar.
They must be fed well and taken care of.
Or else...
gasp!
gasp
gasp!
If you fail to take care of your familiar...
...They will turn on you...
...And become feral.
Treat your familiars with great care. They are your companions now.
They are part of you.

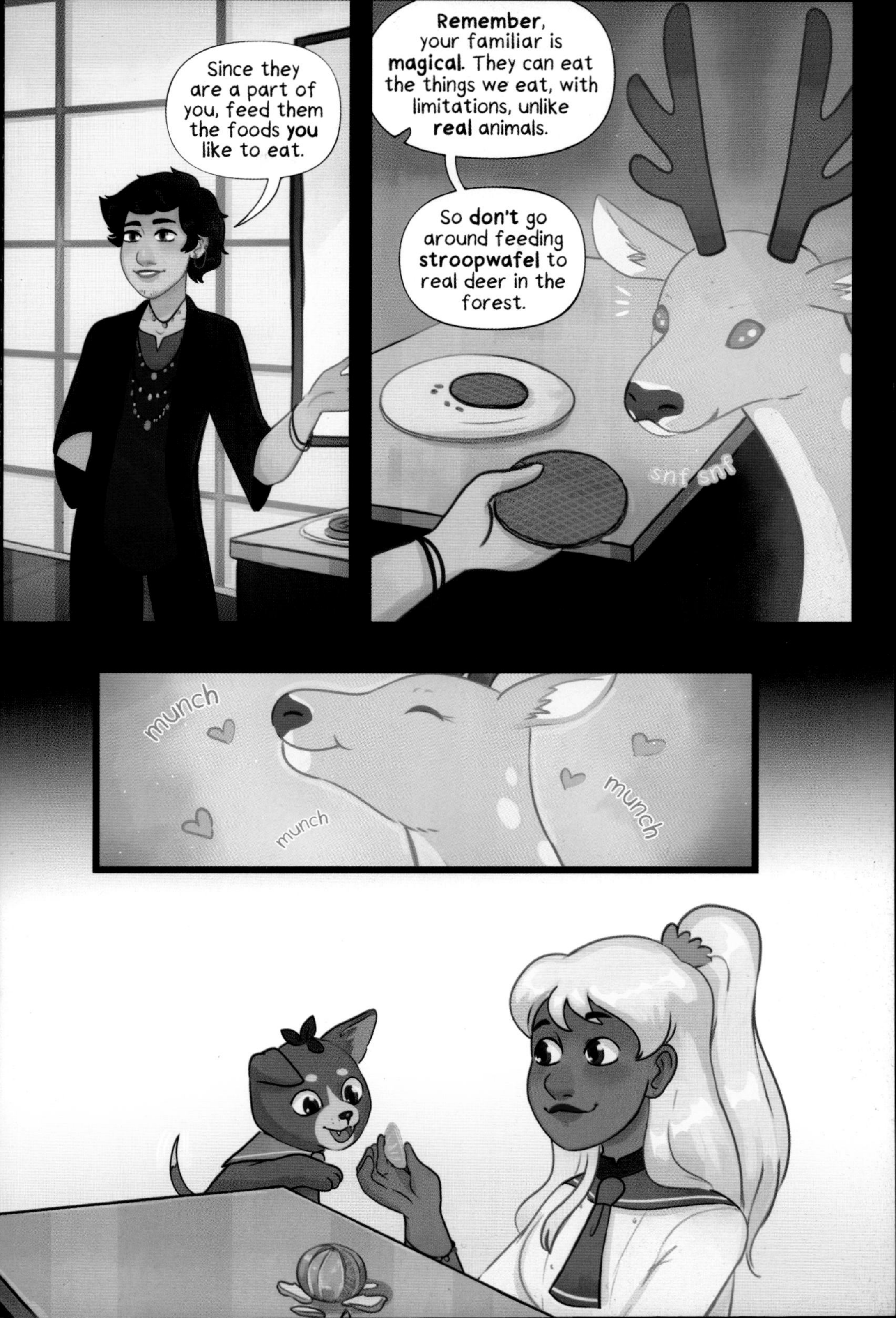
Since they are a part of you, feed them the foods **you** like to eat.
Remember, your familiar is **magical**. They can eat the things we eat, with limitations, unlike **real** animals.
So **don't** go around feeding **stroopwafel** to real deer in the forest.
snf snf
munch
munch
munch

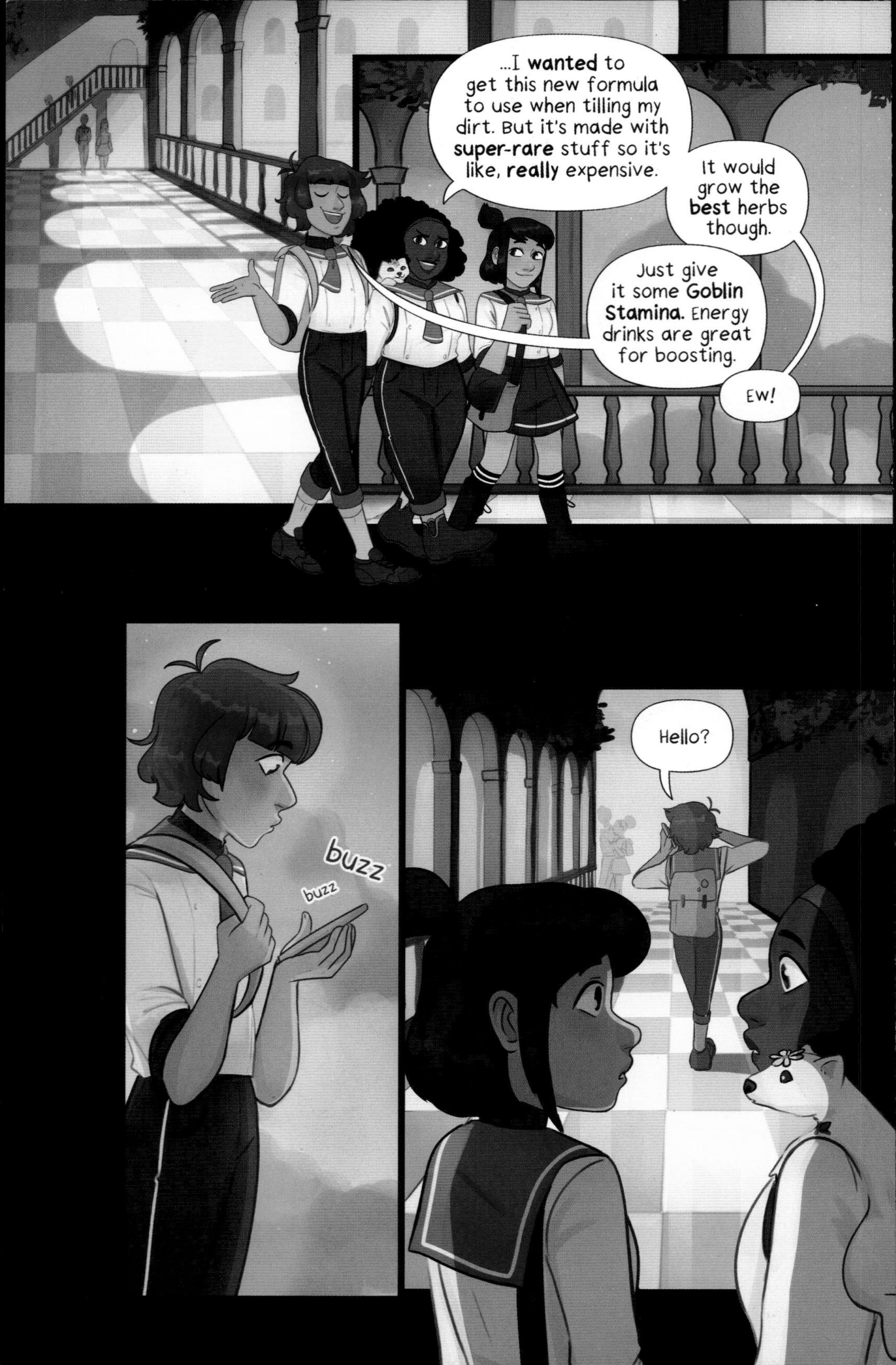
...I **wanted** to get this new formula to use when tilling my dirt. But it's made with **super-rare** stuff so it's like, **really** expensive.
It would grow the **best** herbs though.
Just give it some **Goblin Stamina.** Energy drinks are great for boosting.
EW!
buzz
buzz
Hello?

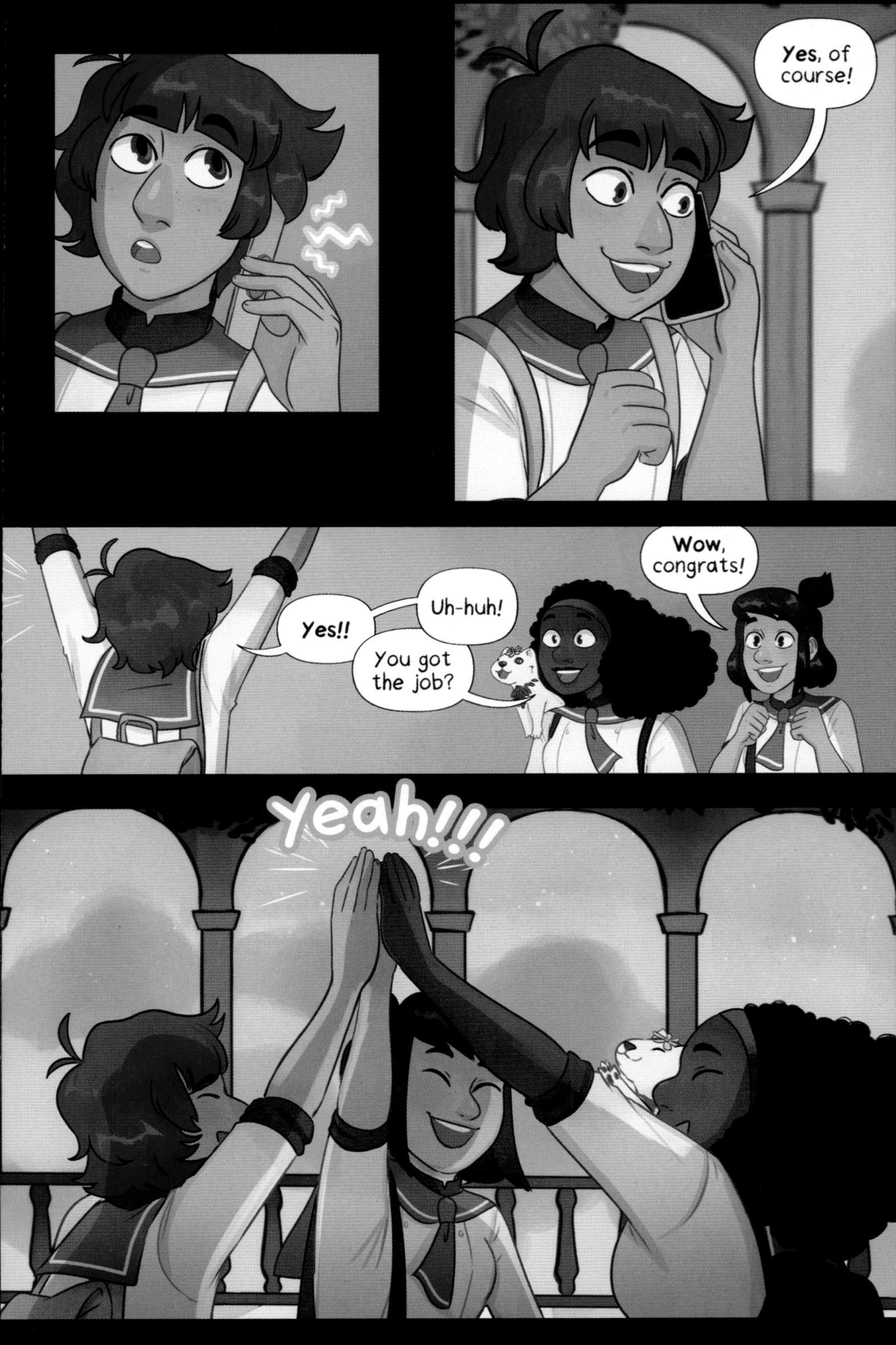
Yes, of course!
Yes!!
Uh-huh!
You got the job?
Wow, congrats!
Yeah!!!

Chapter
THREE

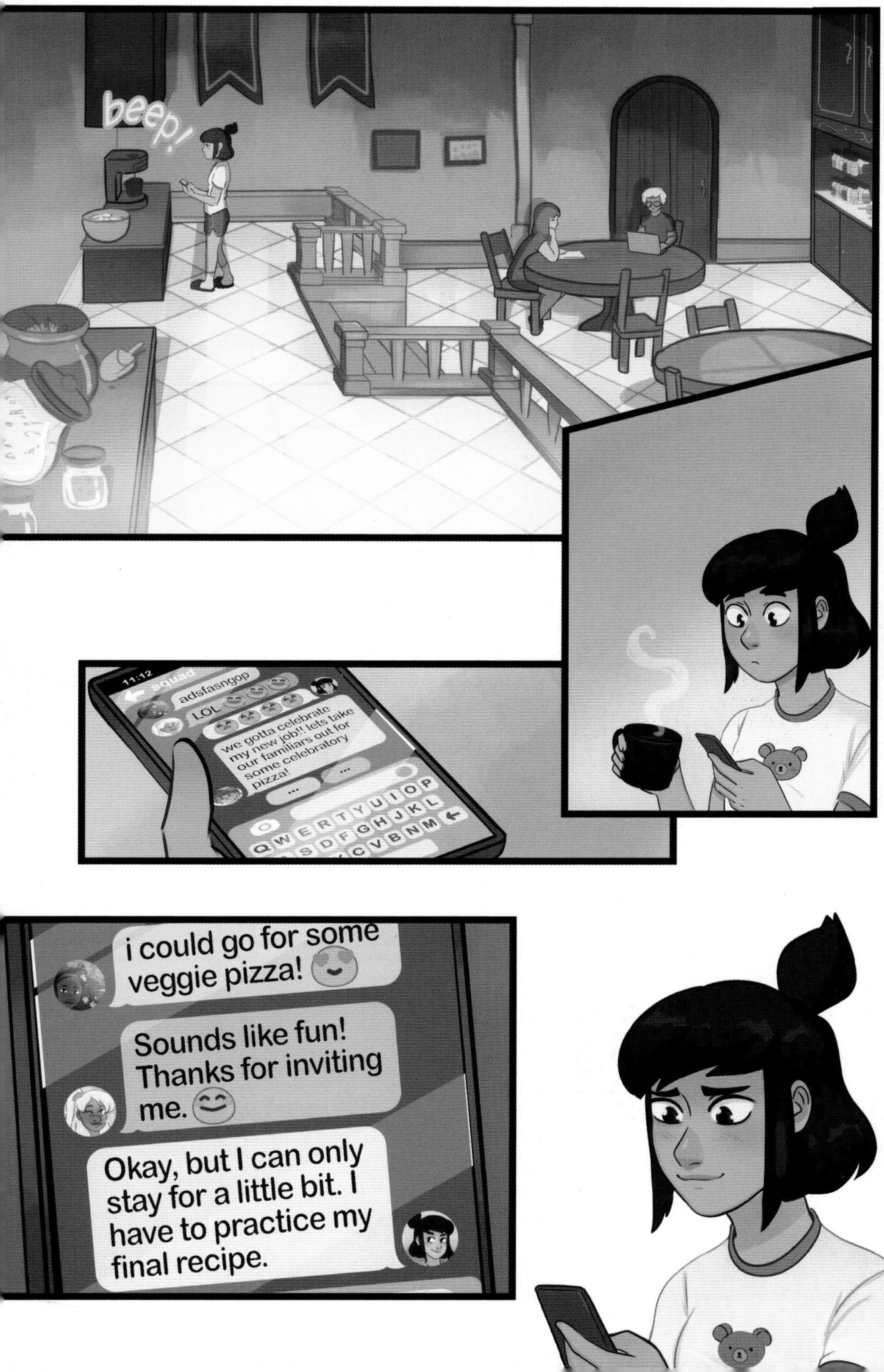

beep!
11:12
squad
adsfasngop
LOL
we gotta celebrate my new job!! lets take our familiars out for some celebratory pizza!
i could go for some veggie pizza!
Sounds like fun! Thanks for inviting me.
Okay, but I can only stay for a little bit. I have to practice my final recipe.

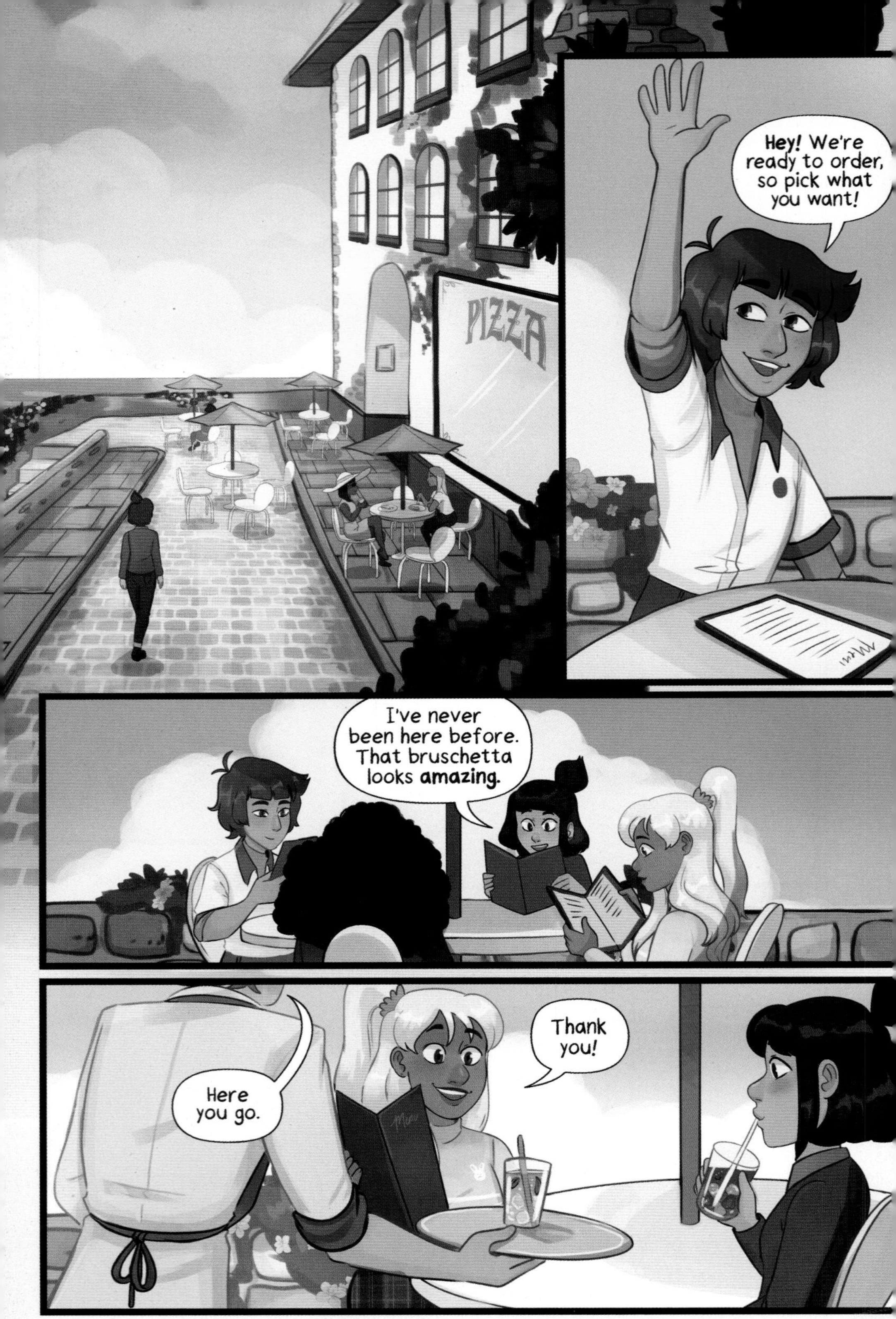
PIZZA
Hey! We're ready to order, so pick what you want!
I've never been here before. That bruschetta looks amazing.
Here you go.
Thank you!

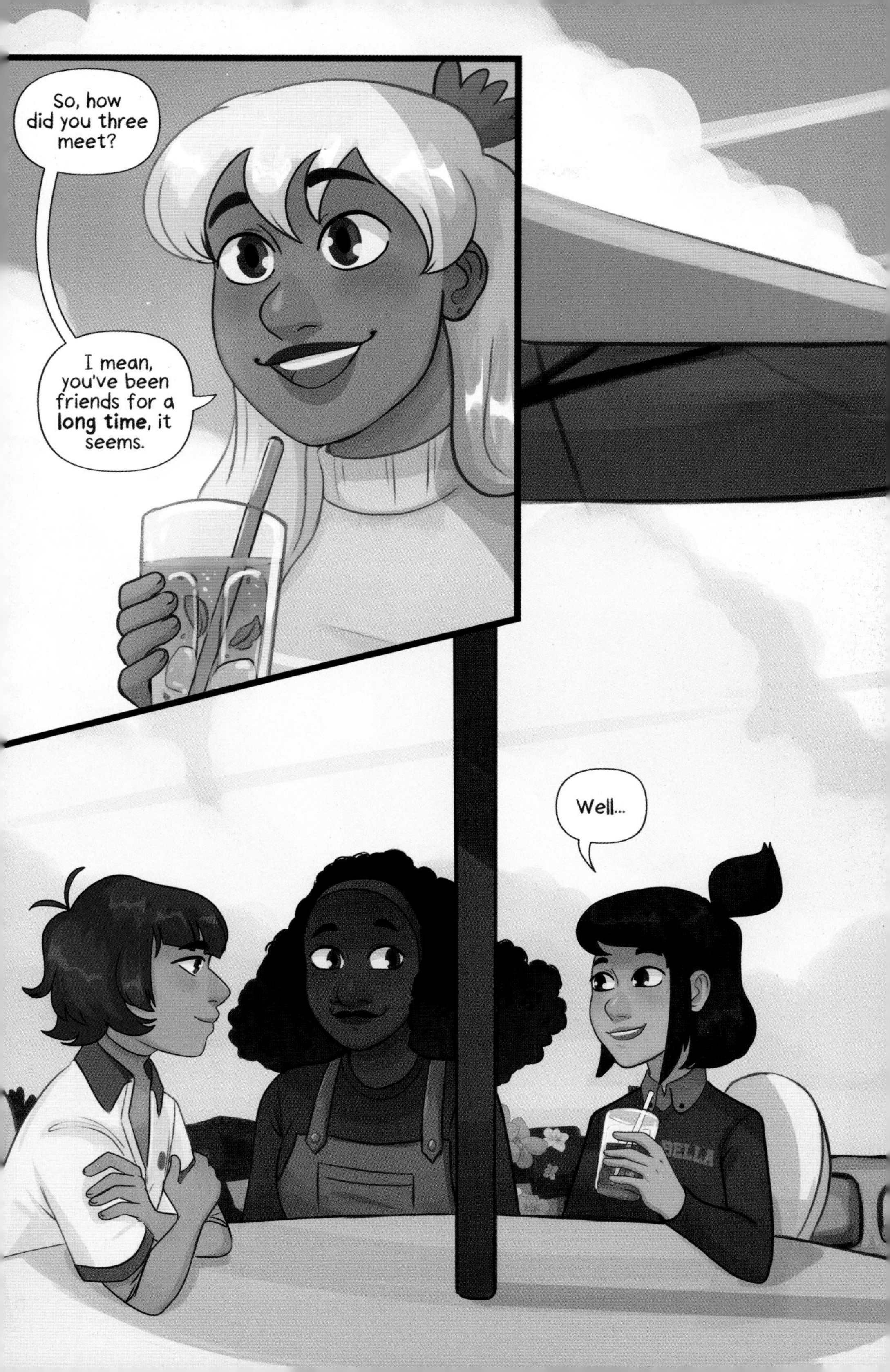
So, how did you three meet?
I mean, you've been friends for a **long time**, it seems.
Well...
BELLA

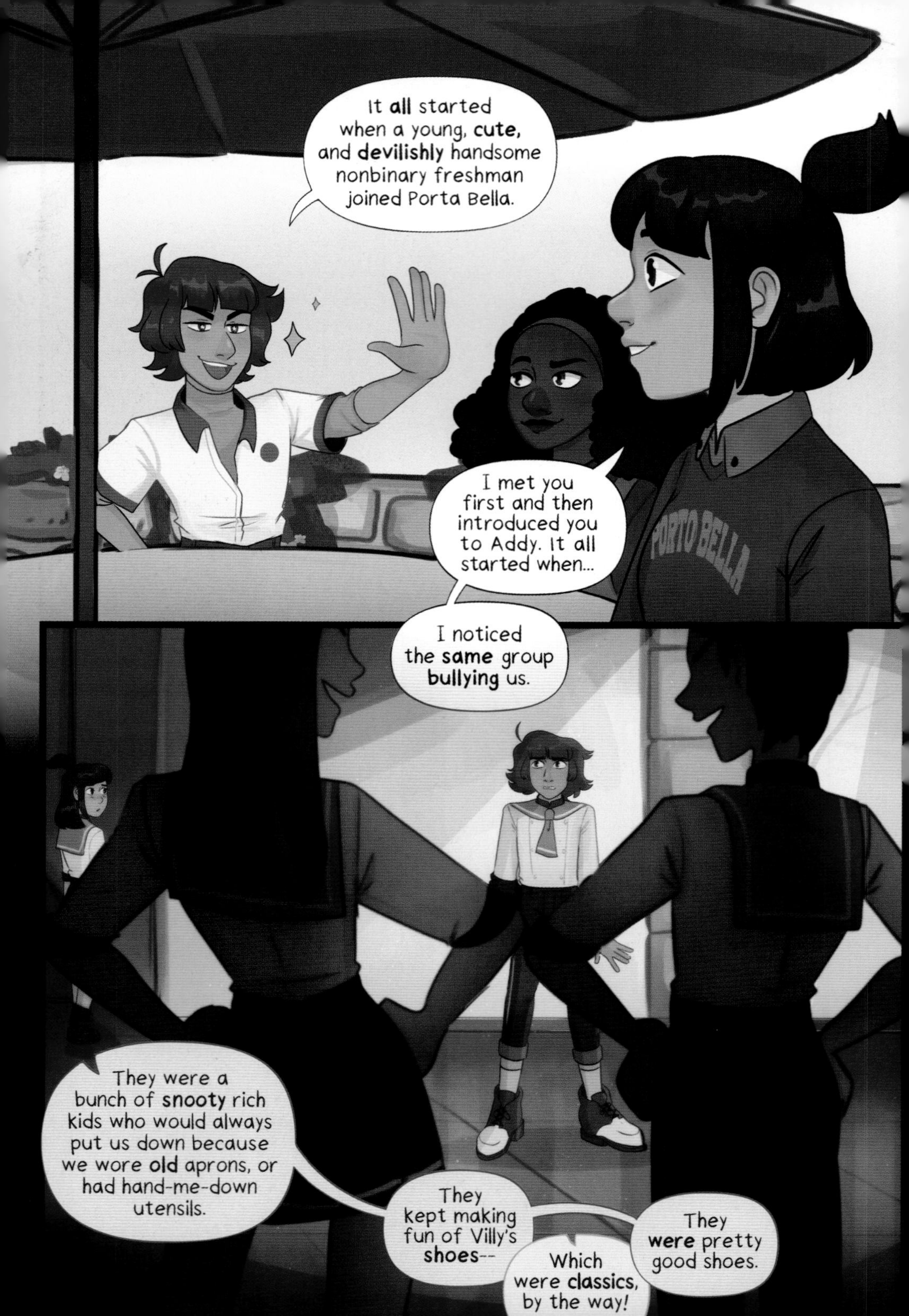
It all started when a young, cute, and devilishly handsome nonbinary freshman joined Porta Bella.
PORTO BELLA
I met you first and then introduced you to Addy. It all started when...
I noticed the same group bullying us.
They were a bunch of snooty rich kids who would always put us down because we wore old aprons, or had hand-me-down utensils.
They kept making fun of Villy's shoes--
Which were classics, by the way!
They were pretty good shoes.

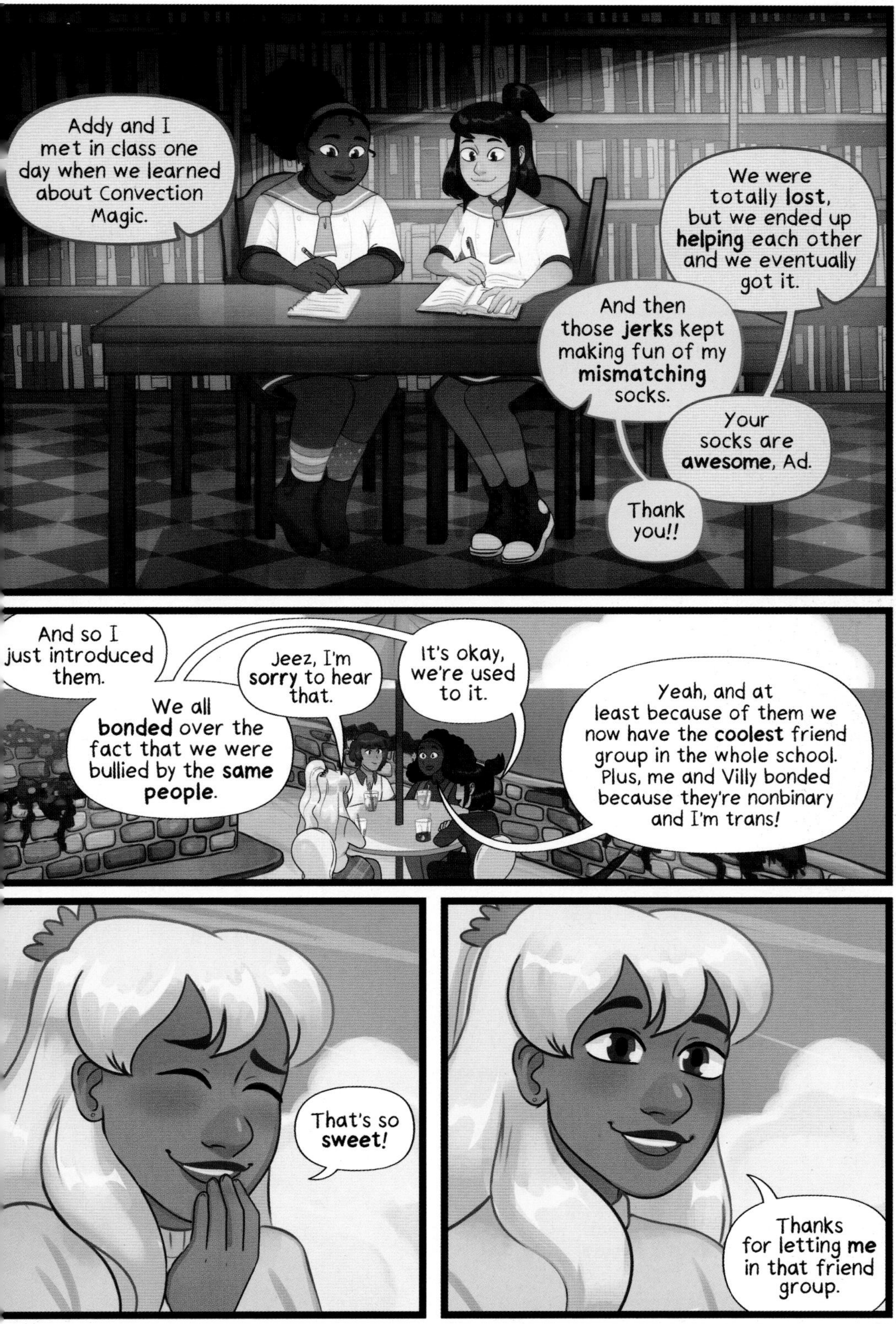
Addy and I met in class one day when we learned about Convection Magic.
We were totally **lost**, but we ended up **helping** each other and we eventually got it.
And then those **jerks** kept making fun of my **mismatching** socks.
Your socks are **awesome**, Ad.
Thank you!!
And so I just introduced them.
We all **bonded** over the fact that we were bullied by the **same people**.
Jeez, I'm **sorry** to hear that.
It's okay, we're used to it.
Yeah, and at least because of them we now have the **coolest** friend group in the whole school. Plus, me and Villy bonded because they're nonbinary and I'm trans!
That's so **sweet**!
Thanks for letting **me** in that friend group.

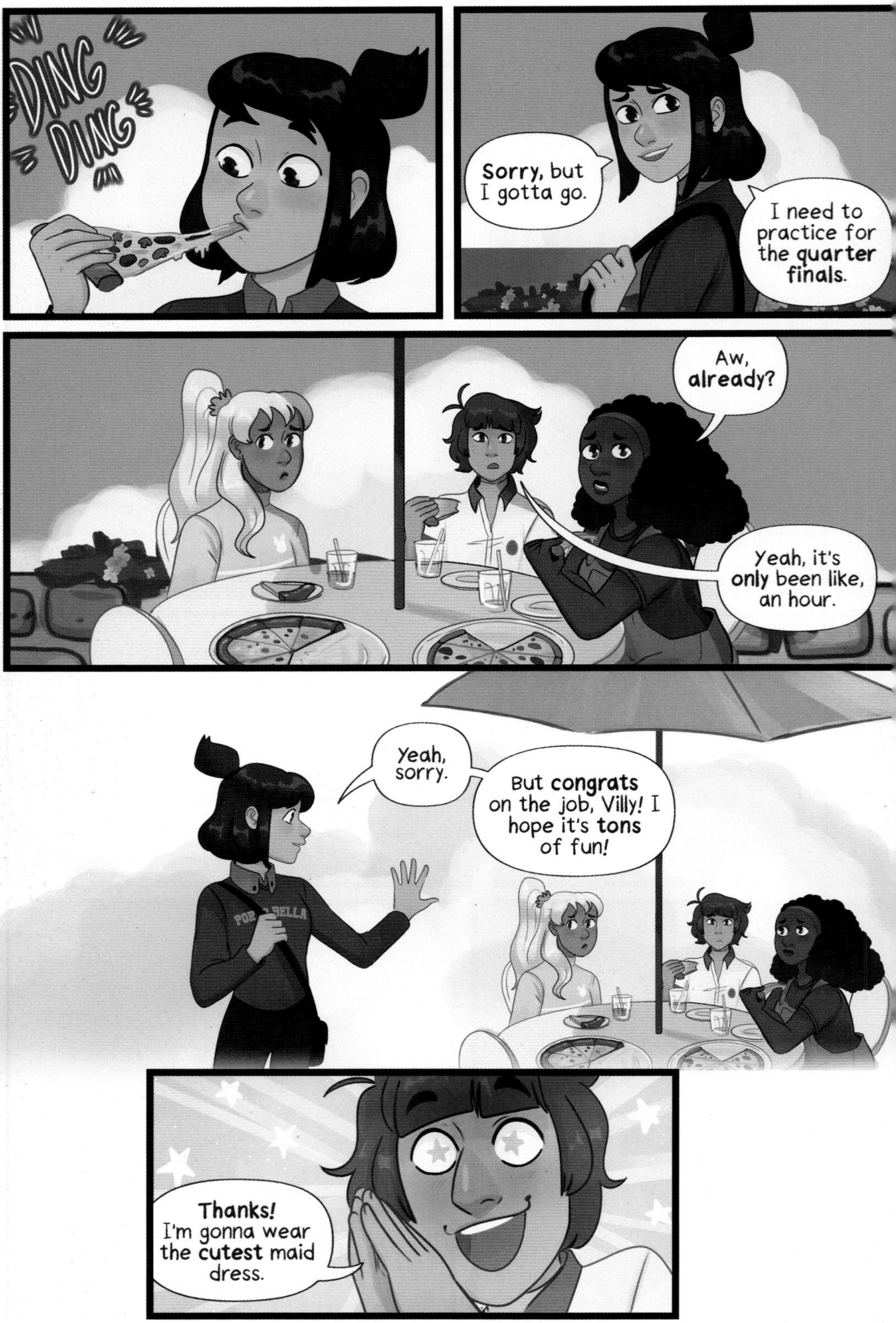
DING DING
Sorry, but I gotta go.
I need to practice for the quarter finals.
Aw, already?
Yeah, it's only been like, an hour.
Yeah, sorry.
But congrats on the job, Villy! I hope it's tons of fun!
Thanks! I'm gonna wear the cutest maid dress.

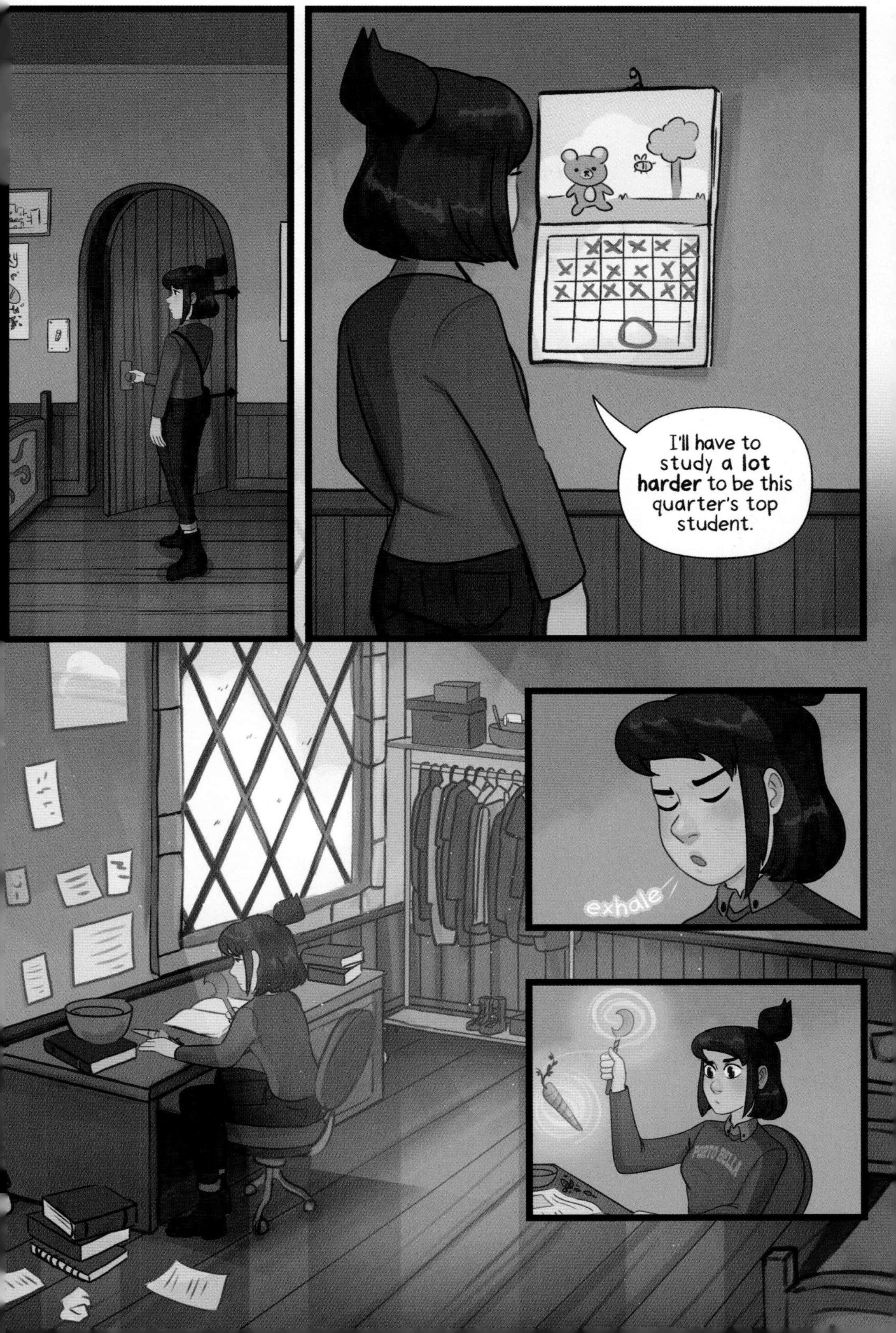
I'll have to study a **lot harder** to be this quarter's top student.
exhale
PORTO BELLA

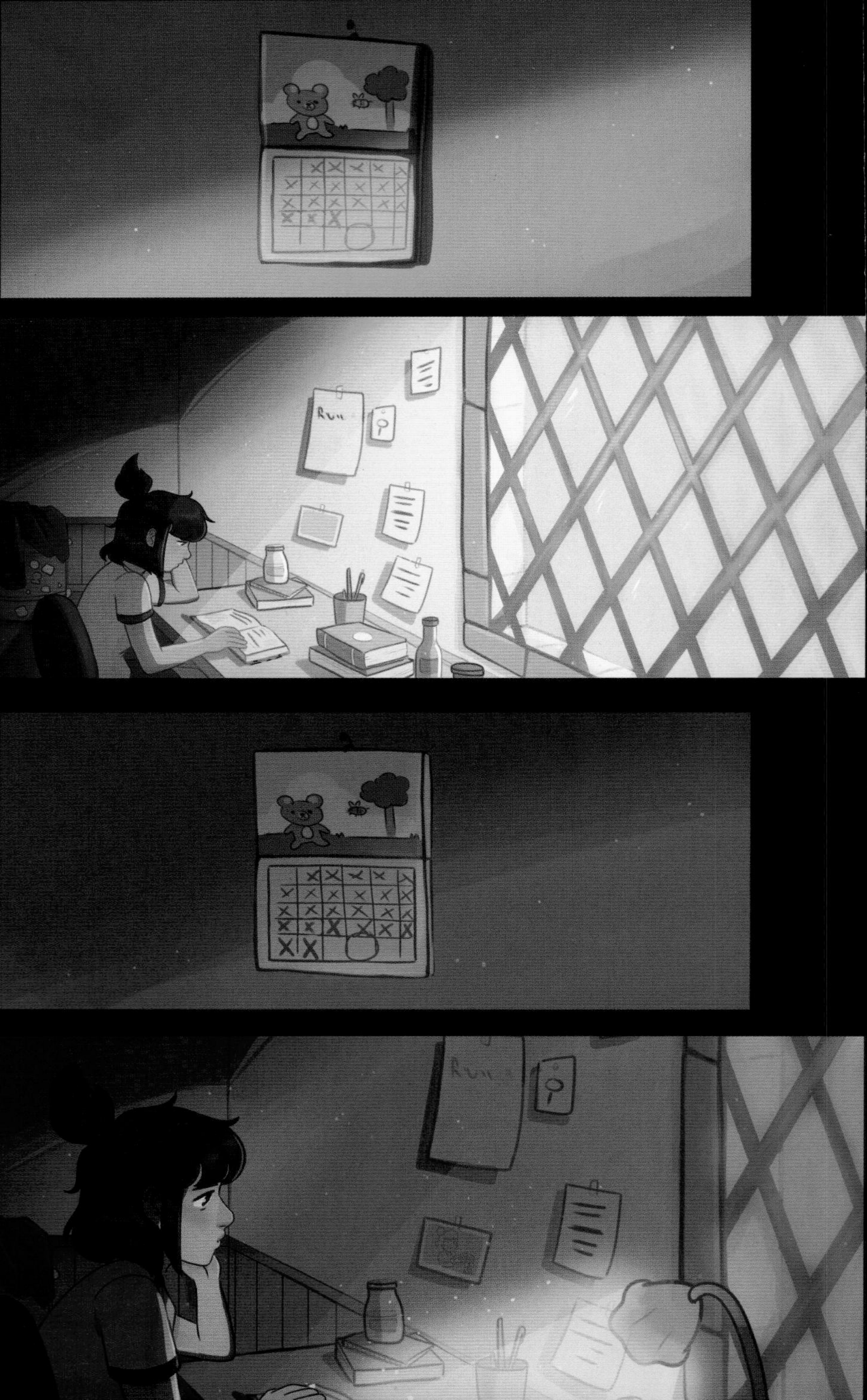
Run

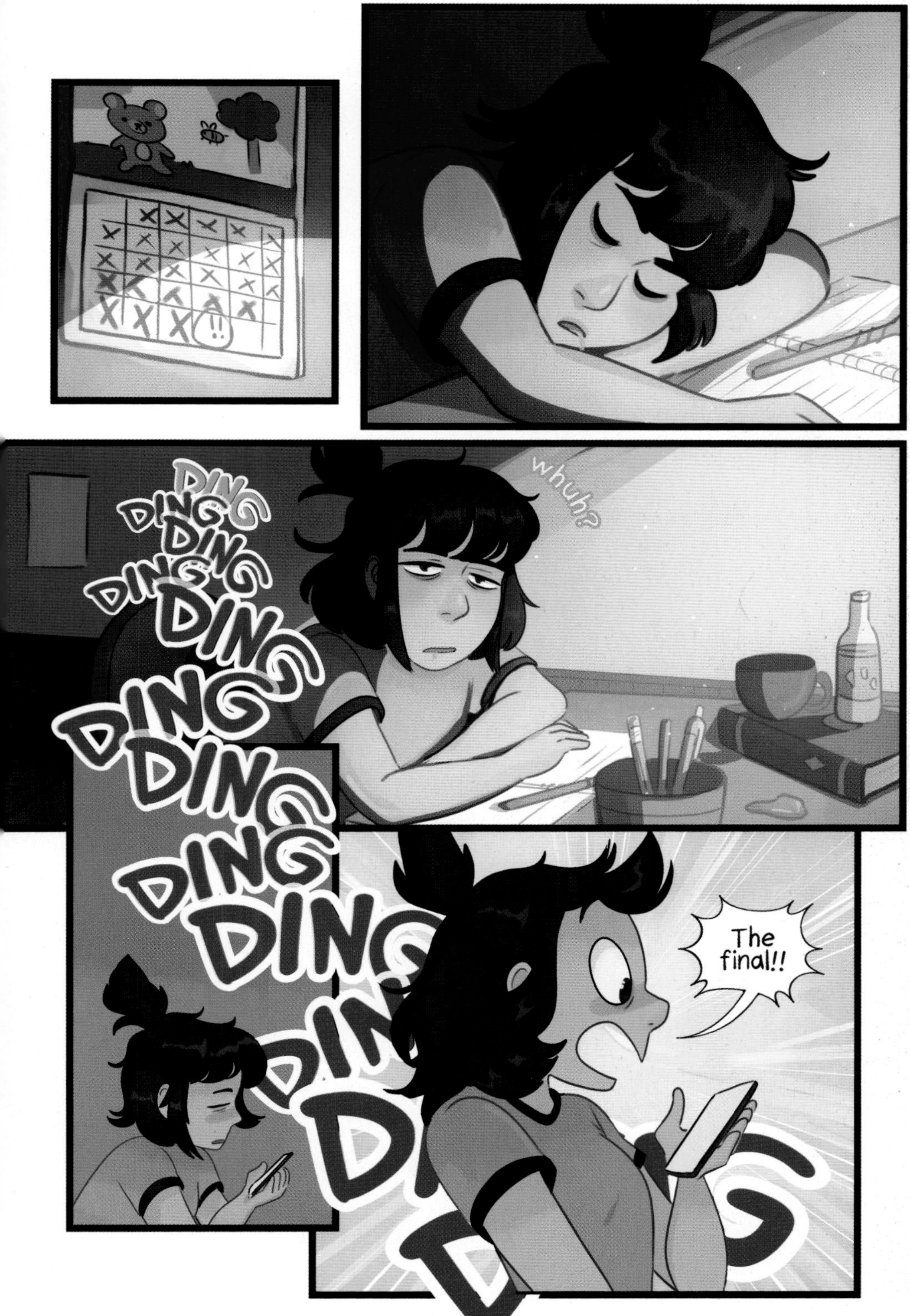

!!
DING
DING
DING
DING
DING
whuh?
DING
DING
DING
DING
DING
DING
The final!!

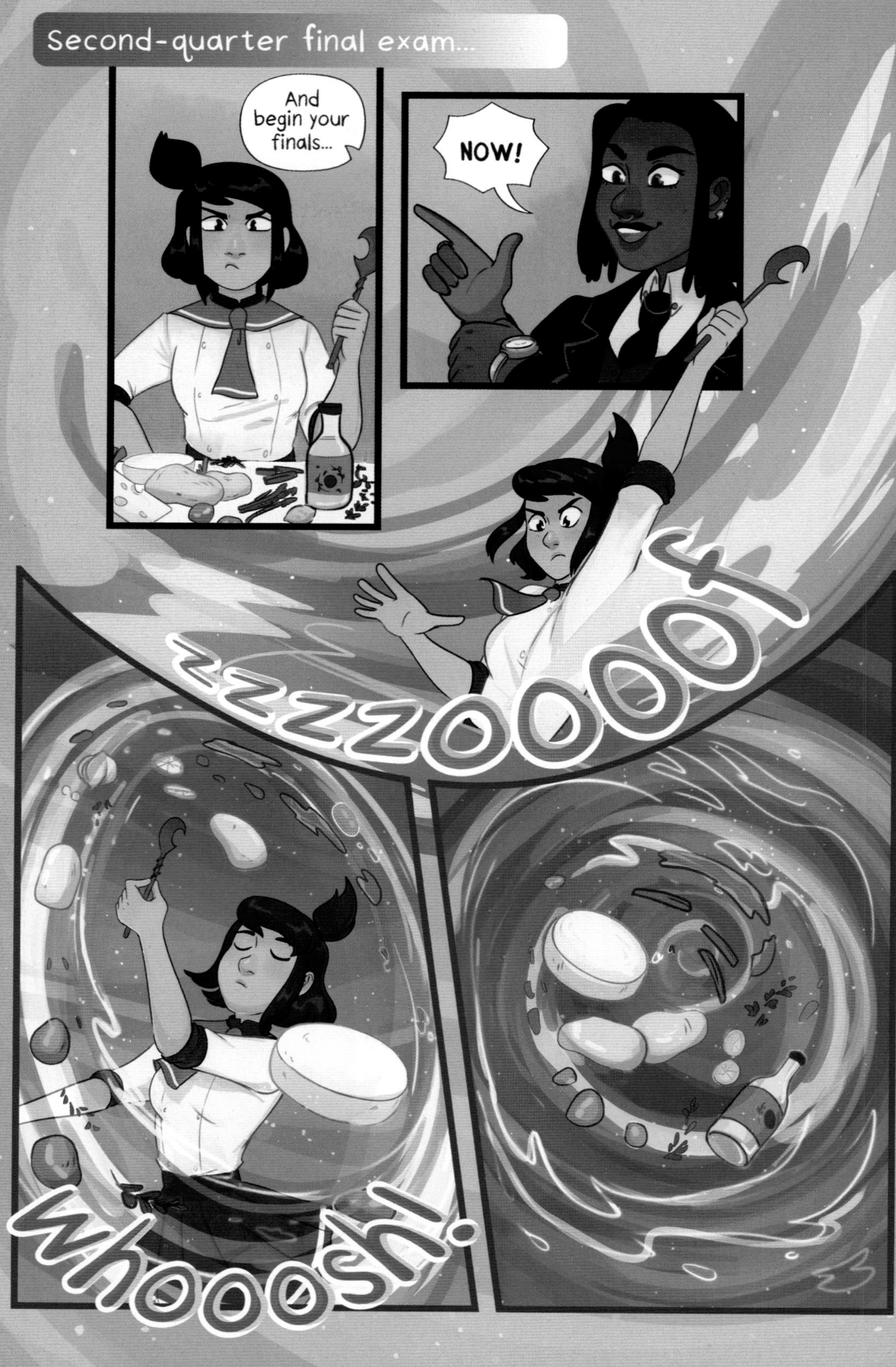

Second-quarter final exam...
And begin your finals...
NOW!
ZZZZOOOOf
WHOOOSH!

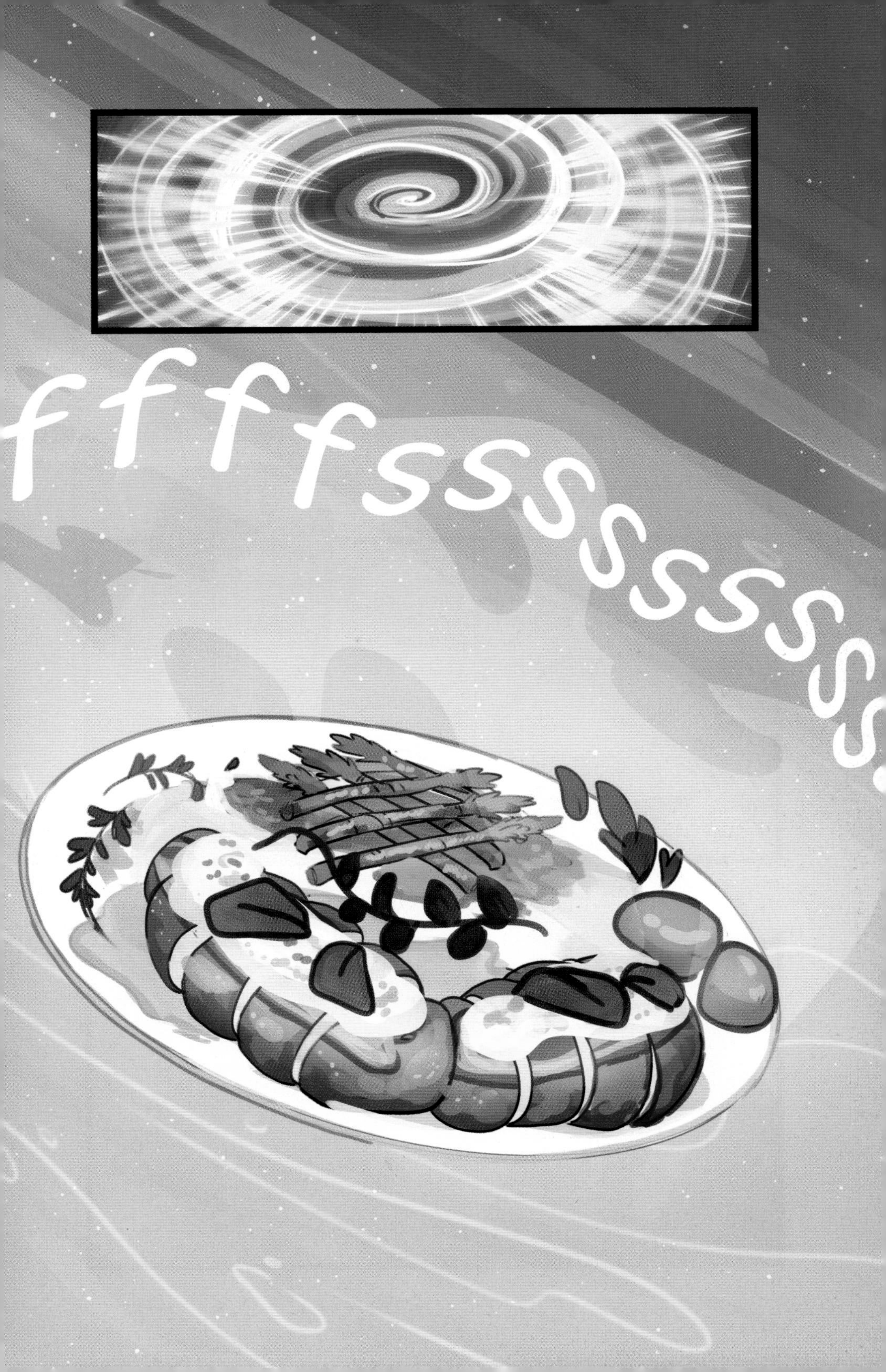
fffssssssss

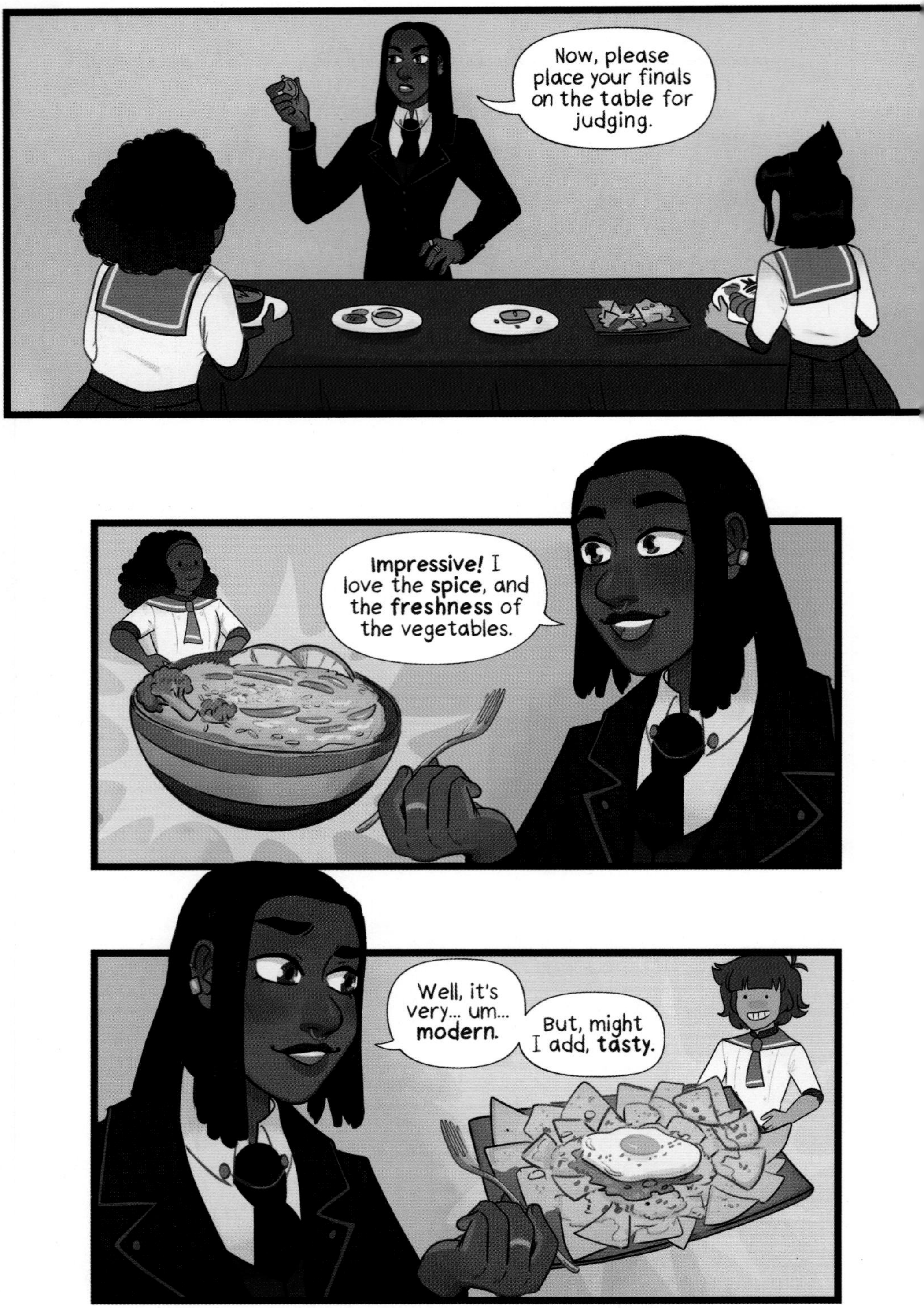
Now, please place your finals on the table for judging.
Impressive! I love the **spice**, and the **freshness** of the vegetables.
Well, it's very... um... **modern**.
But, might I add, **tasty**.

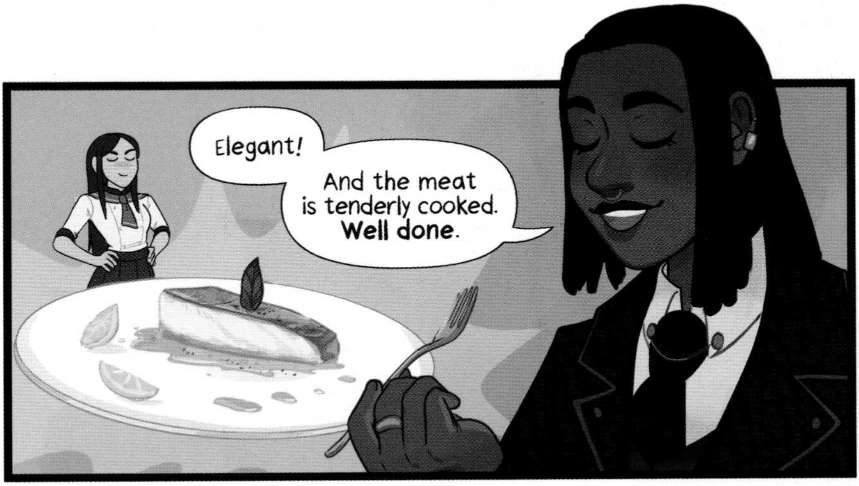
Elegant!
And the meat is tenderly cooked. **Well done**.

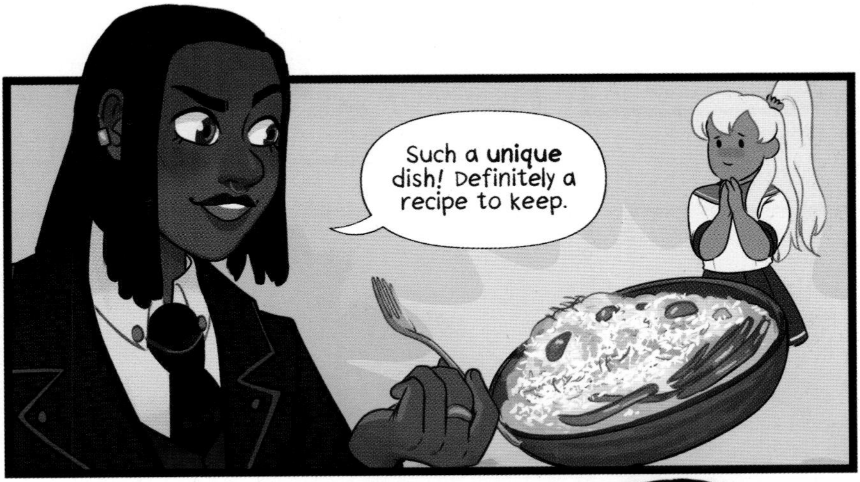
Such a **unique** dish! Definitely a recipe to keep.

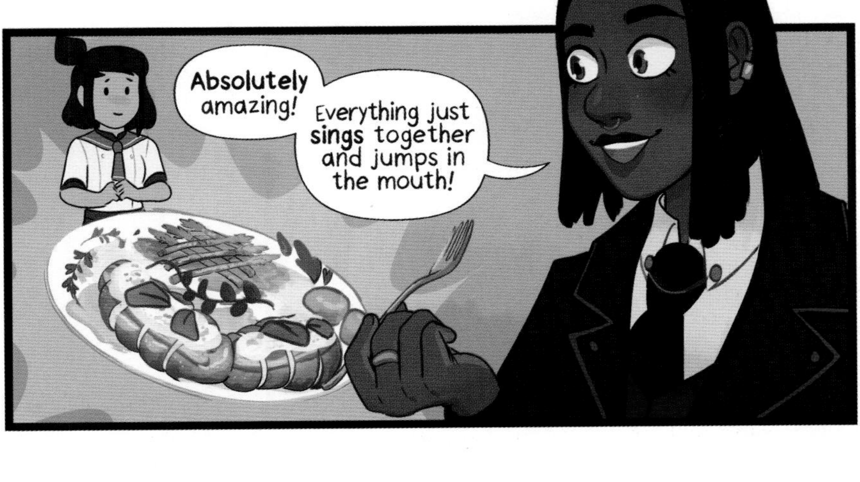
Absolutely amazing!
Everything just **sings** together and jumps in the mouth!

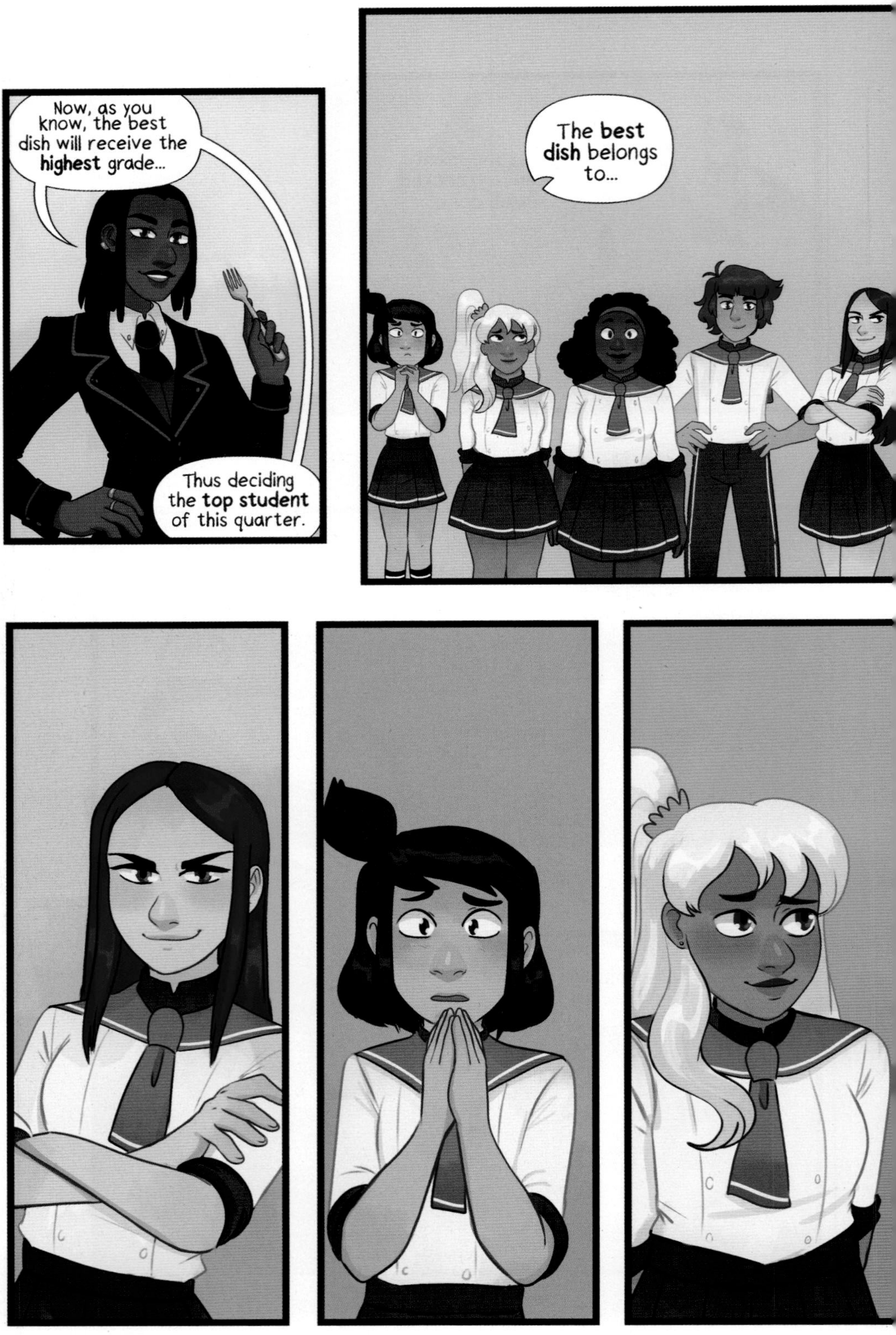

Now, as you know, the best dish will receive the **highest** grade...
Thus deciding the **top student** of this quarter.
The **best dish** belongs to...

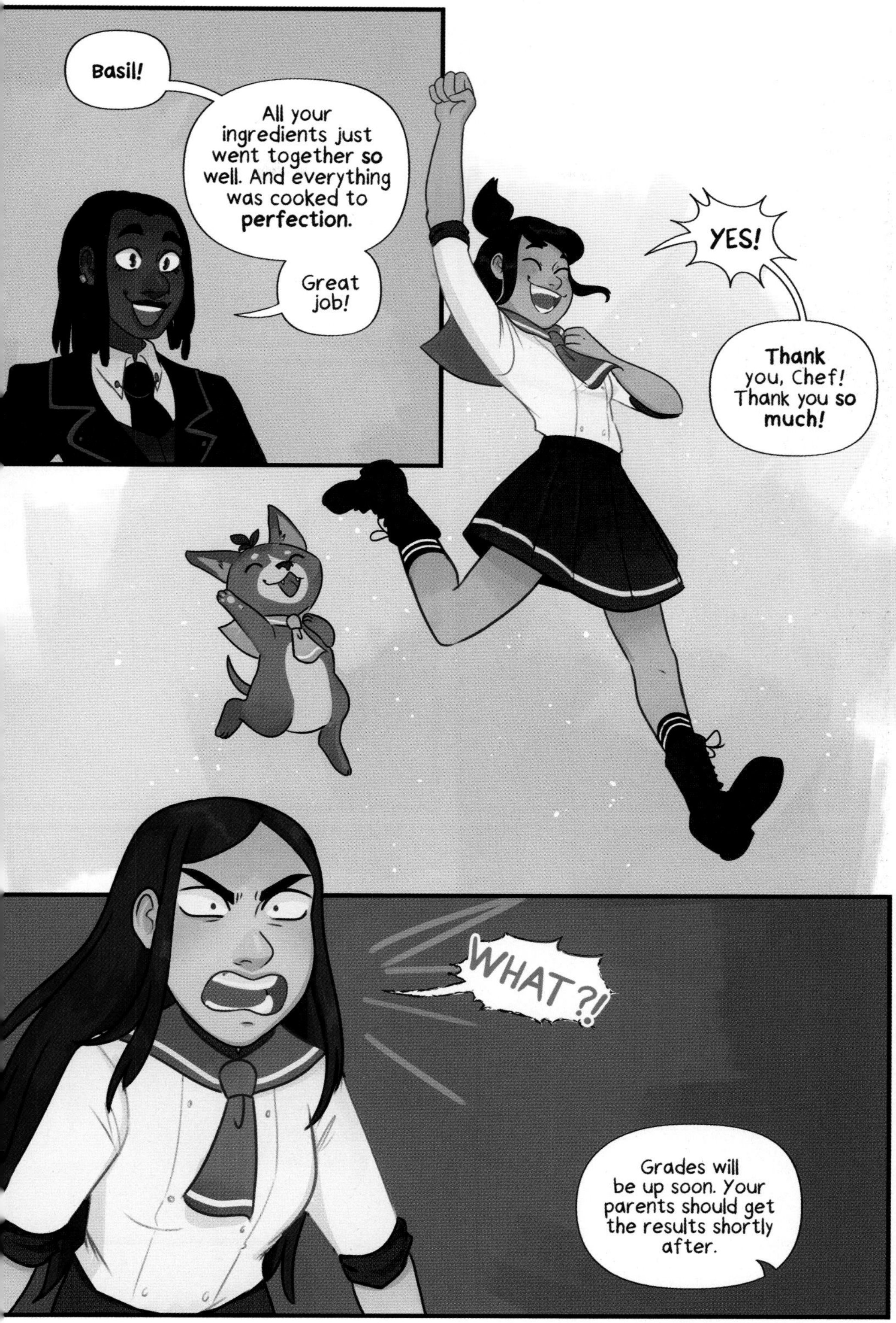

Basil!
All your ingredients just went together so well. And everything was cooked to perfection.
Great job!
YES!
Thank you, Chef! Thank you so much!
WHAT?!
Grades will be up soon. Your parents should get the results shortly after.

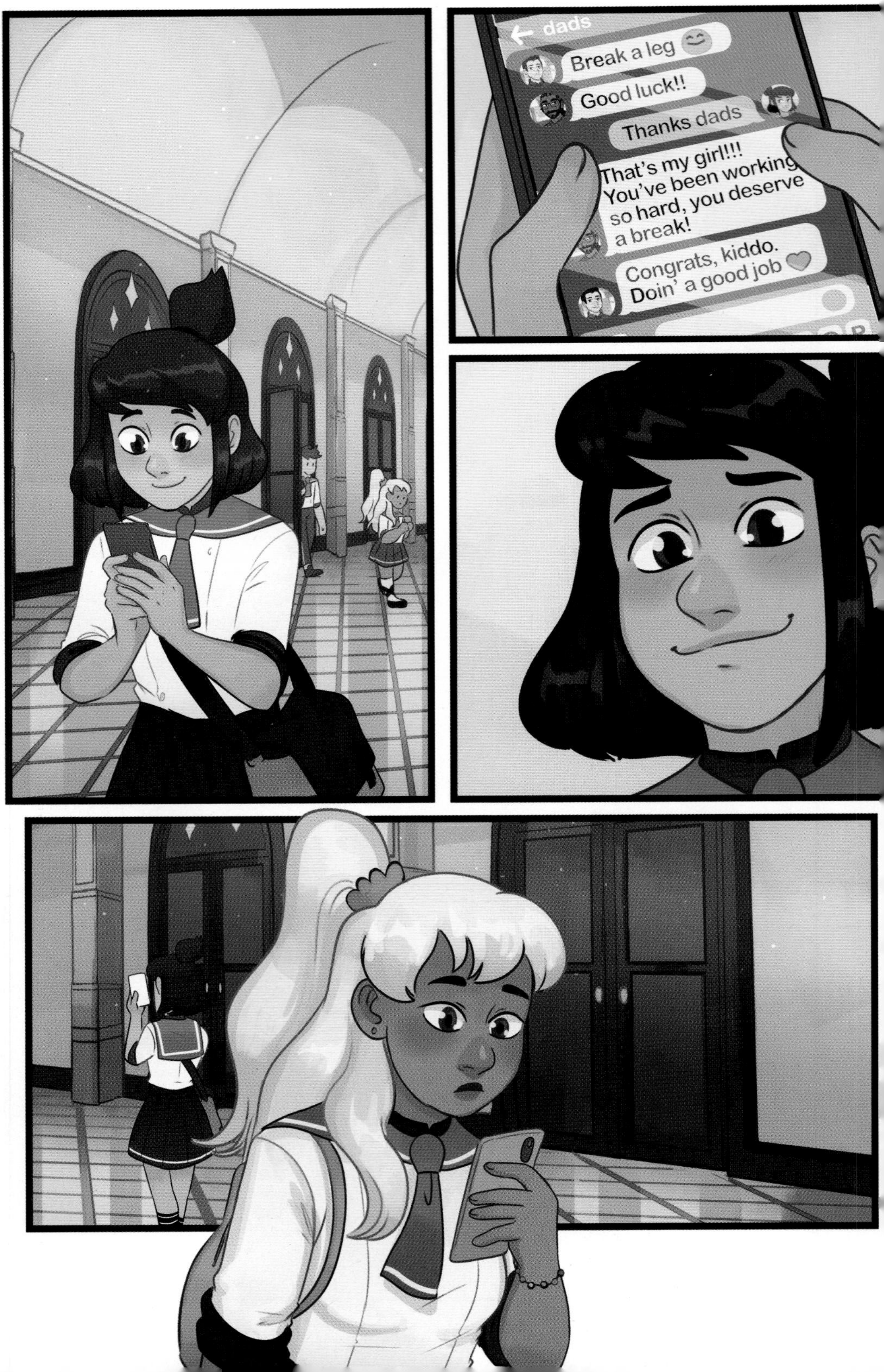

dads
Break a leg
Good luck!!
Thanks dads
That's my girl!!! You've been working so hard, you deserve a break!
Congrats, kiddo. Doin' a good job

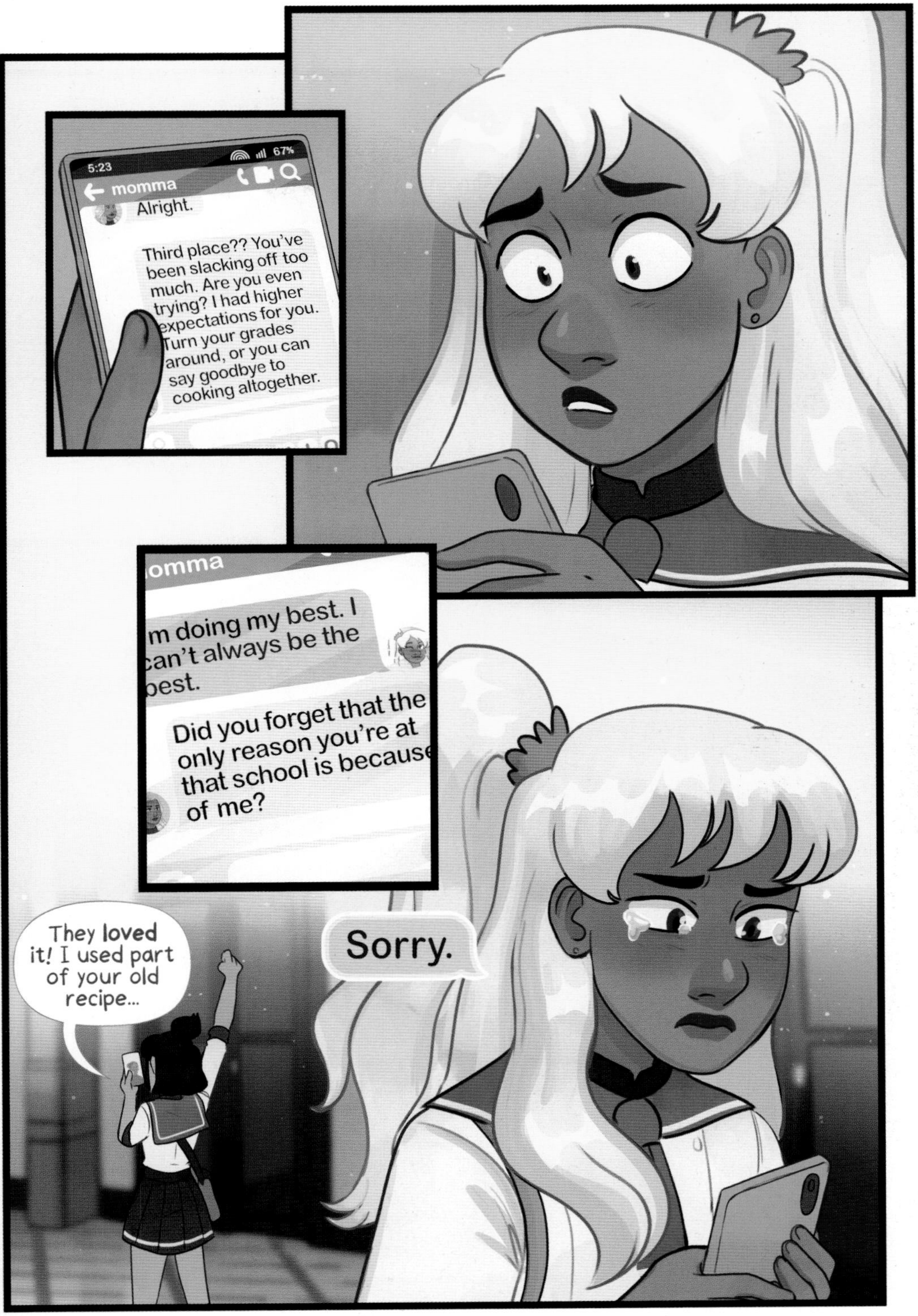
5:23
67%
momma
Alright.
Third place?? You've been slacking off too much. Are you even trying? I had higher expectations for you. Turn your grades around, or you can say goodbye to cooking altogether.
omma
m doing my best. I can't always be the best.
Did you forget that the only reason you're at that school is becaus of me?
They loved it! I used part of your old recipe...
Sorry.

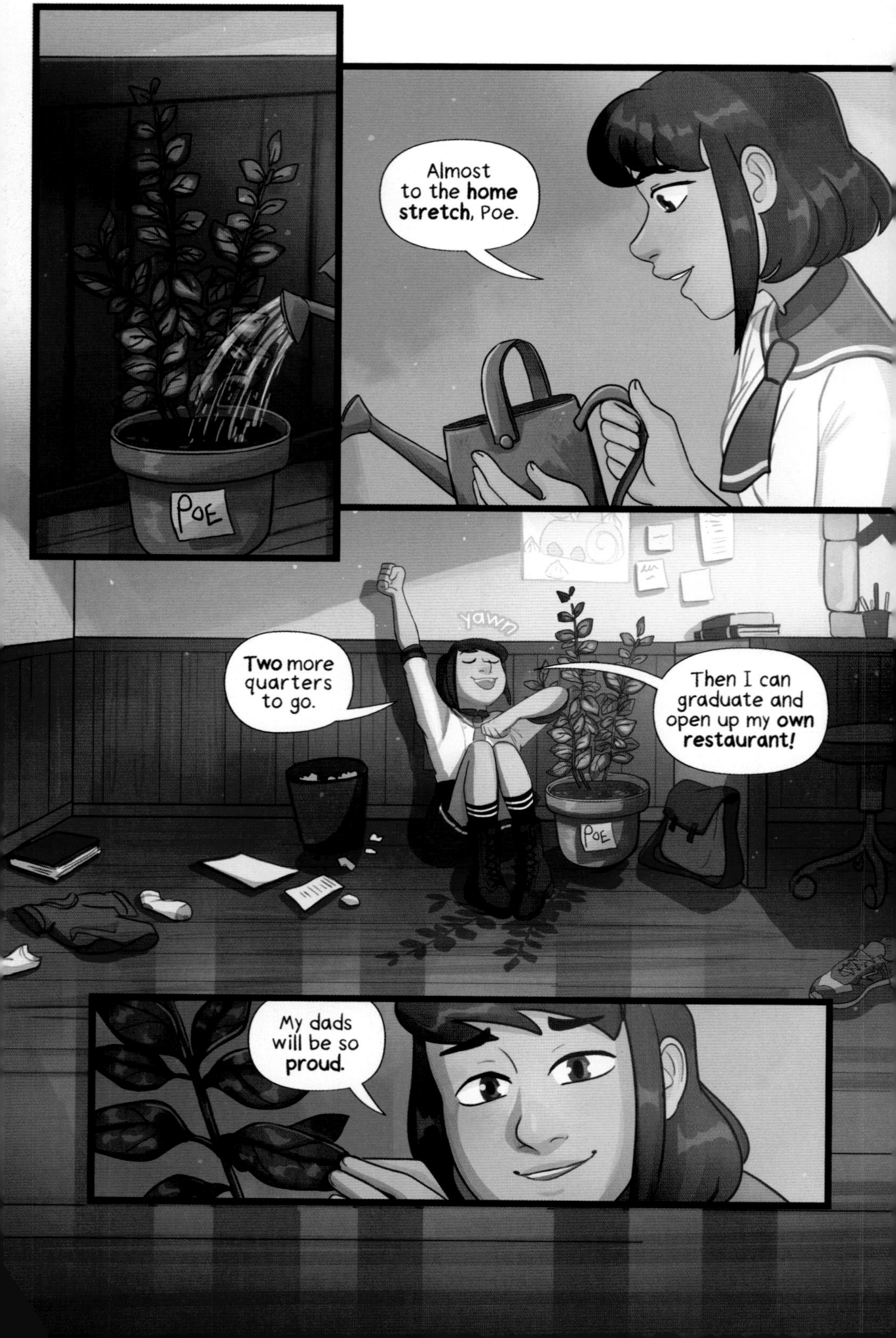
POE
Almost to the home stretch, Poe.
yawn
Two more quarters to go.
Then I can graduate and open up my own restaurant!
POE
My dads will be so proud.

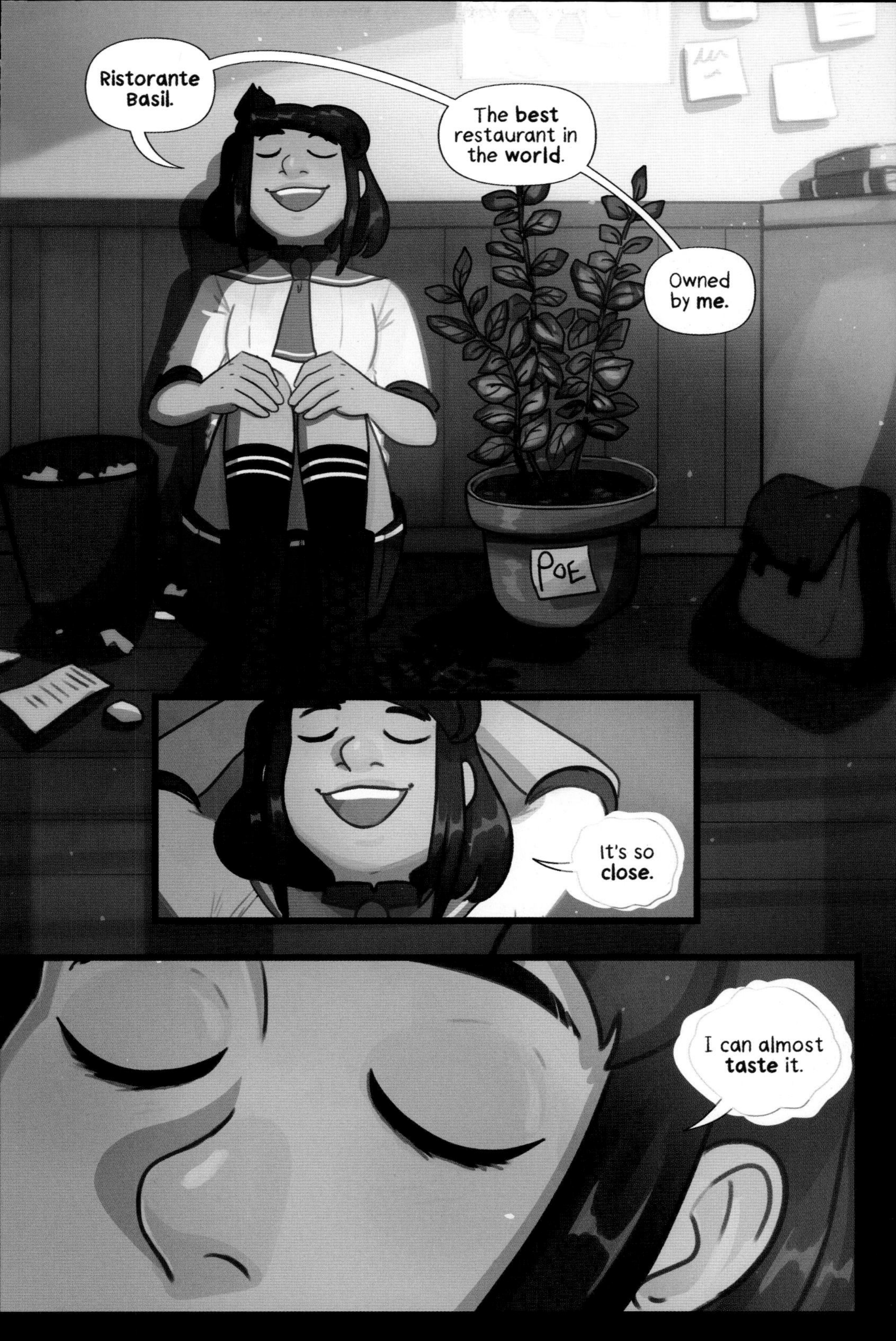
Ristorante Basil.
The best restaurant in the world.
Owned by me.
POE
It's so close.
I can almost taste it.

Chapter
FOUR

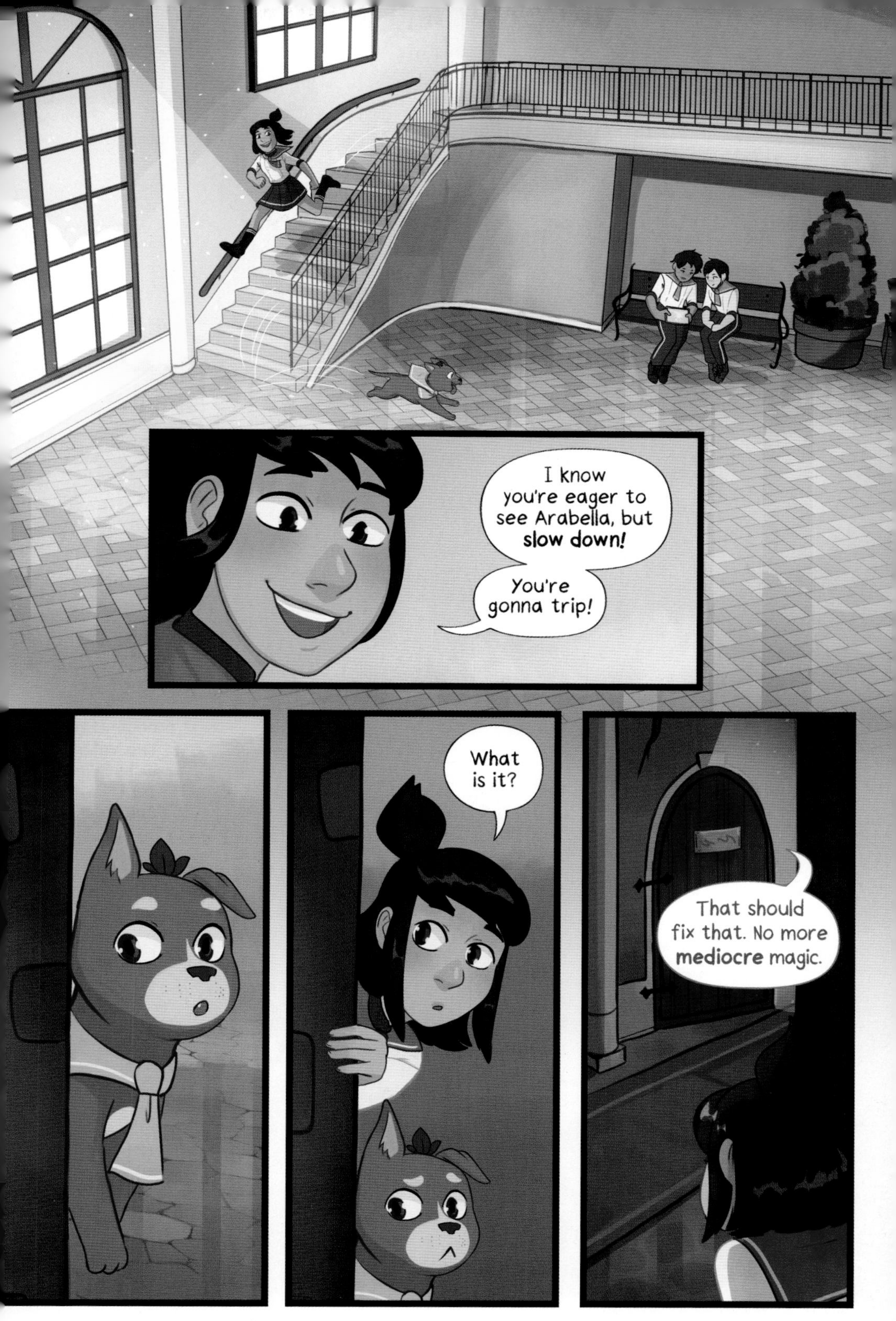
I know you're eager to see Arabella, but **slow down!**
You're gonna trip!
What is it?
That should fix that. No more **mediocre** magic.

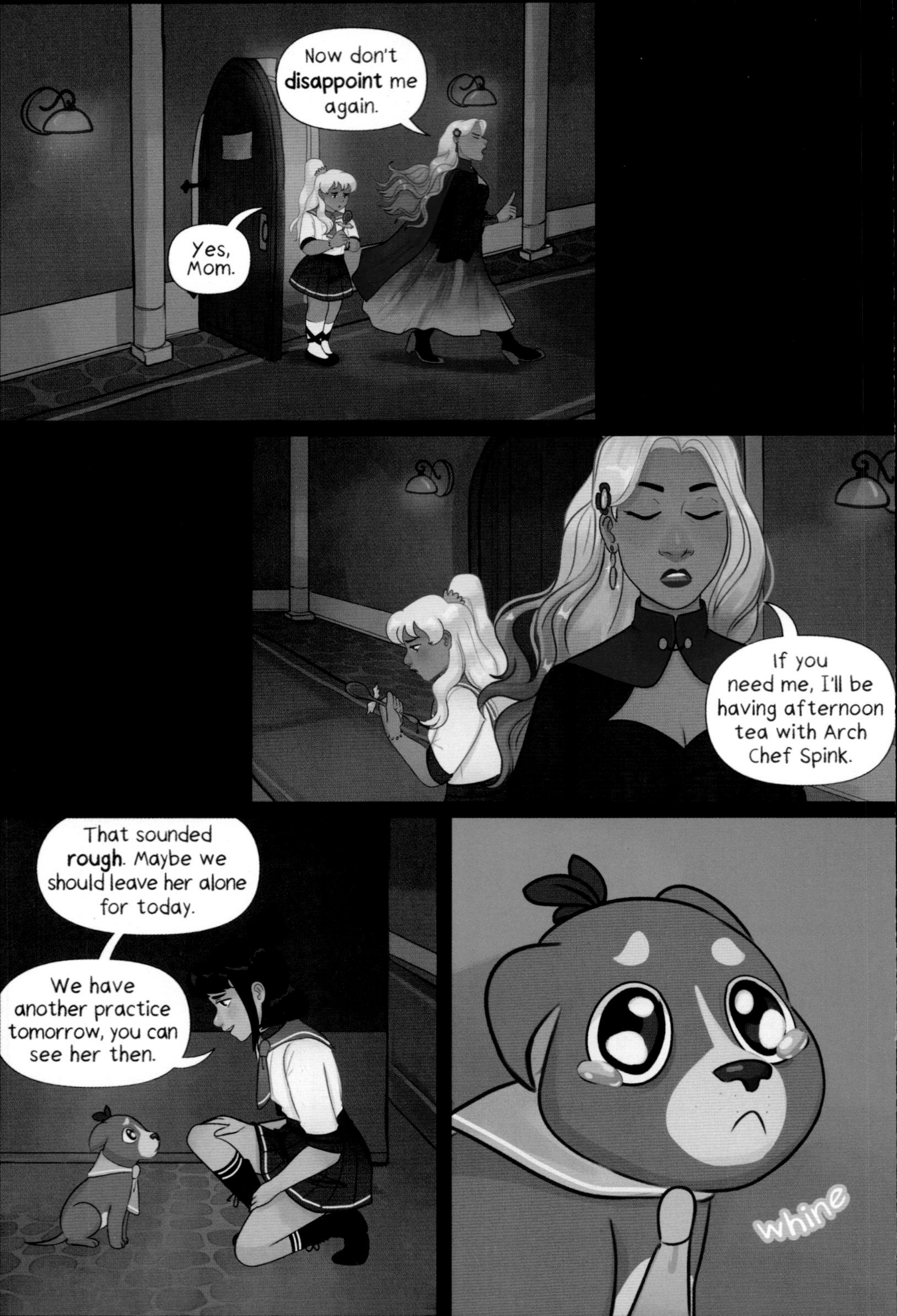
Now don't **disappoint** me again.
Yes, Mom.
If you need me, I'll be having afternoon tea with Arch Chef Spink.
That sounded **rough**. Maybe we should leave her alone for today.
We have another practice tomorrow, you can see her then.
whine

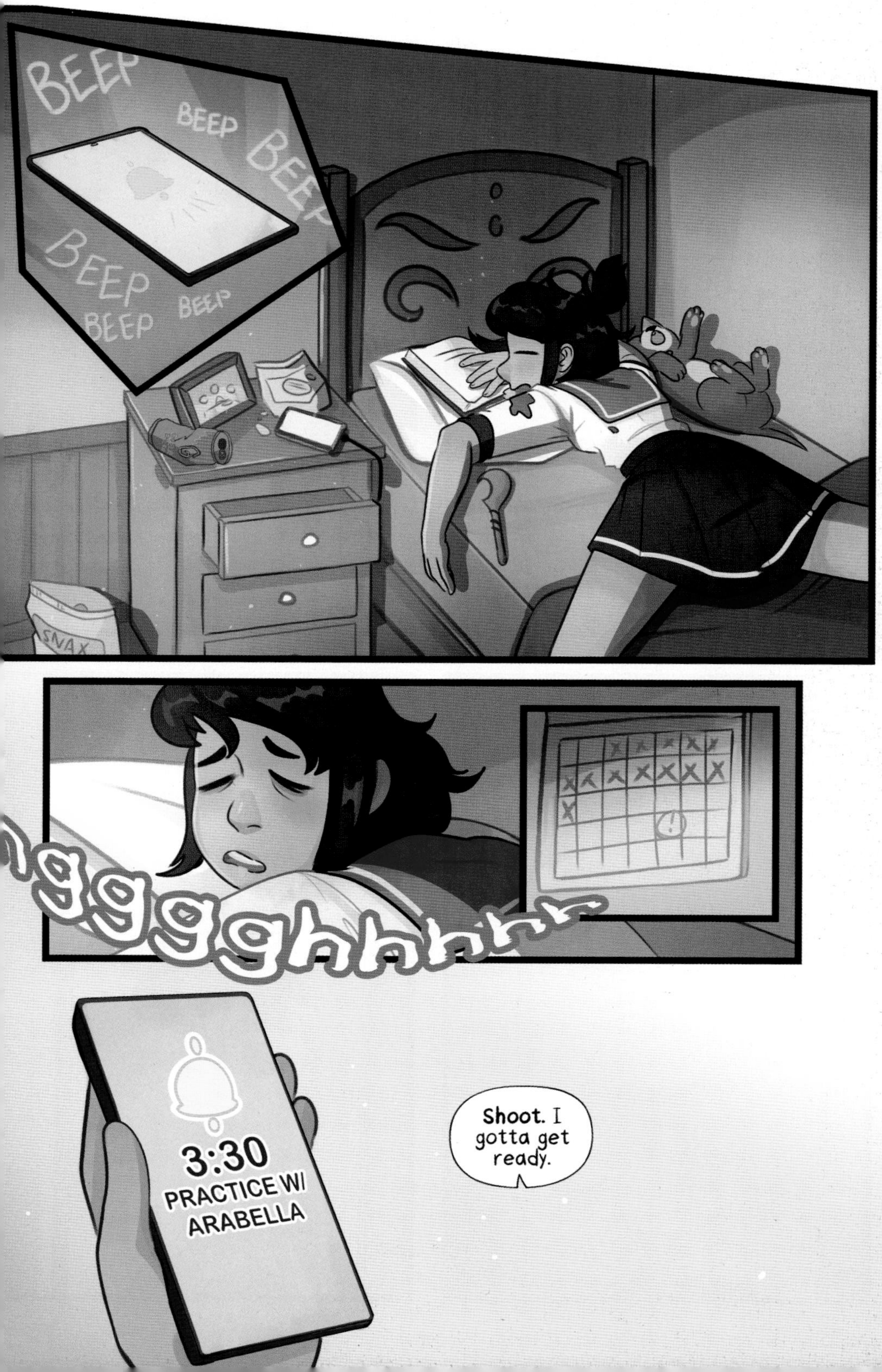
BEEP
BEEP
BEEP
BEEP
BEEP
BEEP
BEEP
SNAX
gggghhhhrr
3:30
PRACTICE W/
ARABELLA
Shoot. I gotta get ready.

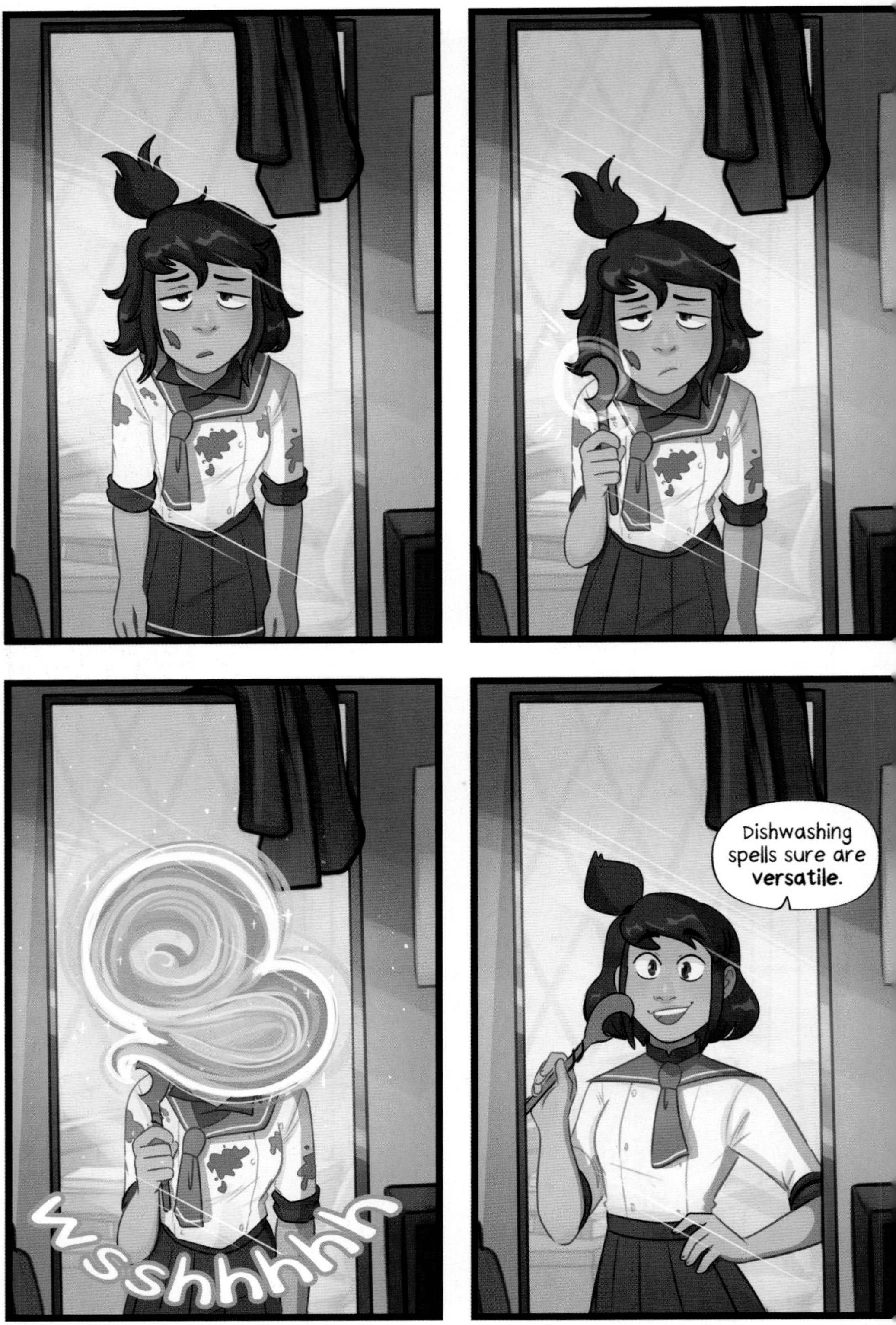
WSSHHHH
Dishwashing spells sure are **versatile.**

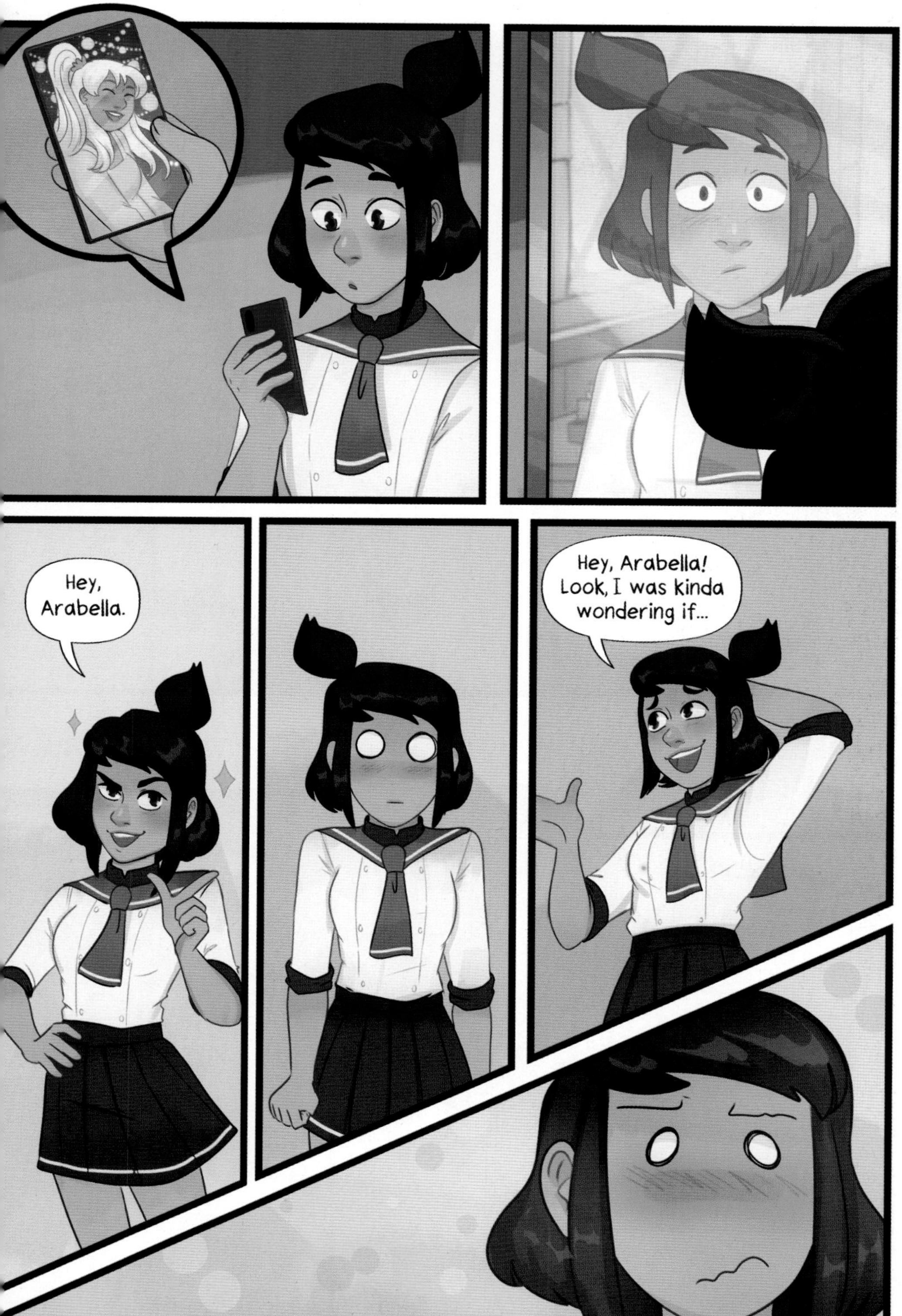
Hey,
Arabella.
Hey, Arabella!
Look, I was kinda
wondering if...

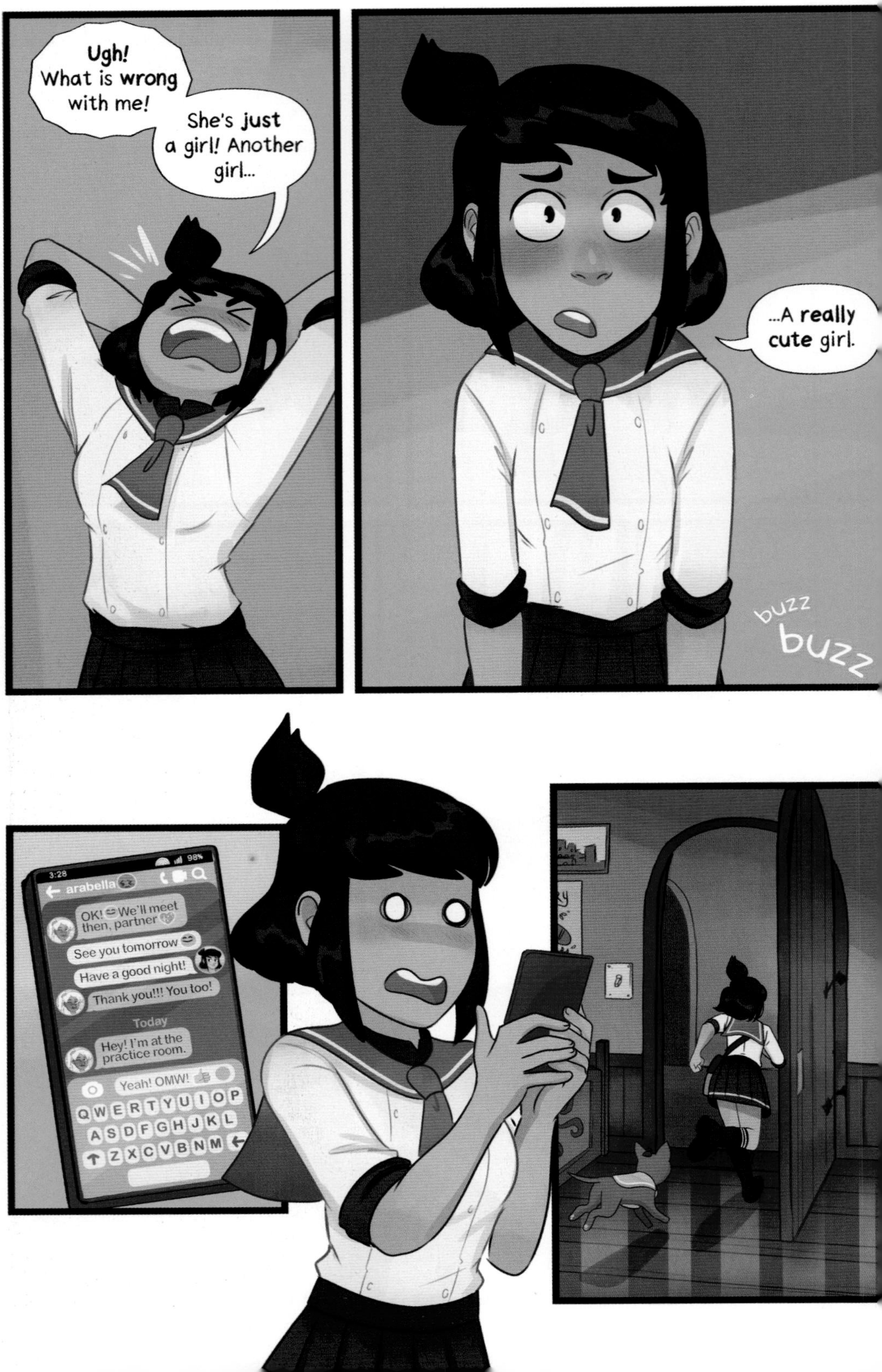
Ugh! What is wrong with me!
She's just a girl! Another girl...
...A really cute girl.
buzz
buzz
3:28
98%
arabella
OK! We'll meet then, partner
See you tomorrow
Have a good night!
Thank you!!! You too!
Today
Hey! I'm at the practice room.
Yeah! OMW!

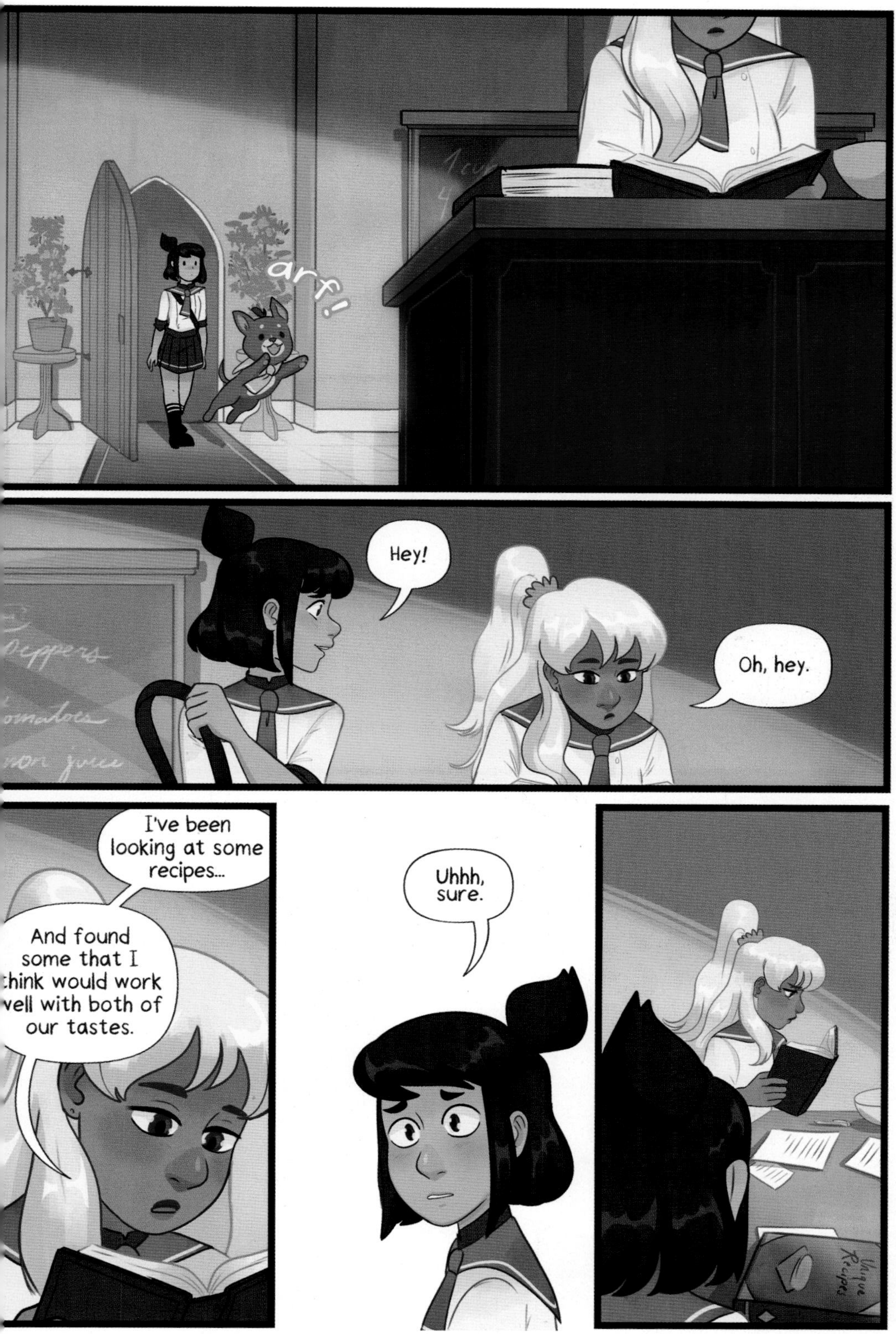
arf!
Hey!
Oh, hey.
I've been looking at some recipes...
And found some that I think would work well with both of our tastes.
Uhhh, sure.
Unique Recipes

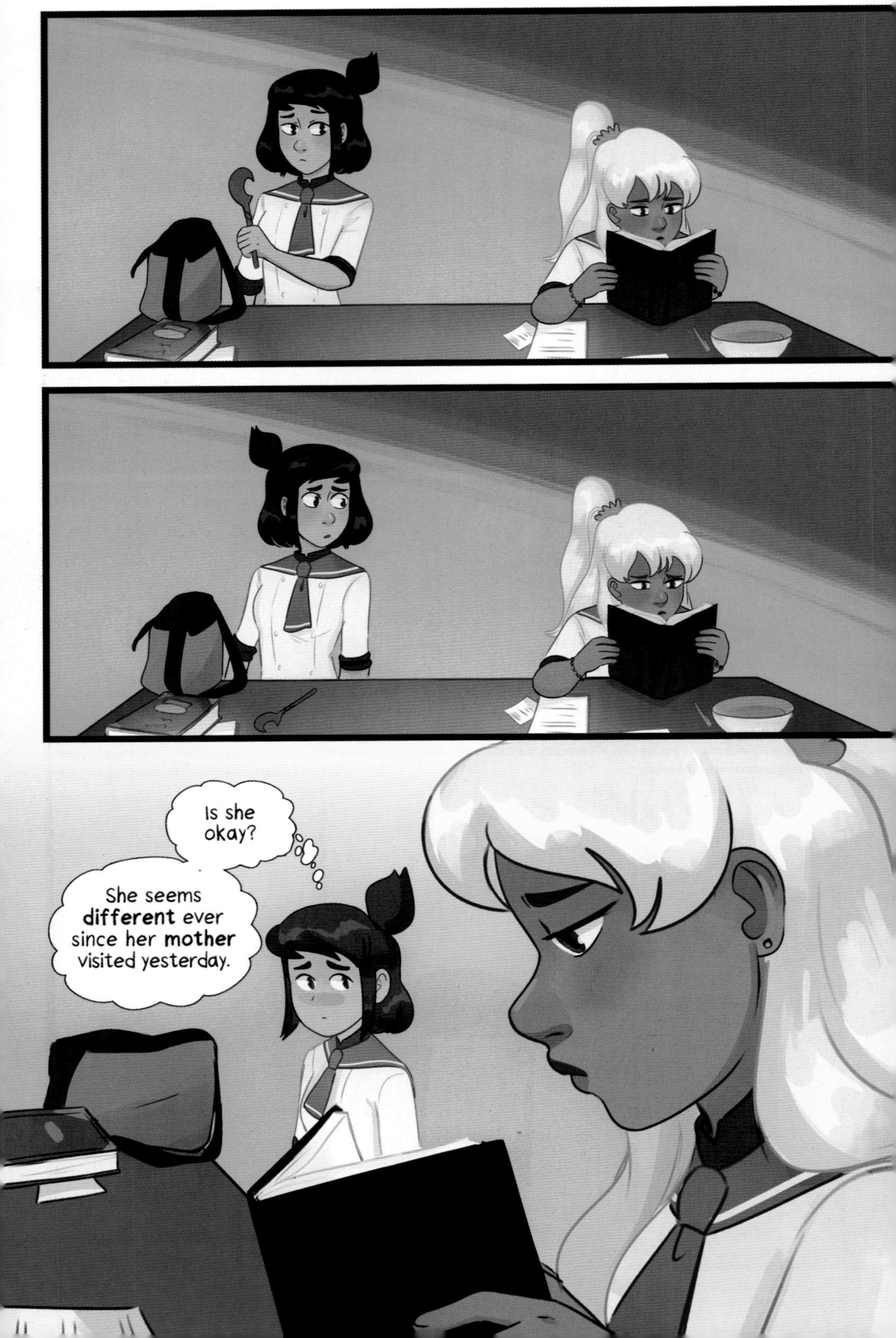
Is she okay?
She seems **different** ever since her **mother** visited yesterday.

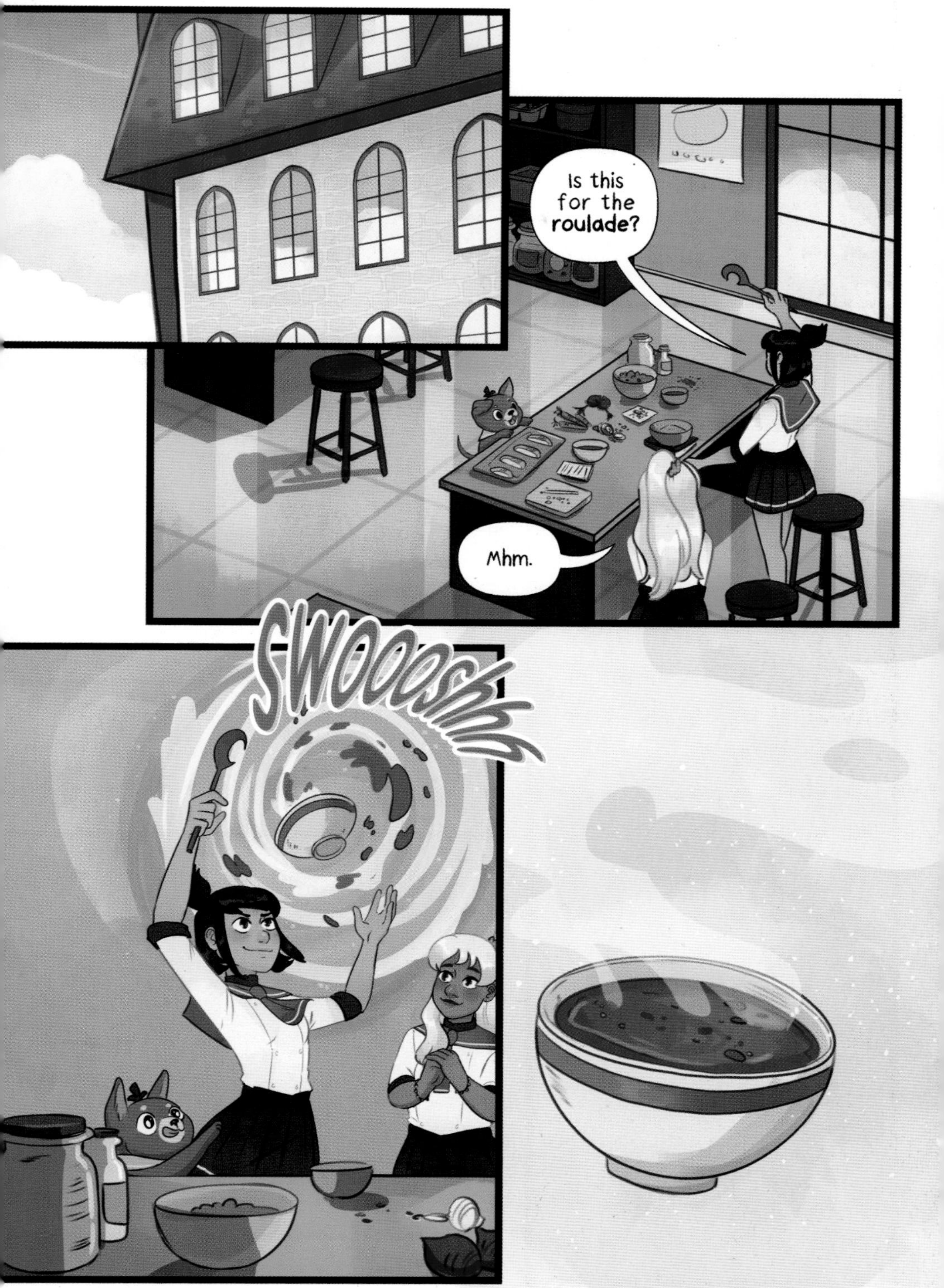

Is this for the **roulade?**
Mhm.
SWOOOSHHH

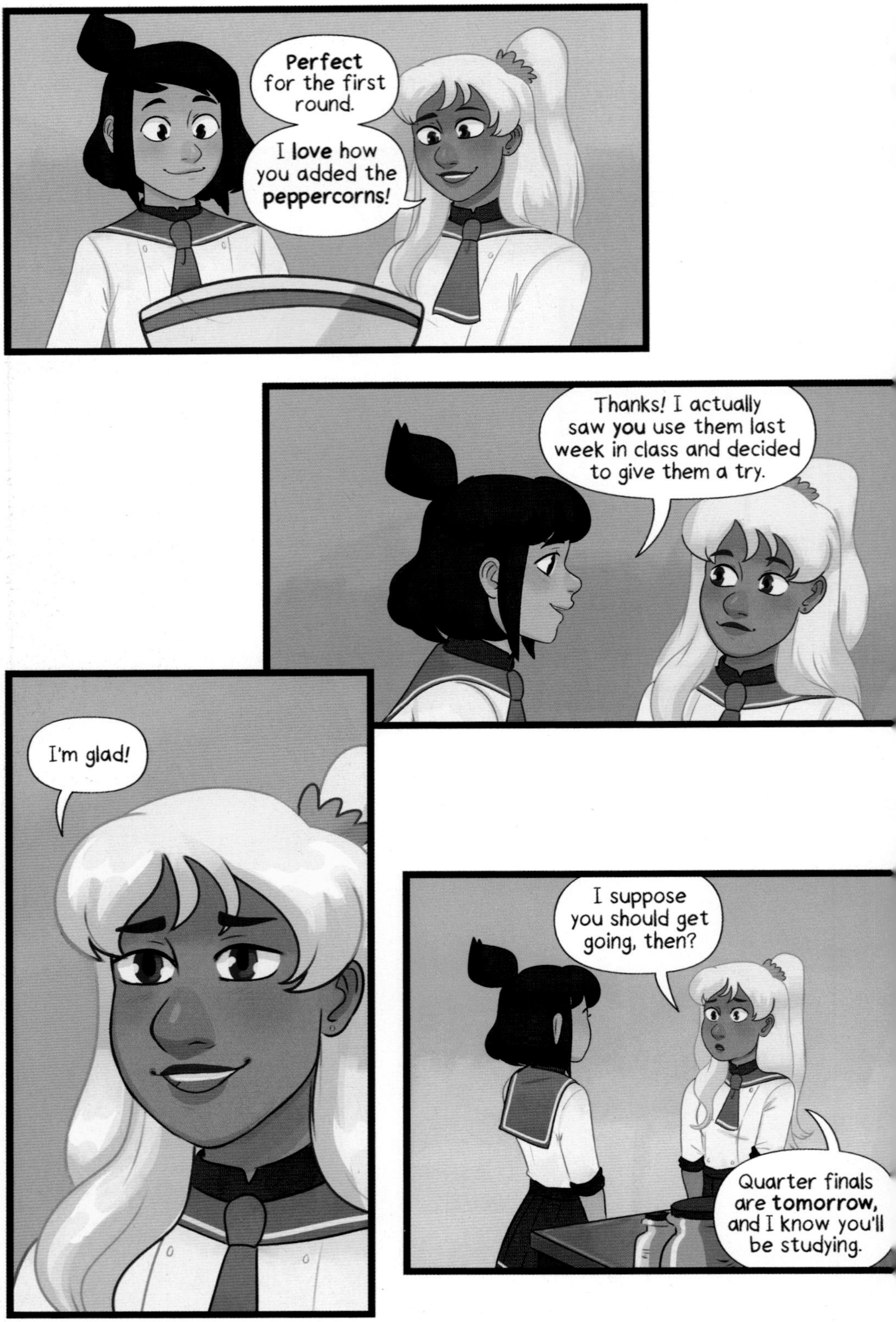

Perfect for the first round.
I love how you added the peppercorns!
Thanks! I actually saw you use them last week in class and decided to give them a try.
I'm glad!
I suppose you should get going, then?
Quarter finals are tomorrow, and I know you'll be studying.

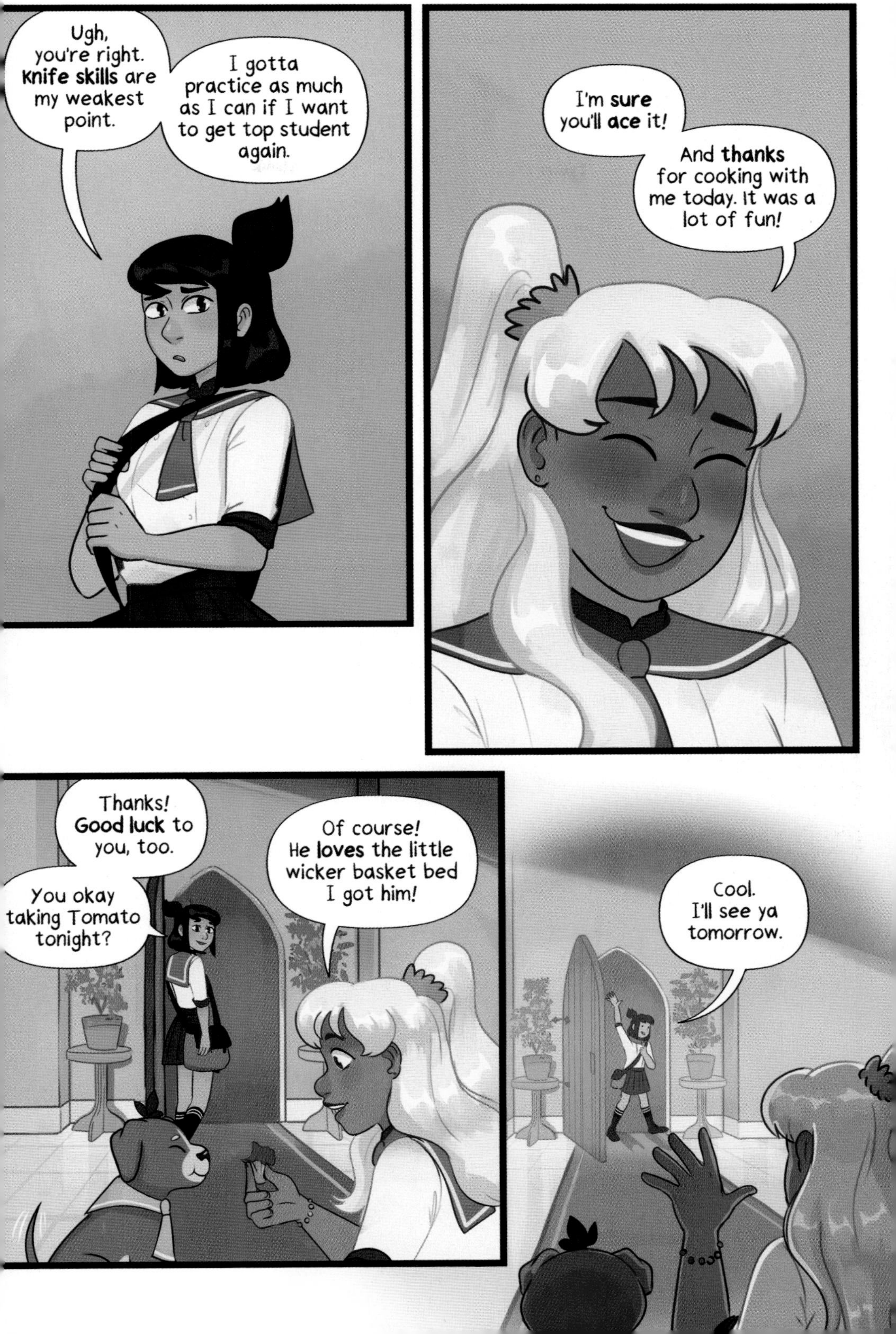
Ugh, you're right. **Knife skills** are my weakest point.
I gotta practice as much as I can if I want to get top student again.
I'm **sure** you'll **ace** it!
And **thanks** for cooking with me today. It was a lot of fun!
Thanks! **Good luck** to you, too.
You okay taking Tomato tonight?
Of course! He **loves** the little wicker basket bed I got him!
Cool. I'll see ya tomorrow.

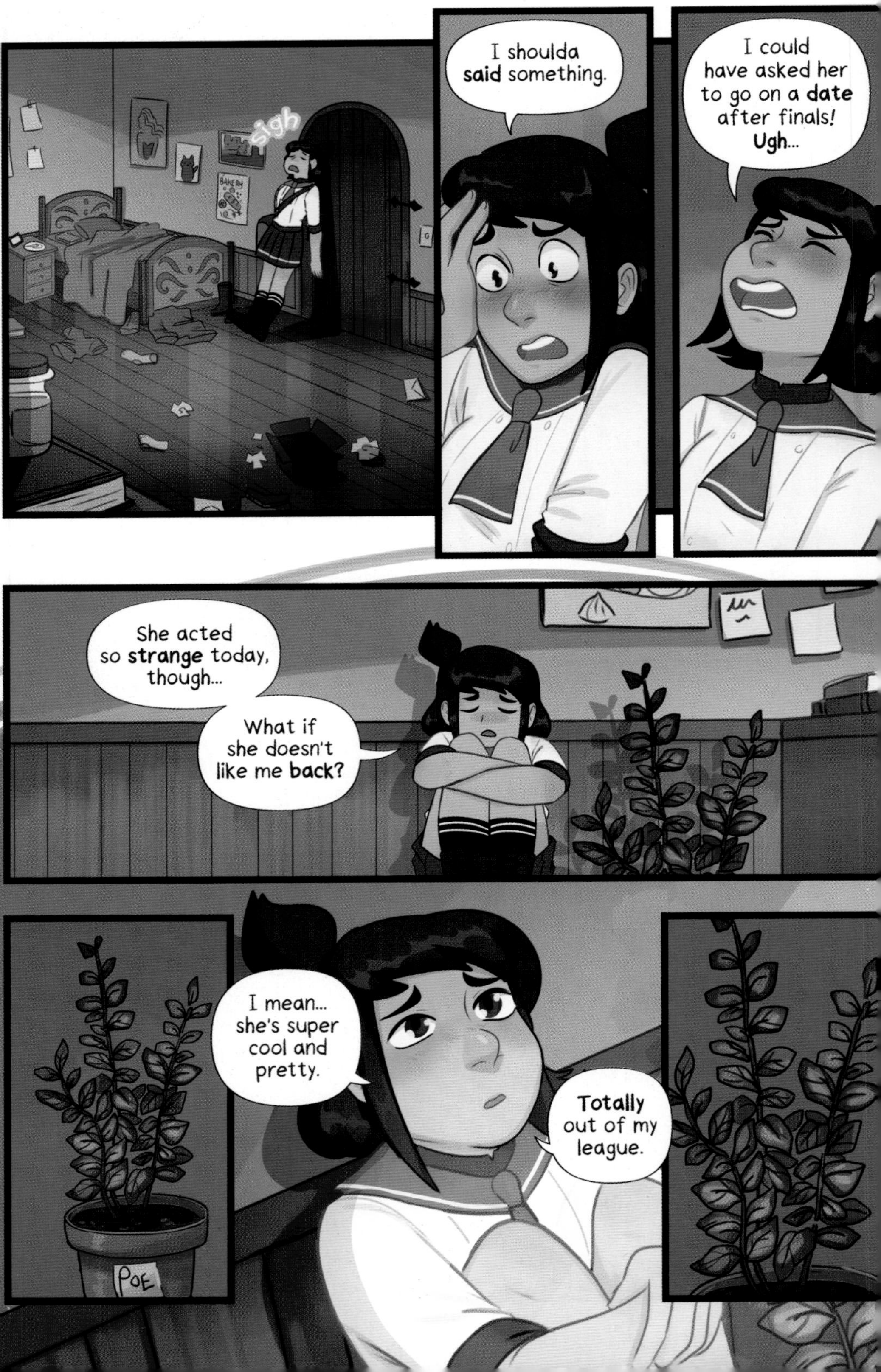
sigh
I shoulda said something.
I could have asked her to go on a date after finals! Ugh...
She acted so strange today, though...
What if she doesn't like me back?
I mean... she's super cool and pretty.
Totally out of my league.
POE

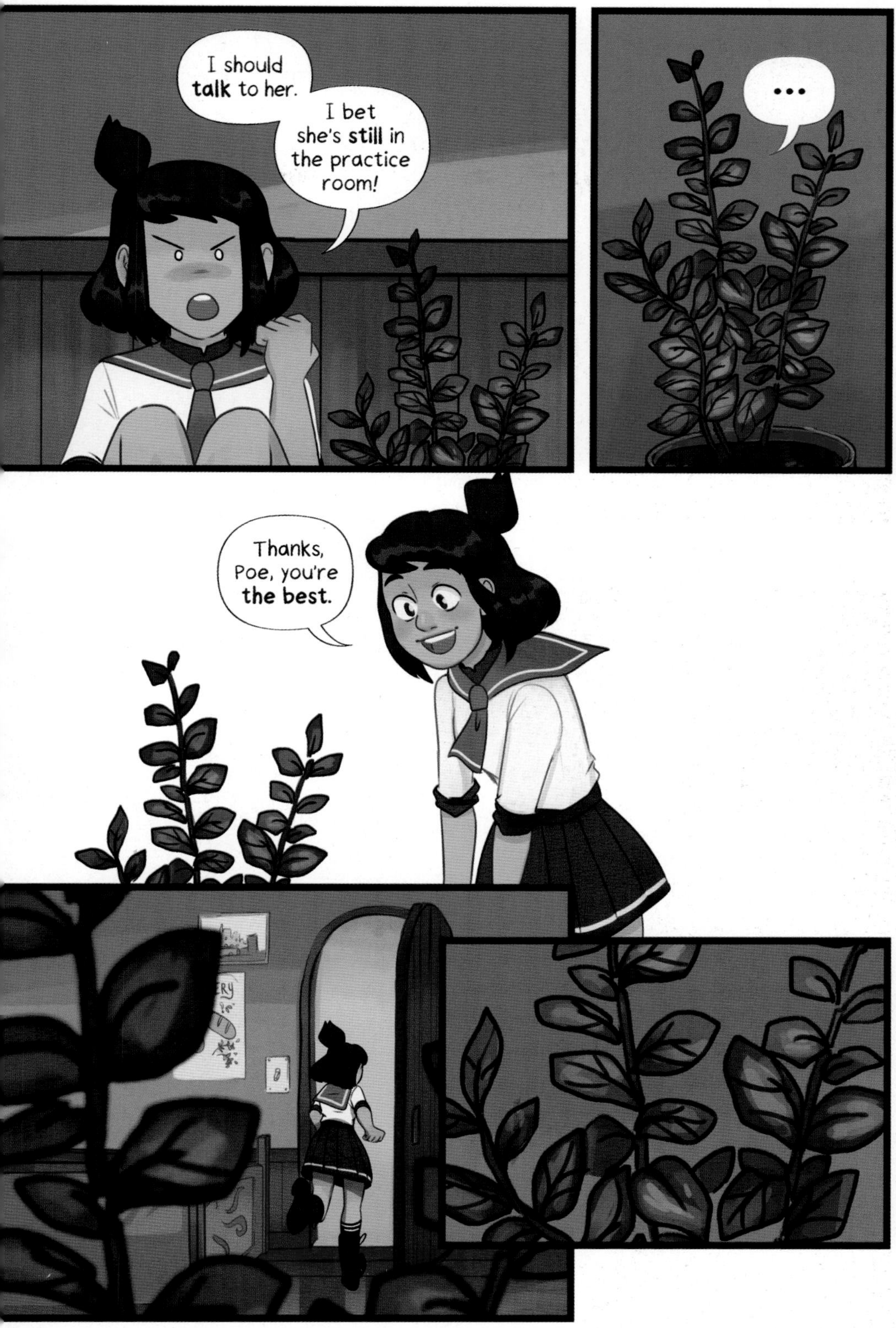
I should **talk** to her.
I bet she's **still** in the practice room!
...
Thanks, Poe, you're **the best**.

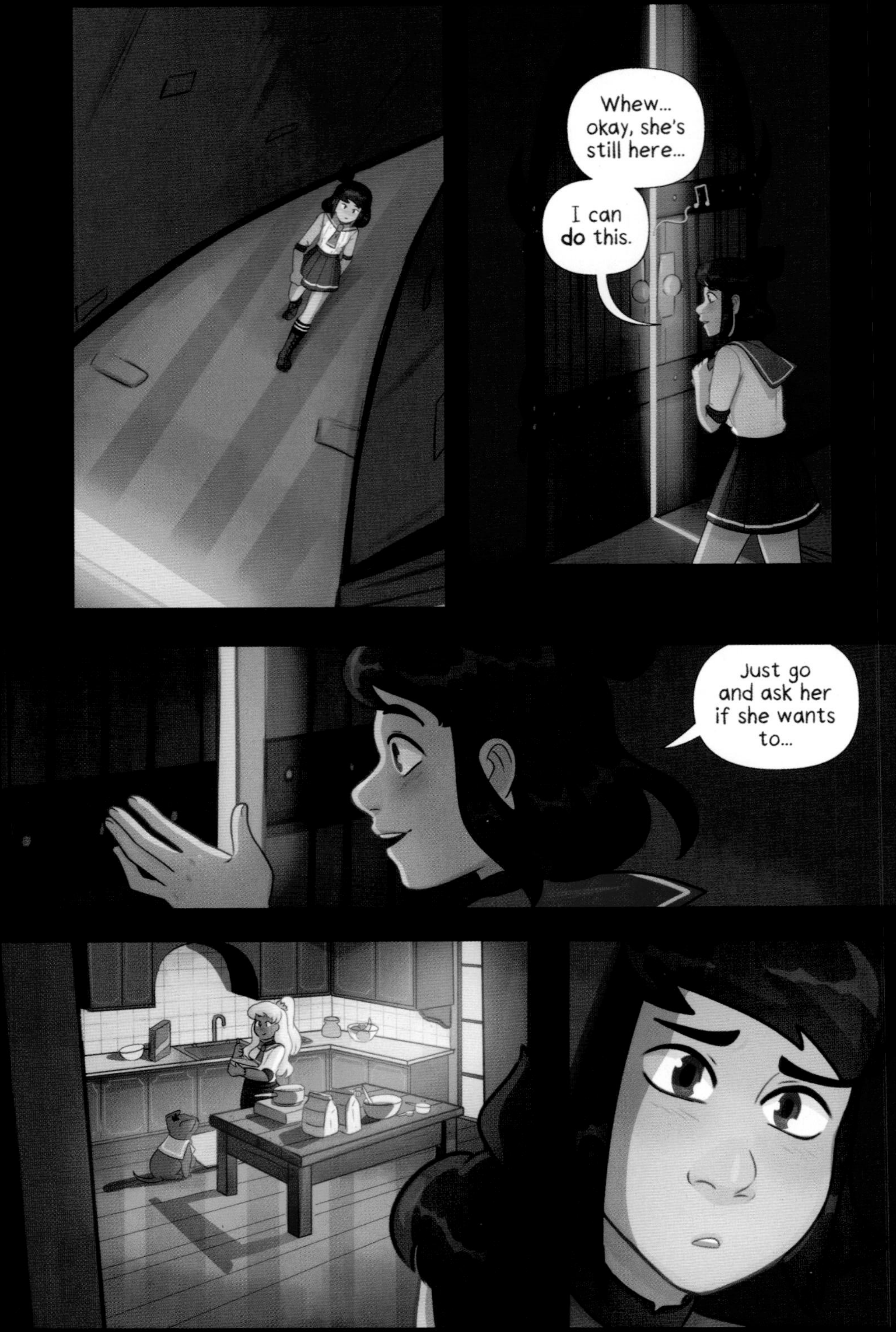
Whew... okay, she's still here...
I can do this.
Just go and ask her if she wants to...

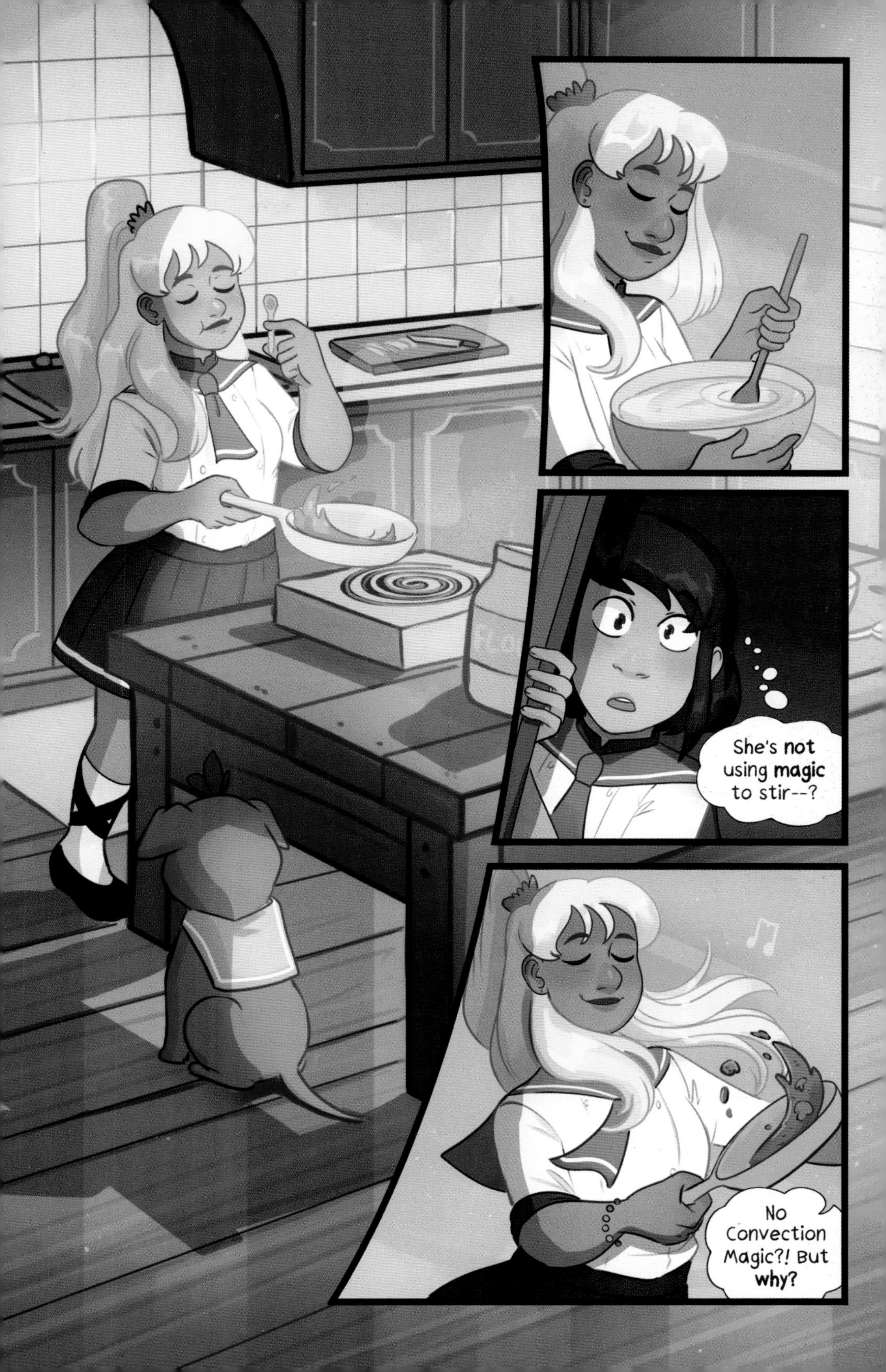

She's **not** using **magic** to stir--?
No Convection Magic?! But **why?**

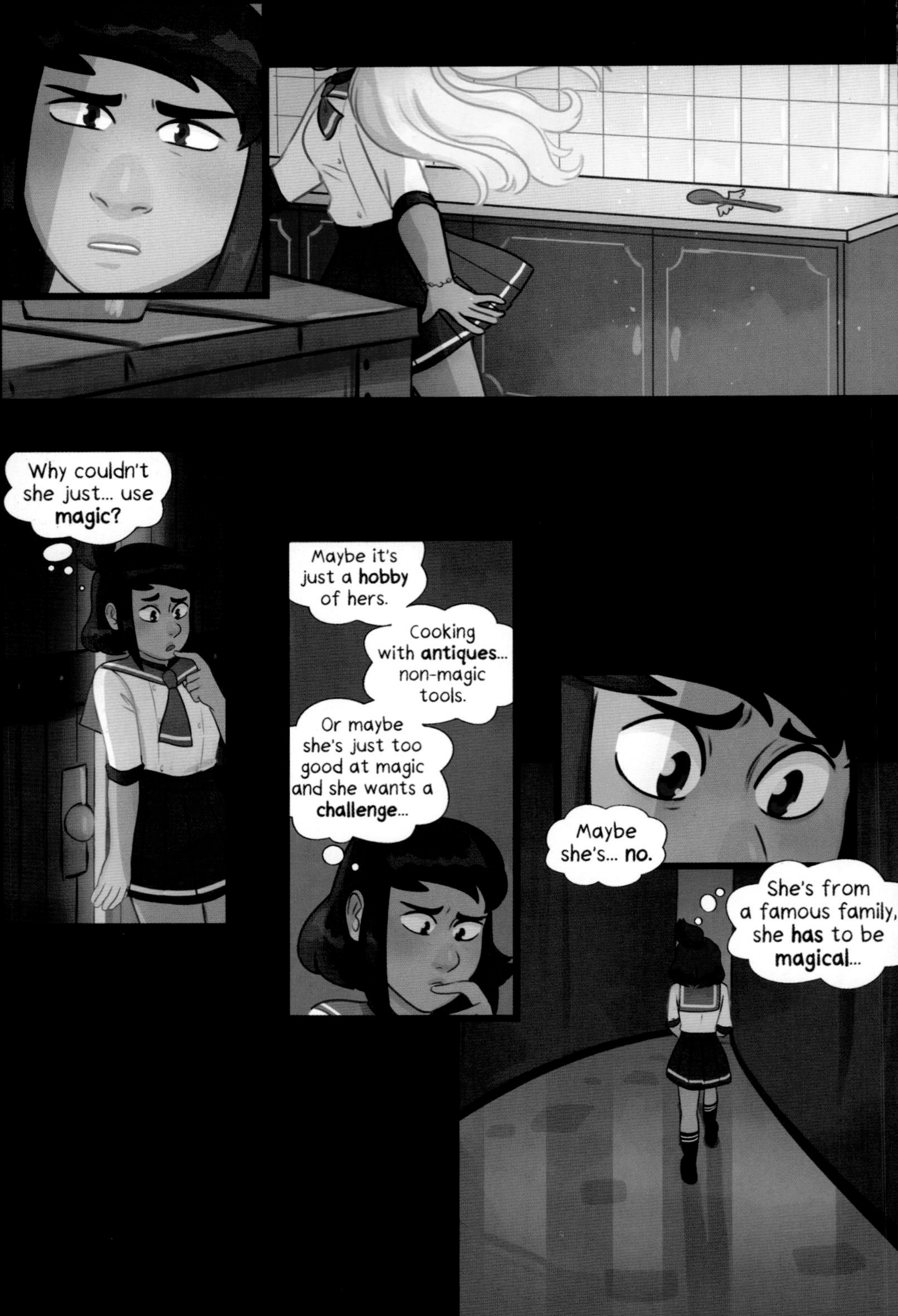
Why couldn't she just... use **magic?**
Maybe it's just a **hobby** of hers.
Cooking with **antiques**... non-magic tools.
Or maybe she's just too good at magic and she wants a **challenge**...
Maybe she's... **no.**
She's from a famous family, she **has** to be **magical**...

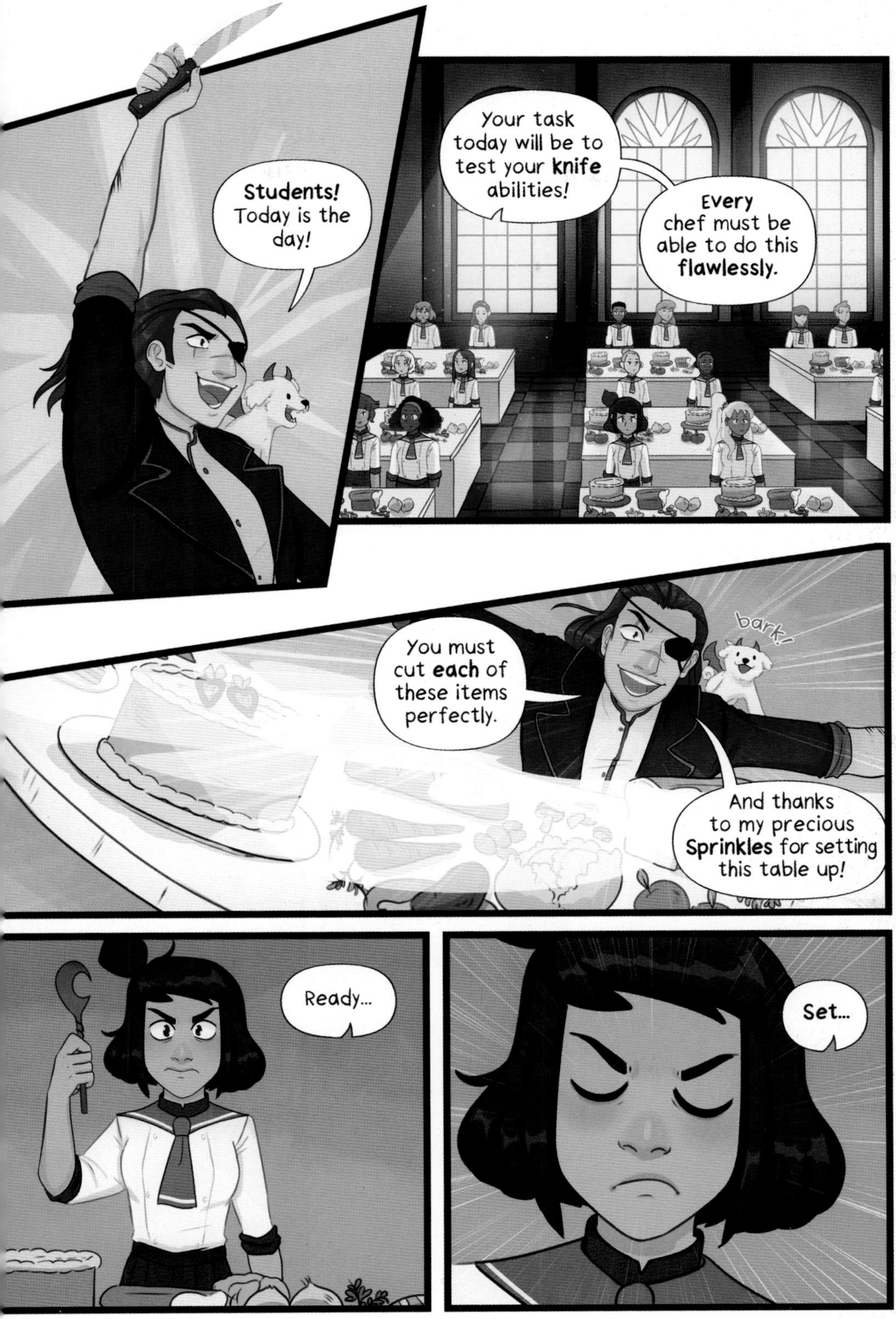

Students! Today is the day!
Your task today will be to test your knife abilities!
Every chef must be able to do this flawlessly.
You must cut each of these items perfectly.
bark!
And thanks to my precious Sprinkles for setting this table up!
Ready...
Set...

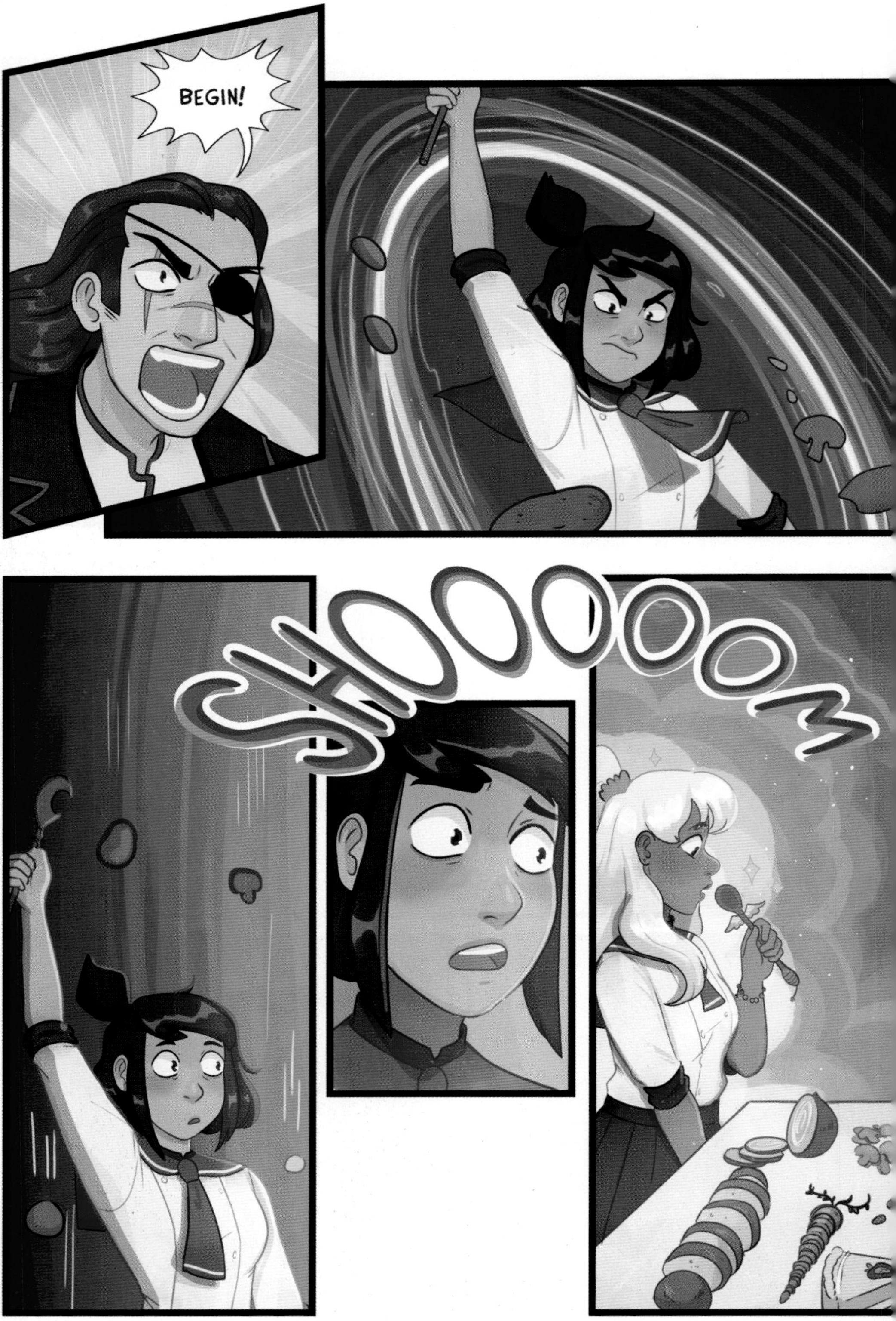
BEGIN!
SHOOOOOM

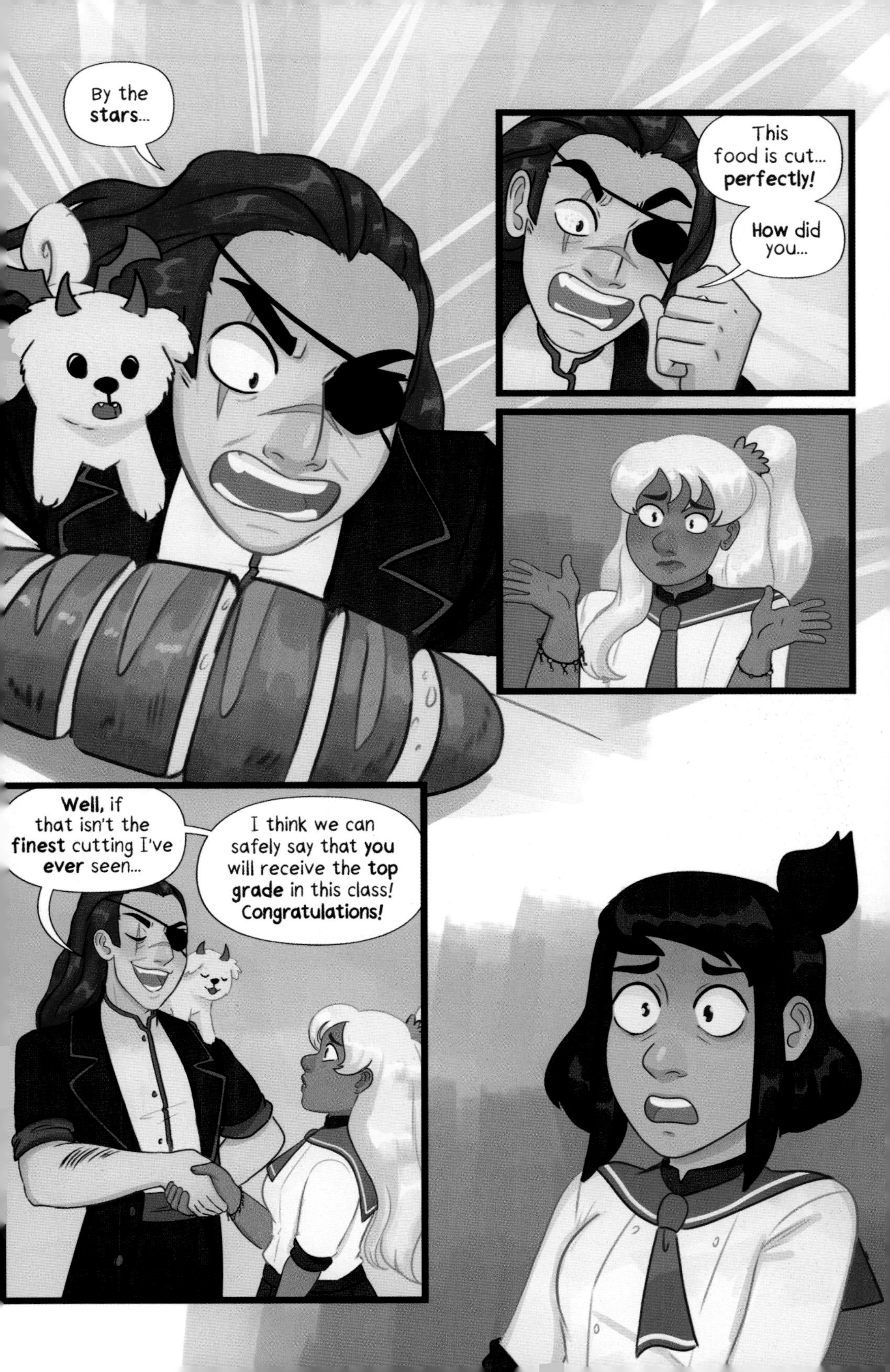
By the stars...
This food is cut... perfectly!
How did you...
Well, if that isn't the finest cutting I've ever seen...
I think we can safely say that you will receive the top grade in this class! Congratulations!

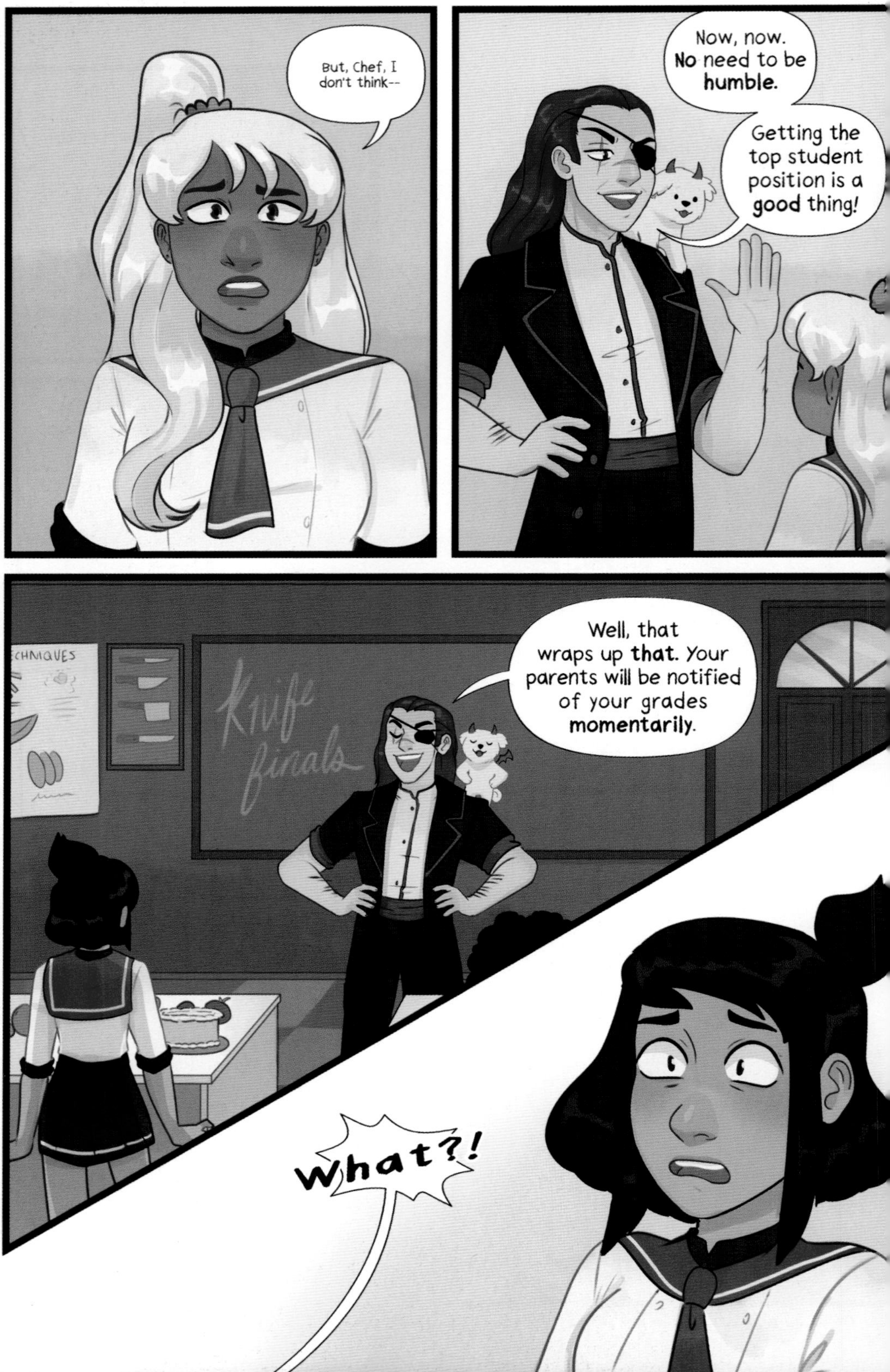
But, Chef, I don't think--
Now, now. No need to be humble.
Getting the top student position is a good thing!
CHNIQUES
Knife finals
Well, that wraps up that. Your parents will be notified of your grades momentarily.
What?!

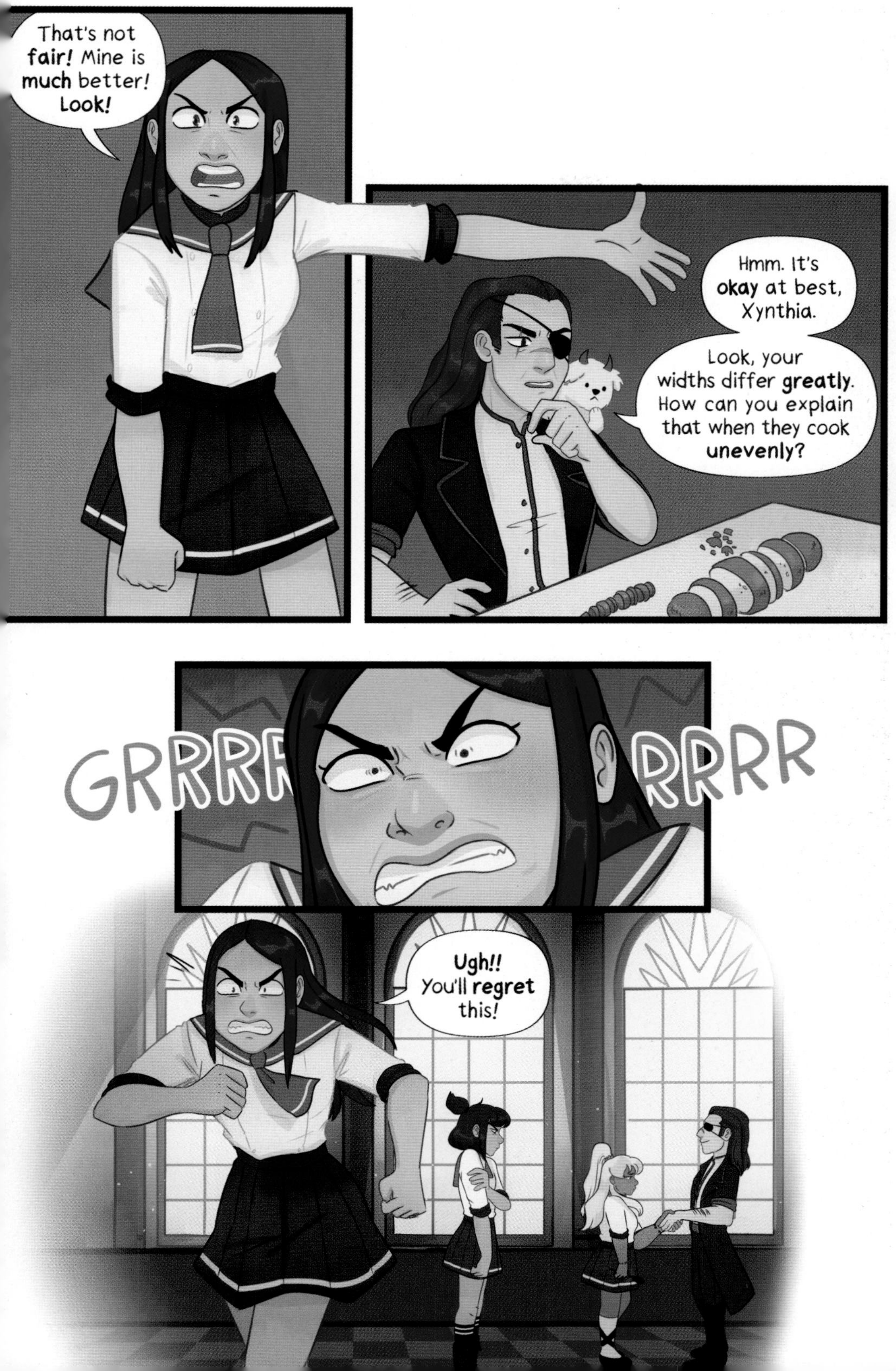
That's not fair! Mine is much better! Look!
Hmm. It's okay at best, Xynthia.
Look, your widths differ greatly. How can you explain that when they cook unevenly?
GRRRRRRRRR
Ugh!! You'll regret this!

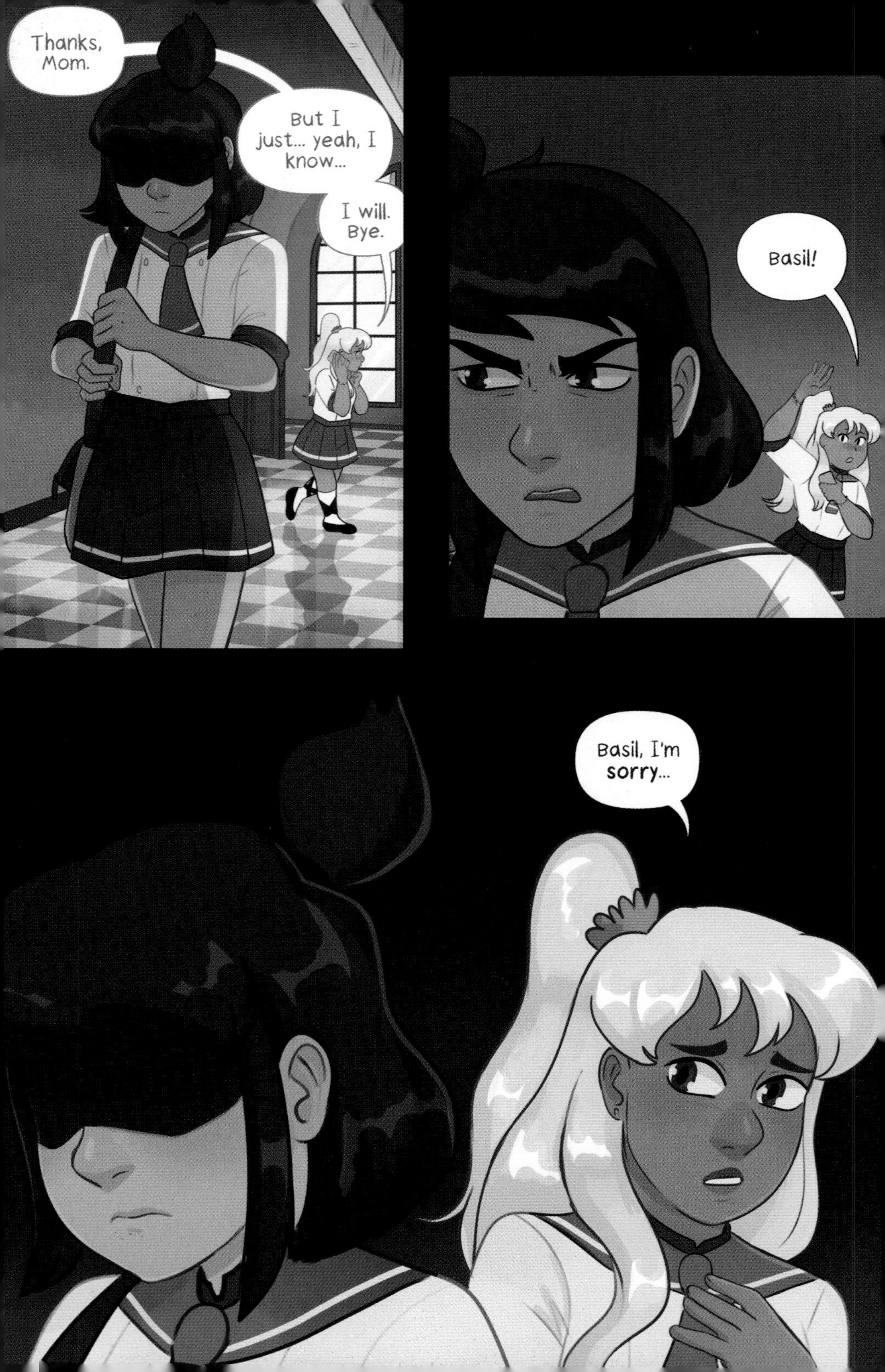
Thanks, Mom.
But I just... yeah, I know...
I will. Bye.
Basil!
Basil, I'm **sorry**...

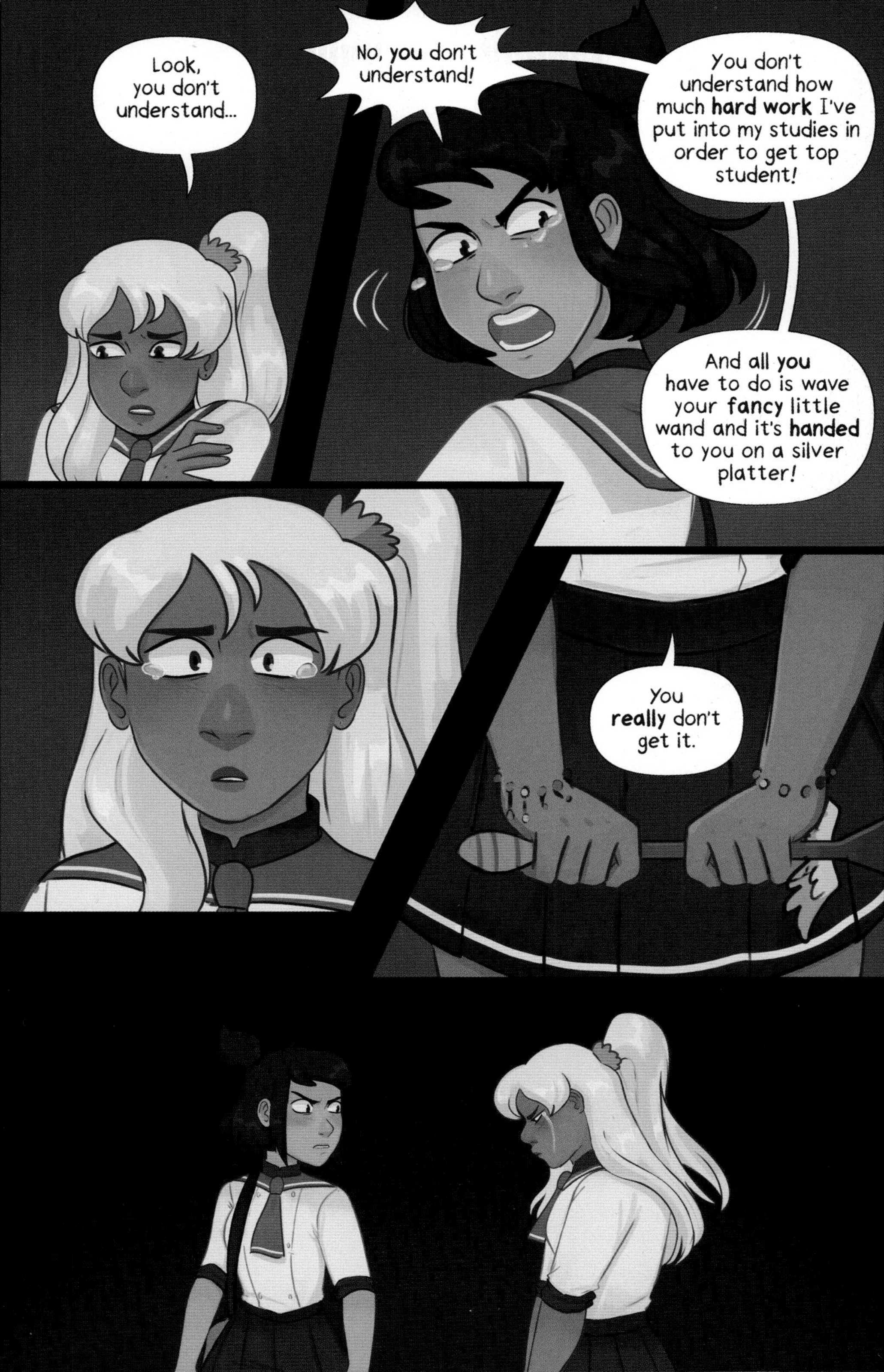
Look, you don't understand...
No, you don't understand!
You don't understand how much hard work I've put into my studies in order to get top student!
And all you have to do is wave your fancy little wand and it's handed to you on a silver platter!
You really don't get it.

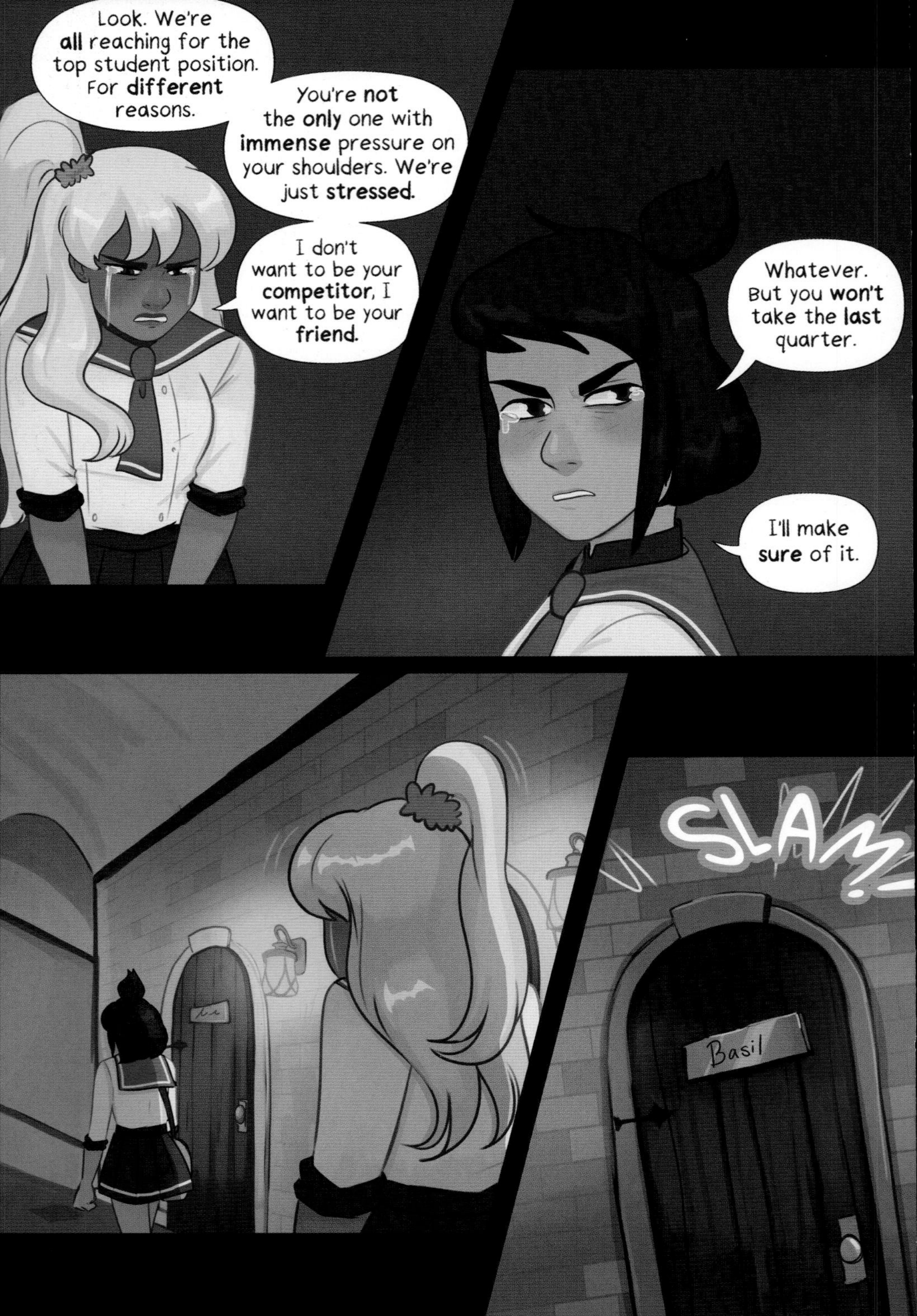
Look. We're **all** reaching for the top student position. For **different** reasons.
You're **not** the **only** one with **immense** pressure on your shoulders. We're just **stressed**.
I don't want to be your **competitor**, I want to be your **friend**.
Whatever. But you **won't** take the **last** quarter.
I'll make **sure** of it.
SLAM!
Basil

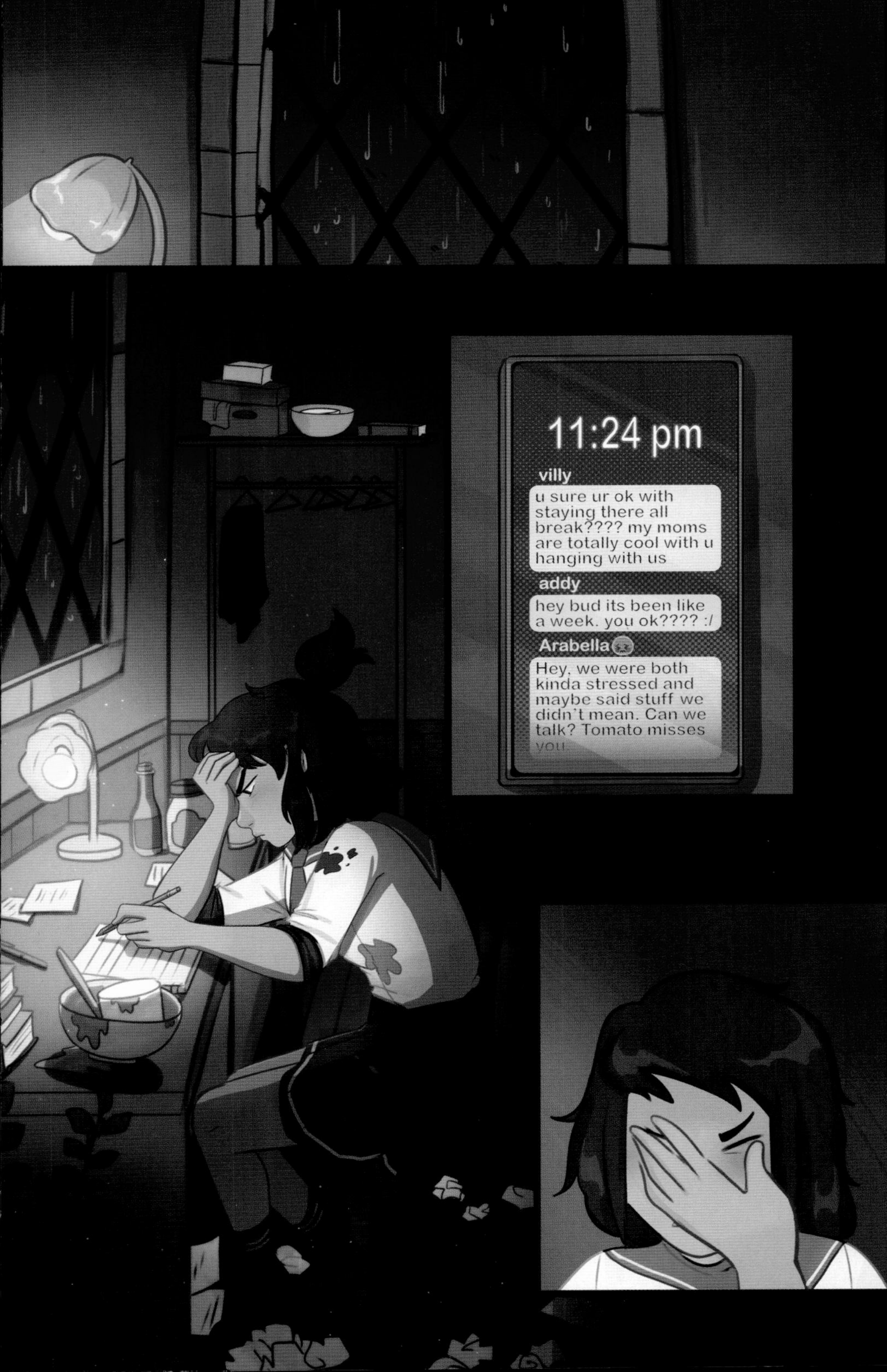
11:24 pm
villy
u sure ur ok with staying there all break???? my moms are totally cool with u hanging with us
addy
hey bud its been like a week. you ok???? :/
Arabella
Hey, we were both kinda stressed and maybe said stuff we didn't mean. Can we talk? Tomato misses you

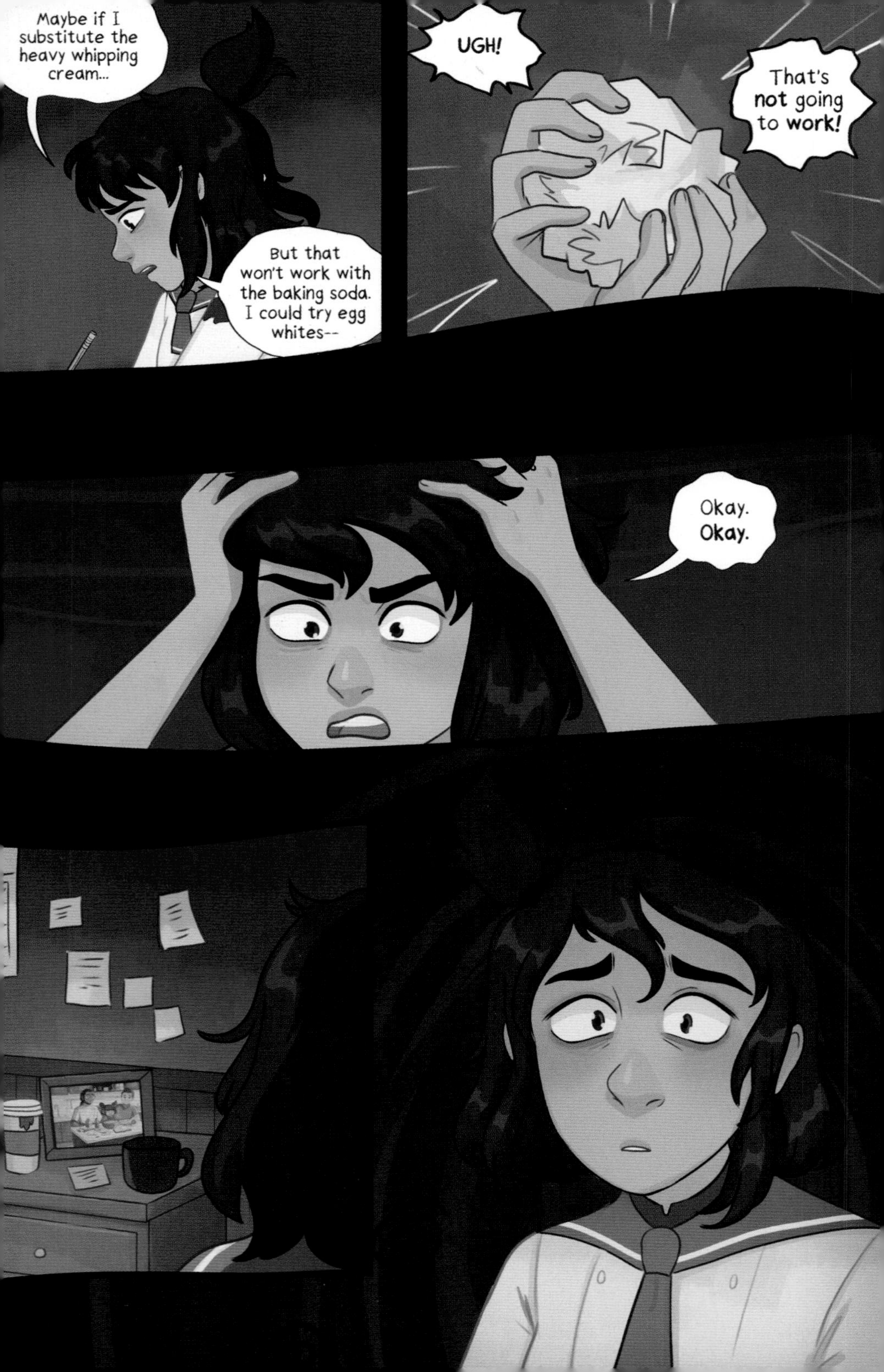
Maybe if I substitute the heavy whipping cream...
But that won't work with the baking soda. I could try egg whites--
UGH!
That's **not** going to **work!**
Okay. **Okay.**

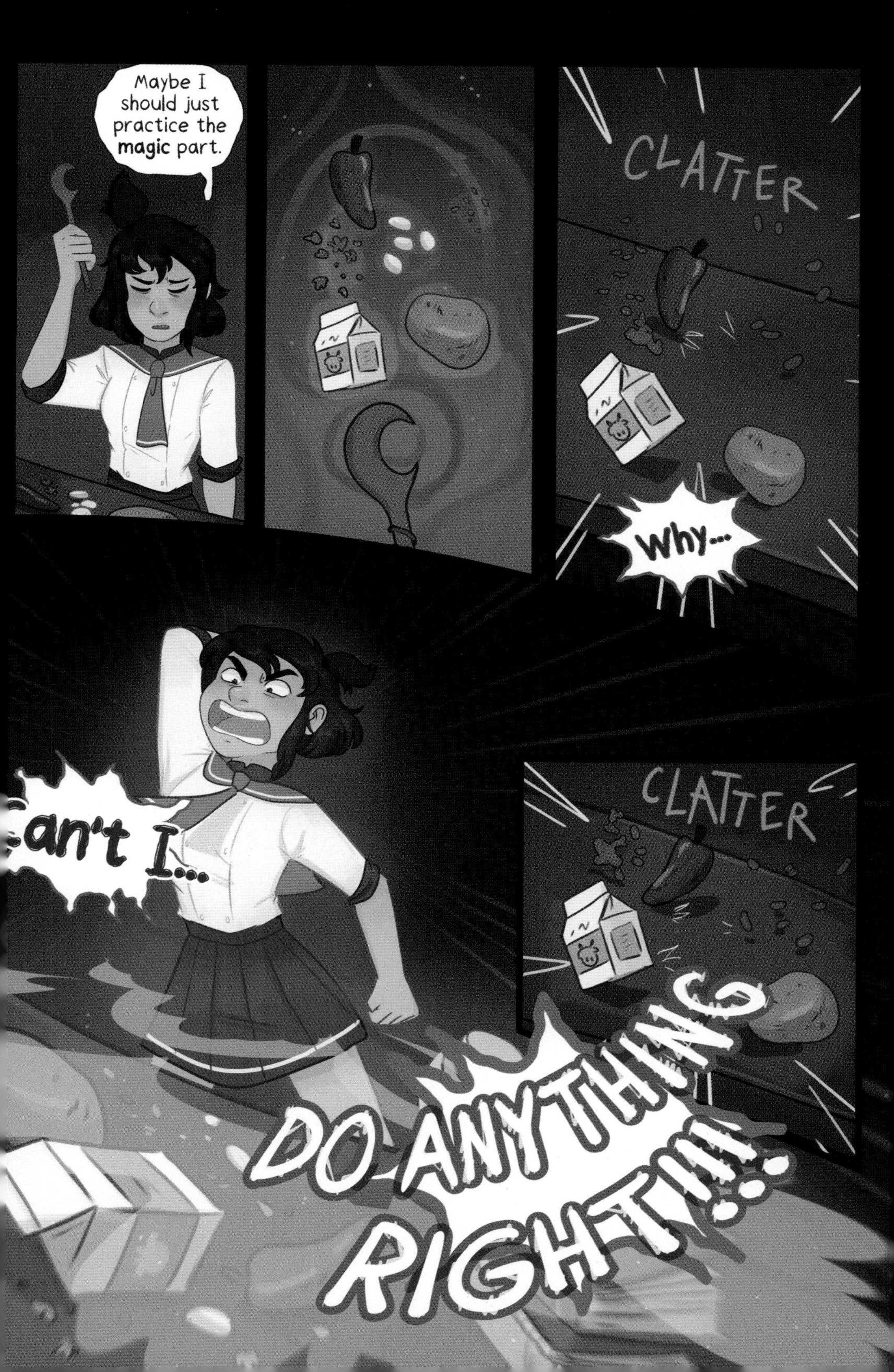
Maybe I should just practice the **magic** part.
CLATTER
Why...
can't I...
CLATTER
DO ANYTHING RIGHT!!!!

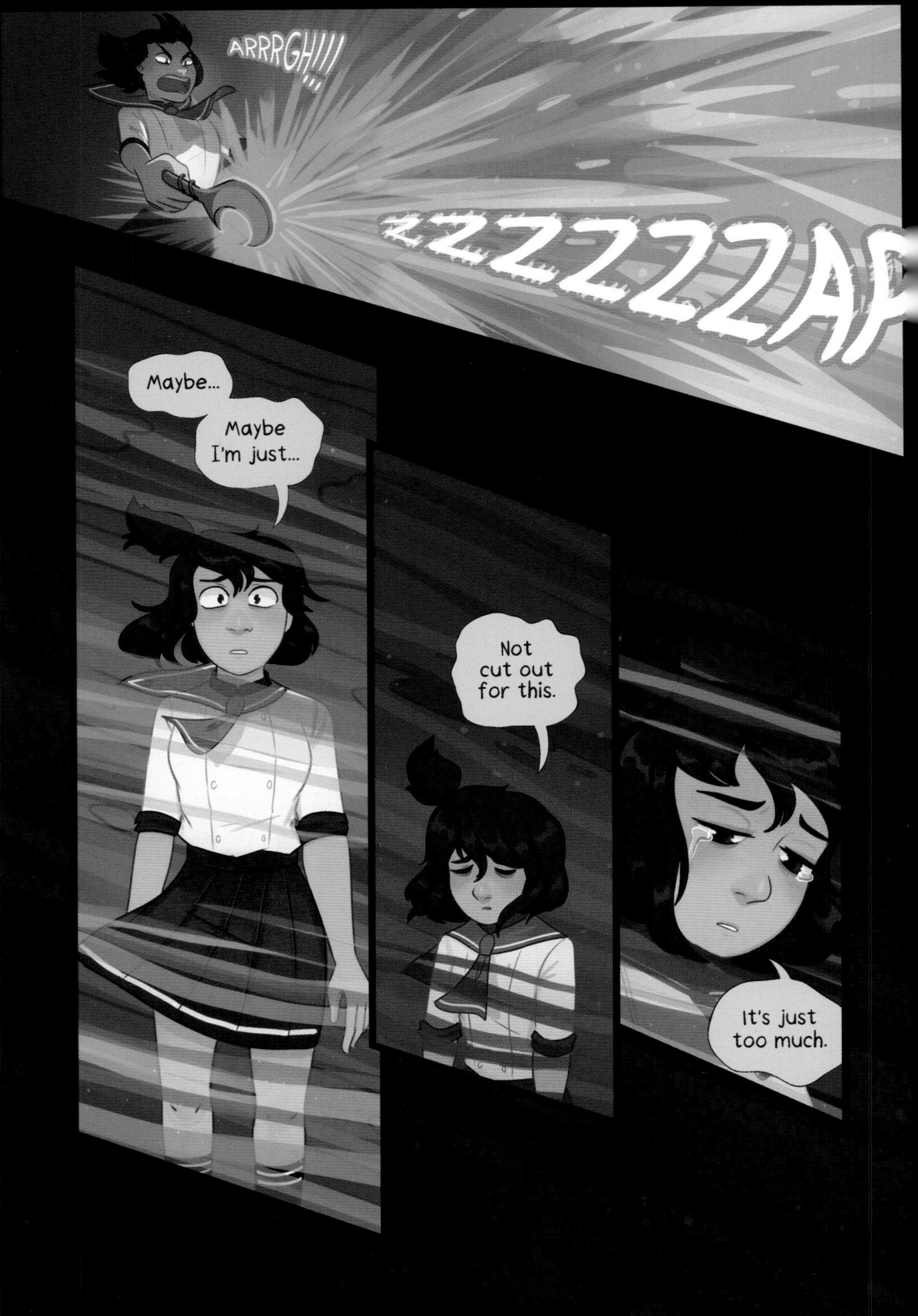
ARRRGH!!!
zZZZZZZAP
Maybe...
Maybe I'm just...
Not cut out for this.
It's just too much.

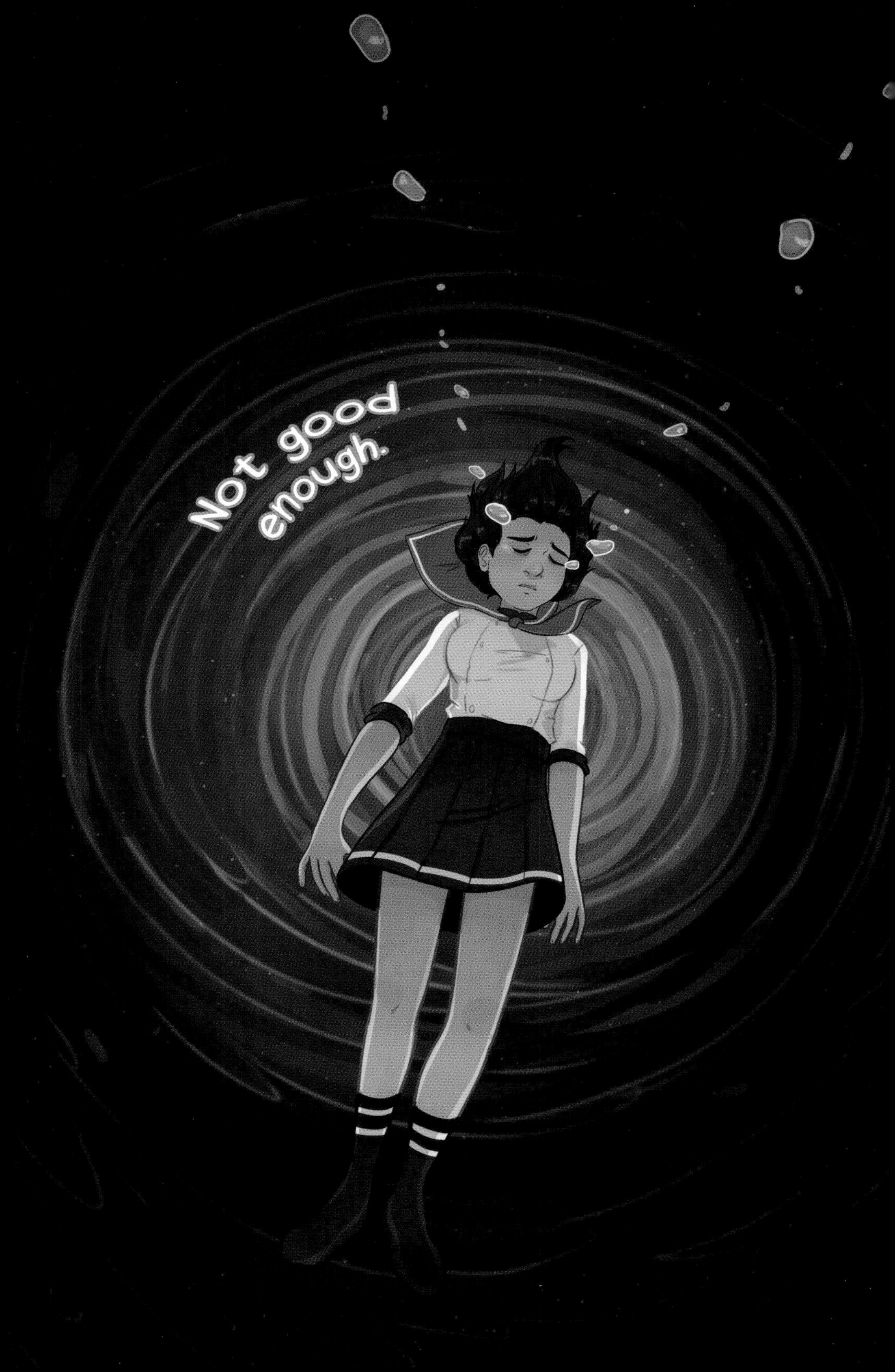
Not good enough.

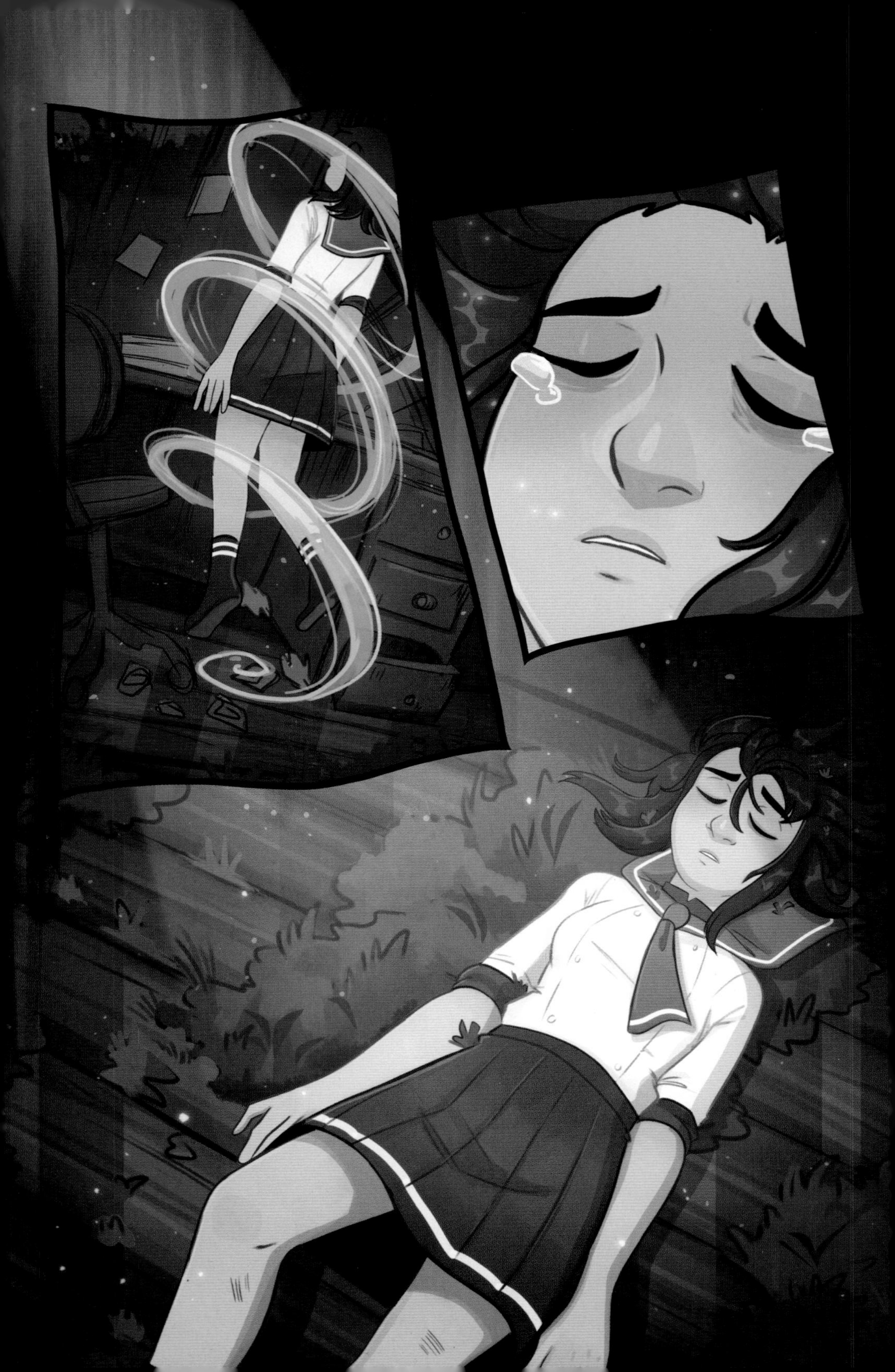

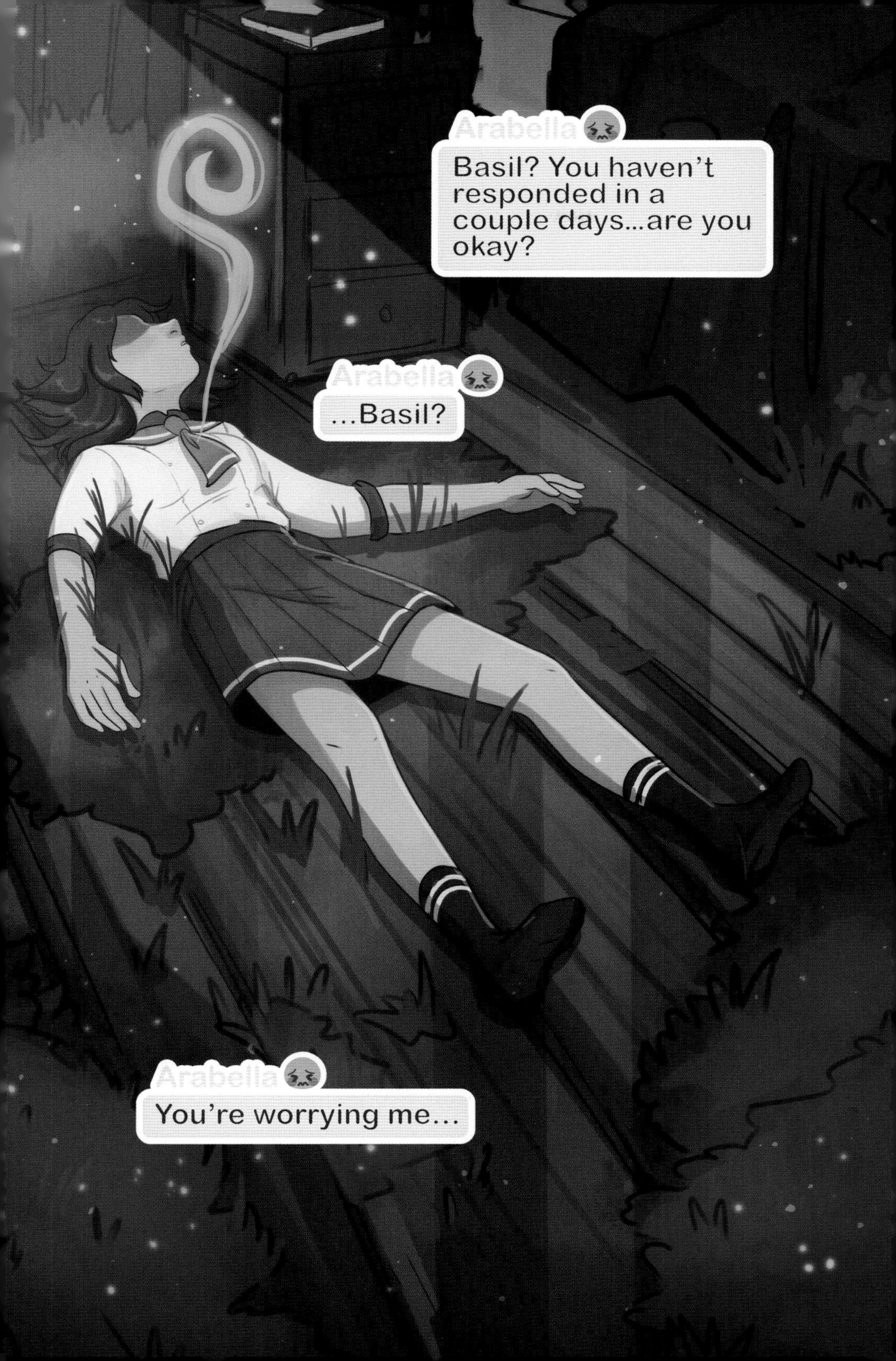
Arabella
Basil? You haven't responded in a couple days...are you okay?
Arabella
...Basil?
Arabella
You're worrying me...

Chapter
FIVE

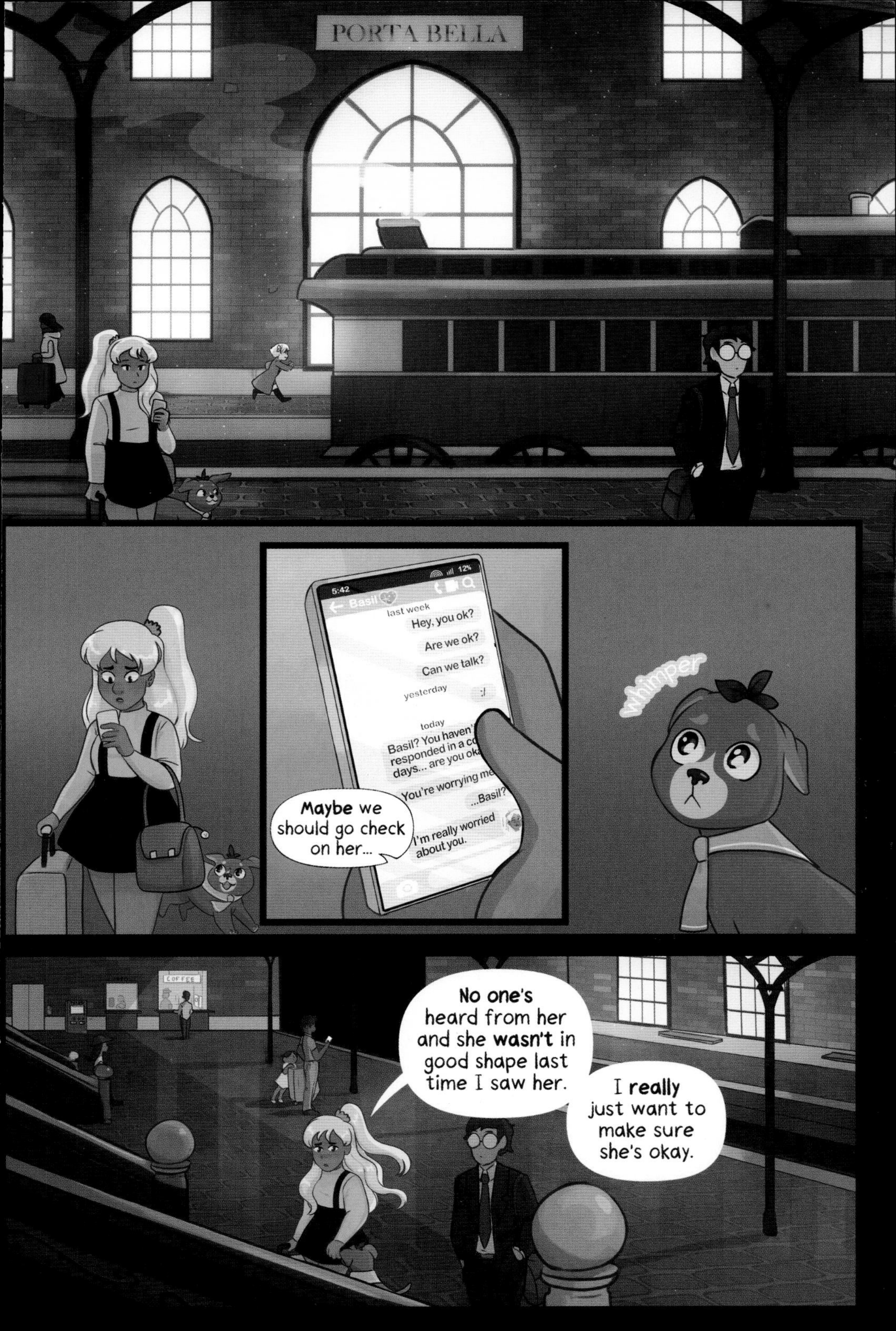
PORTA BELLA
5:42
12%
Basil
last week
Hey, you ok?
Are we ok?
Can we talk?
yesterday
:/
today
Basil? You haven't
responded in a co
days... are you oka
You're worrying me
...Basil?
I'm really worried
about you.
Maybe we should go check on her...
whimper
COFFEE
No one's heard from her and she wasn't in good shape last time I saw her.
I really just want to make sure she's okay.

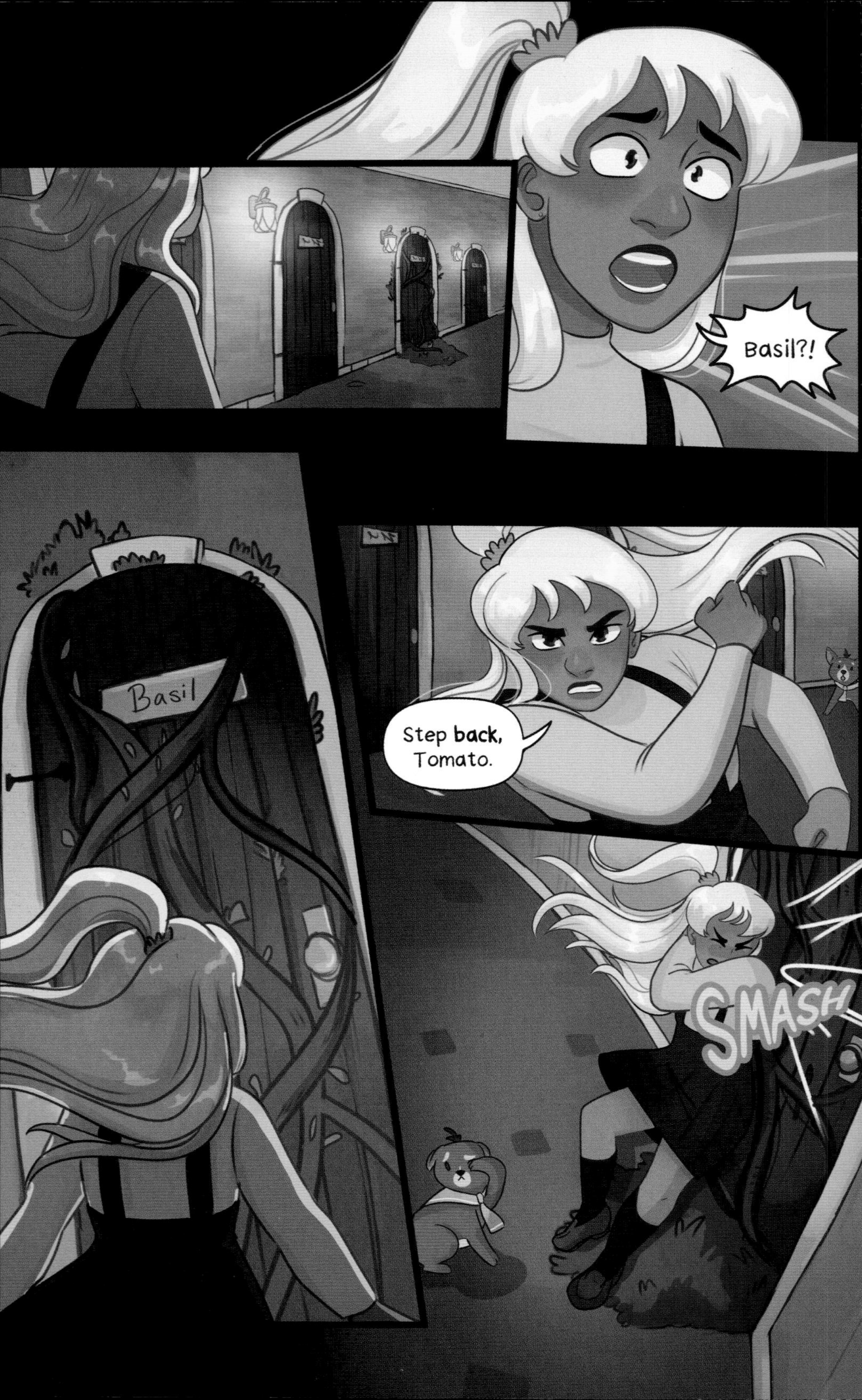

Basil?!
Basil
Step back, Tomato.
SMASH

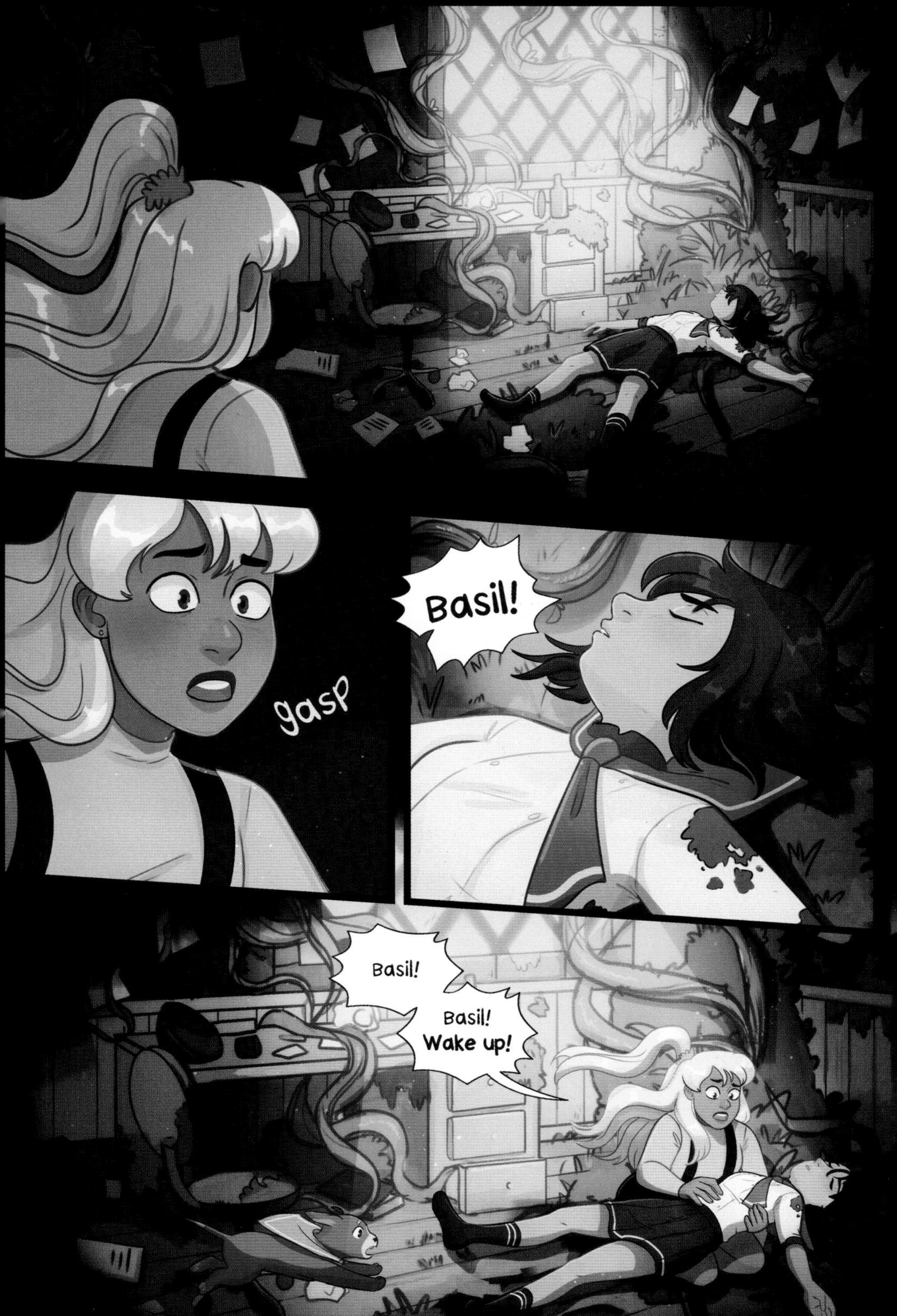
gasp
Basil!
Basil!
Basil!
Wake up!

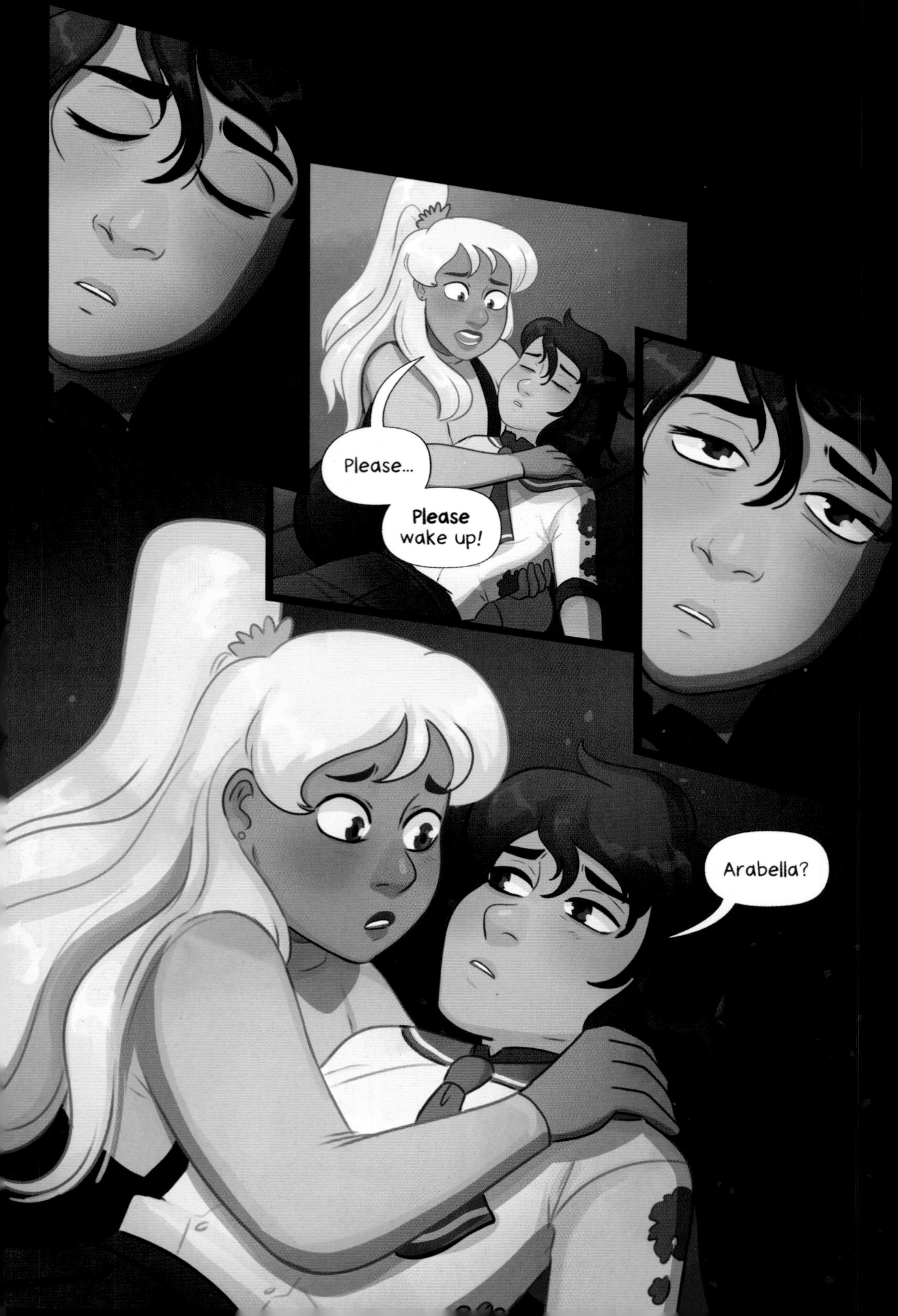
Please...
Please wake up!
Arabella?

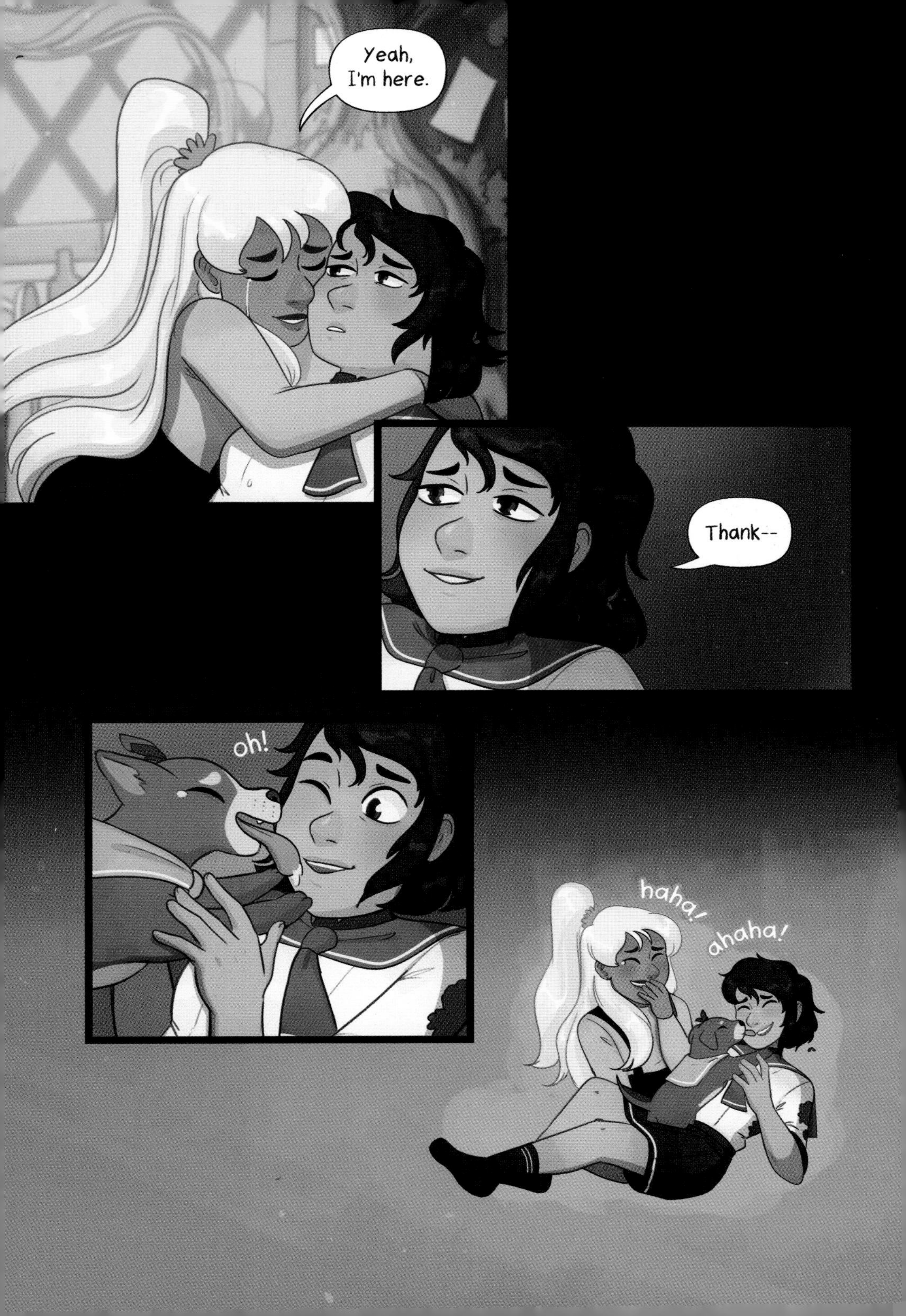
Yeah,
I'm here.
Thank--
oh!
haha!
ahaha!

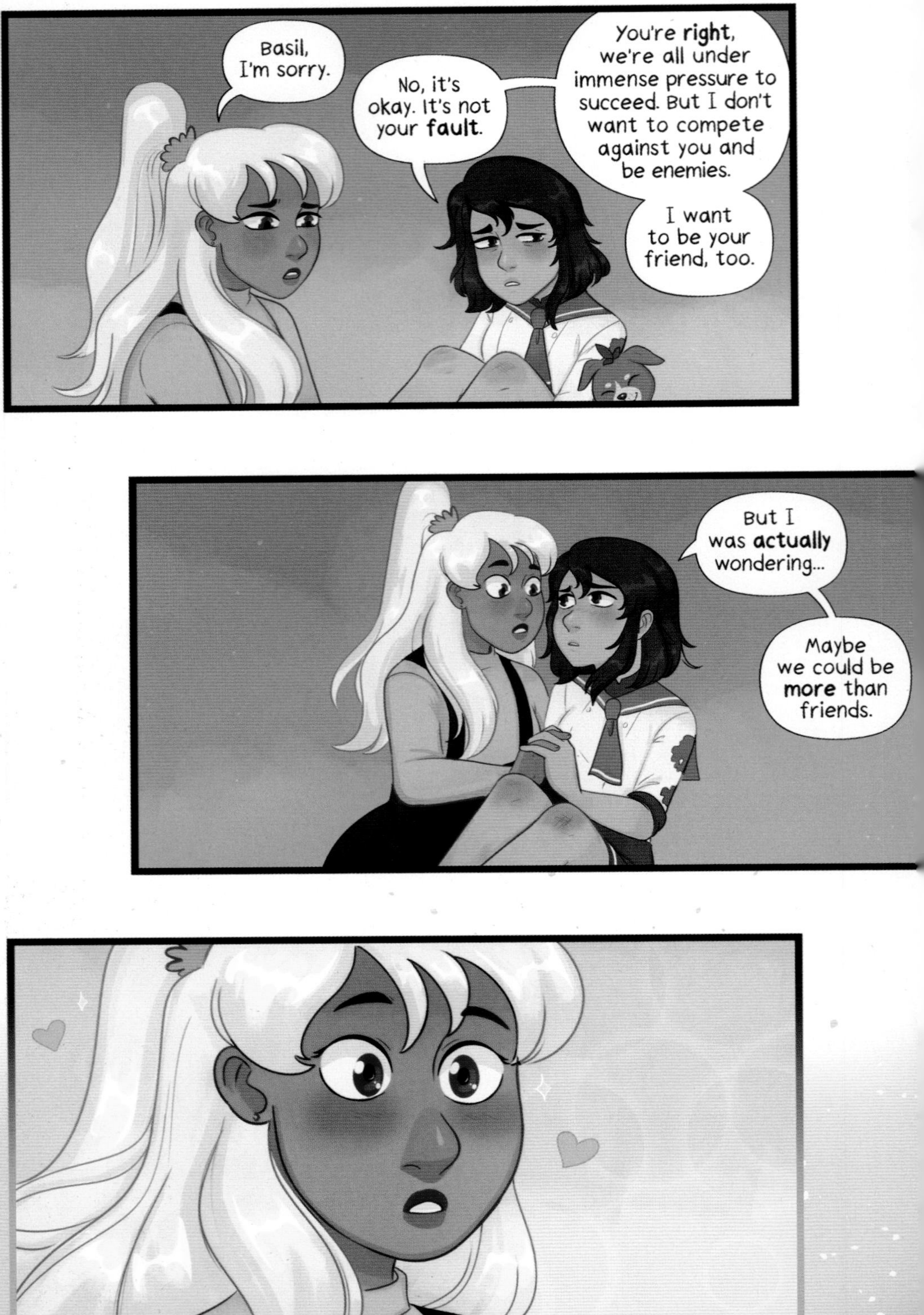
Basil,
I'm sorry.
No, it's
okay. It's not
your **fault**.
You're **right**,
we're all under
immense pressure to
succeed. But I don't
want to compete
against you and
be enemies.
I want
to be your
friend, too.
But I
was **actually**
wondering...
Maybe
we could be
more than
friends.

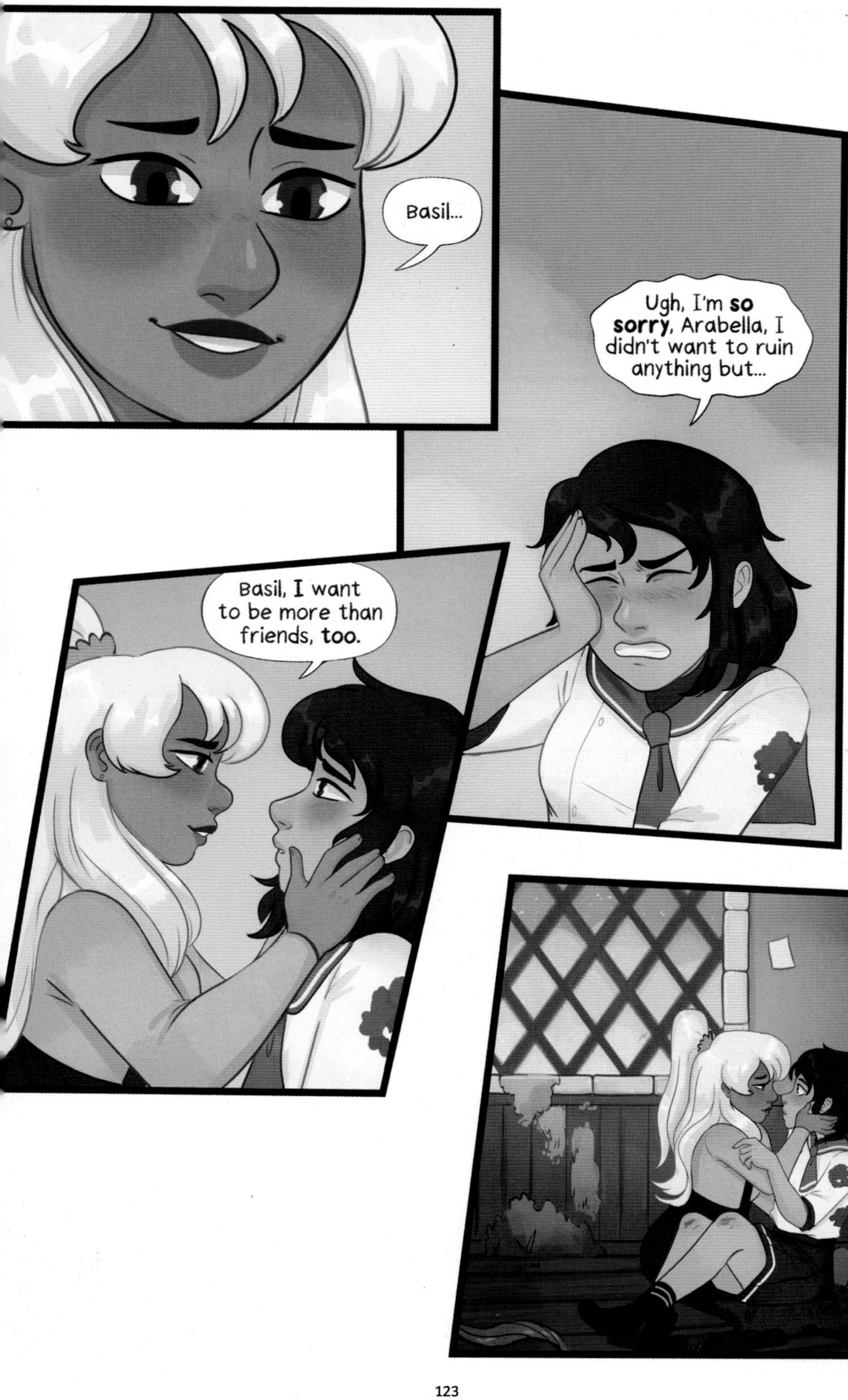
Basil...
Ugh, I'm **so sorry**, Arabella, I didn't want to ruin anything but...
Basil, I want to be more than friends, **too.**

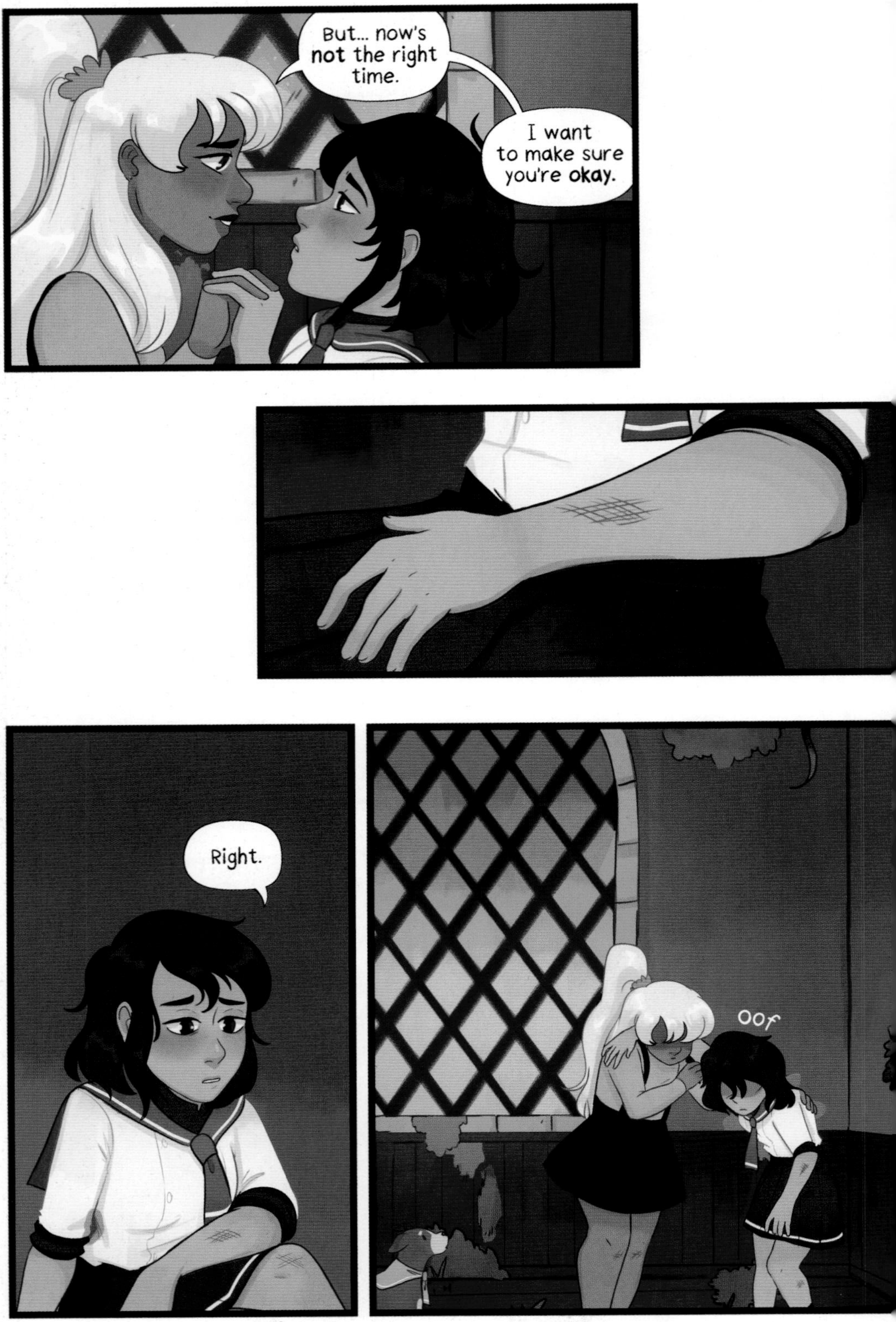
But... now's **not** the right time.
I want to make sure you're **okay**.
Right.
Oof

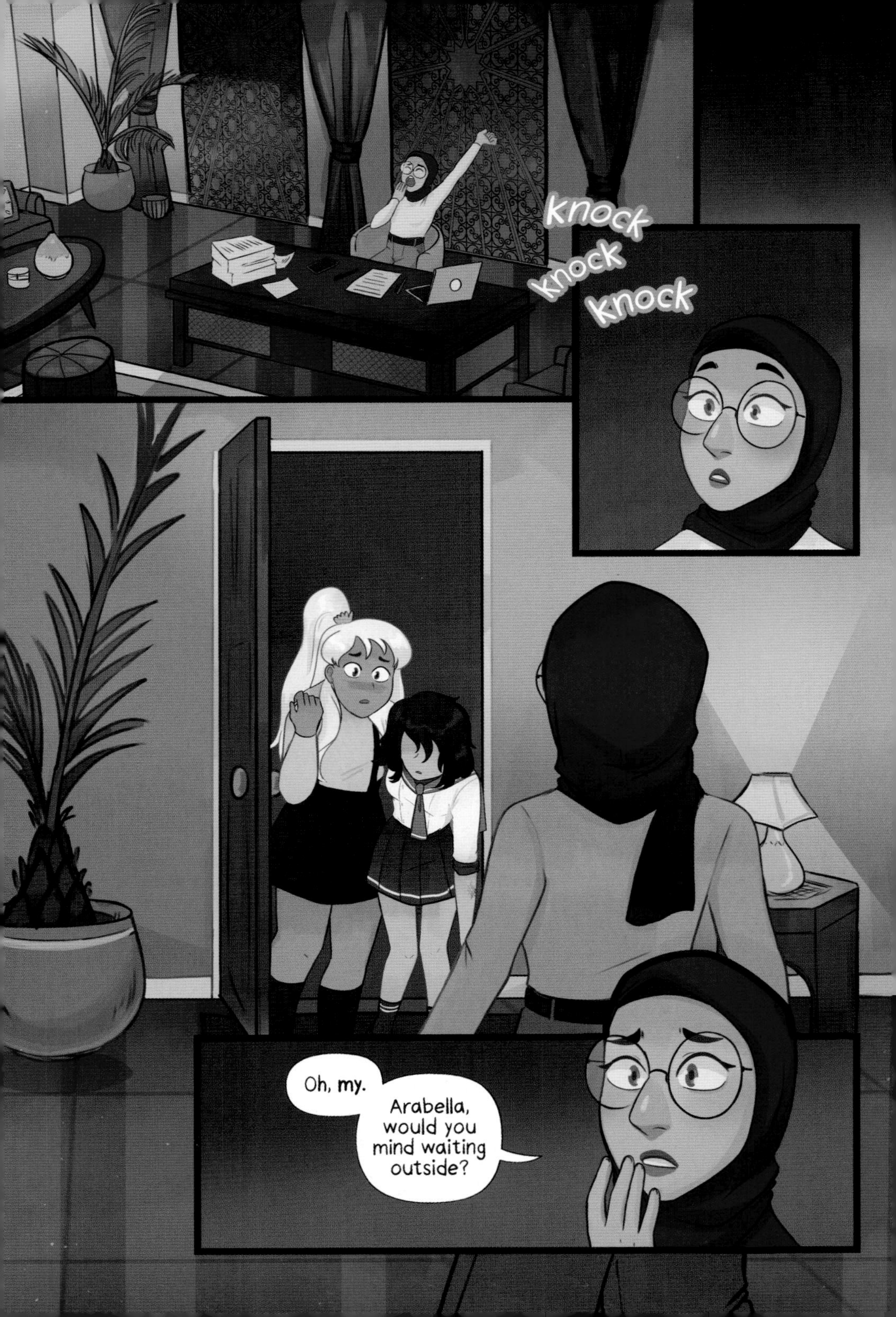
knock
knock
knock
Oh, my.
Arabella, would you mind waiting outside?

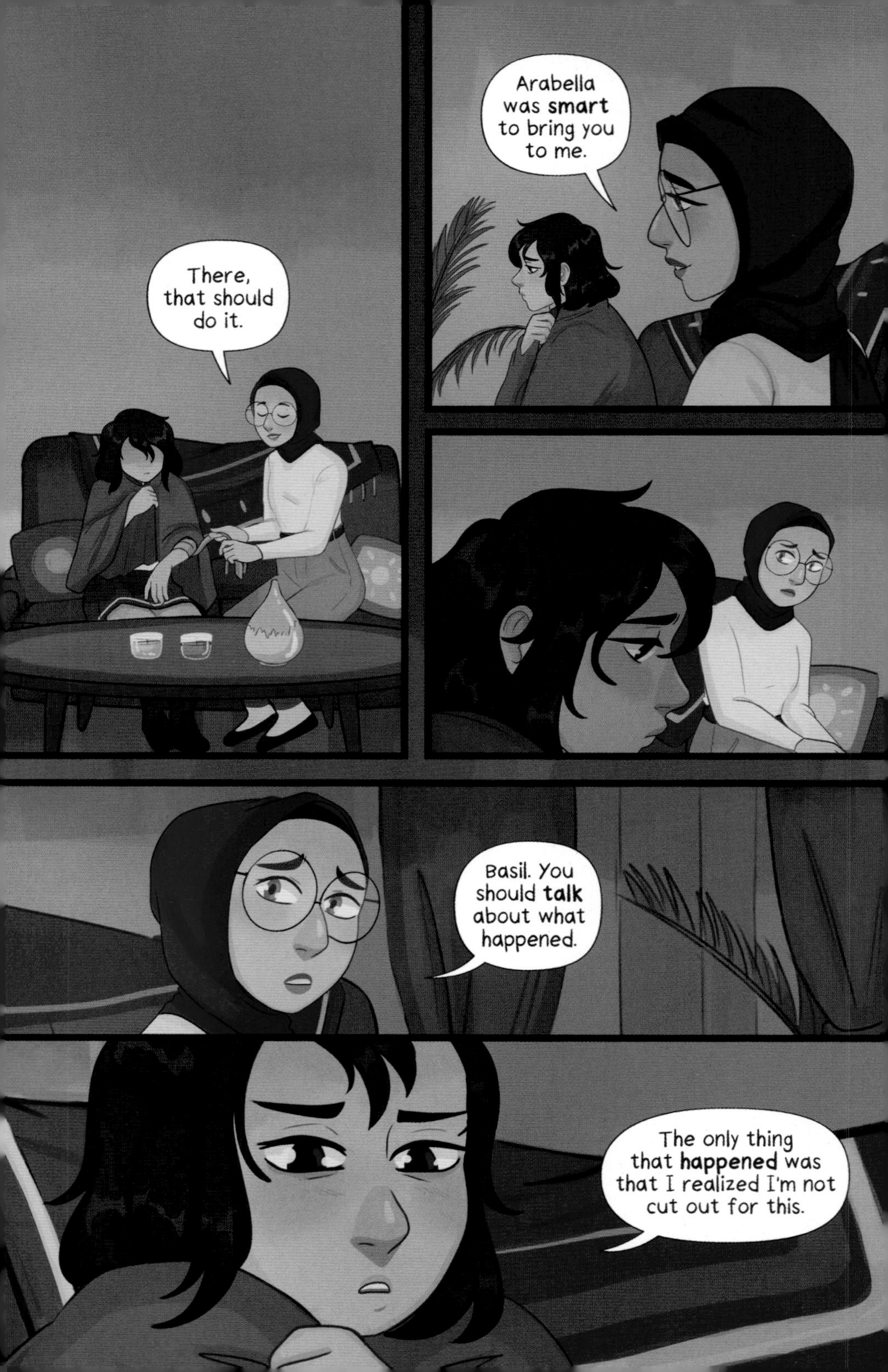
There, that should do it.
Arabella was **smart** to bring you to me.
Basil. You should **talk** about what happened.
The only thing that **happened** was that I realized I'm not cut out for this.

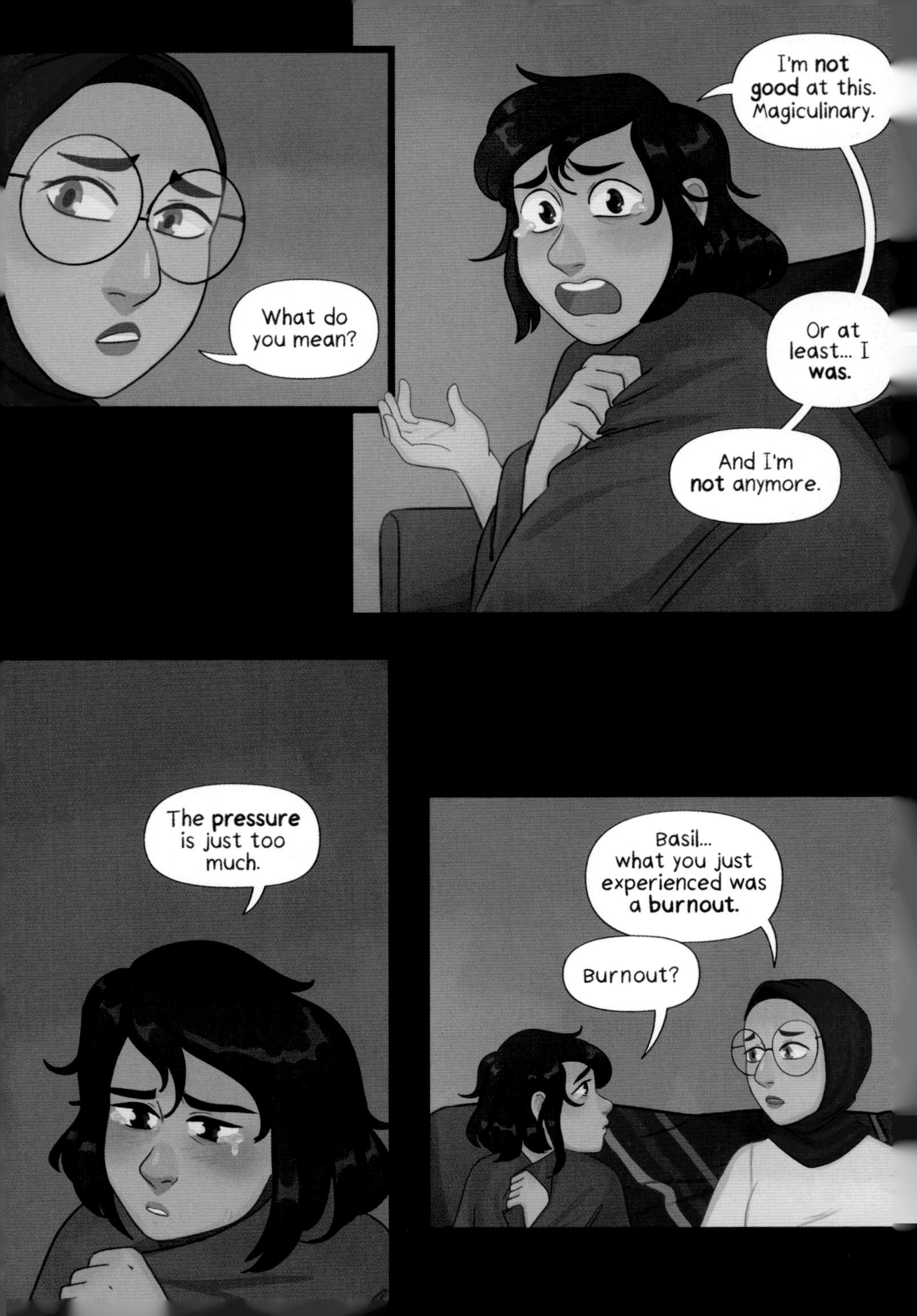
What do you mean?
I'm **not** **good** at this. Magiculinary.
Or at least... I **was.**
And I'm **not** anymore.
The **pressure** is just too much.
Basil... what you just experienced was a **burnout.**
Burnout?

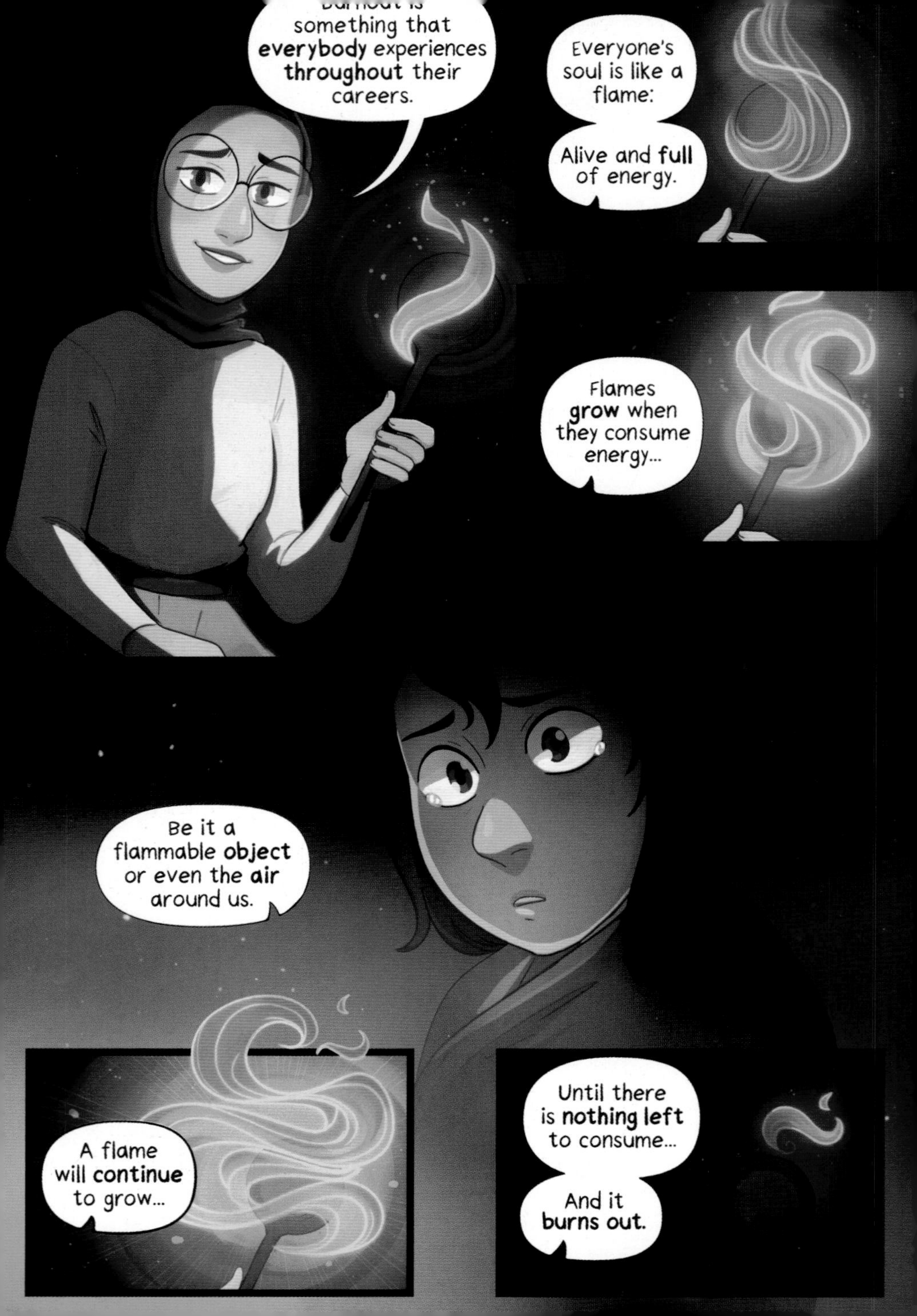
something that **everybody** experiences **throughout** their careers.
Everyone's soul is like a flame:
Alive and **full** of energy.
Flames **grow** when they consume energy...
Be it a flammable **object** or even the **air** around us.
A flame will **continue** to grow...
Until there is **nothing left** to consume...
And it **burns out.**

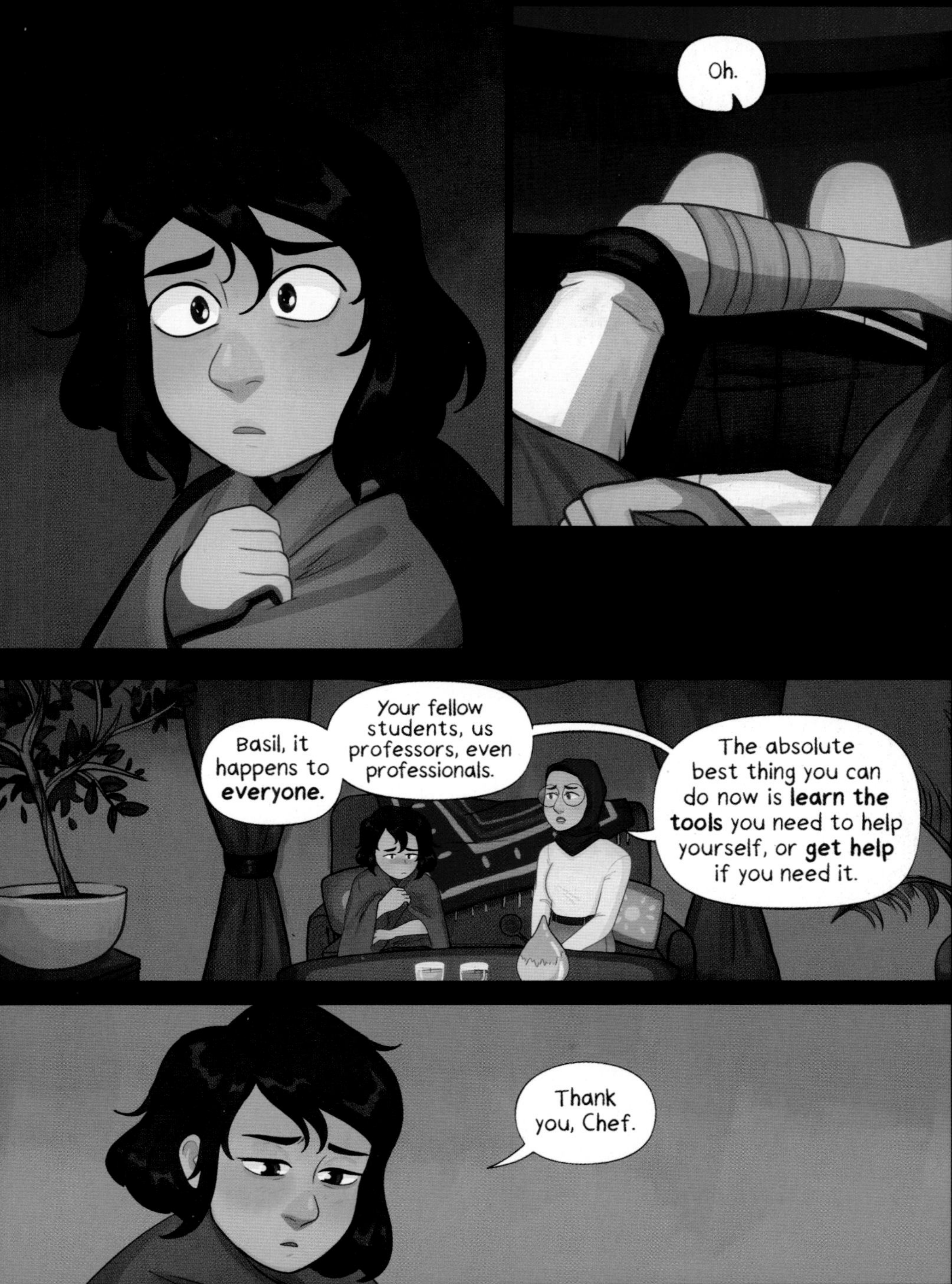
Oh.
Basil, it happens to **everyone.**
Your fellow students, us professors, even professionals.
The absolute best thing you can do now is **learn the tools** you need to help yourself, or **get help** if you need it.
Thank you, Chef.

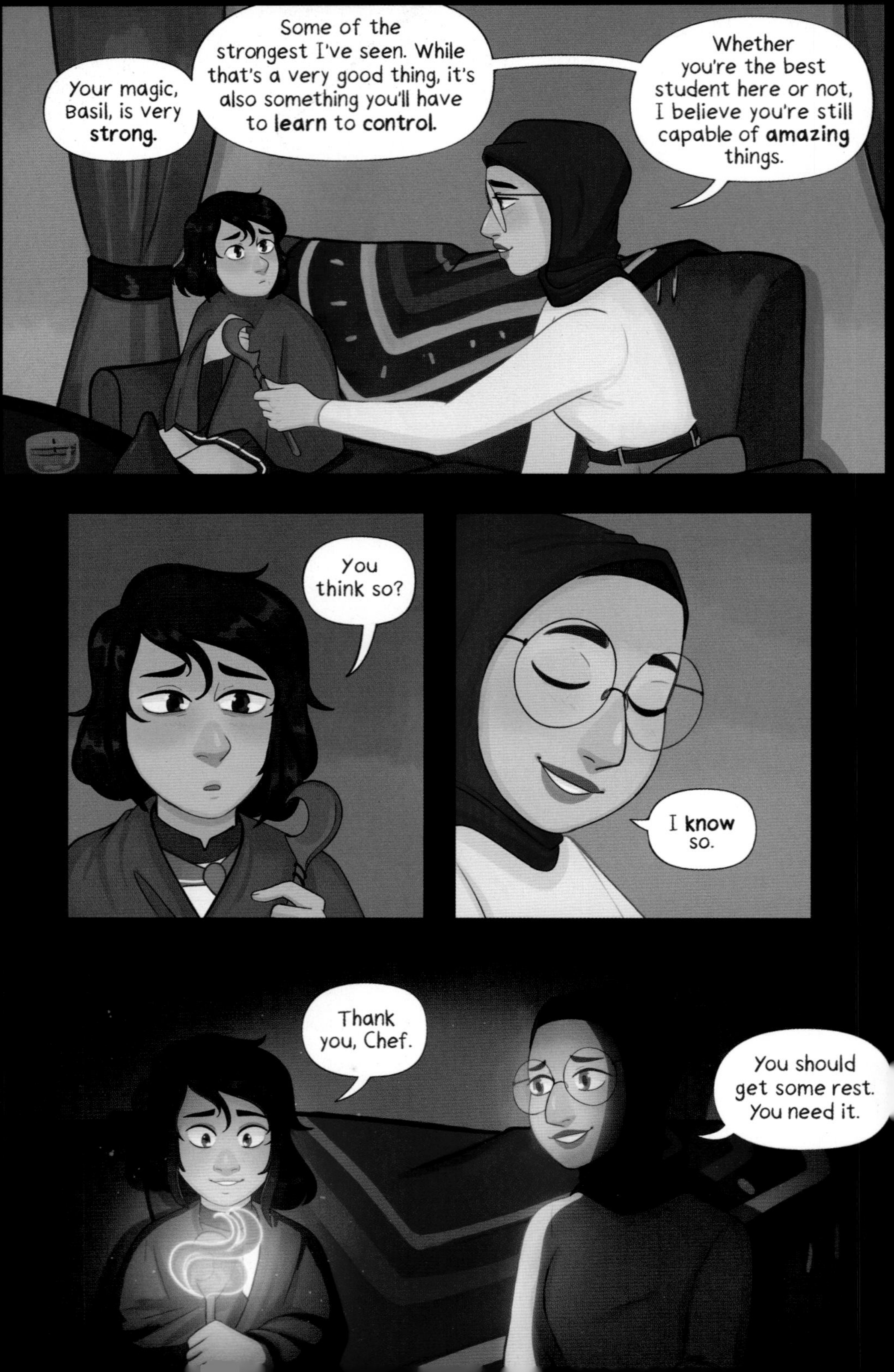
Your magic, Basil, is very **strong.**
Some of the strongest I've seen. While that's a very good thing, it's also something you'll have to **learn** to **control.**
Whether you're the best student here or not, I believe you're still capable of **amazing** things.
You think so?
I **know** so.
Thank you, Chef.
You should get some rest. You need it.

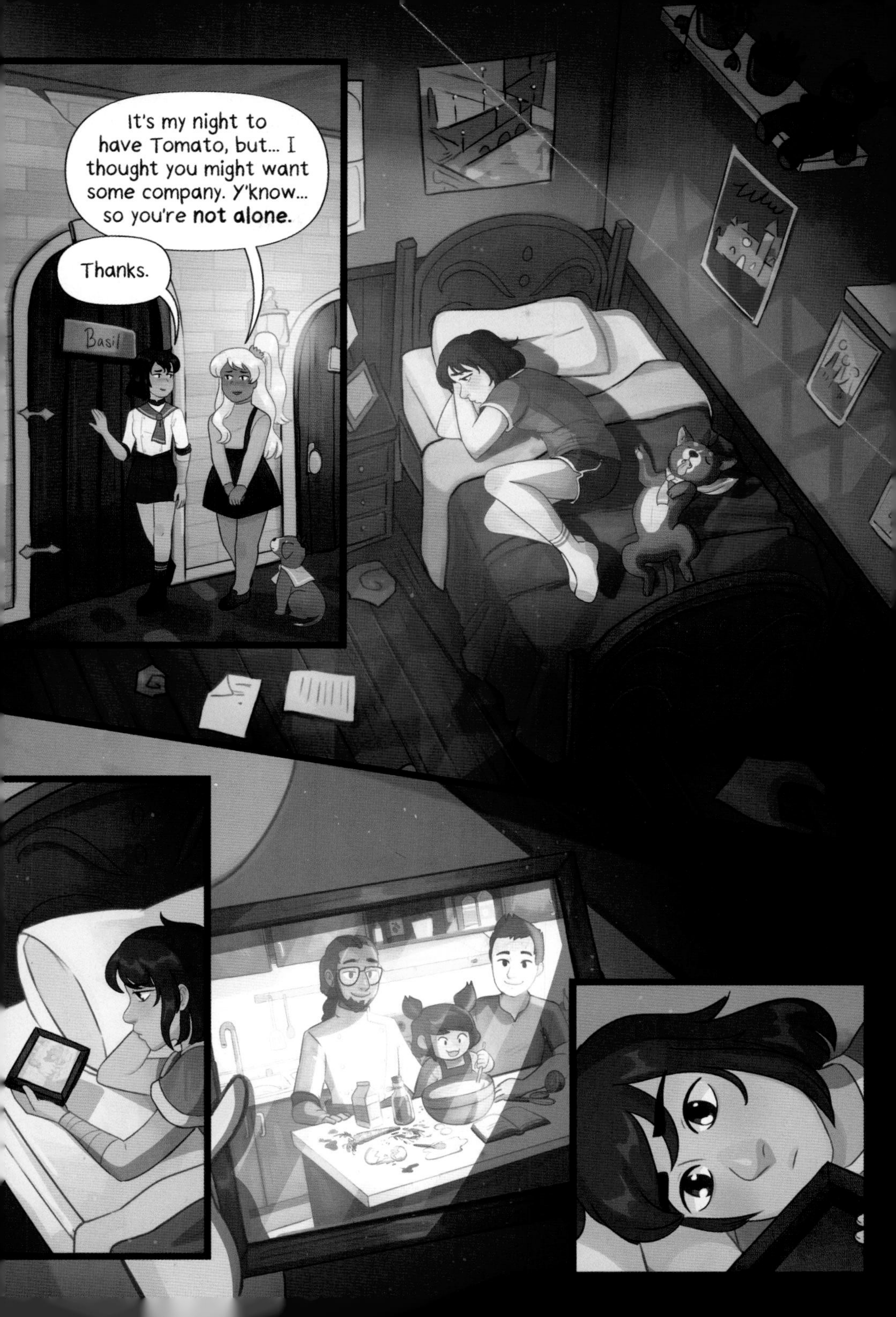
It's my night to have Tomato, but... I thought you might want some company. Y'know... so you're **not alone.**
Thanks.
Basil

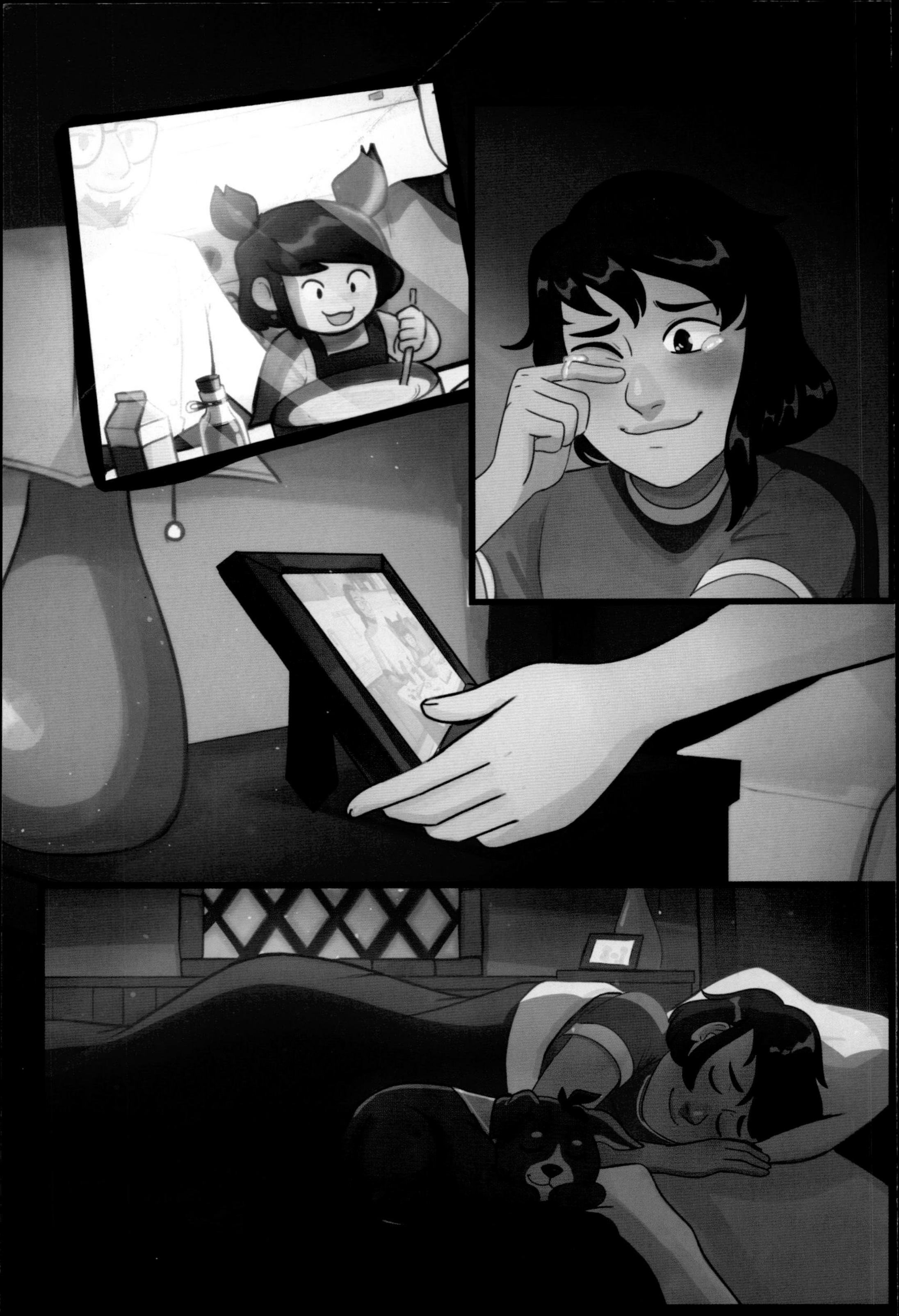

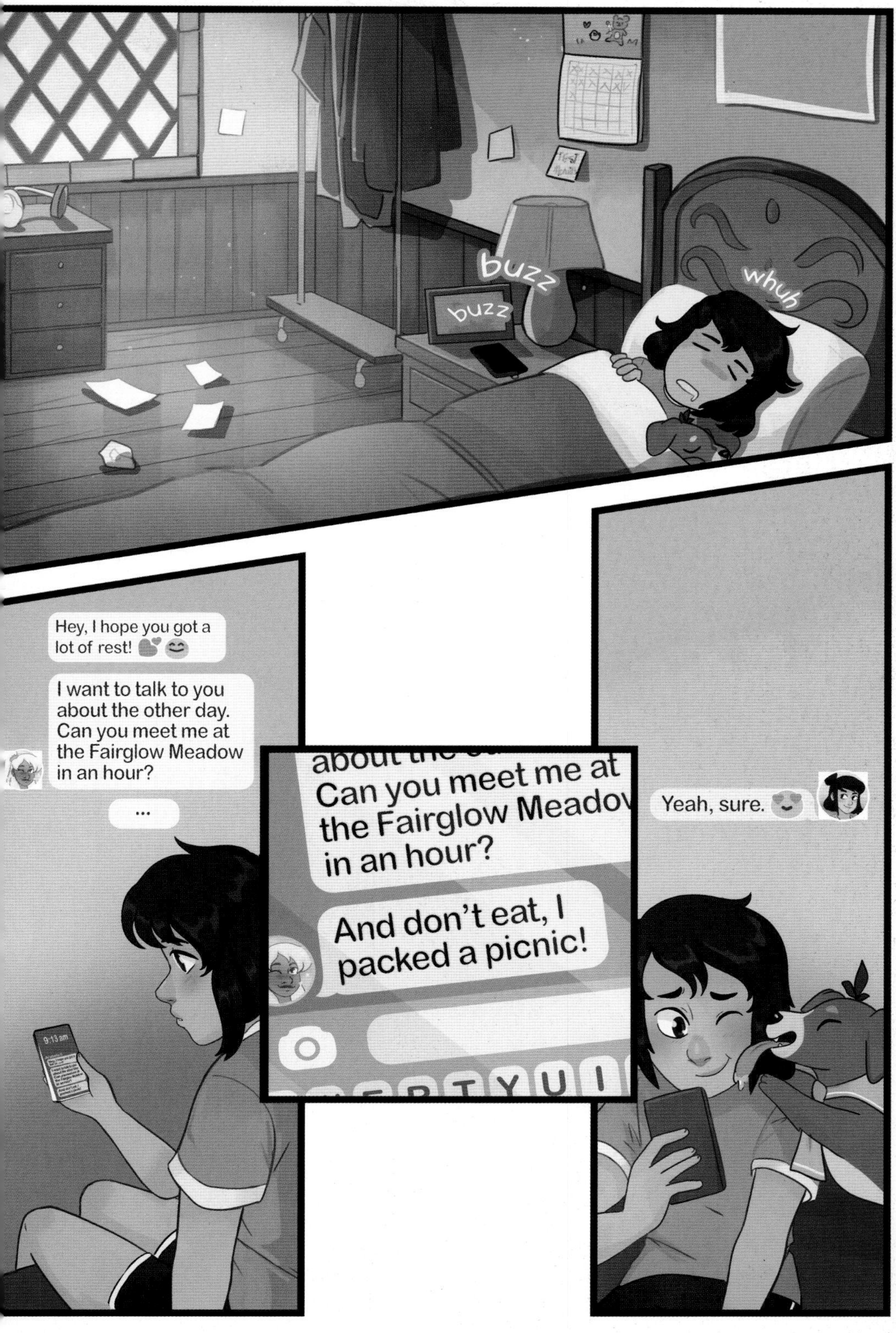
buzz
buzz
whuh
Hey, I hope you got a lot of rest!
I want to talk to you about the other day. Can you meet me at the Fairglow Meadow in an hour?
...
Can you meet me at the Fairglow Meadow in an hour?
And don't eat, I packed a picnic!
Yeah, sure.

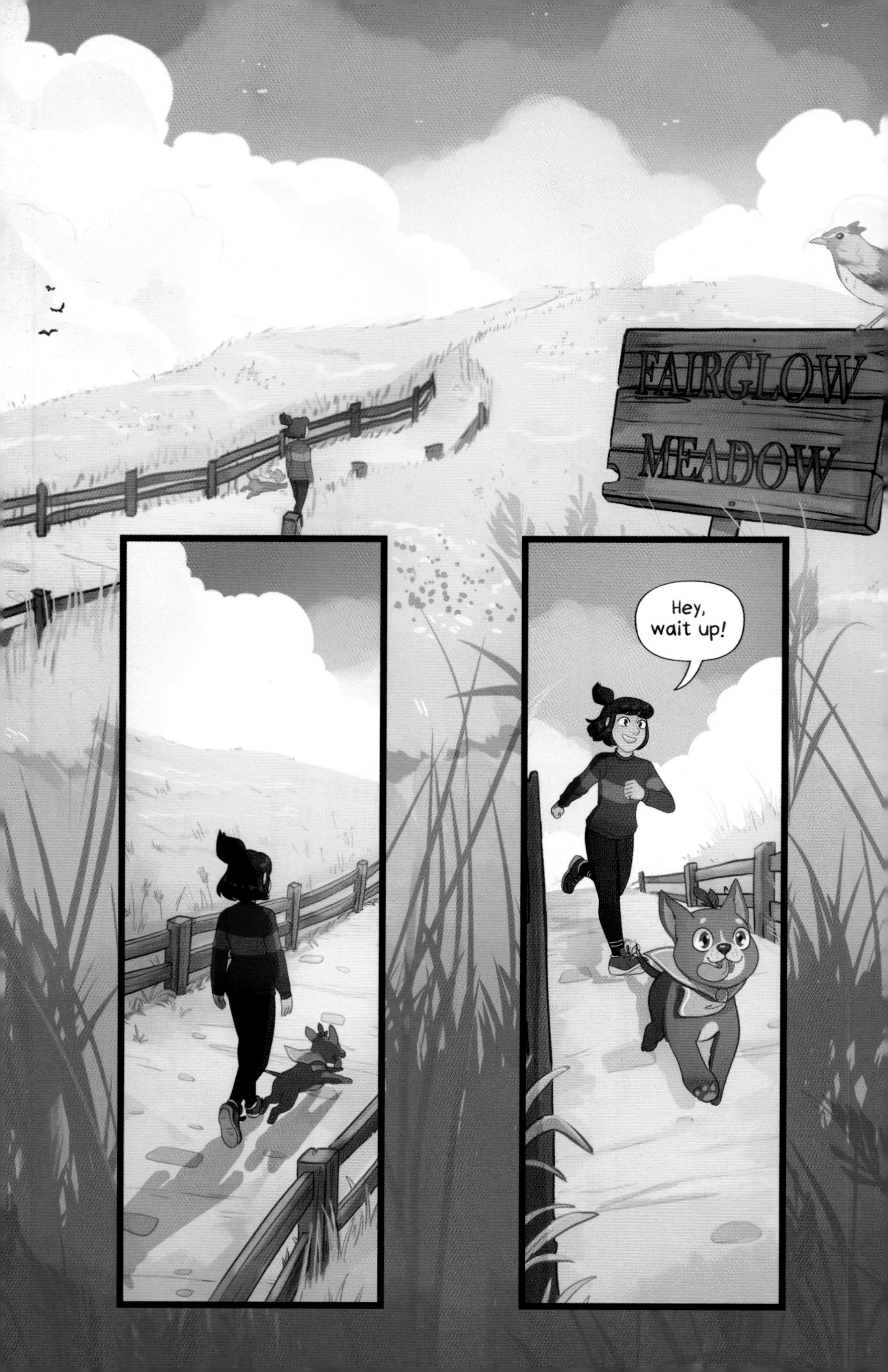
FAIRGLOW MEADOW
Hey, wait up!

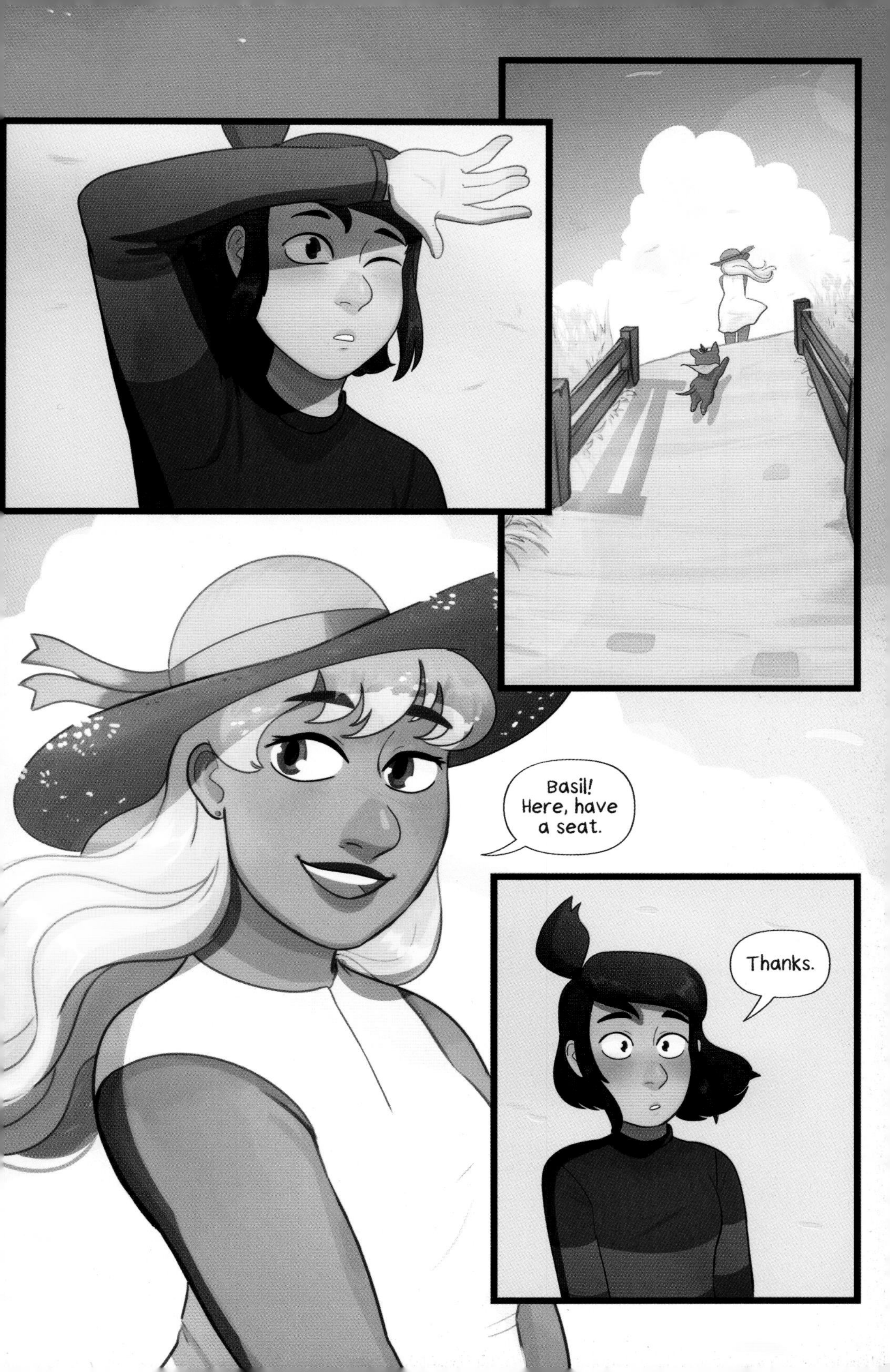
Basil! Here, have a seat.
Thanks.

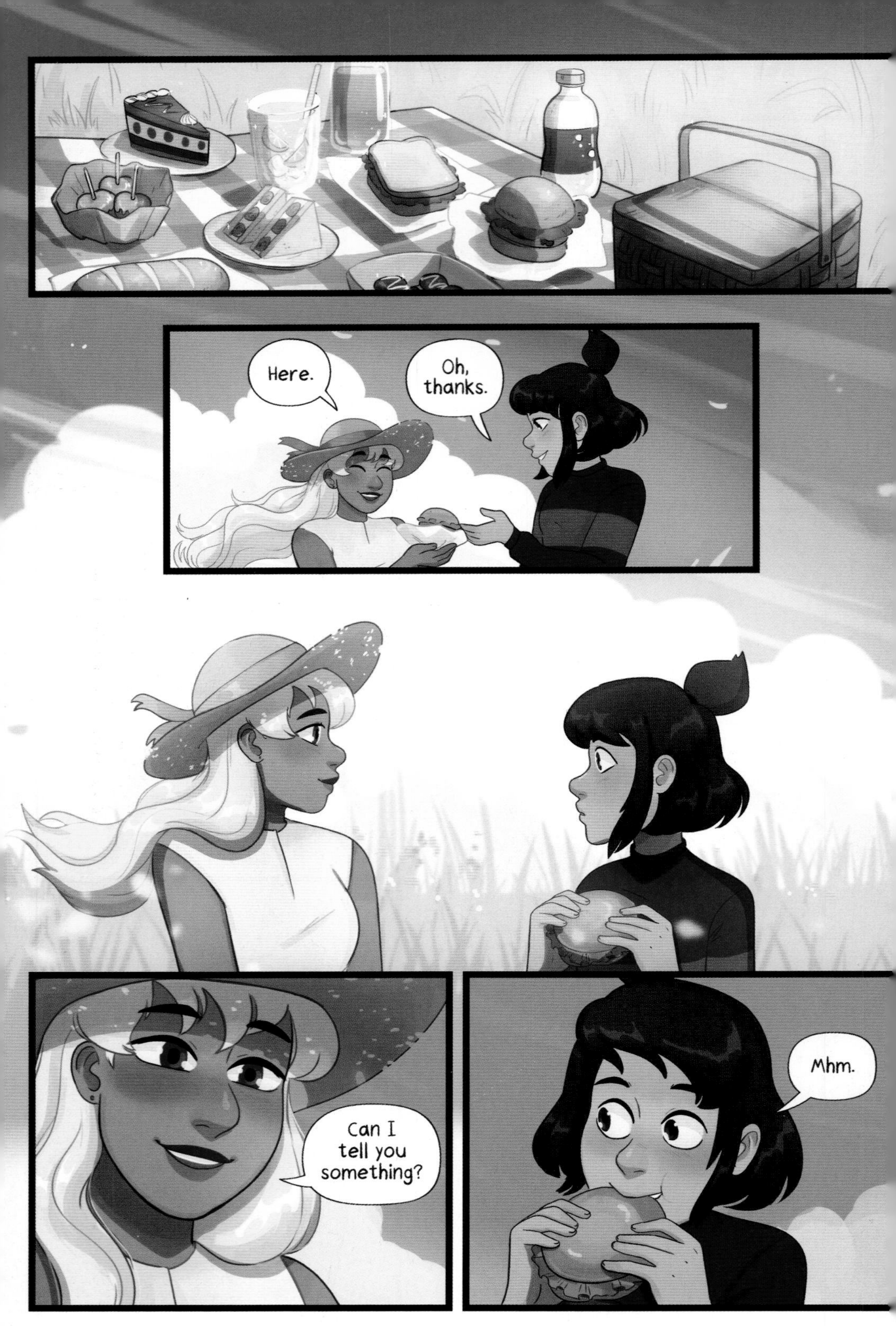
Here.
Oh, thanks.
Can I tell you something?
Mhm.

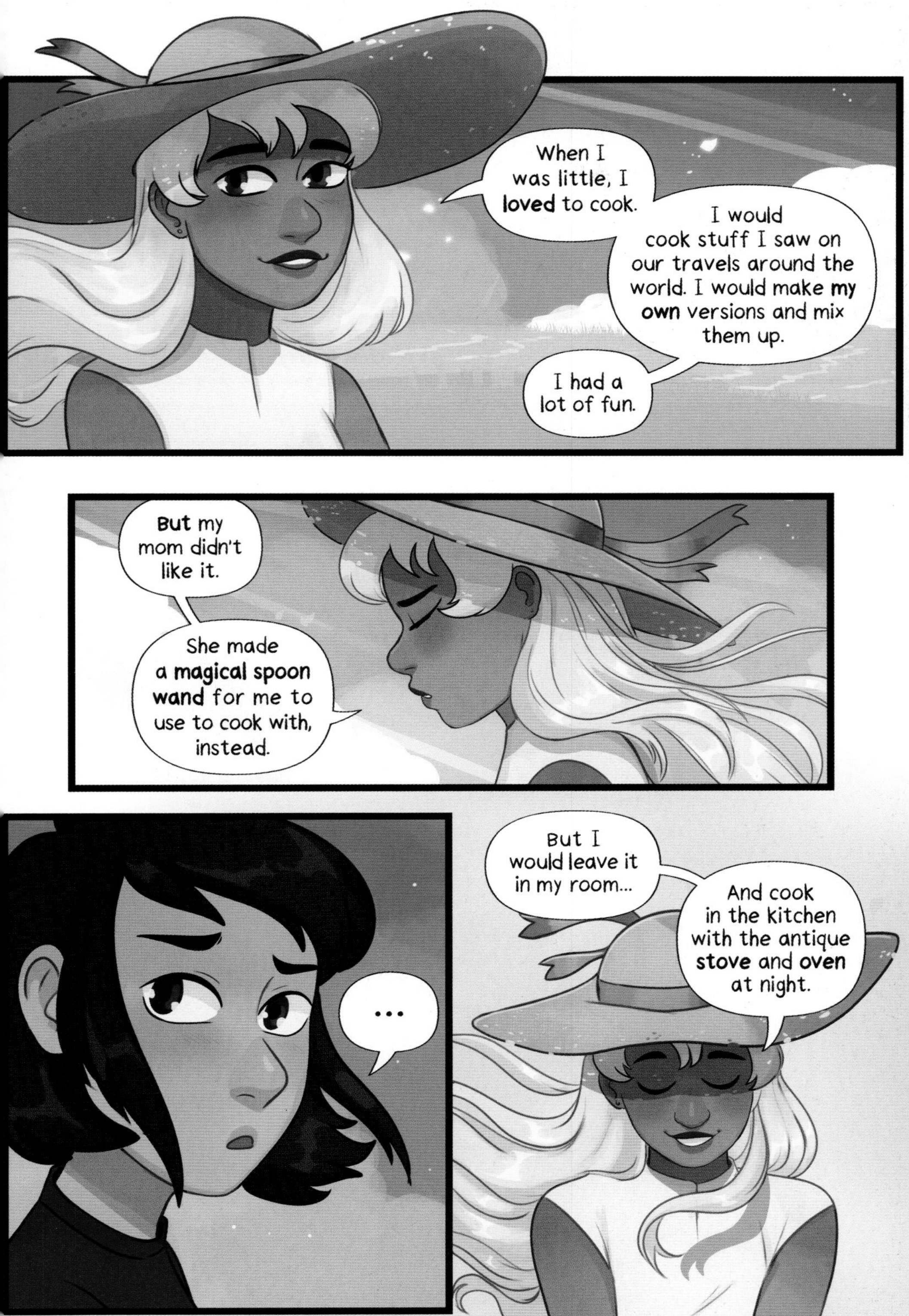
When I was little, I **loved** to cook.
I would cook stuff I saw on our travels around the world. I would make **my own** versions and mix them up.
I had a lot of fun.
But my mom didn't like it.
She made a **magical spoon wand** for me to use to cook with, instead.
...
But I would leave it in my room...
And cook in the kitchen with the antique **stove** and **oven** at night.

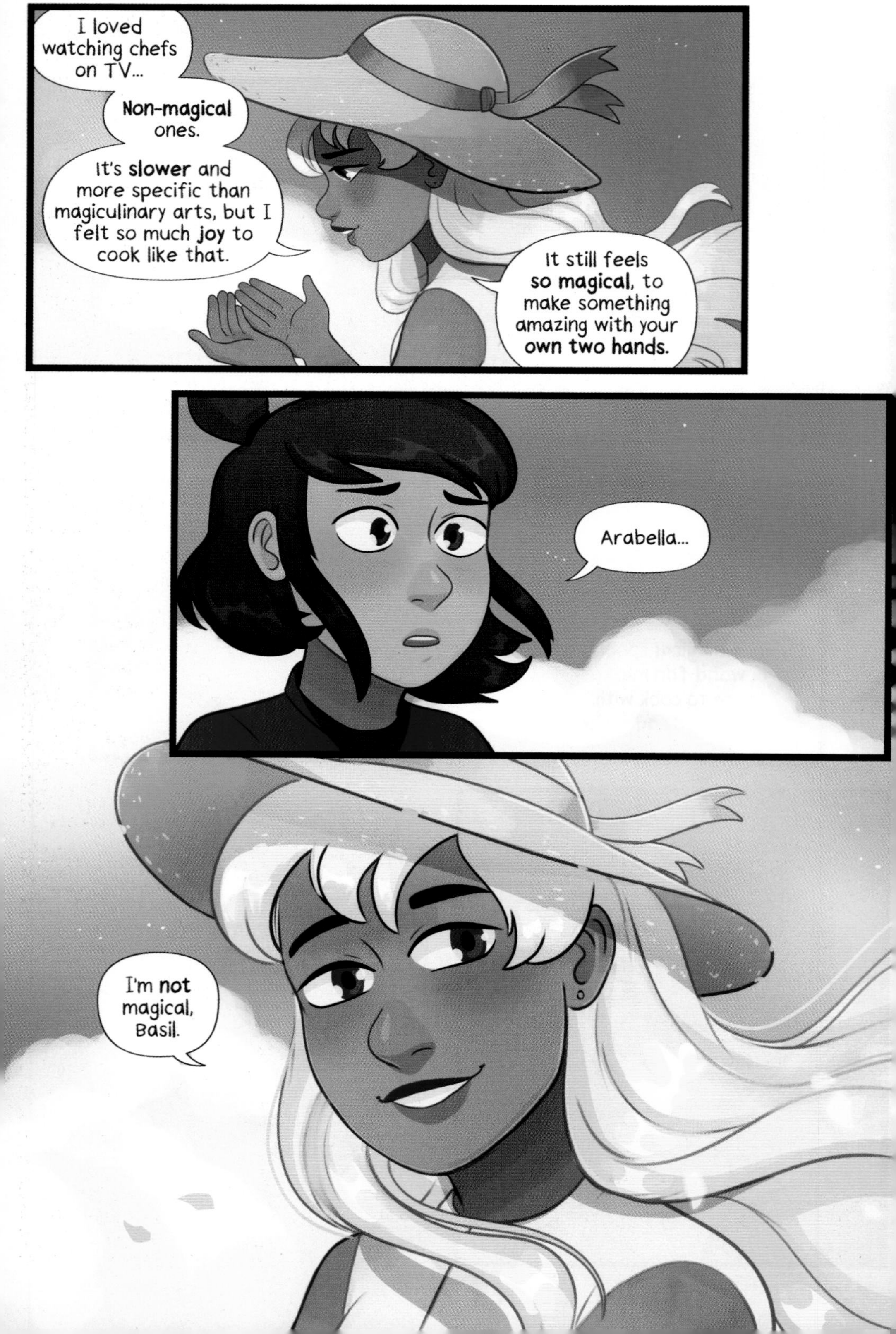
I loved watching chefs on TV...
Non-magical ones.
It's **slower** and more specific than magiculinary arts, but I felt so much **joy** to cook like that.
It still feels **so magical**, to make something amazing with your **own two hands.**
Arabella...
I'm **not** magical, Basil.

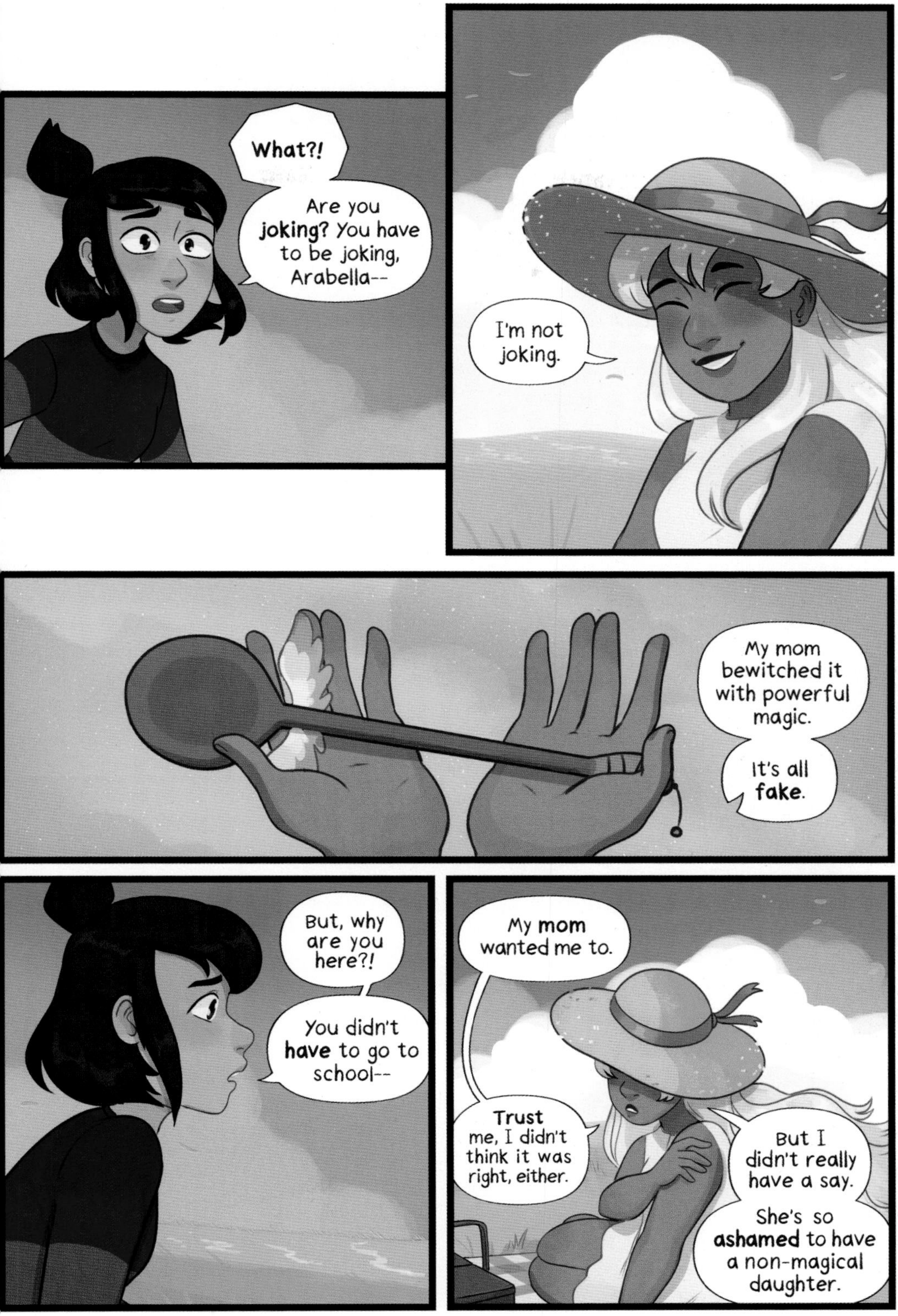
What?!
Are you joking? You have to be joking, Arabella--
I'm not joking.
My mom bewitched it with powerful magic.
It's all fake.
But, why are you here?!
You didn't have to go to school--
My mom wanted me to.
Trust me, I didn't think it was right, either.
But I didn't really have a say.
She's so ashamed to have a non-magical daughter.

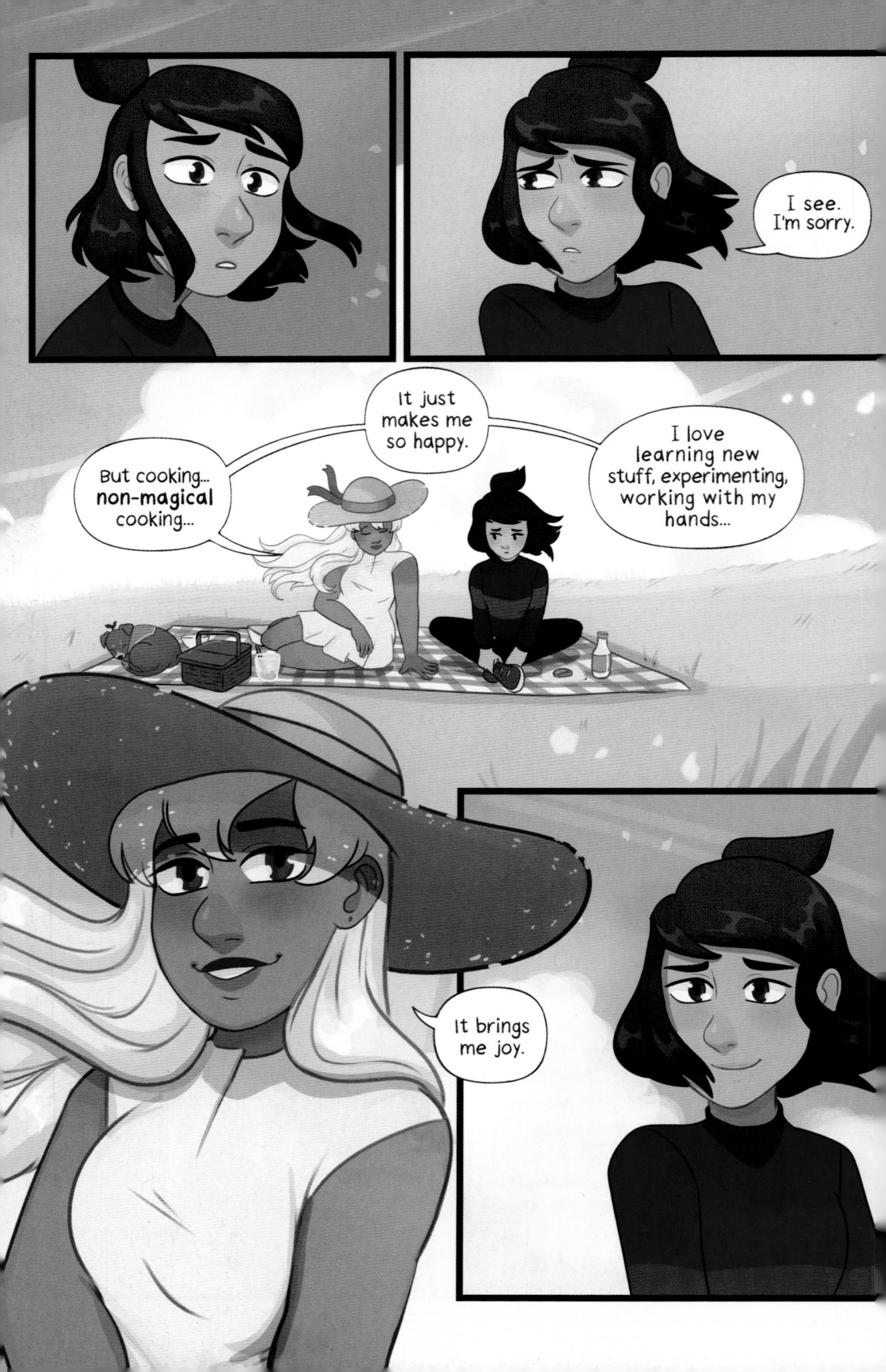
I see. I'm sorry.
But cooking... **non-magical** cooking...
It just makes me so happy.
I love **learning** new stuff, experimenting, working with my hands...
It brings me joy.

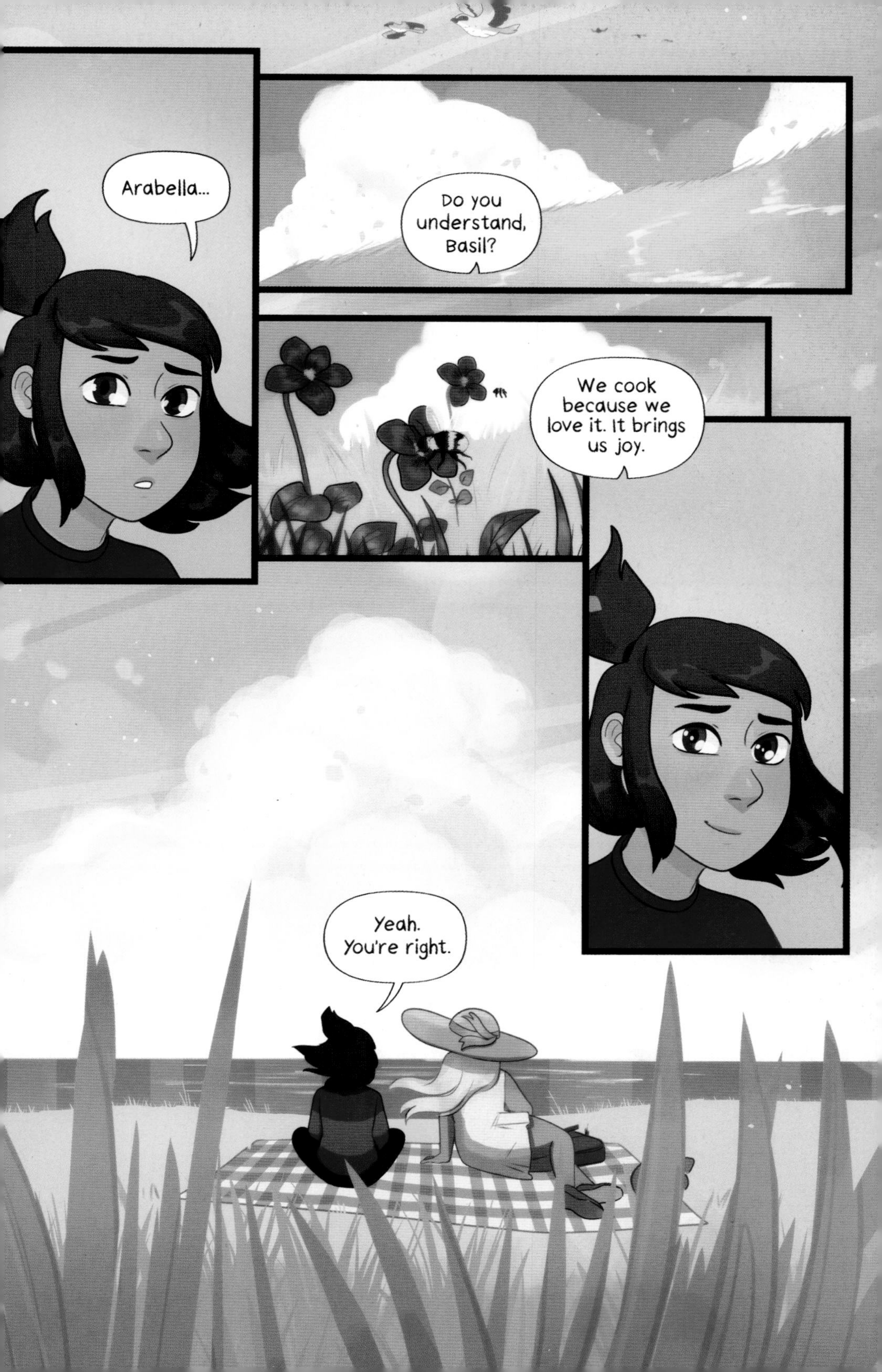
Arabella...
Do you understand, Basil?
We cook because we love it. It brings us joy.
Yeah. You're right.

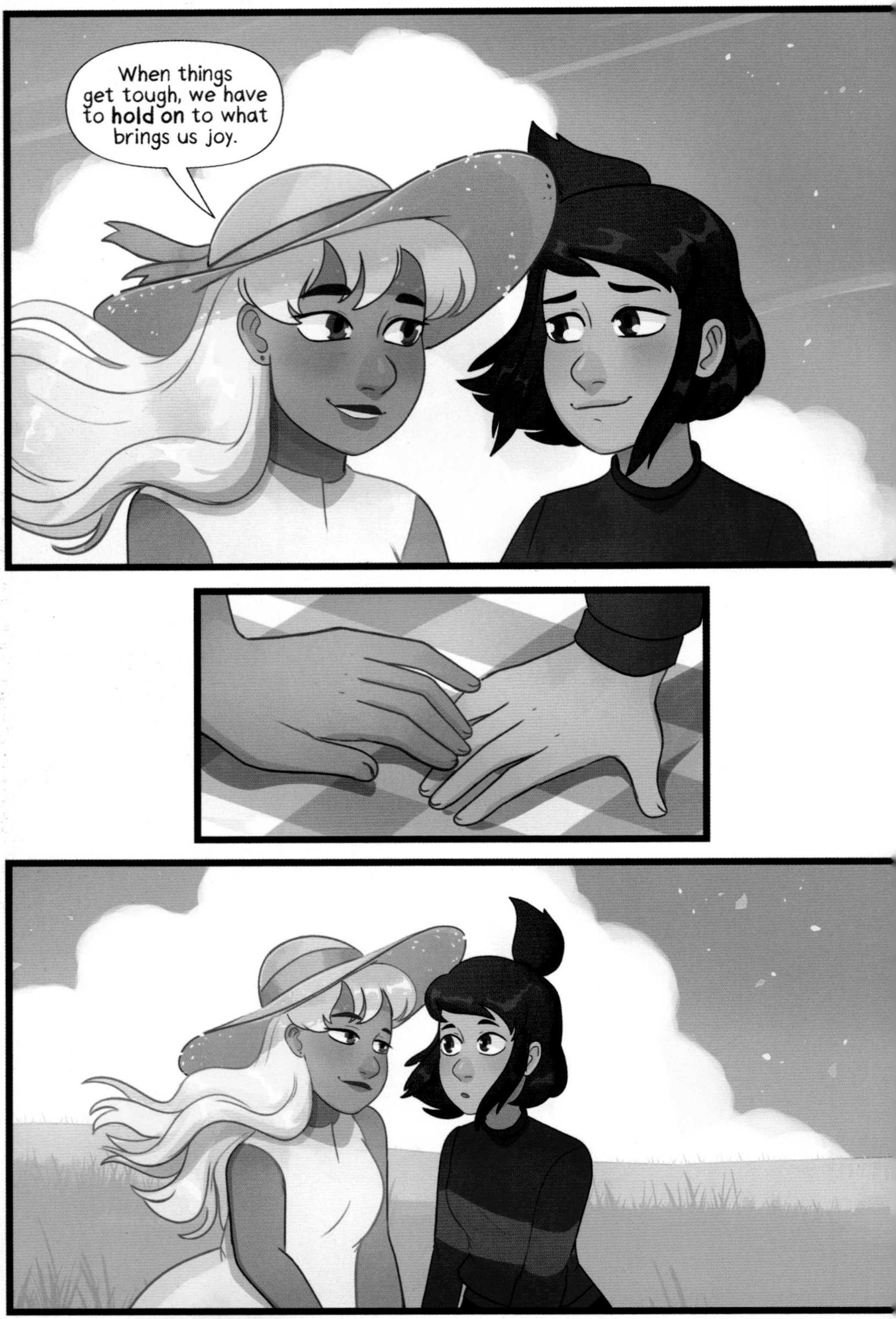
When things get tough, we have to **hold on** to what brings us joy.

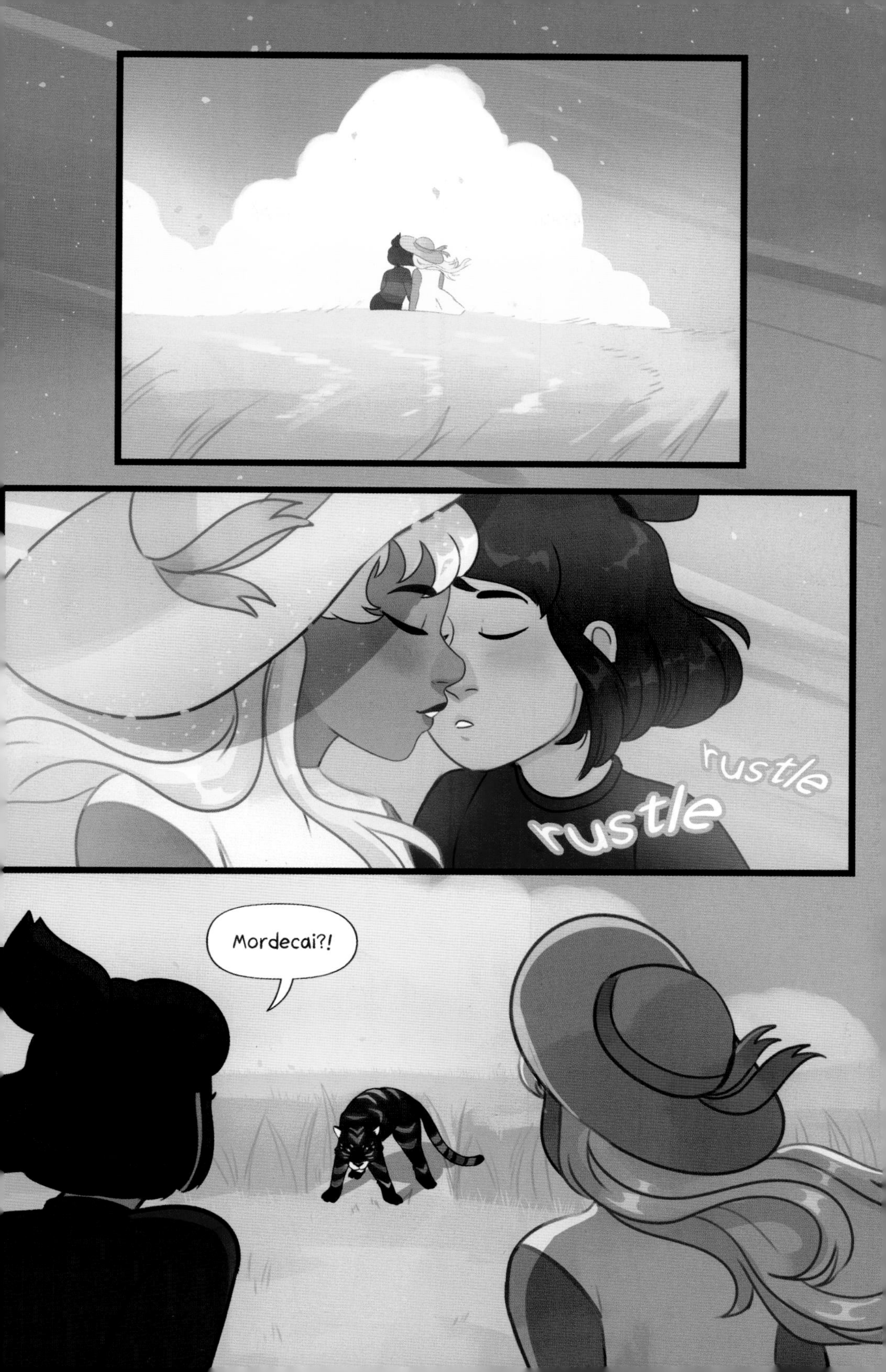
rustle
rustle
Mordecai?!

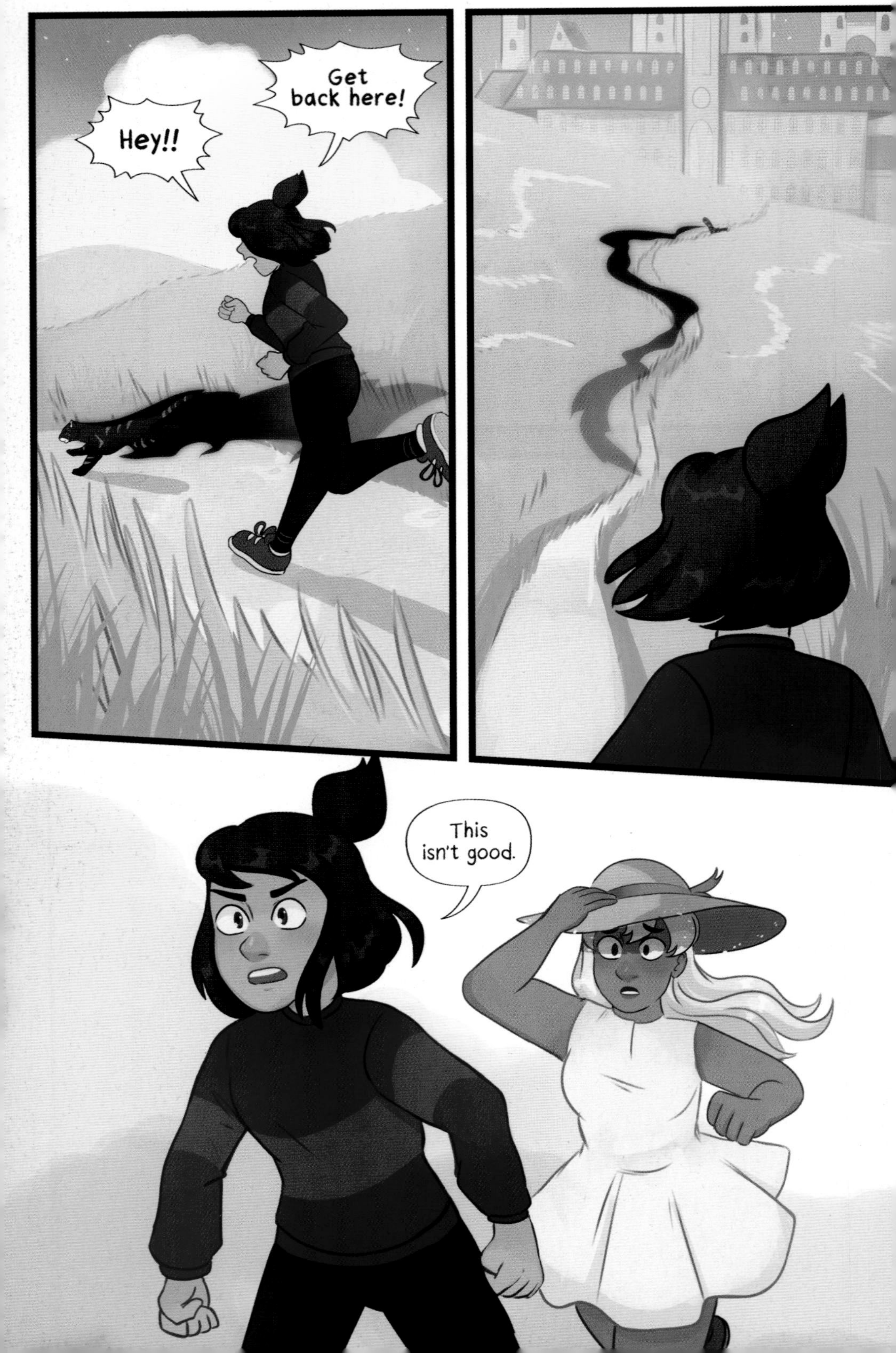
Hey!!
Get back here!
This isn't good.

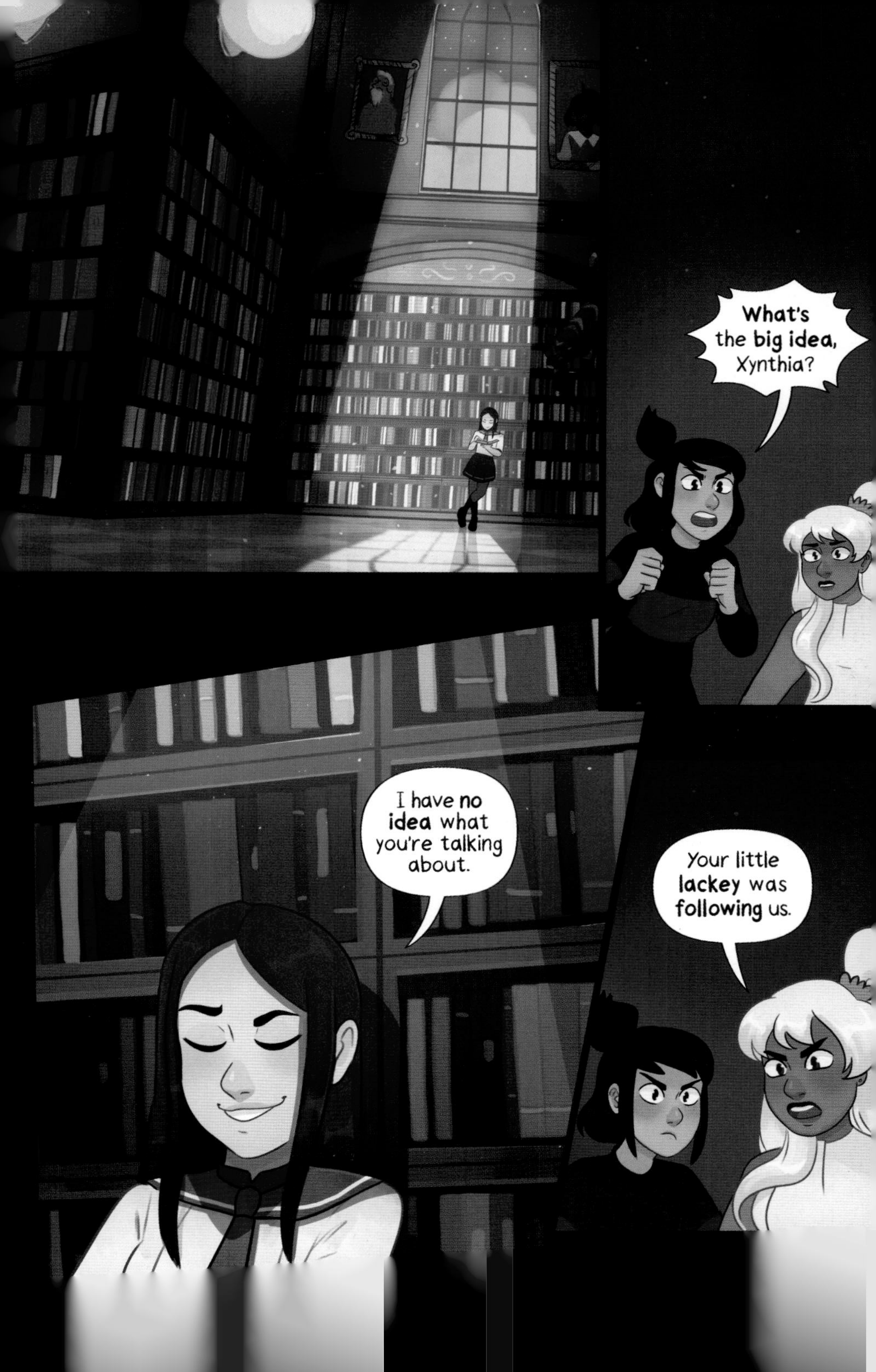
What's the big idea, Xynthia?
I have no idea what you're talking about.
Your little lackey was following us.

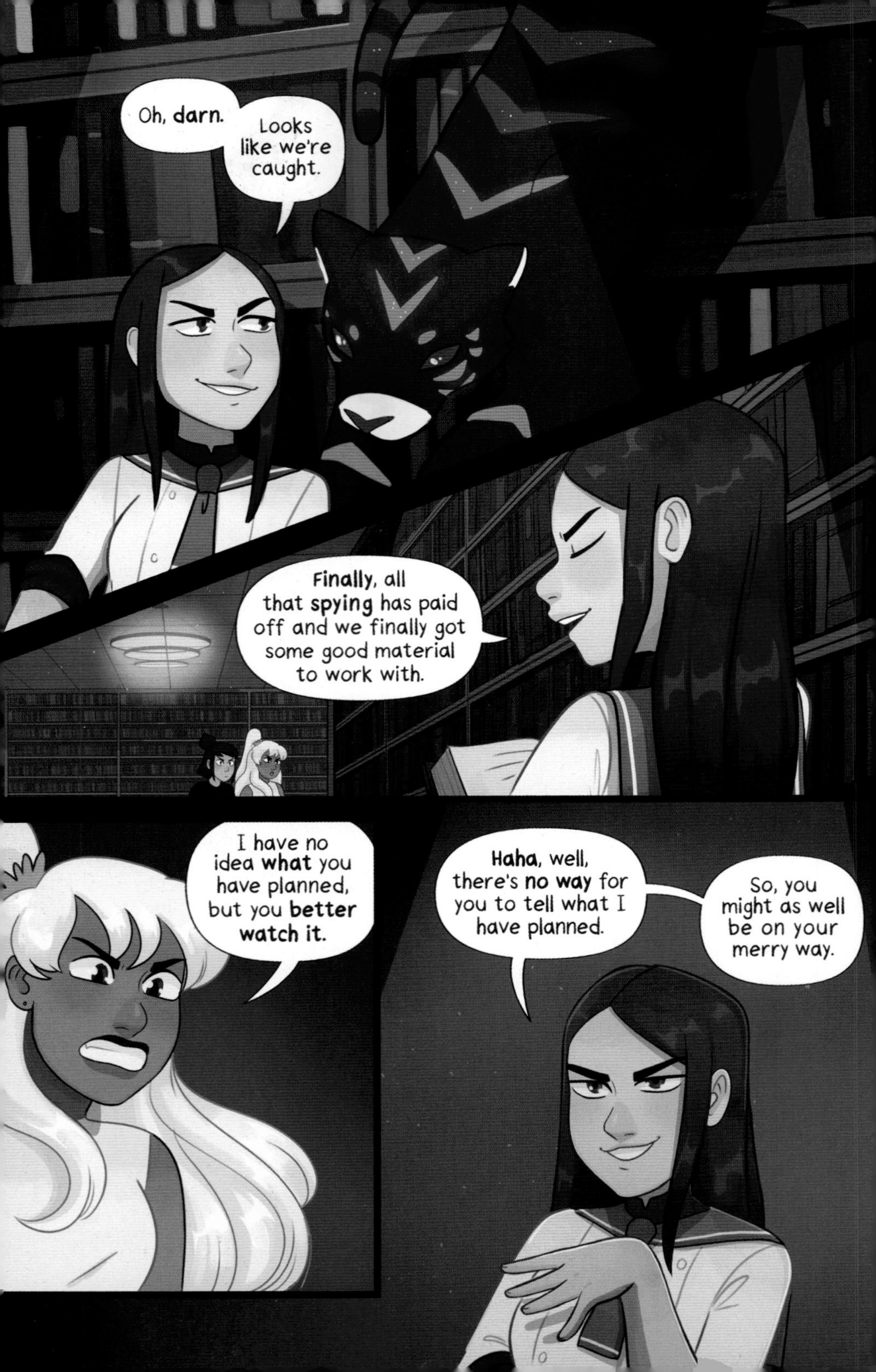
Oh, darn.
Looks like we're caught.
Finally, all that spying has paid off and we finally got some good material to work with.
I have no idea what you have planned, but you better watch it.
Haha, well, there's no way for you to tell what I have planned.
So, you might as well be on your merry way.

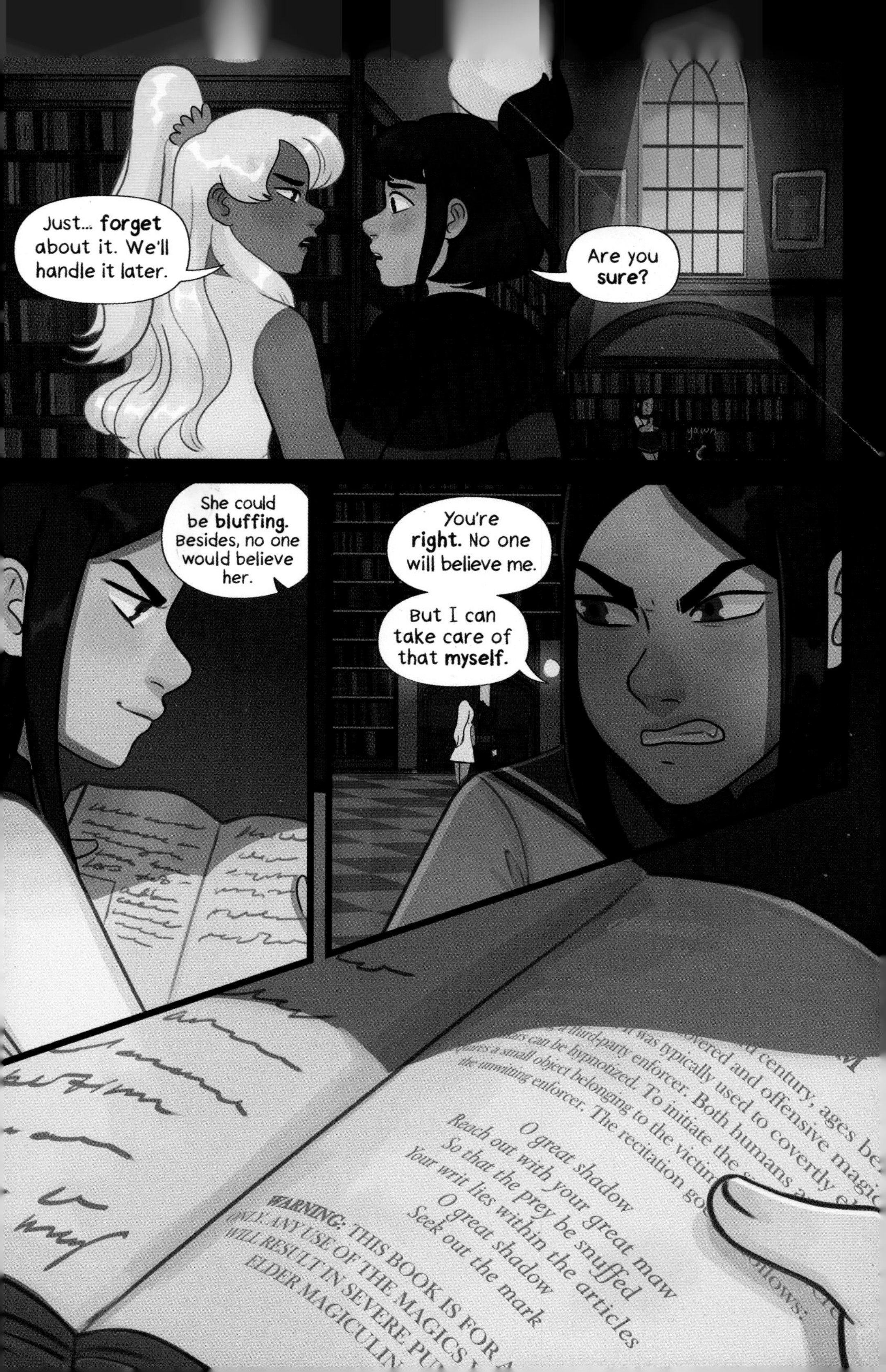
Just... **forget** about it. We'll handle it later.
Are you **sure?**
She could be **bluffing.** Besides, no one would believe her.
You're **right.** No one will believe me.
But I can take care of that **myself.**
O great shadow
Reach out with your great maw
So that the prey be snuffed
Your writ lies within the articles
O great shadow
Seek out the mark

Chapter
SIX

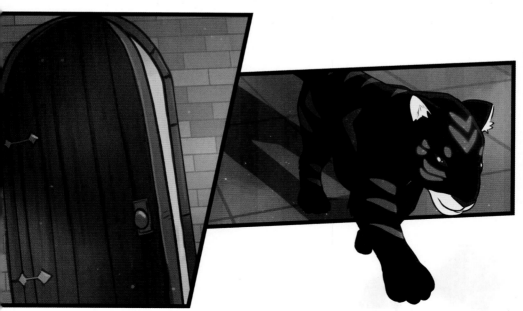

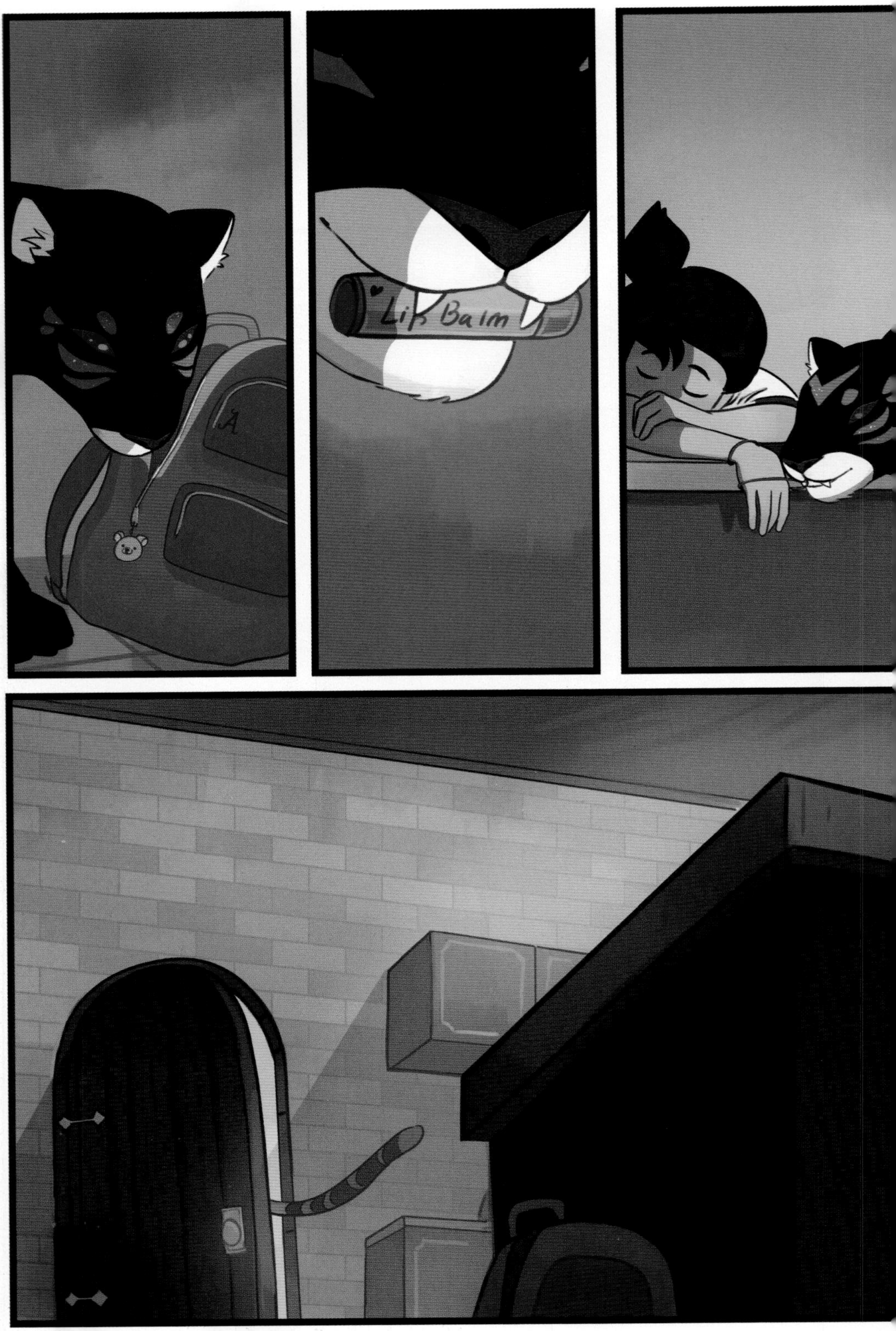
Lip Balm

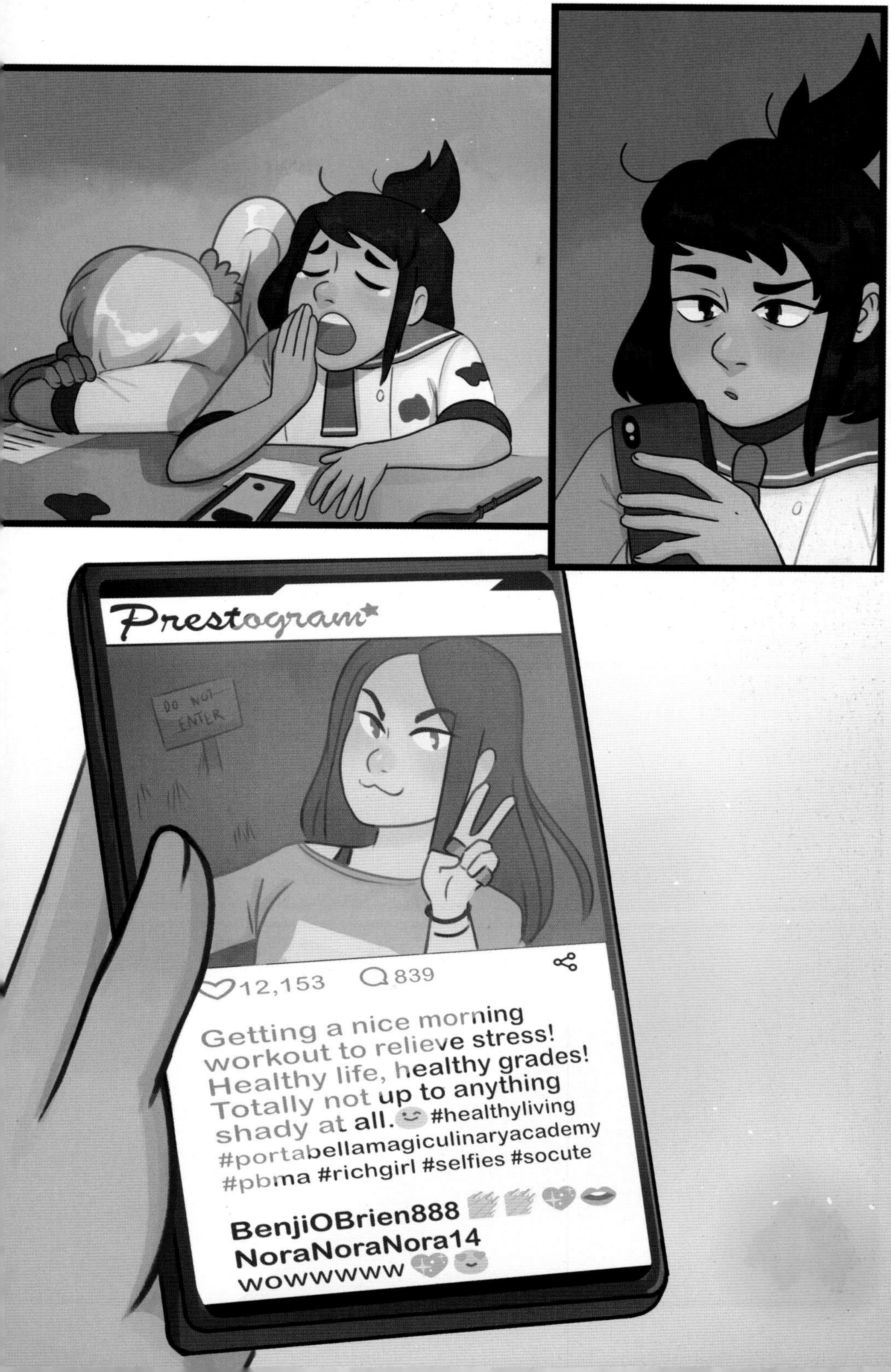
Prestogram
DO NOT ENTER
12,153
839
Getting a nice morning workout to relieve stress! Healthy life, healthy grades! Totally not up to anything shady at all. #healthyliving #portabellamagiculinaryacademy #pbma #richgirl #selfies #socute
BenjiOBrien888
NoraNoraNora14
WOWWWWW

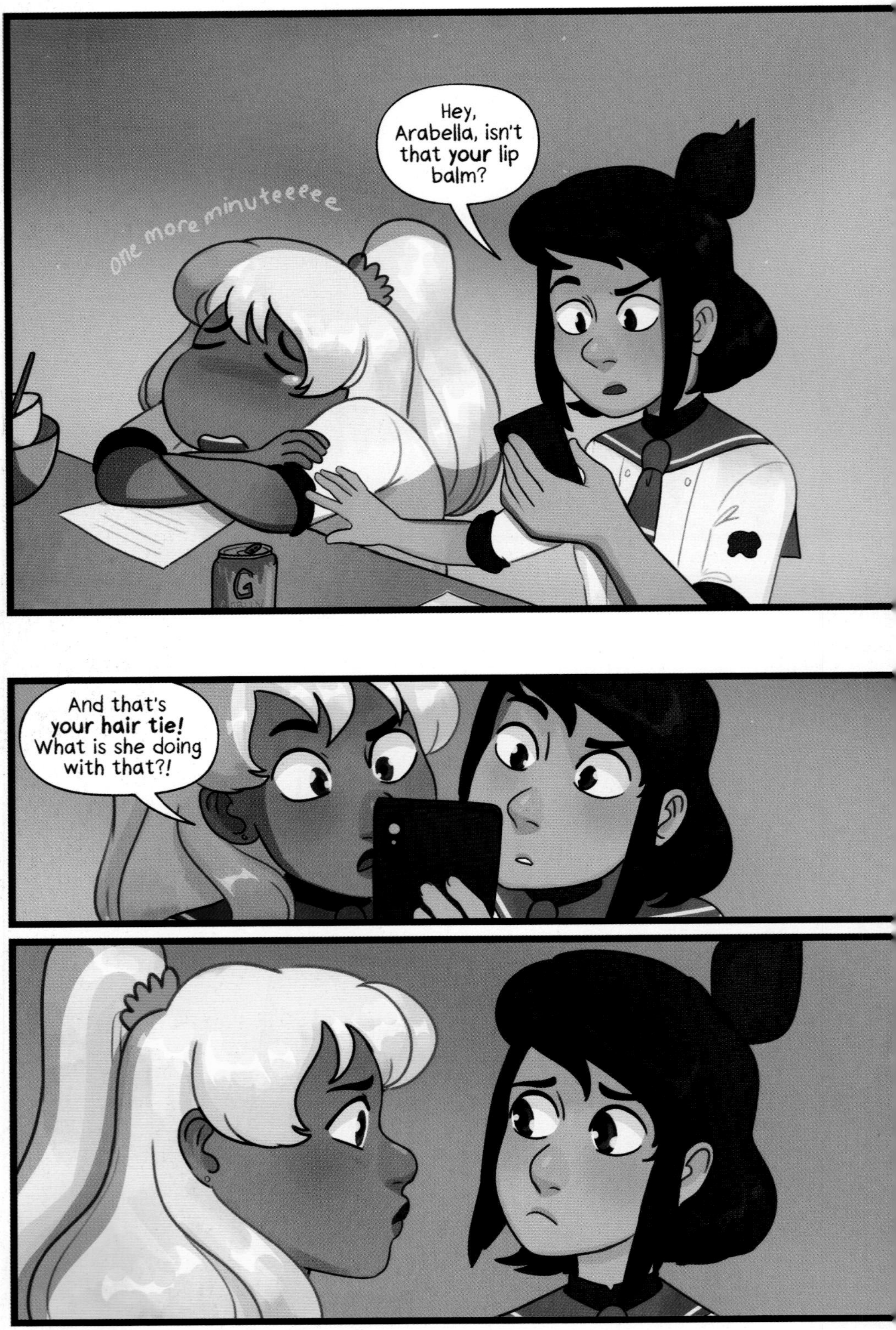

one more minuteeeee
Hey, Arabella, isn't that your lip balm?
And that's **your hair tie!** What is she doing with that?!

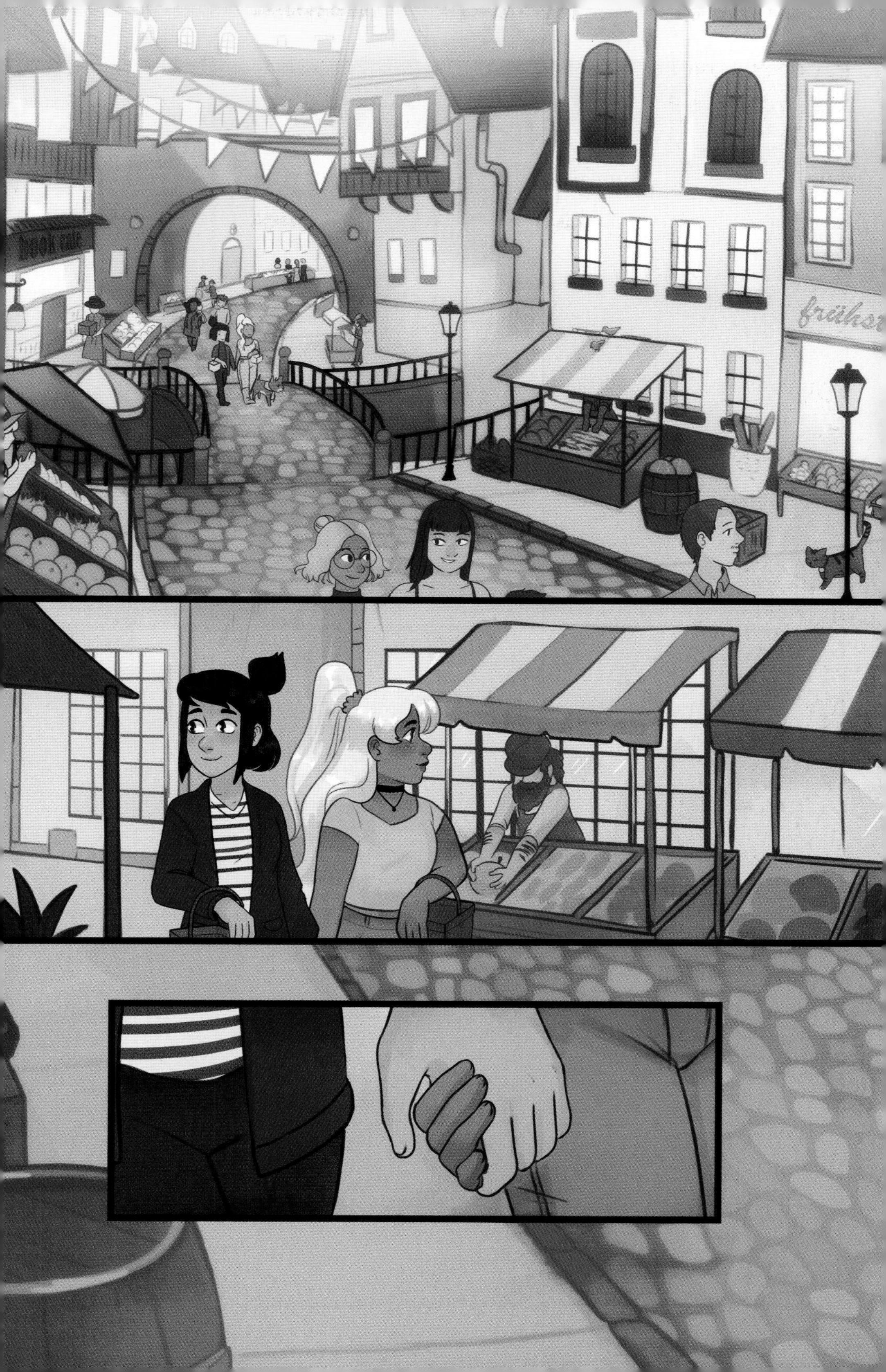
book cafe

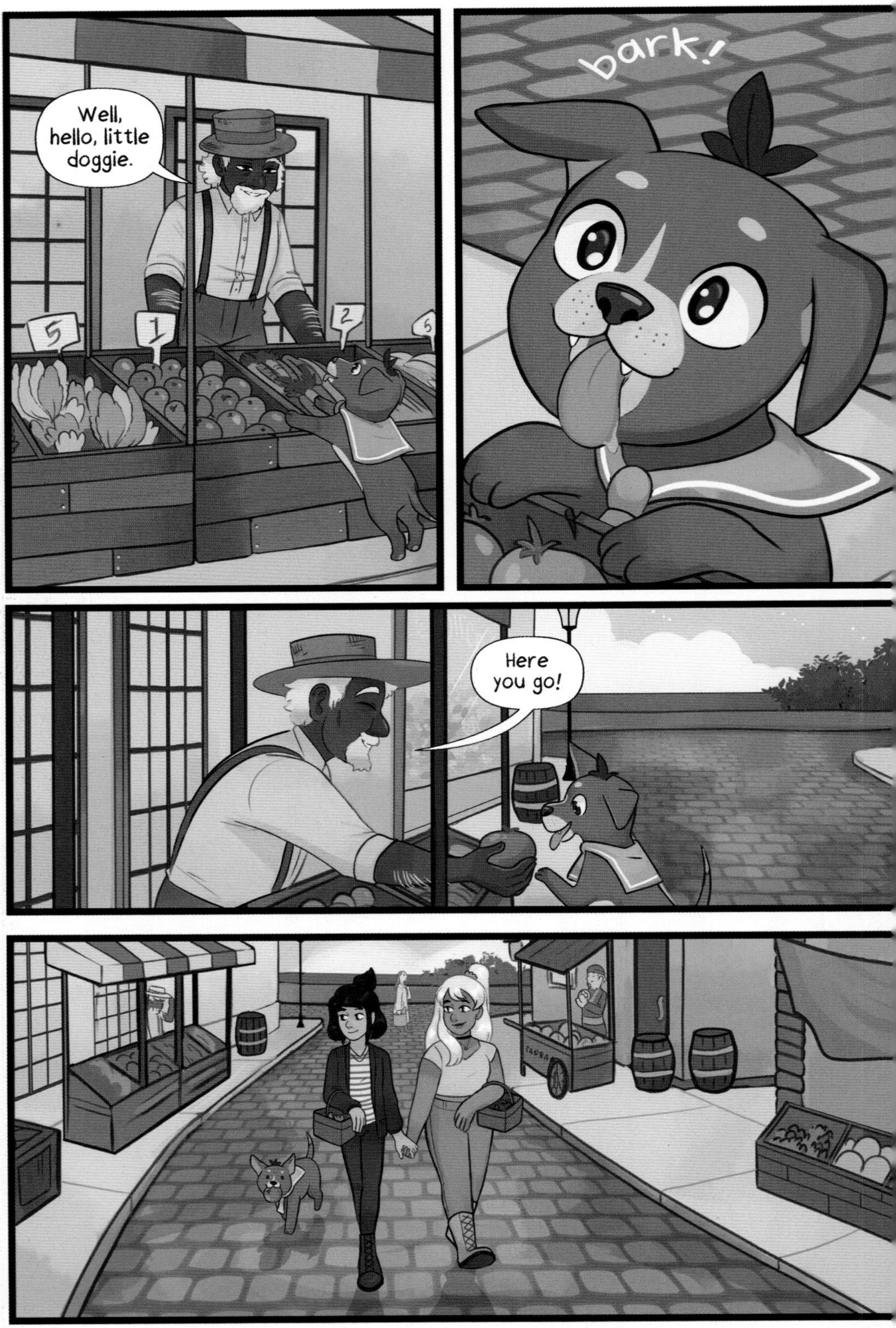
Well, hello, little doggie.
5
1
2
5
bark!
Here you go!

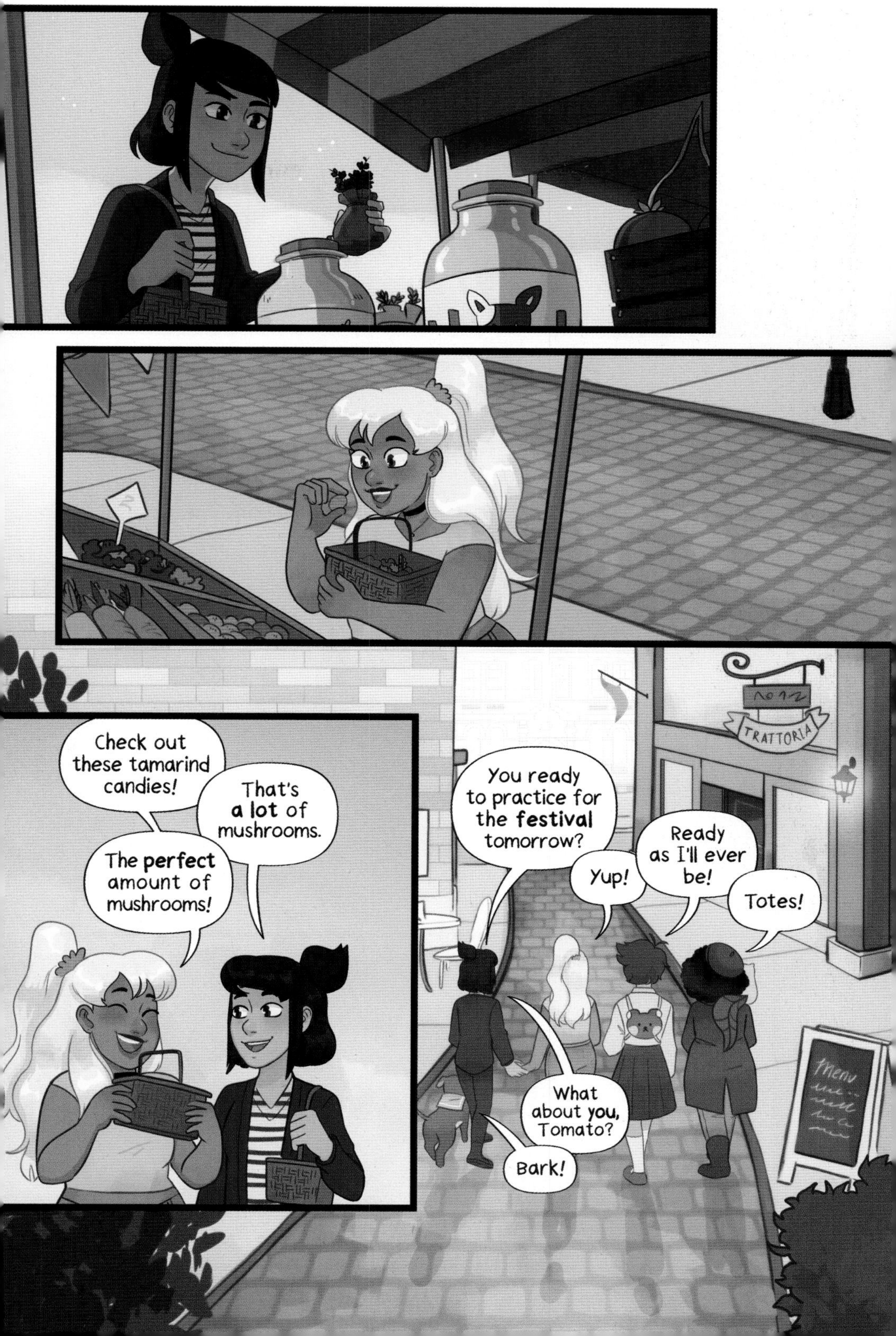
Check out these tamarind candies!
That's **a lot** of mushrooms.
The **perfect** amount of mushrooms!
TRATTORIA
You ready to practice for the **festival** tomorrow?
Yup!
Ready as I'll ever be!
Totes!
What about **you,** Tomato?
Bark!
menu

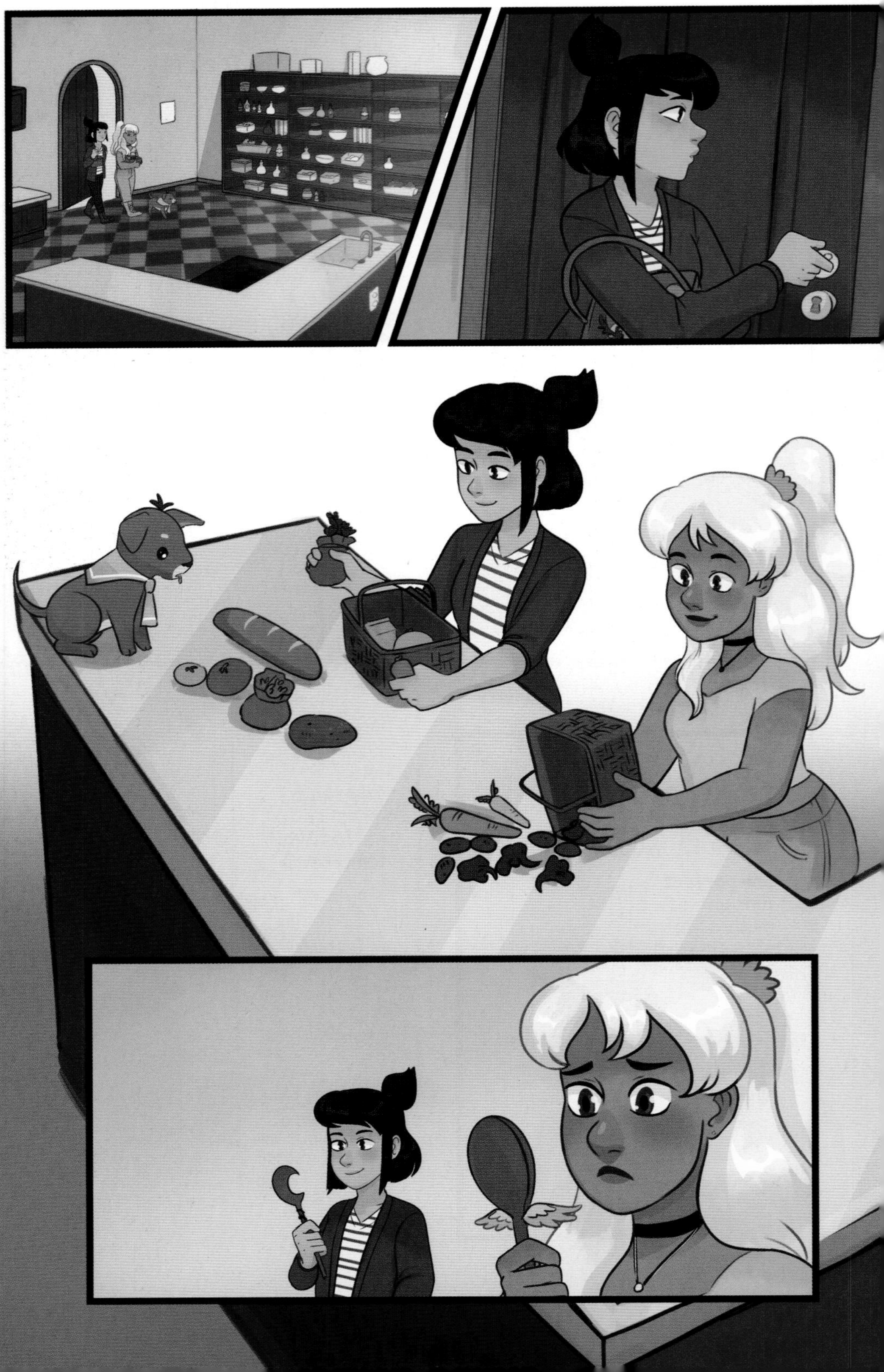

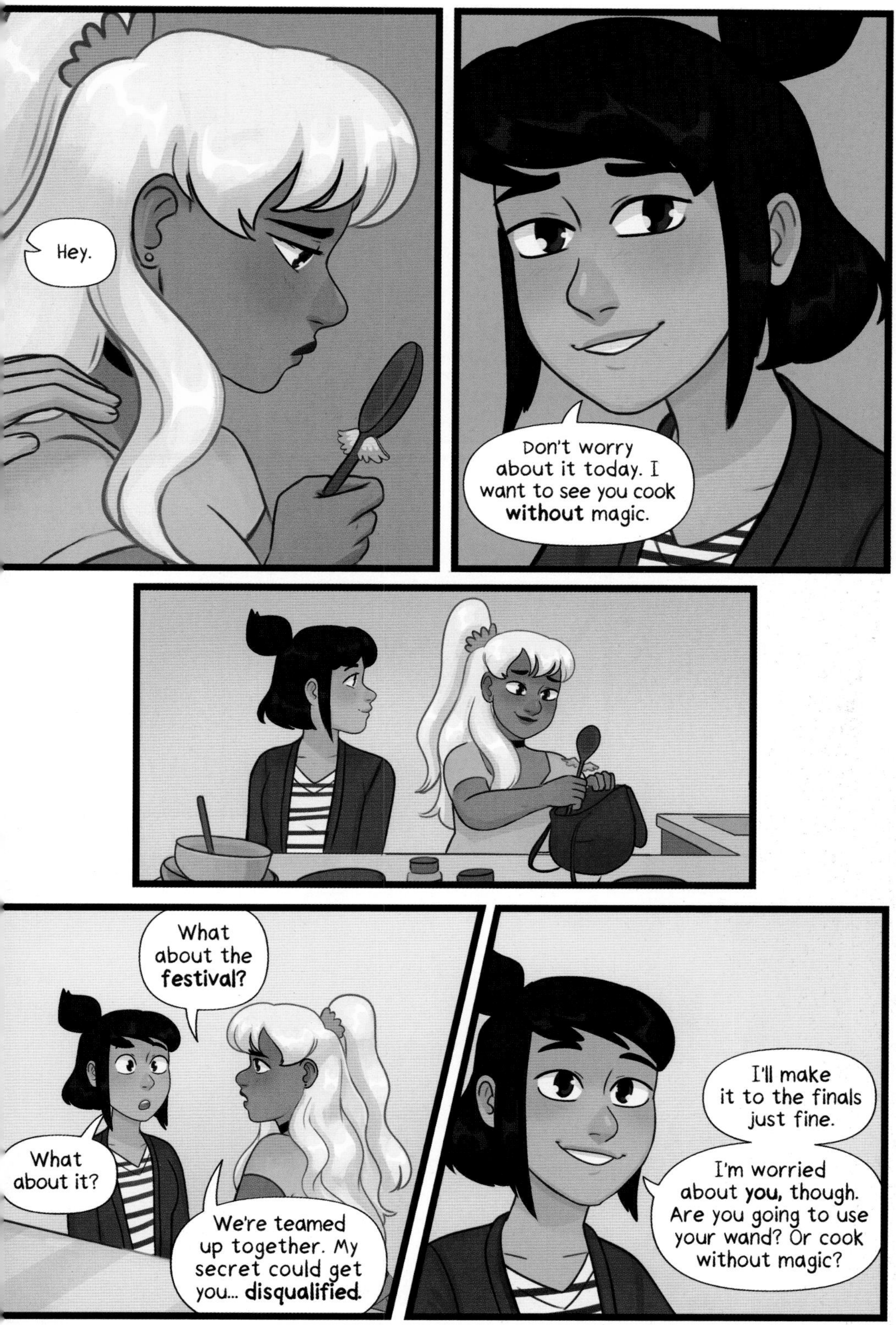
Hey.
Don't worry about it today. I want to see you cook **without** magic.
What about the **festival?**
What about it?
We're teamed up together. My secret could get you... **disqualified.**
I'll make it to the finals just fine.
I'm worried about **you,** though. Are you going to use your wand? Or cook without magic?

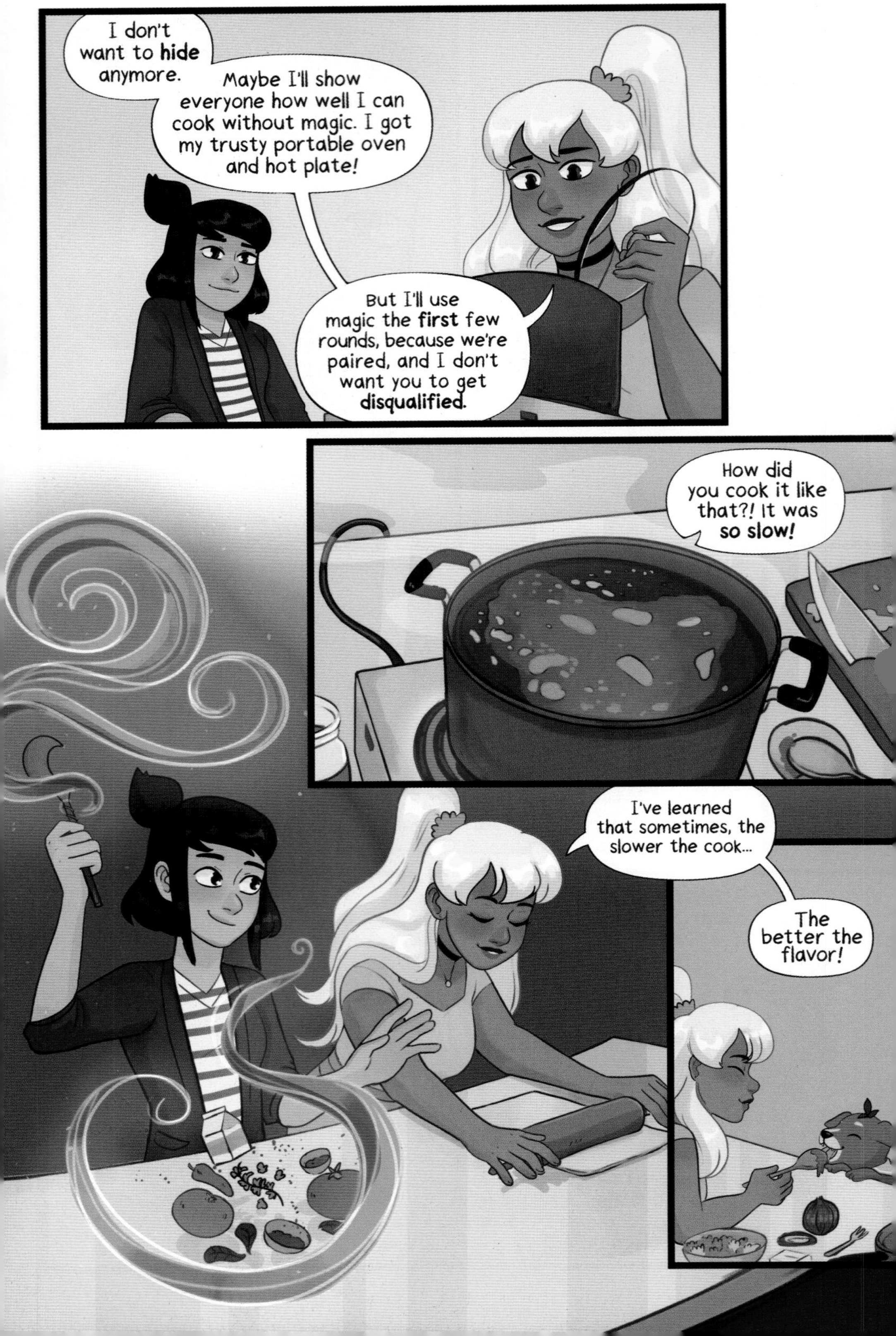
I don't want to **hide** anymore.
Maybe I'll show everyone how well I can cook without magic. I got my trusty portable oven and hot plate!
But I'll use magic the **first** few rounds, because we're paired, and I don't want you to get **disqualified**.
How did you cook it like that?! It was **so slow!**
I've learned that sometimes, the slower the cook...
The better the flavor!

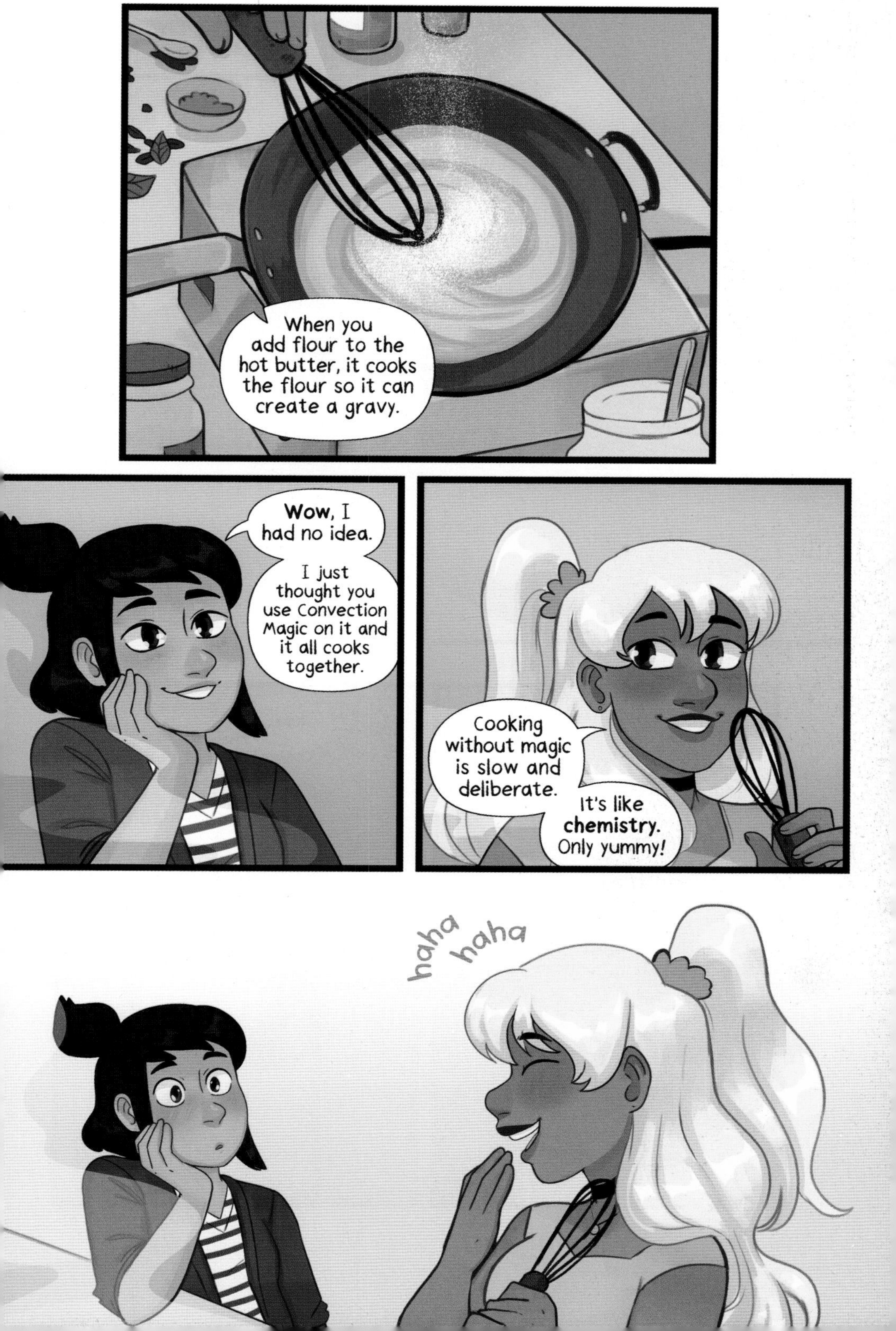
When you add flour to the hot butter, it cooks the flour so it can create a gravy.
Wow, I had no idea.
I just thought you use Convection Magic on it and it all cooks together.
Cooking without magic is slow and deliberate.
It's like **chemistry.** Only yummy!
haha haha

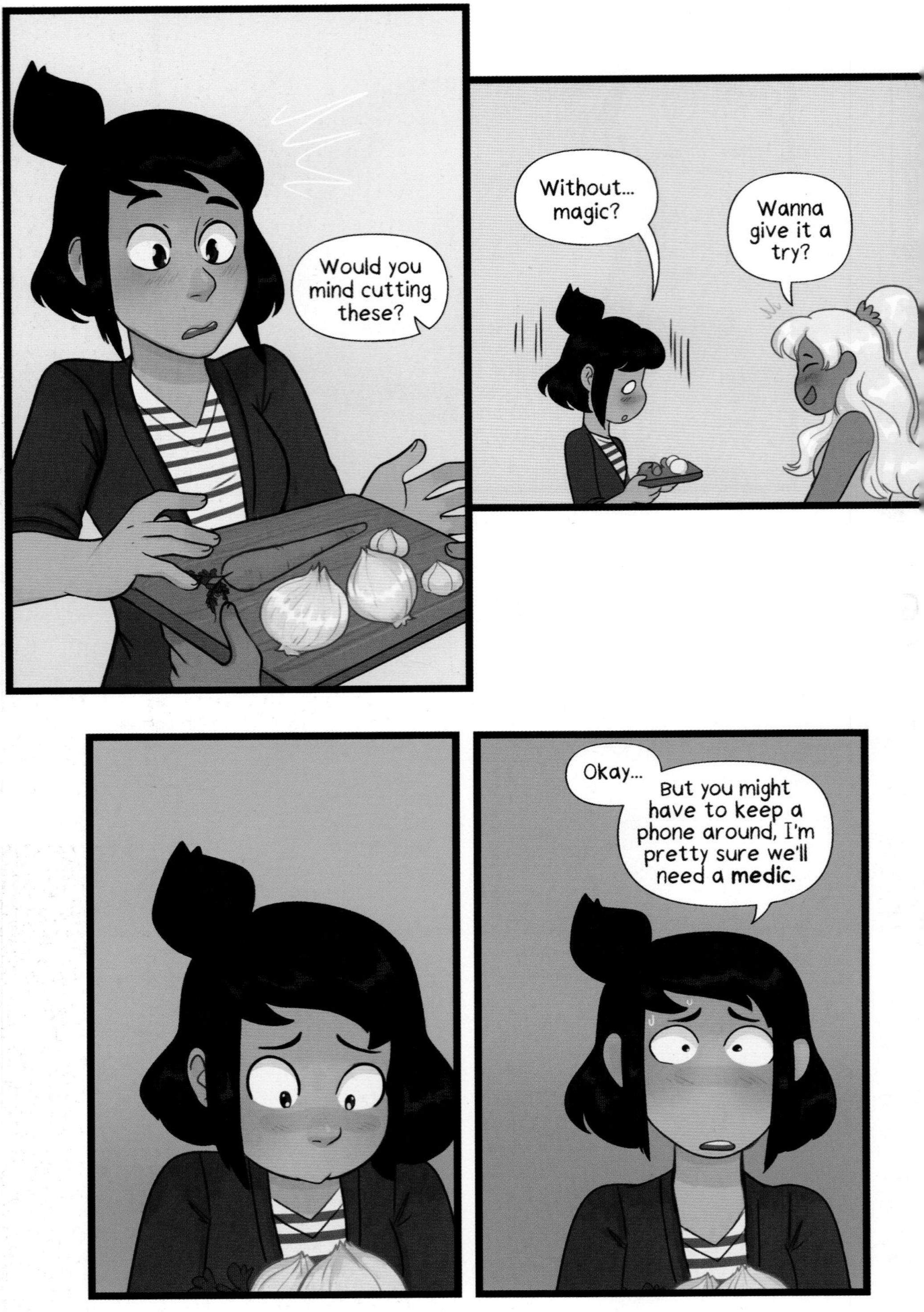
Would you mind cutting these?
Without... magic?
Wanna give it a try?
Okay...
But you might have to keep a phone around, I'm pretty sure we'll need a medic.

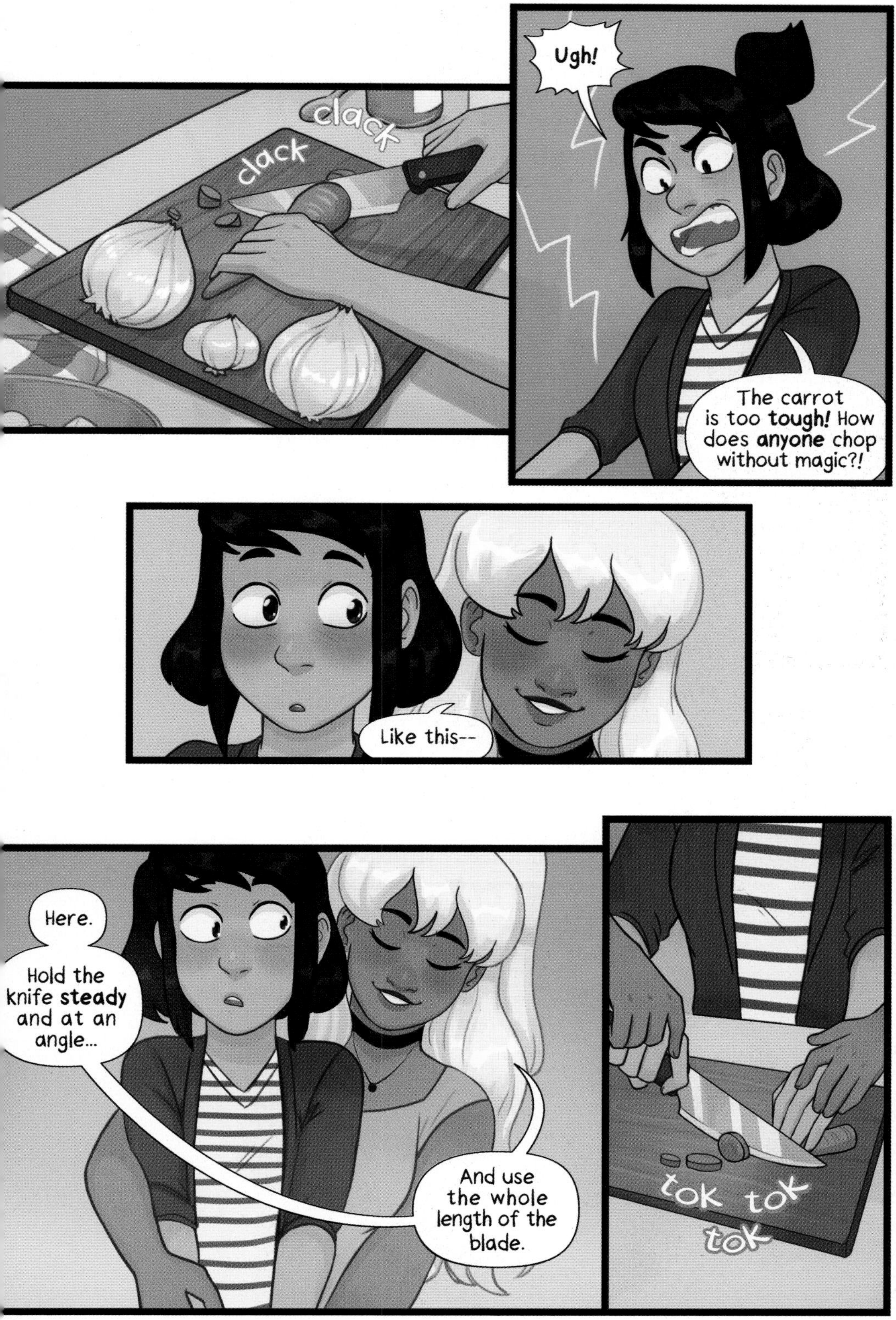
clack
clack
Ugh!
The carrot is too **tough!** How does **anyone** chop without magic?!
Like this--
Here.
Hold the knife **steady** and at an angle...
And use the whole length of the blade.
tok tok tok

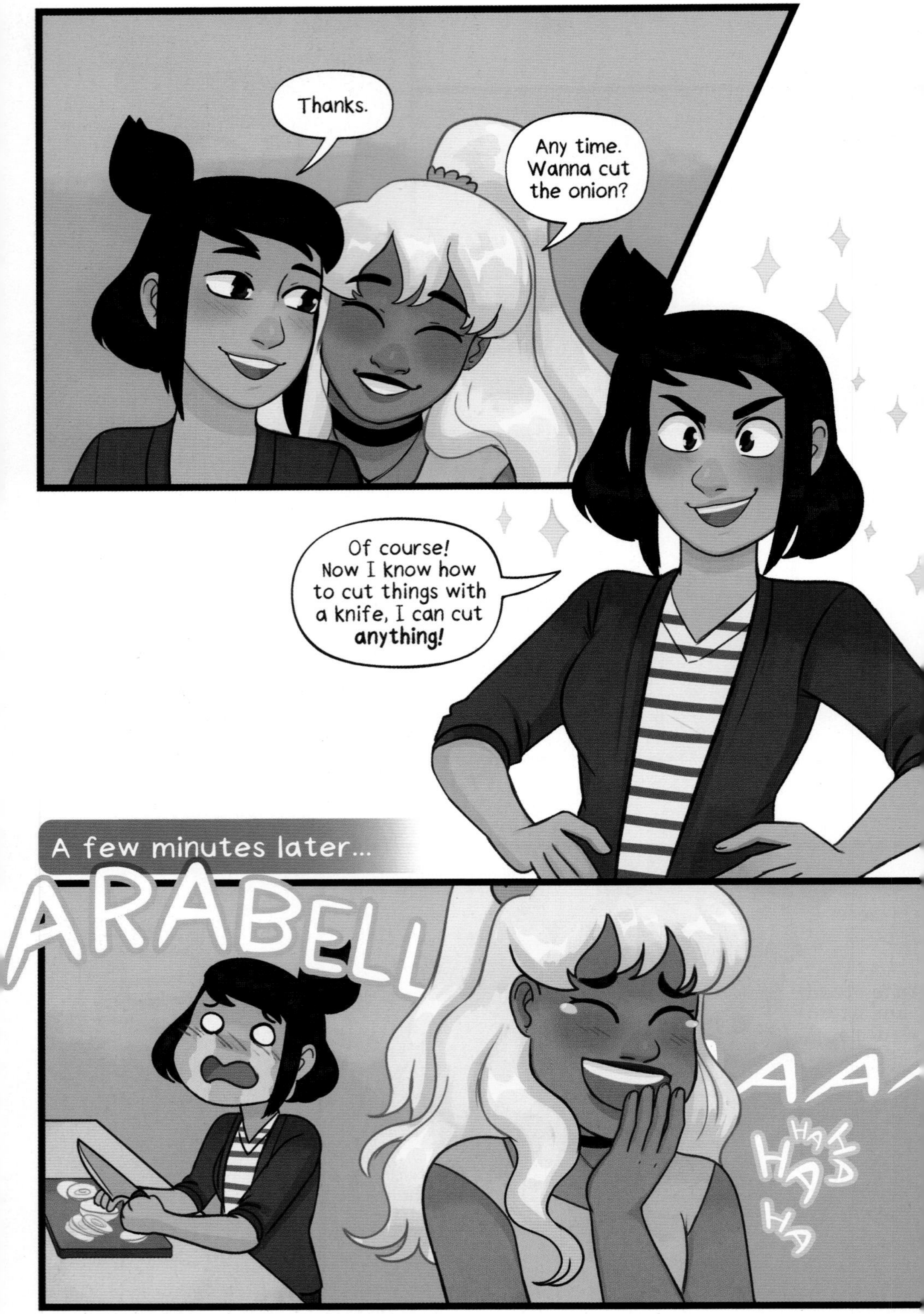
Thanks.
Any time. Wanna cut the onion?
Of course! Now I know how to cut things with a knife, I can cut **anything!**
A few minutes later...
ARABELL
HA HA HA HA

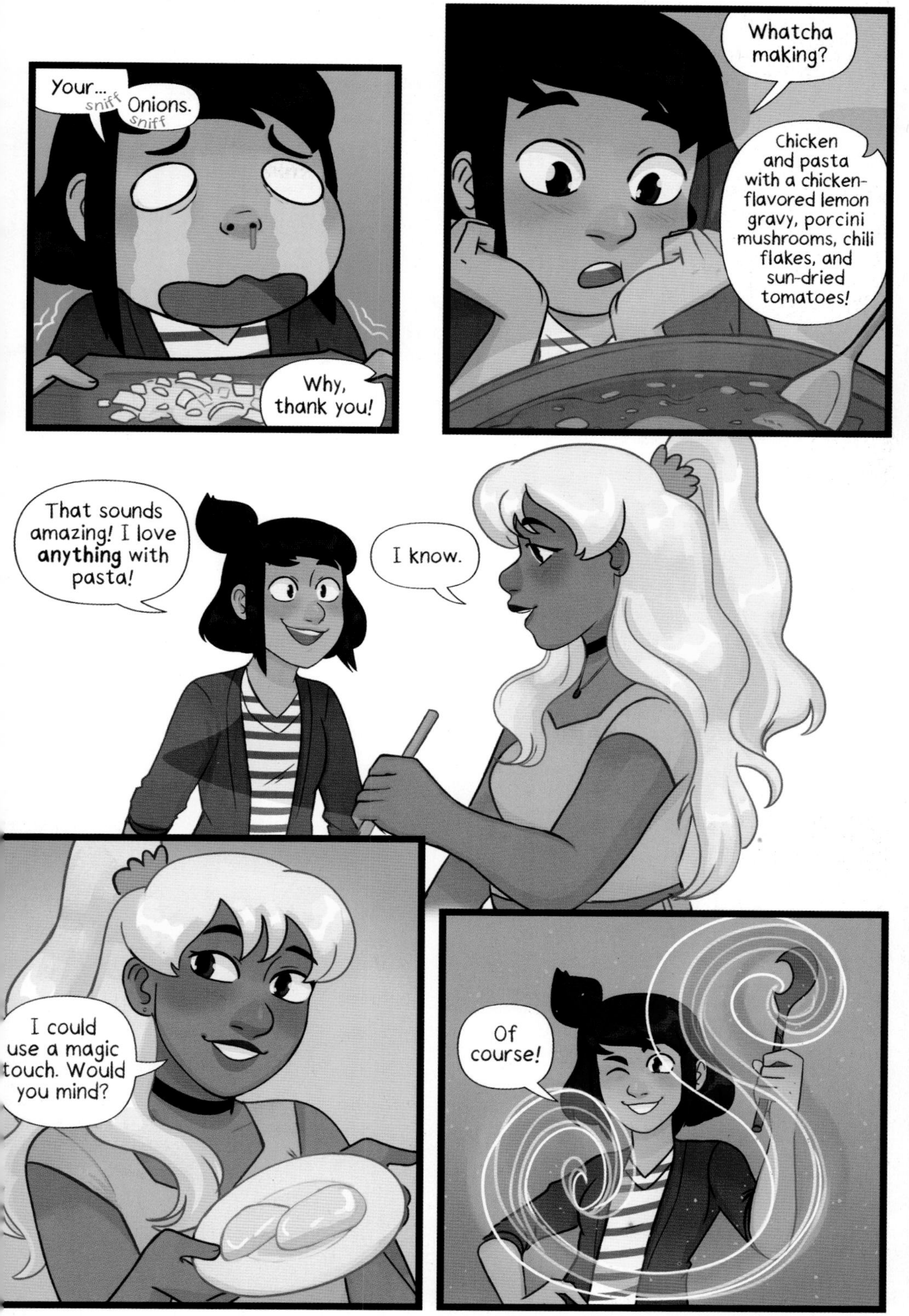
Your...
sniff
Onions.
sniff
Why, thank you!
Whatcha making?
Chicken and pasta with a chicken-flavored lemon gravy, porcini mushrooms, chili flakes, and sun-dried tomatoes!
That sounds amazing! I love **anything** with pasta!
I know.
I could use a magic touch. Would you mind?
Of course!

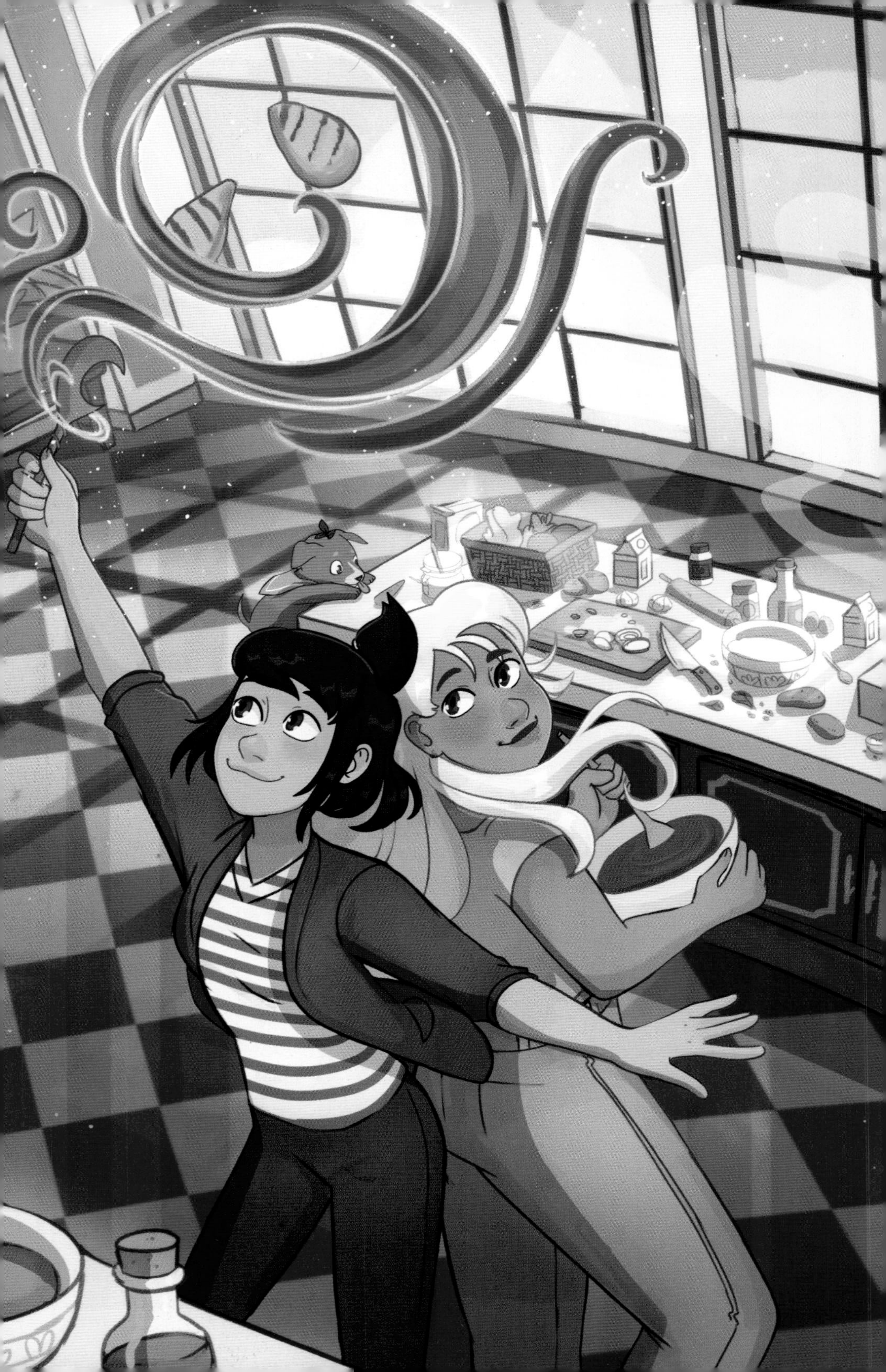

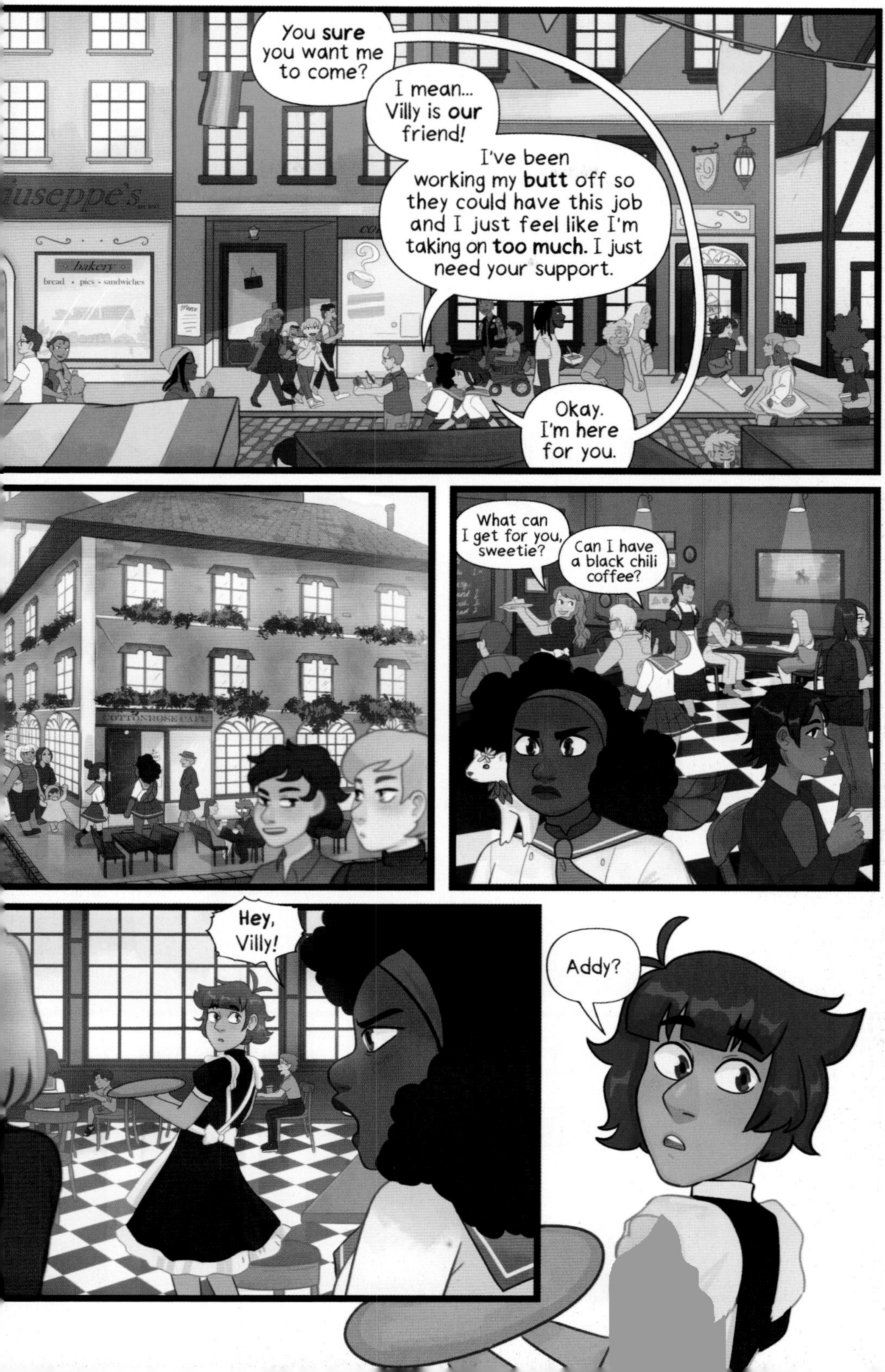
You **sure** you want me to come?
I mean... Villy is **our** friend!
I've been working my **butt** off so they could have this job and I just feel like I'm taking on **too much.** I just need your support.
Okay. I'm here for you.
bakery
bread • pies • sandwiches
COTTONROSE CAFE
What can I get for you, sweetie?
Can I have a black chili coffee?
Hey, Villy!
Addy?

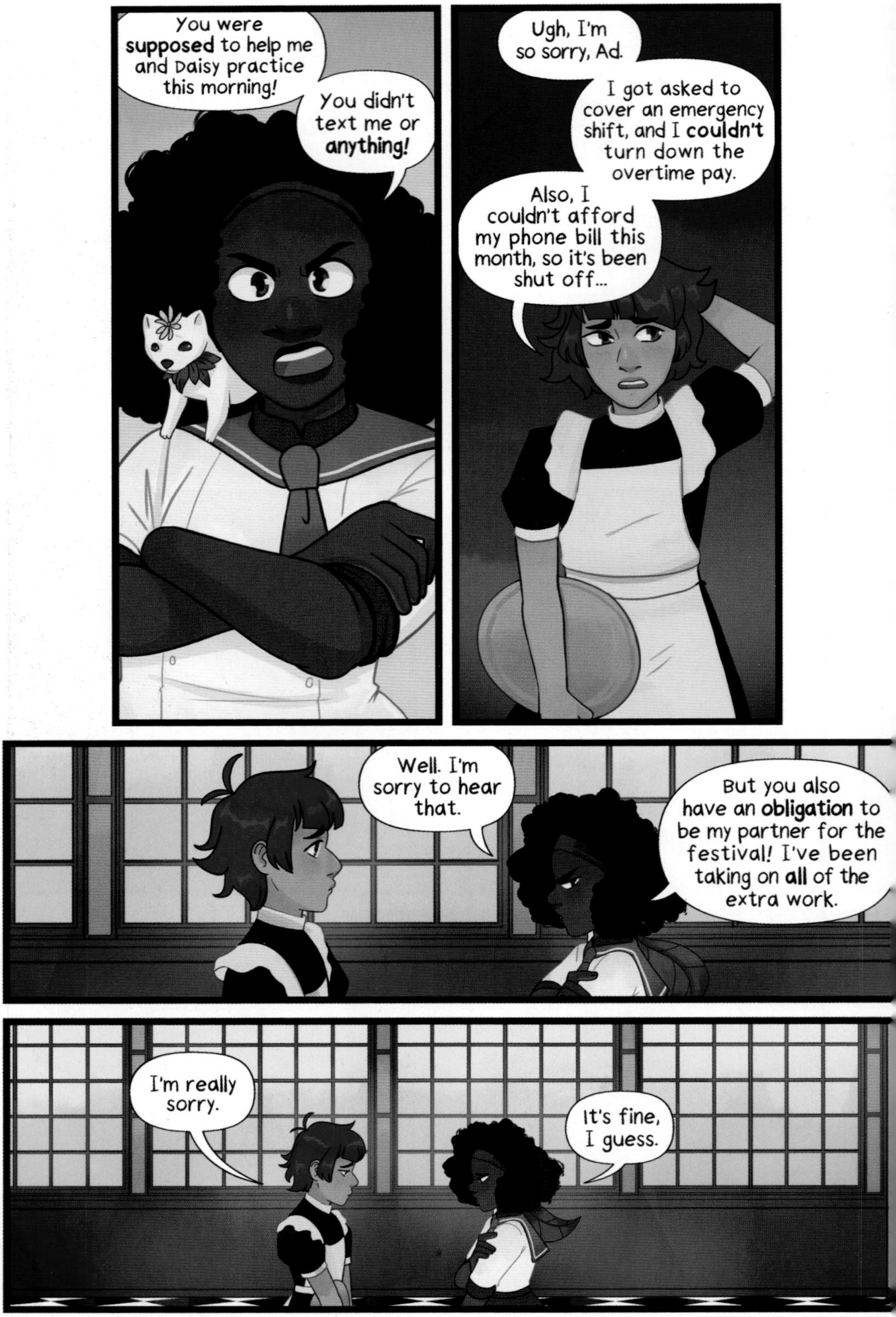
You were supposed to help me and Daisy practice this morning!
You didn't text me or anything!
Ugh, I'm so sorry, Ad.
I got asked to cover an emergency shift, and I couldn't turn down the overtime pay.
Also, I couldn't afford my phone bill this month, so it's been shut off...
Well. I'm sorry to hear that.
But you also have an obligation to be my partner for the festival! I've been taking on all of the extra work.
I'm really sorry.
It's fine, I guess.

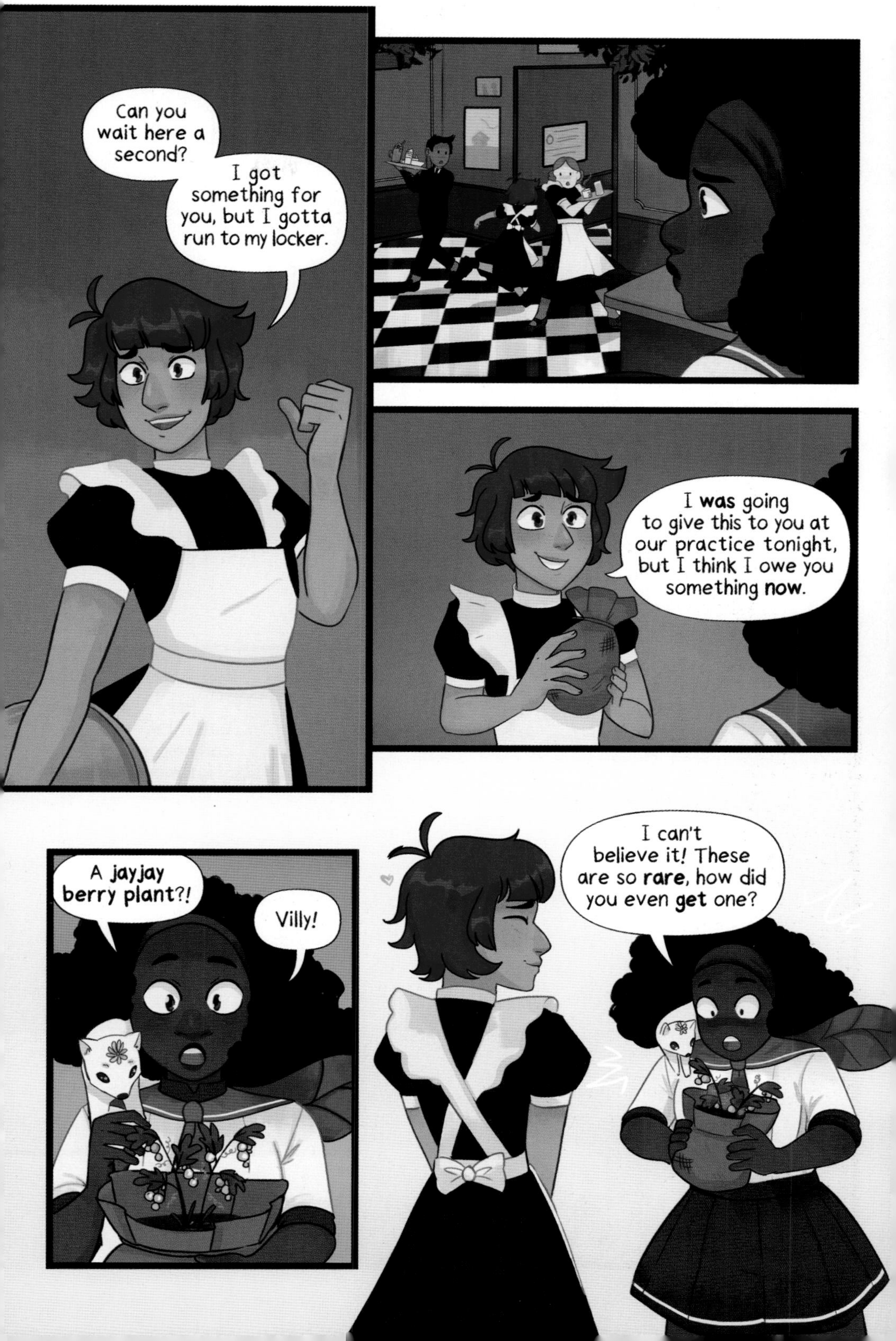
Can you wait here a second?
I got something for you, but I gotta run to my locker.
I **was** going to give this to you at our practice tonight, but I think I owe you something **now**.
A **jayjay berry plant**?!
Villy!
I can't believe it! These are so **rare**, how did you even **get** one?

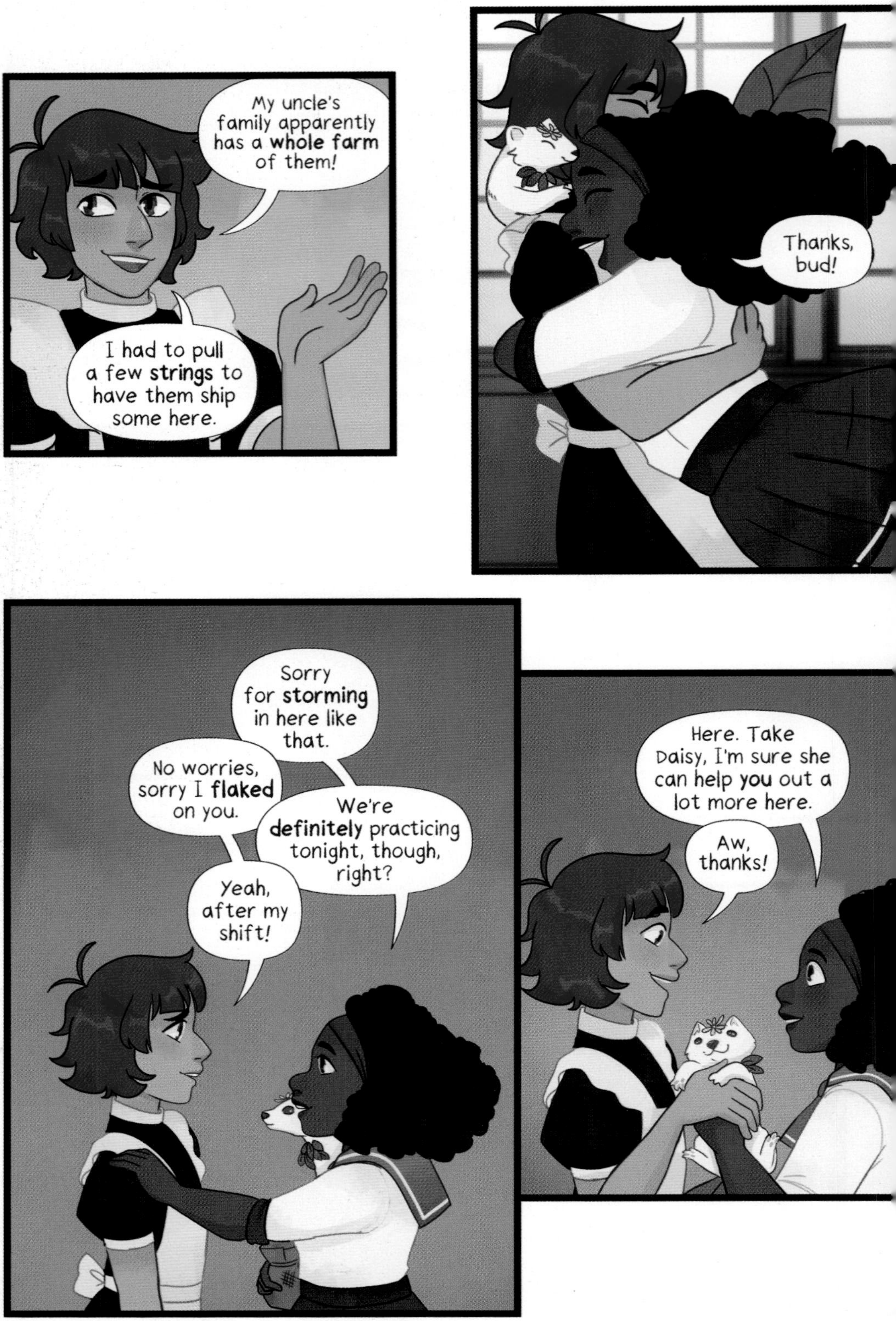
My uncle's family apparently has a **whole farm** of them!
I had to pull a few **strings** to have them ship some here.
Thanks, bud!
Sorry for **storming** in here like that.
No worries, sorry I **flaked** on you.
We're **definitely** practicing tonight, though, right?
Yeah, after my shift!
Here. Take Daisy, I'm sure she can help **you** out a lot more here.
Aw, thanks!

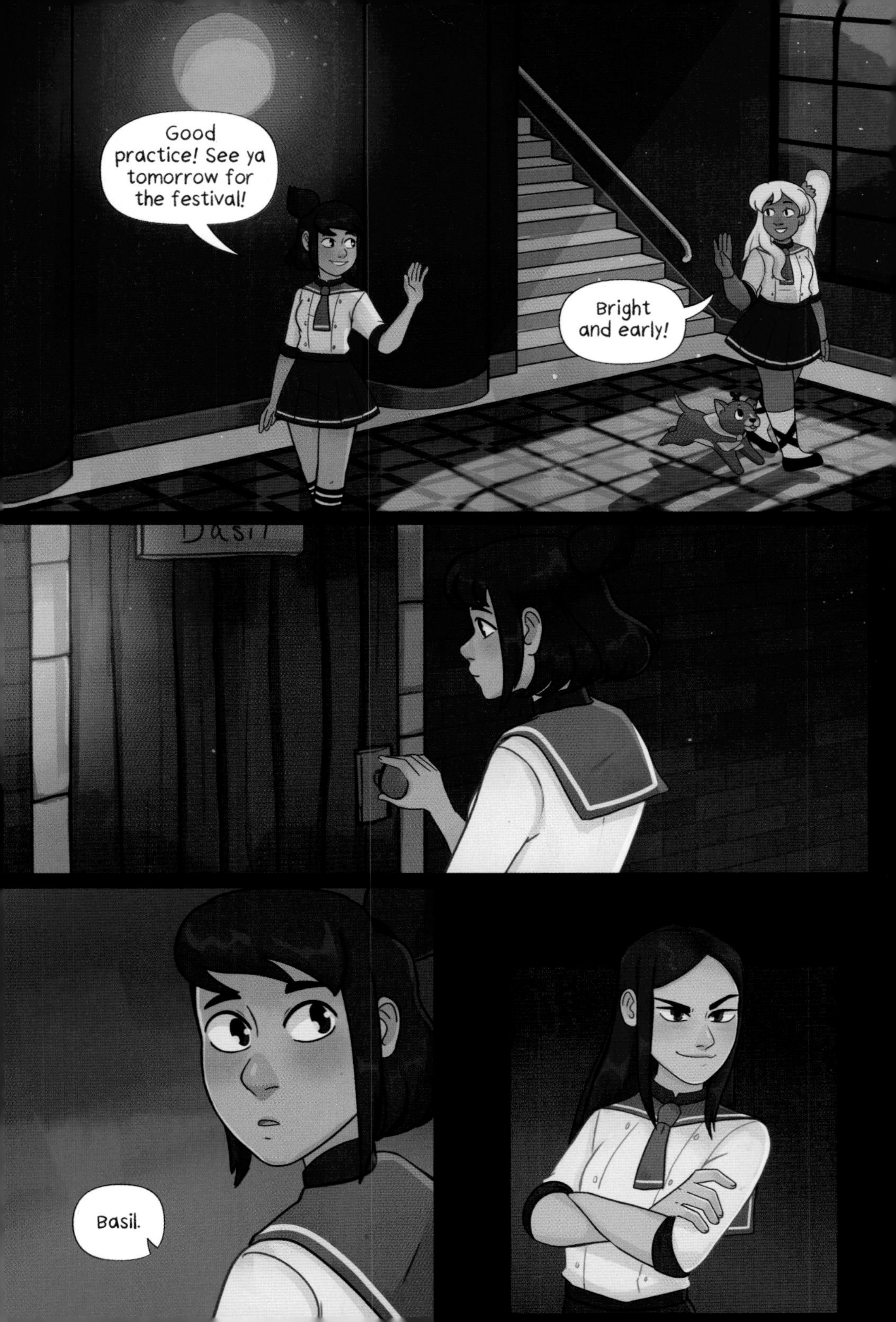
Good practice! See ya tomorrow for the festival!
Bright and early!
Basil.

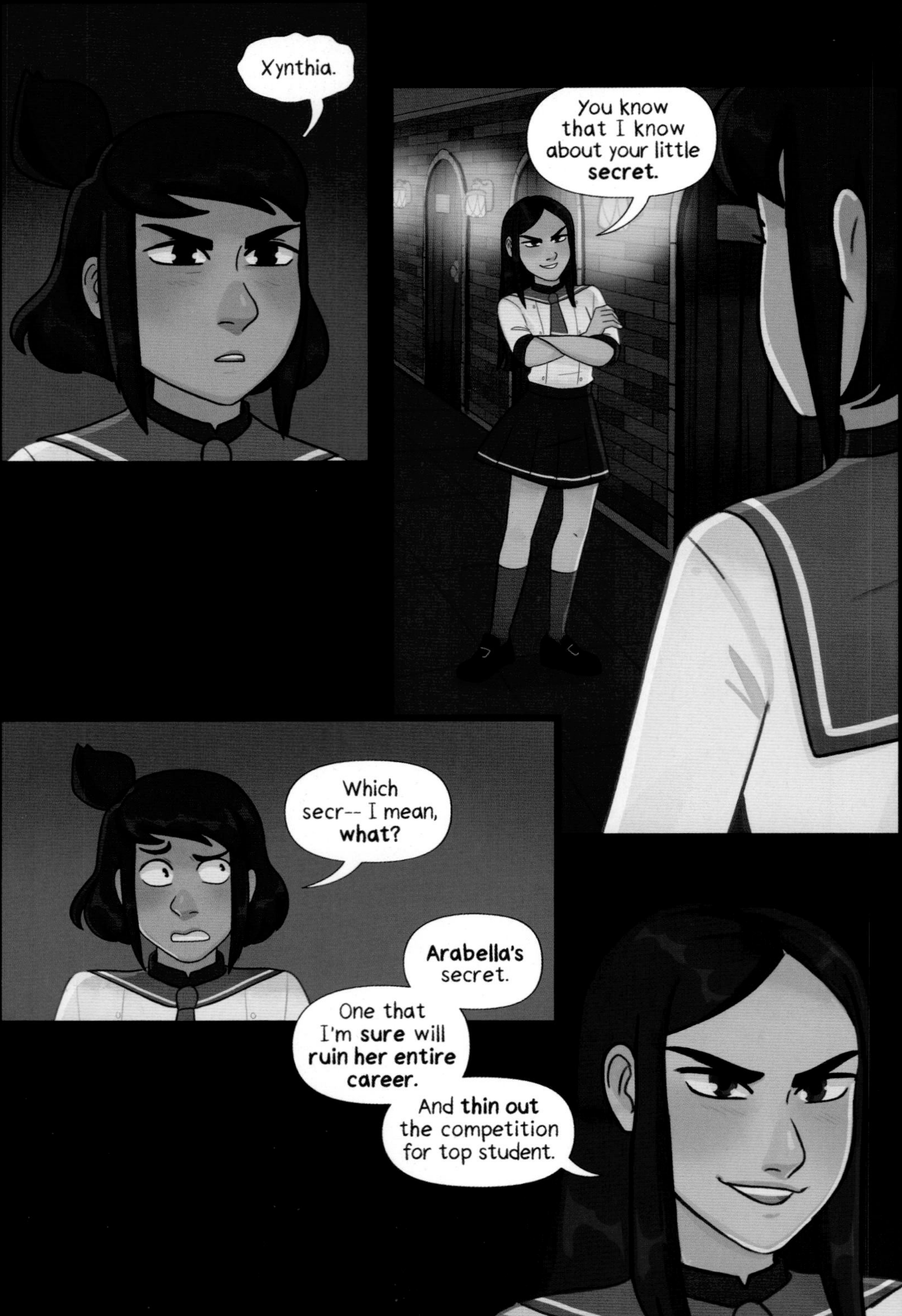
Xynthia.
You know that I know about your little **secret.**
Which secr-- I mean, **what?**
Arabella's secret.
One that I'm **sure** will **ruin her entire career.**
And **thin out** the competition for top student.

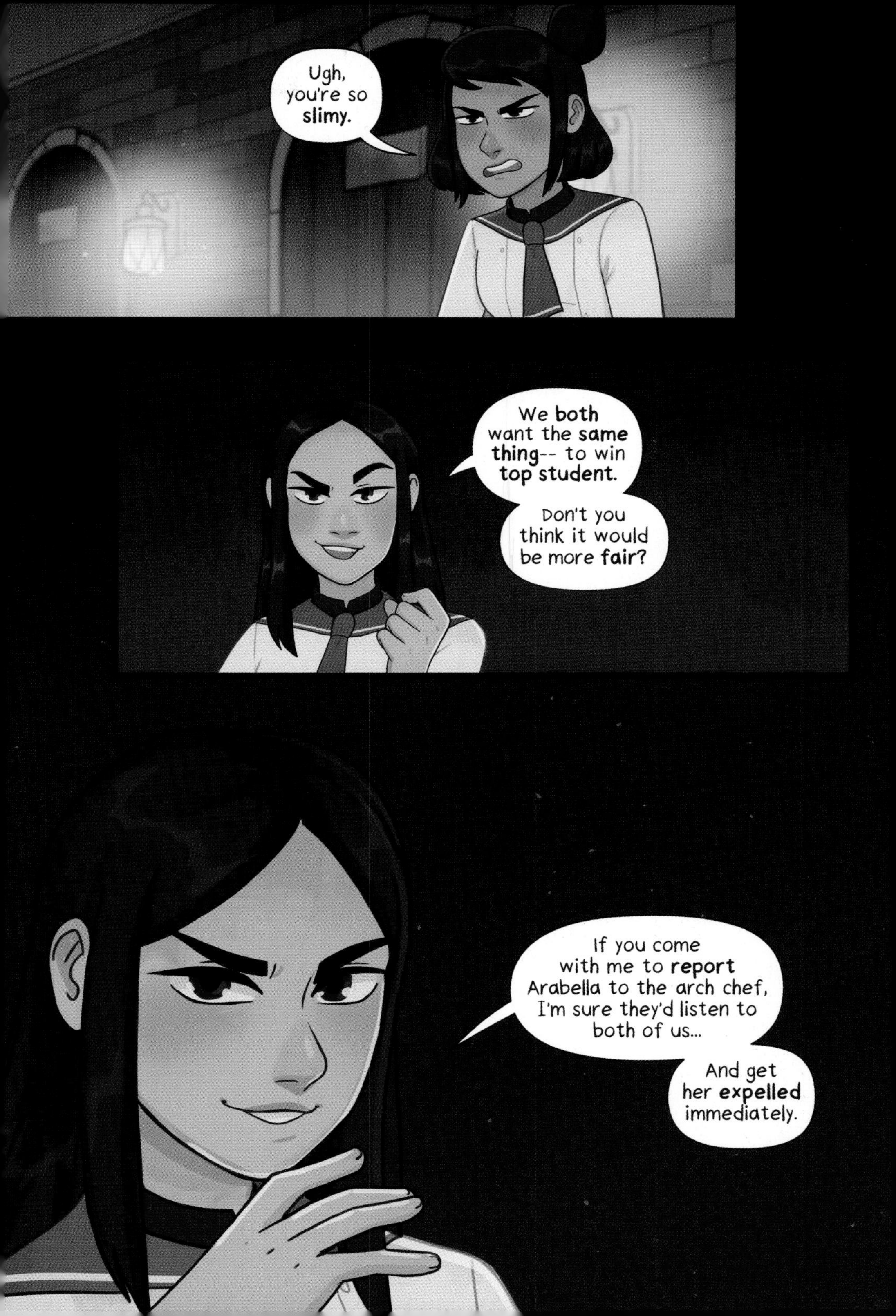
Ugh, you're so slimy.
We both want the same thing-- to win top student.
Don't you think it would be more fair?
If you come with me to report Arabella to the arch chef, I'm sure they'd listen to both of us...
And get her expelled immediately.

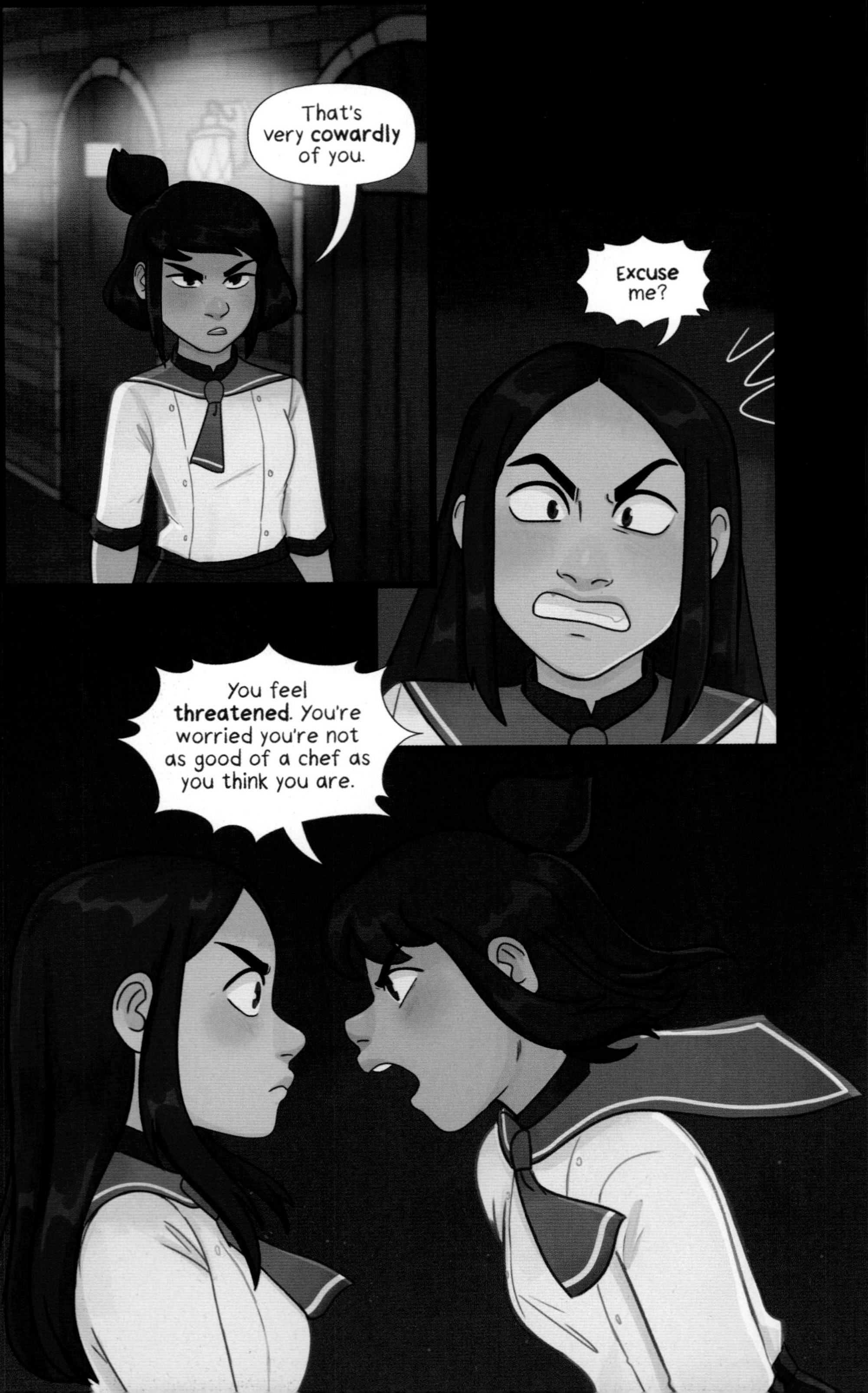
That's very **cowardly** of you.
Excuse me?
You feel **threatened**. You're worried you're not as good of a chef as you think you are.

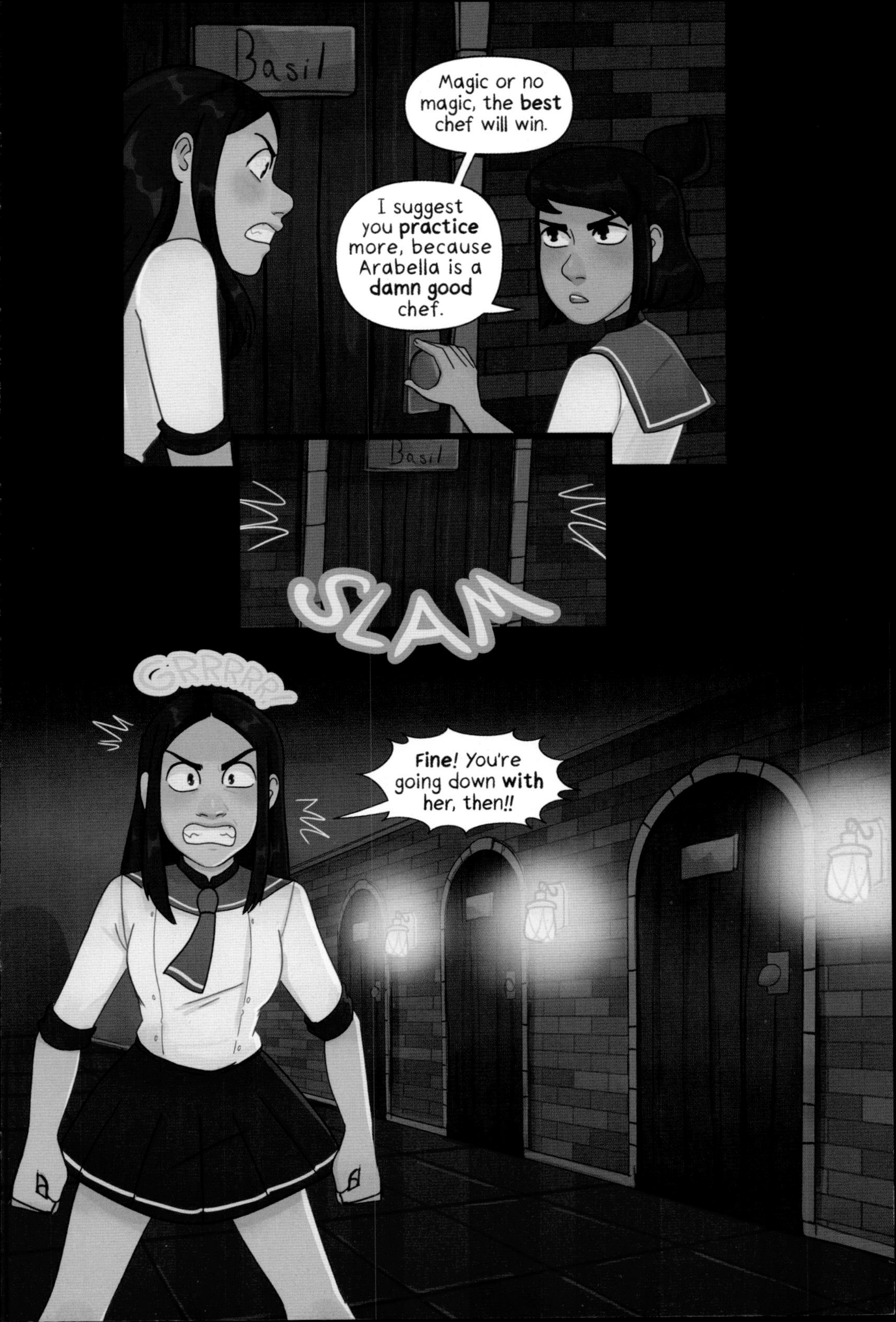
Basil
Magic or no magic, the **best** chef will win.
I suggest you **practice** more, because Arabella is a **damn good** chef.
Basil
SLAM
GRRRRR!
Fine! You're going down **with** her, then!!

Chapter
SEVEN

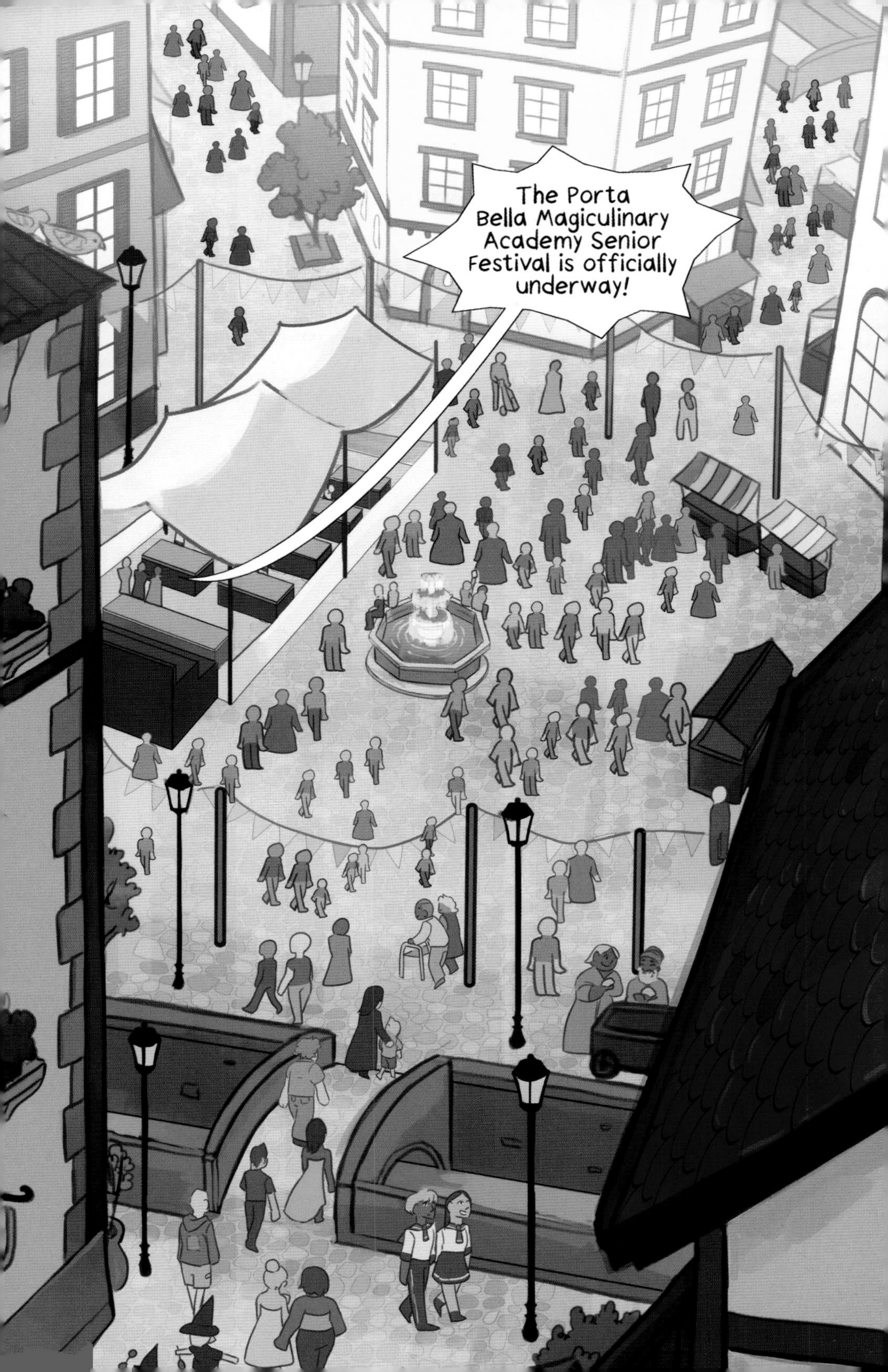
The Porta Bella Magiculinary Academy Senior Festival is officially underway!

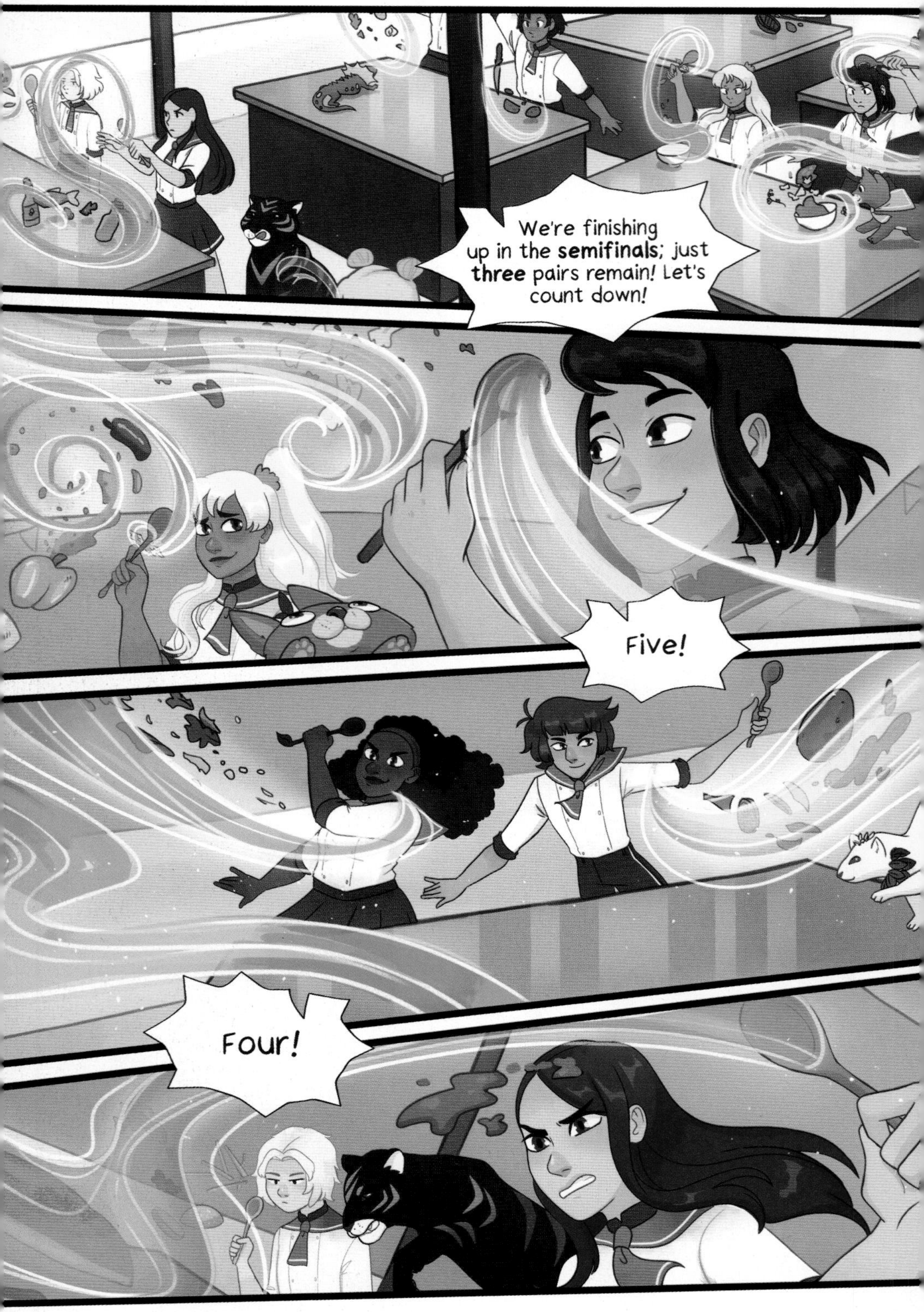
We're finishing up in the **semifinals**; just **three** pairs remain! Let's count down!
Five!
Four!

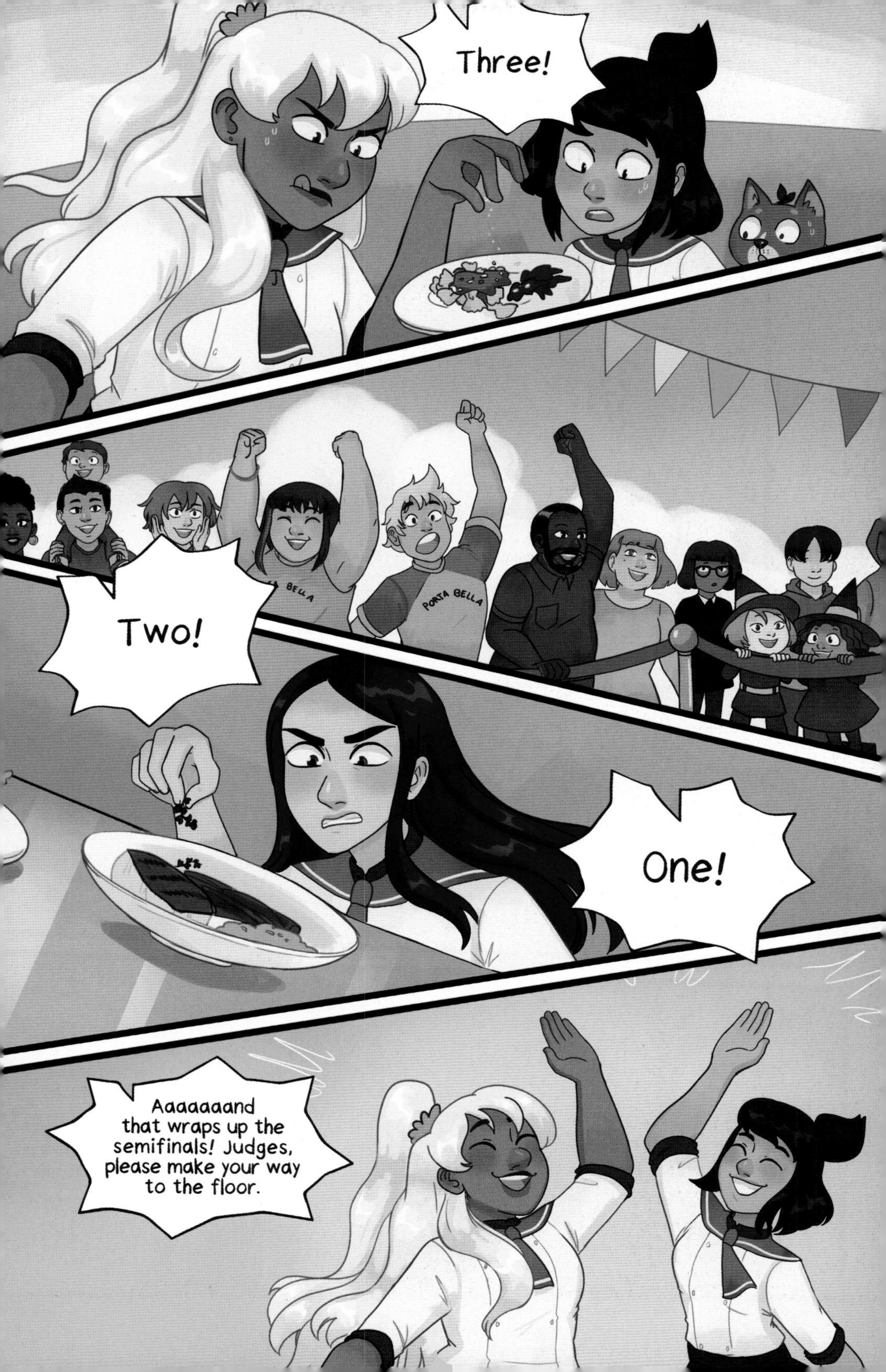
Three!
PORTA BELLA
Two!
One!
Aaaaaaand that wraps up the semifinals! Judges, please make your way to the floor.

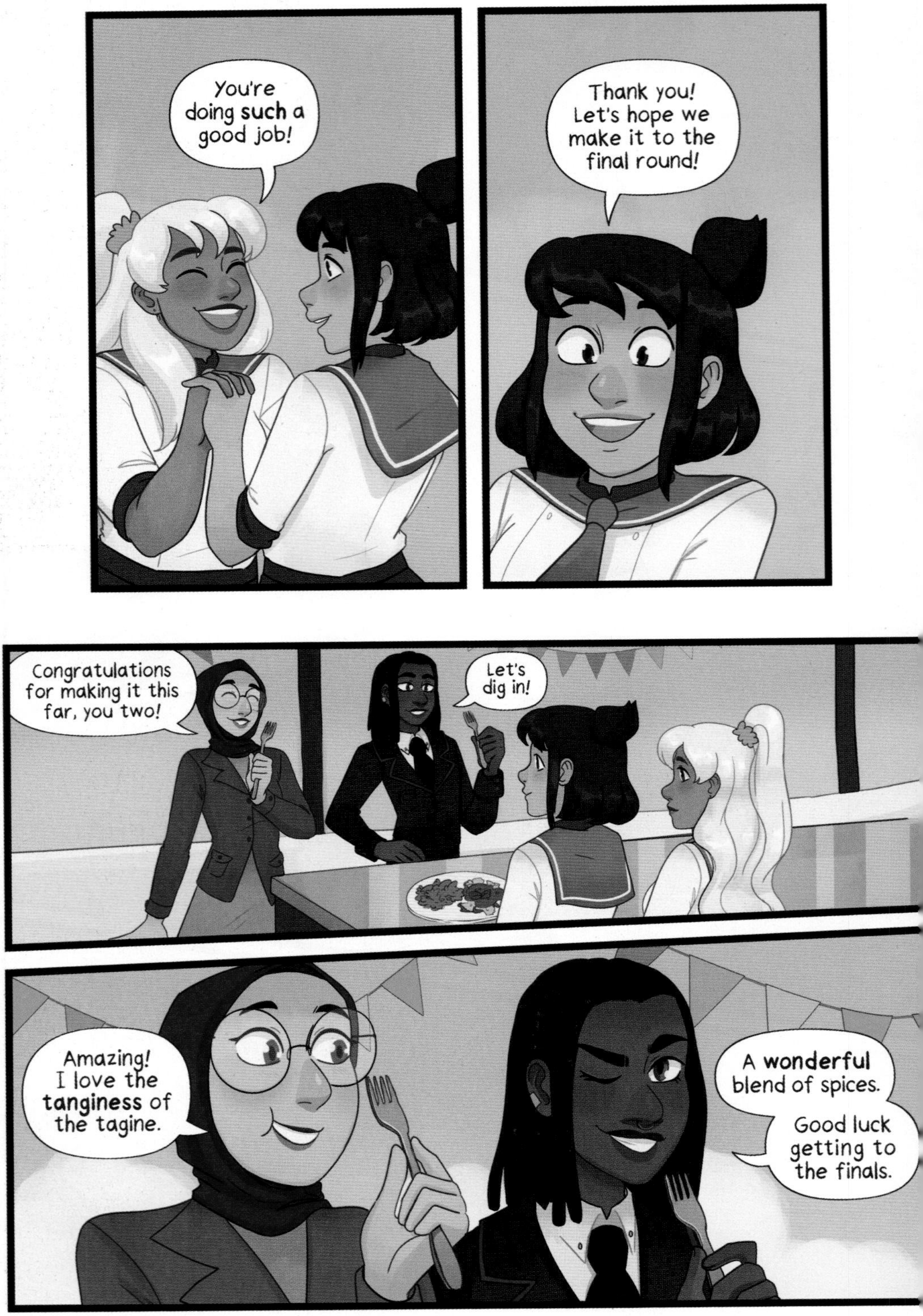
You're doing **such** a good job!
Thank you! Let's hope we make it to the final round!
Congratulations for making it this far, you two!
Let's dig in!
Amazing! I love the **tanginess** of the tagine.
A **wonderful** blend of spices.
Good luck getting to the finals.

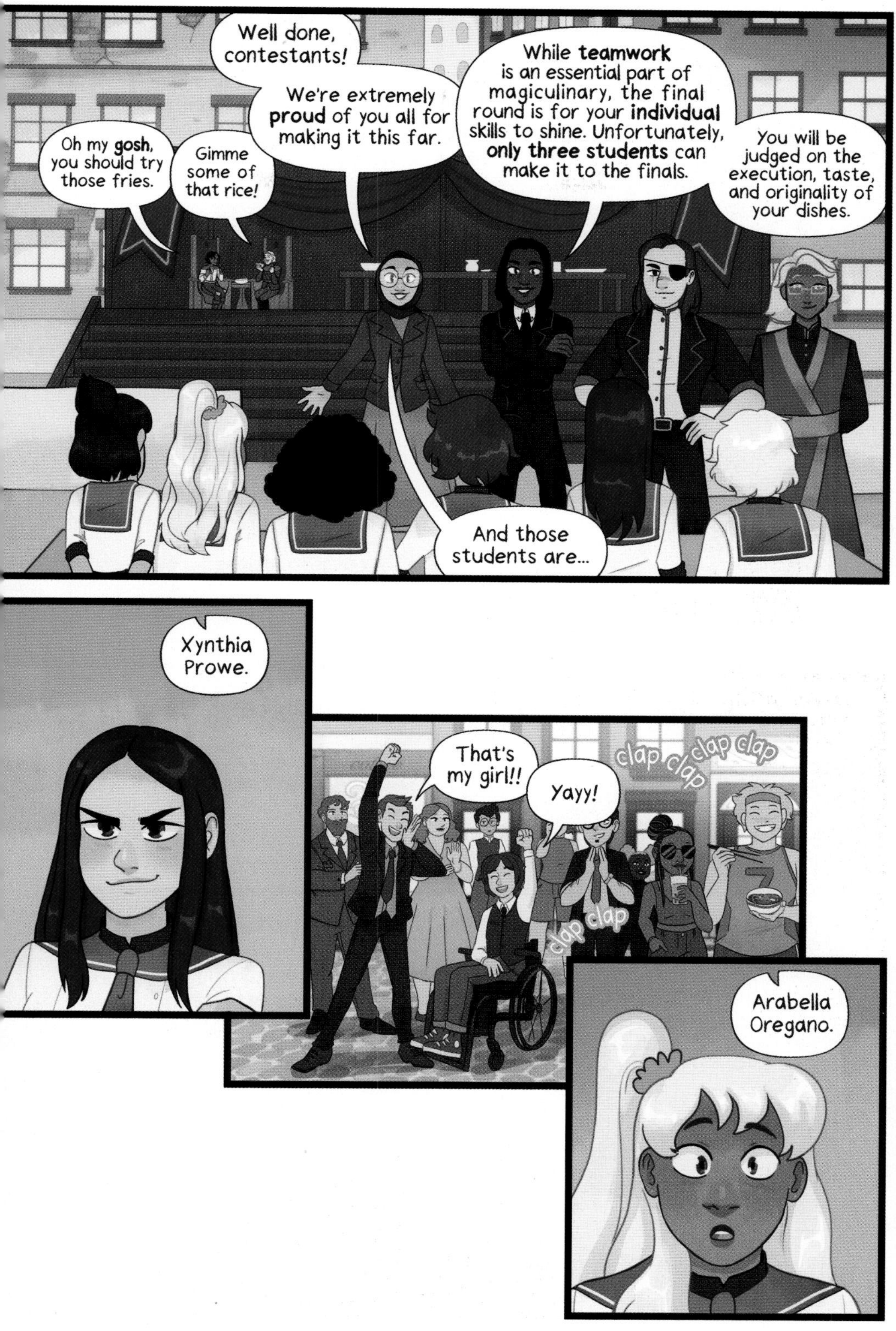
Well done, contestants!
We're extremely proud of you all for making it this far.
Oh my gosh, you should try those fries.
Gimme some of that rice!
While teamwork is an essential part of magiculinary, the final round is for your individual skills to shine. Unfortunately, only three students can make it to the finals.
You will be judged on the execution, taste, and originality of your dishes.
And those students are...
Xynthia Prowe.
That's my girl!!
Yayy!
clap clap clap clap
clap clap
Arabella Oregano.

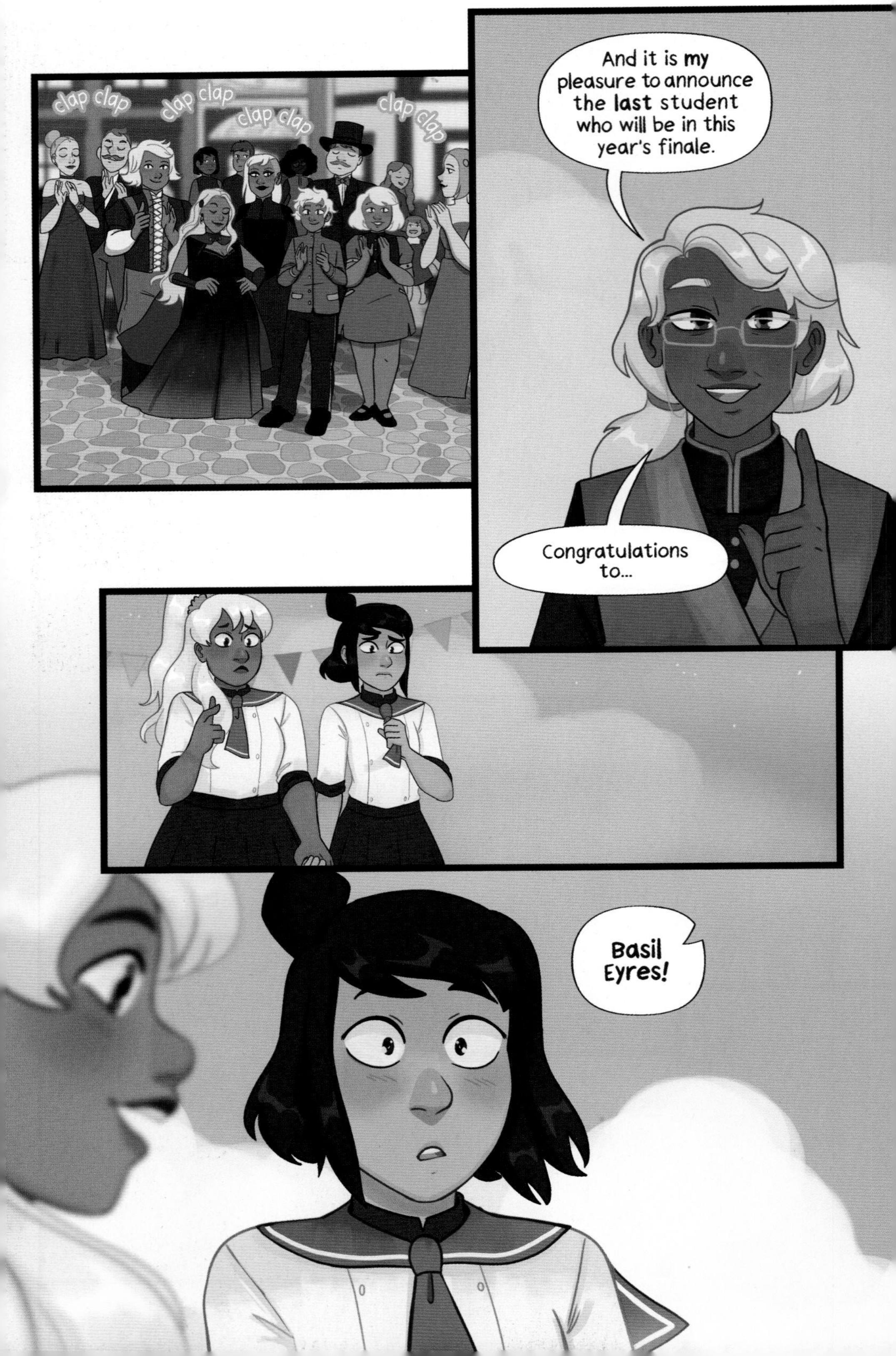

clap clap
clap clap
clap clap
clap clap
And it is my pleasure to announce the last student who will be in this year's finale.
Congratulations to...
Basil Eyres!

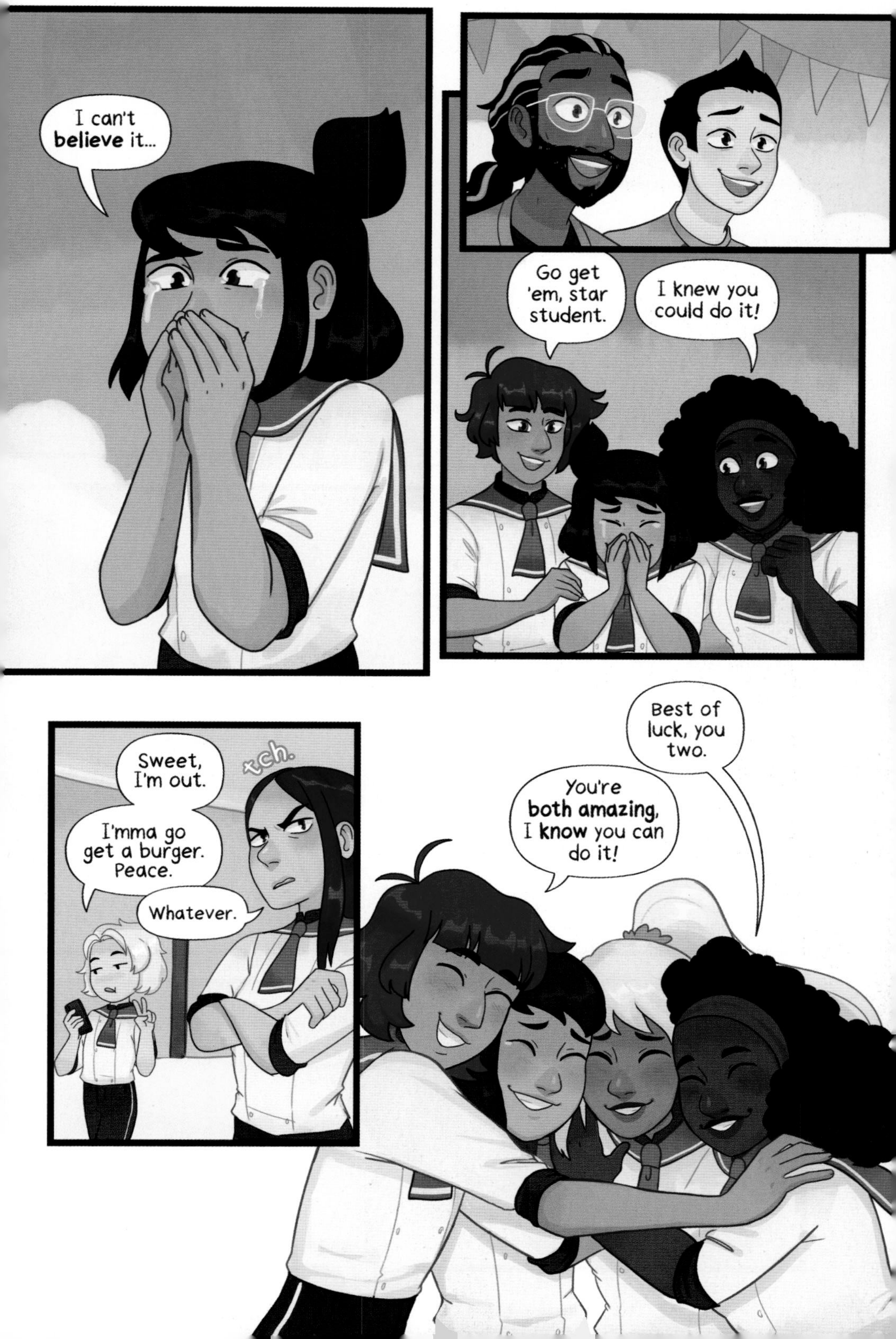

I can't **believe** it...
Go get 'em, star student.
I knew you could do it!
Sweet, I'm out.
I'mma go get a burger. Peace.
xch.
Whatever.
Best of luck, you two.
You're **both amazing**, I **know** you can do it!

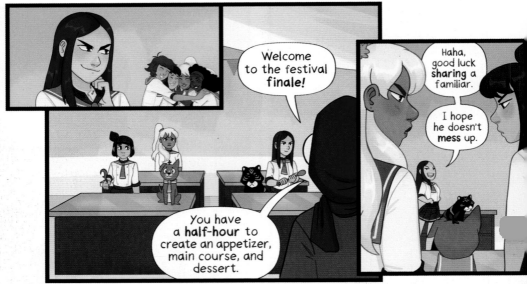

Welcome to the festival **finale!**

You have a **half-hour** to create an appetizer, main course, and dessert.

Haha, good luck **sharing a** familiar.

I hope he doesn't **mess up.**

Ready...

Let the cooking commence...

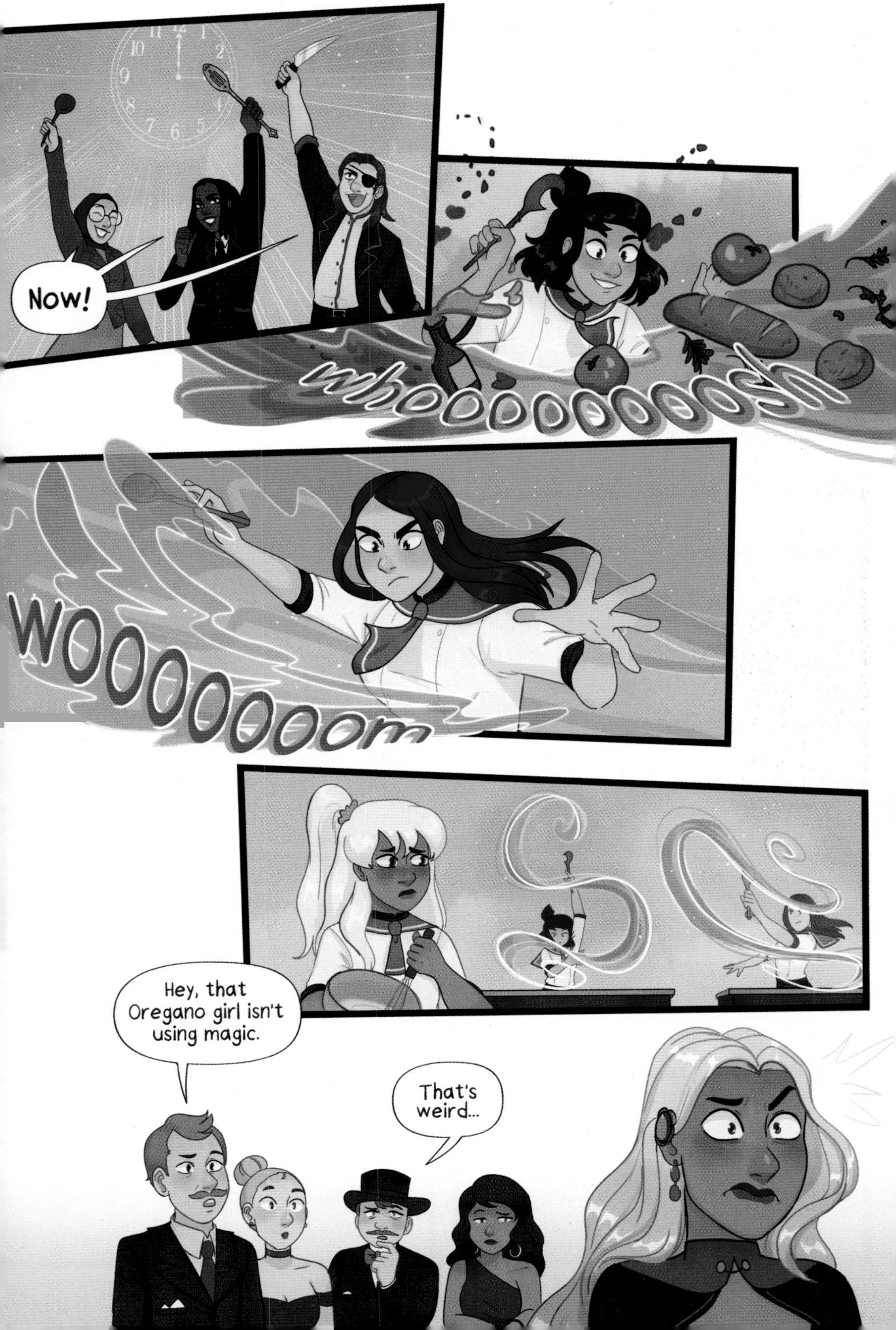
Now!
whoooooooosh
WOOOOOOOOm
Hey, that Oregano girl isn't using magic.
That's weird...

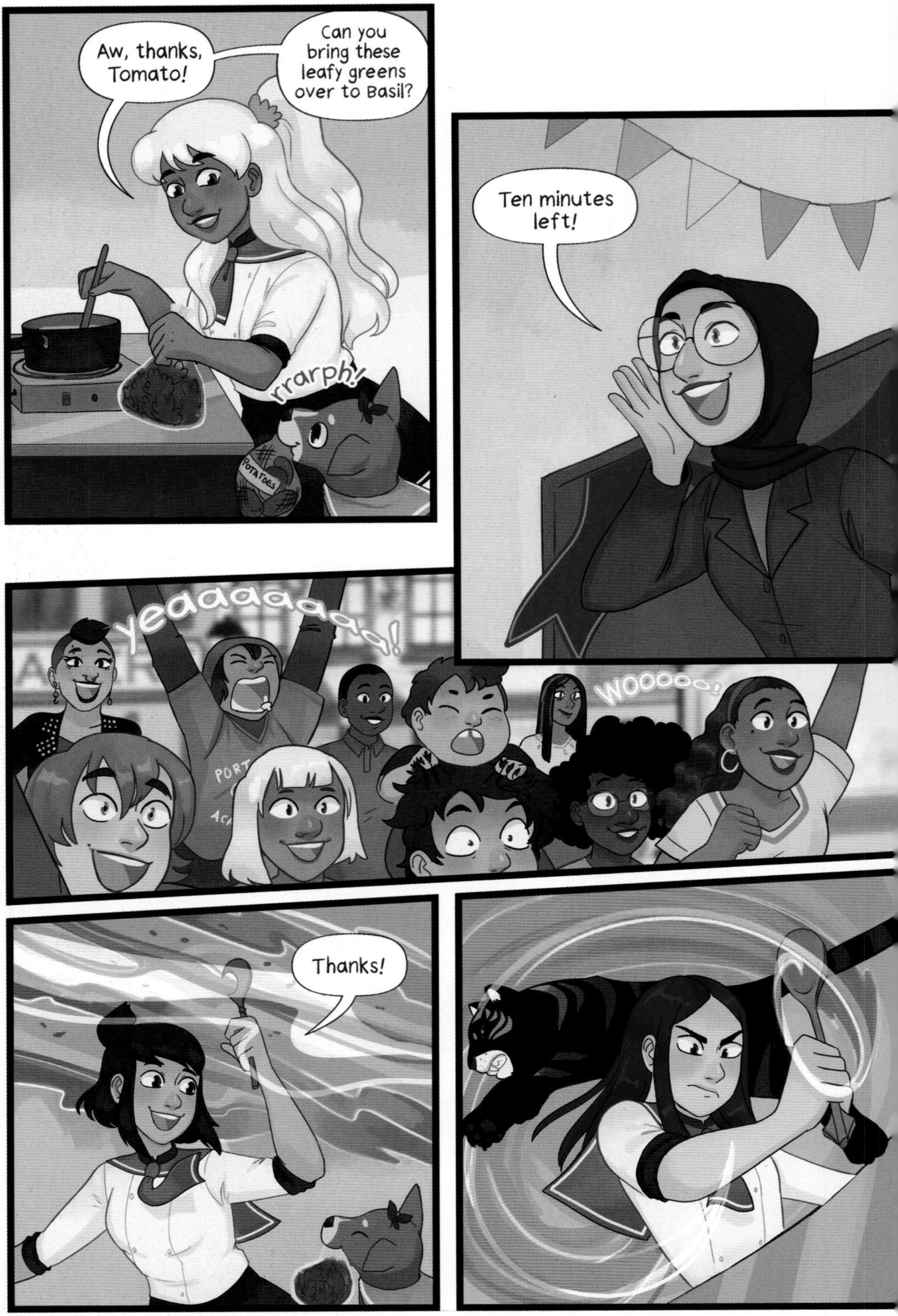
Aw, thanks, Tomato!
Can you bring these leafy greens over to Basil?
POTATOES
rrarph!
Ten minutes left!
yeaaaaaaa!
WOOOOO!
Thanks!

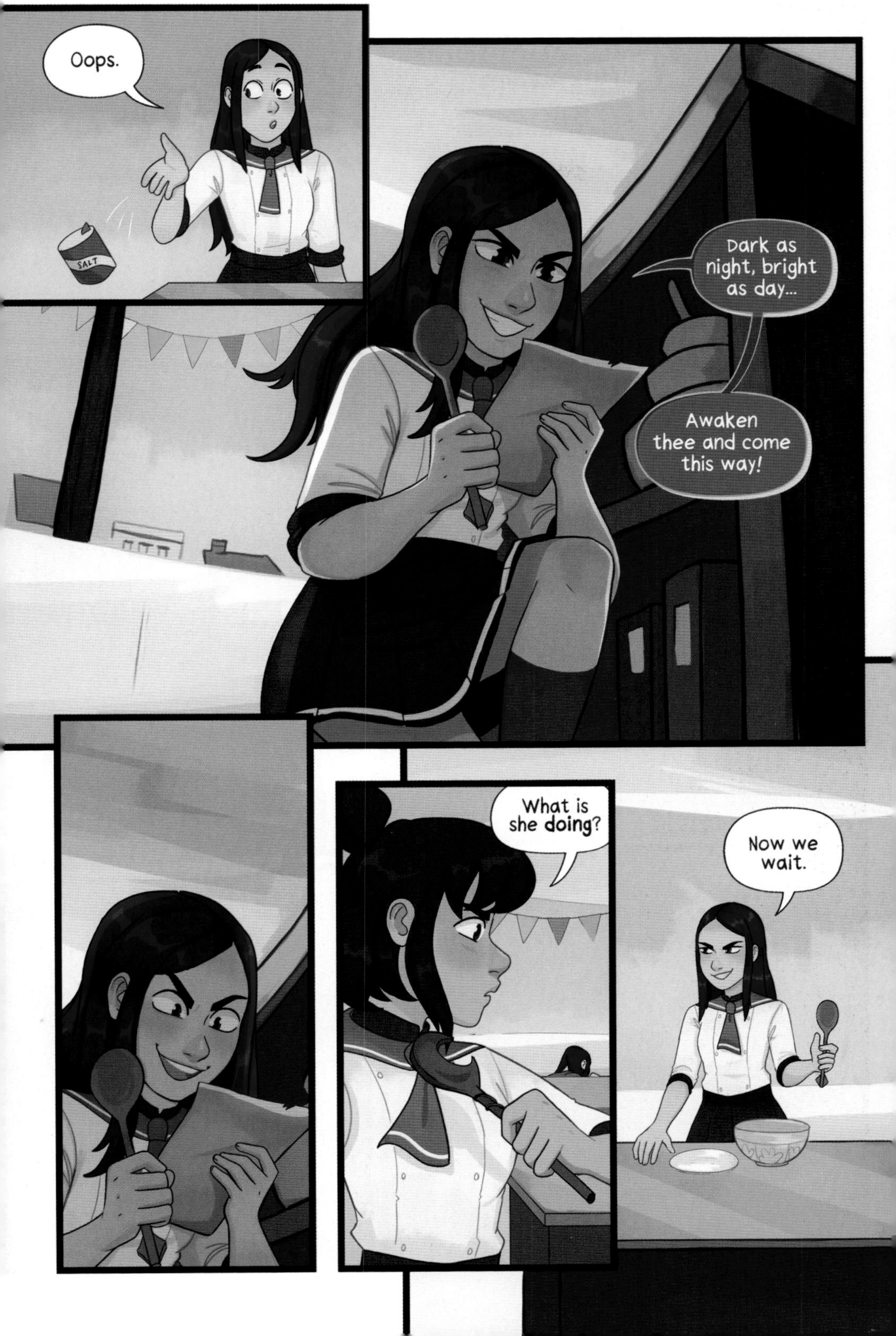

Oops.
SALT
Dark as night, bright as day...
Awaken thee and come this way!
What is she doing?
Now we wait.

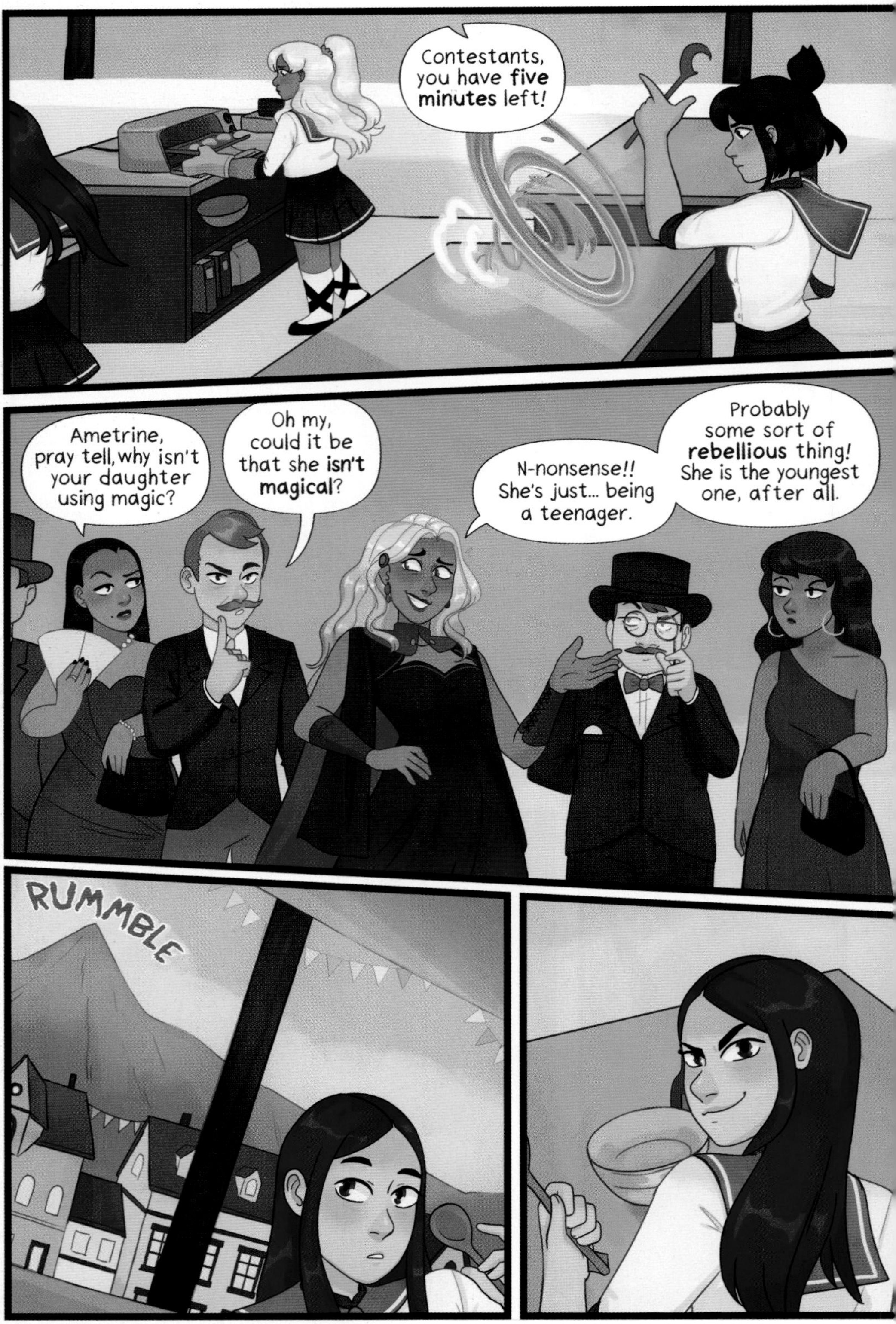
Contestants, you have **five minutes** left!
Ametrine, pray tell, why isn't your daughter using magic?
Oh my, could it be that she **isn't magical**?
N-nonsense!! She's just... being a teenager.
Probably some sort of **rebellious** thing! She is the youngest one, after all.
RUMMBLE

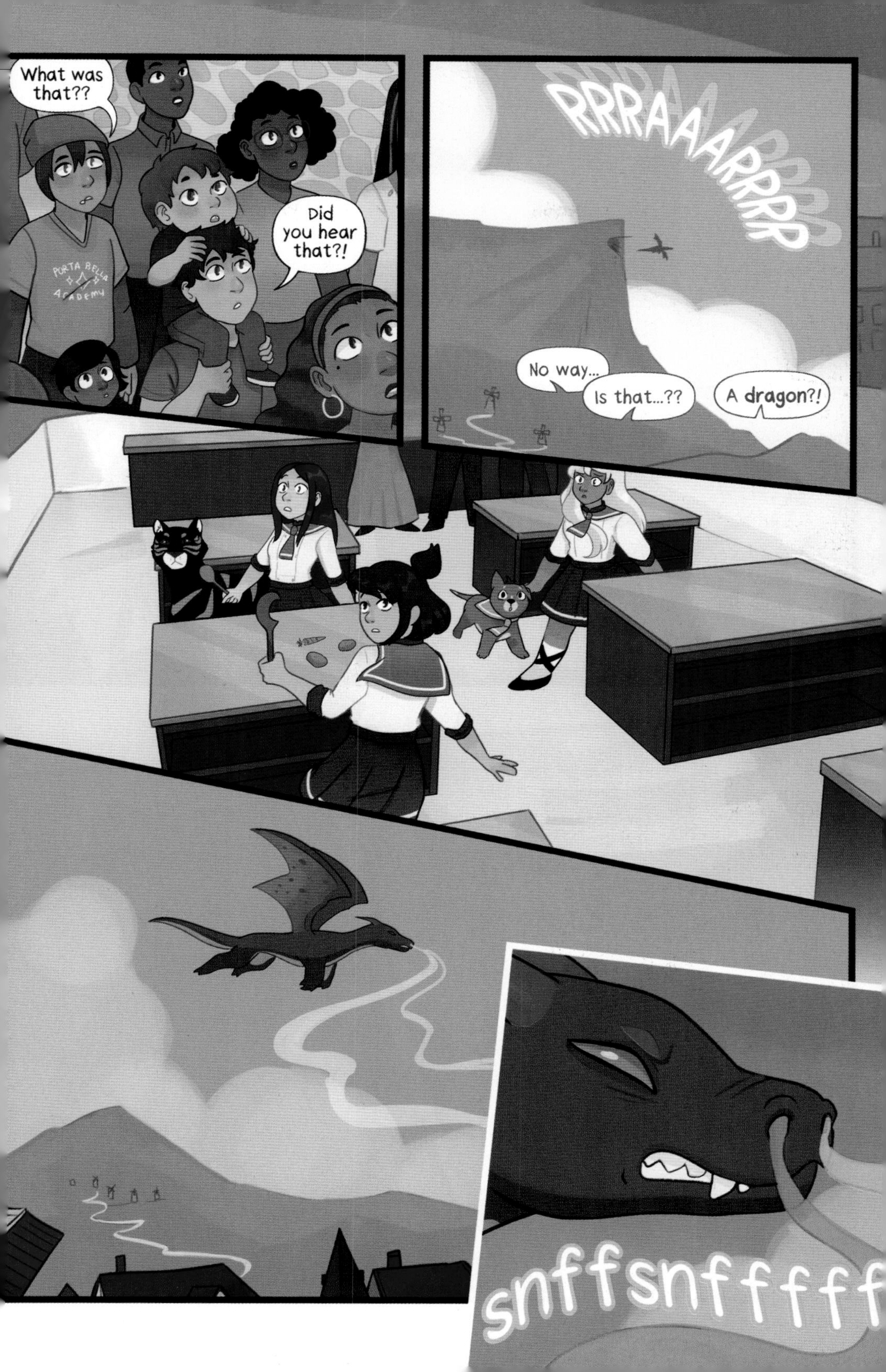
What was that??
Did you hear that?!
RRRAAAARRRRP
No way...
Is that...??
A dragon?!
snffsnfffff

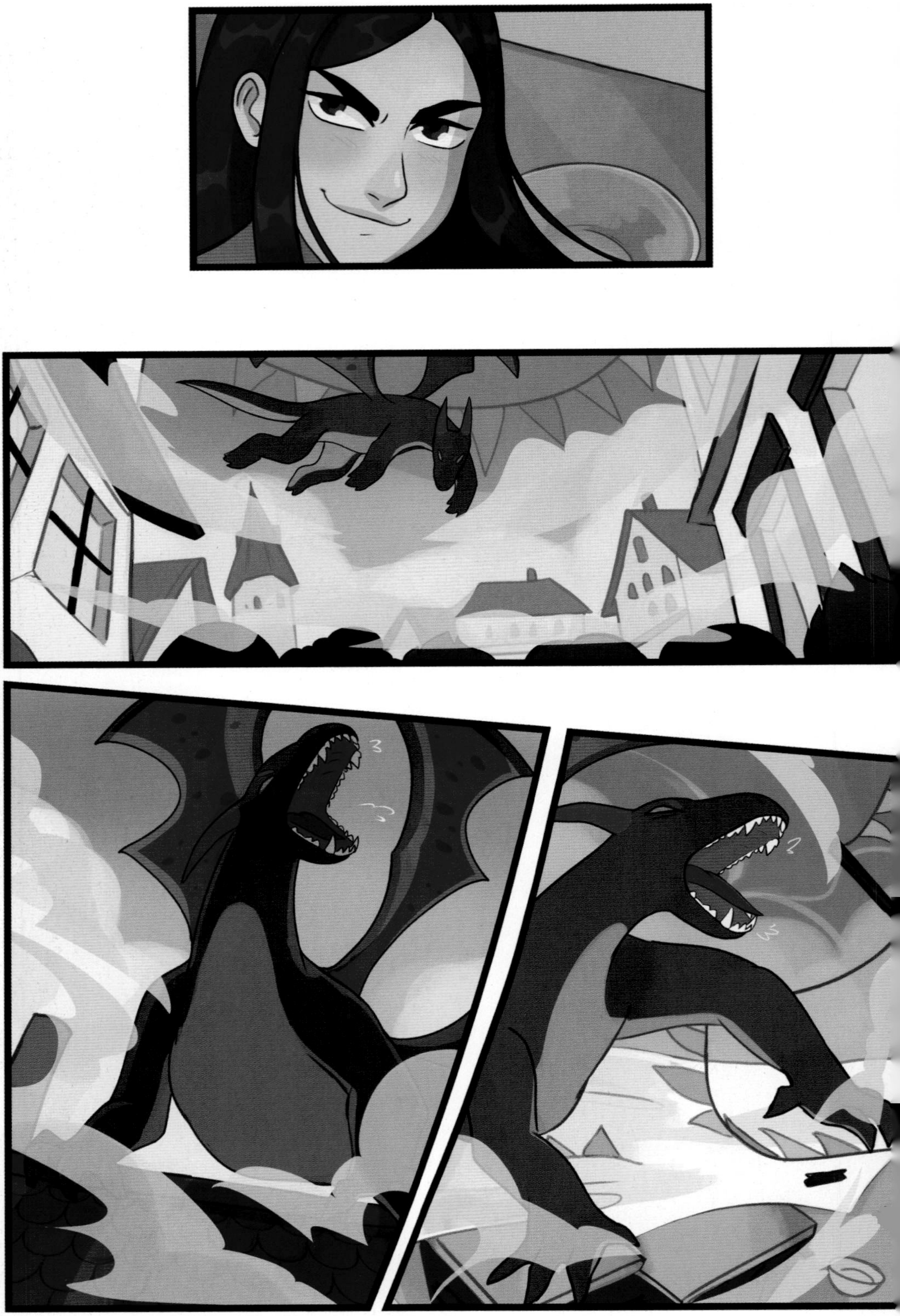

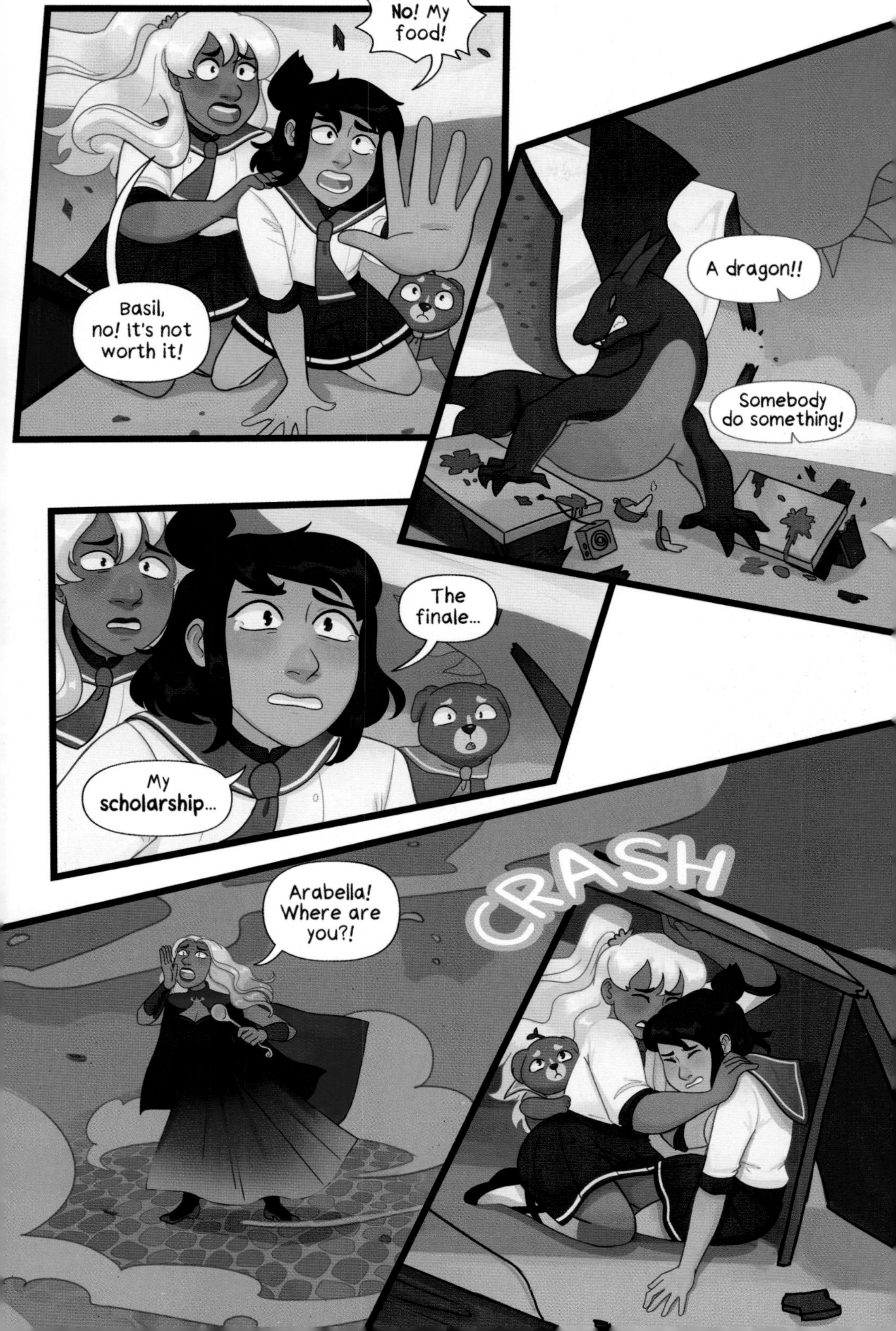
No! My food!
Basil, no! It's not worth it!
A dragon!!
Somebody do something!
The finale...
My scholarship...
Arabella! Where are you?!
CRASH

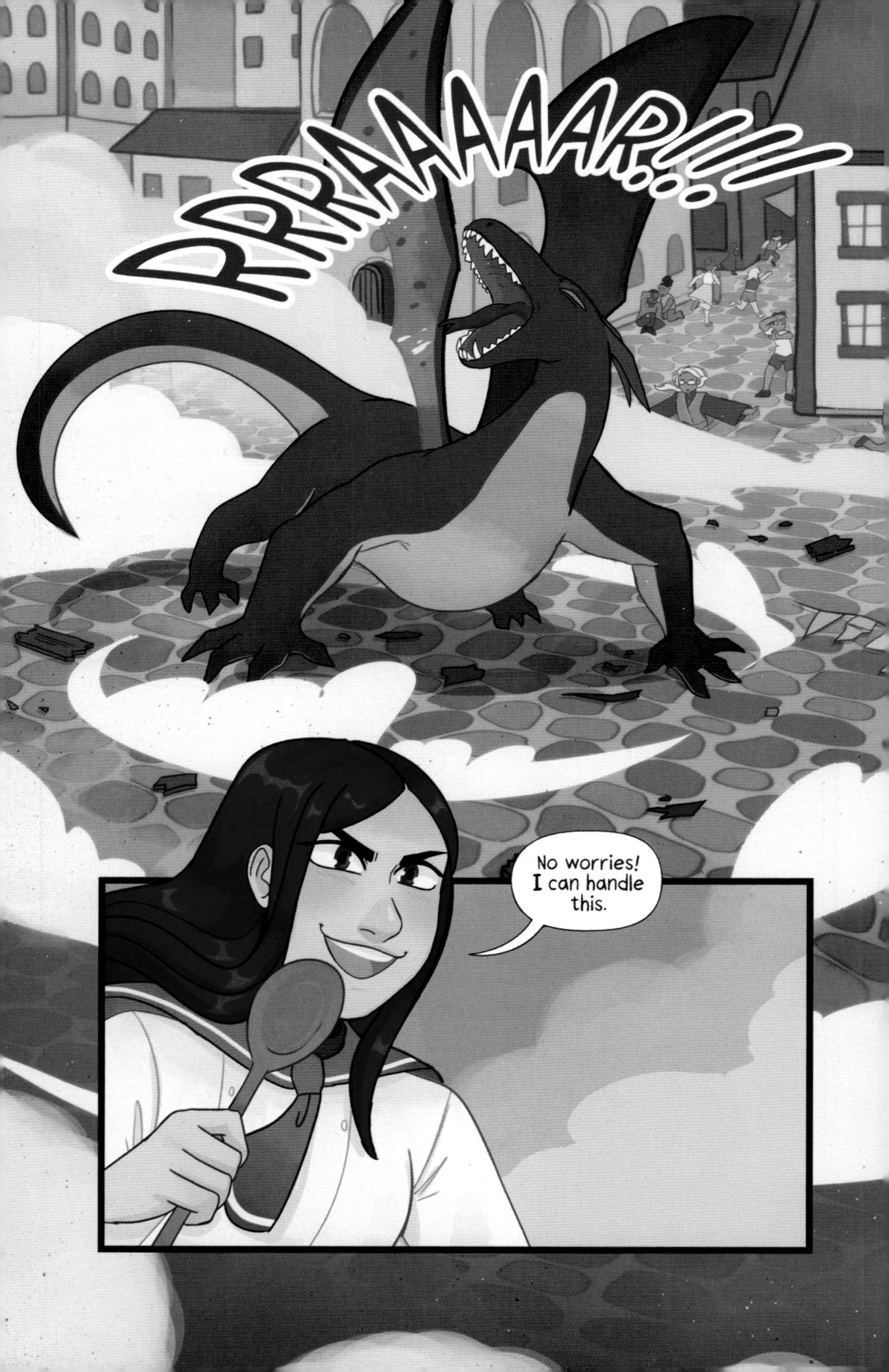
RRRAAAAAR!!!!
No worries! I can handle this.

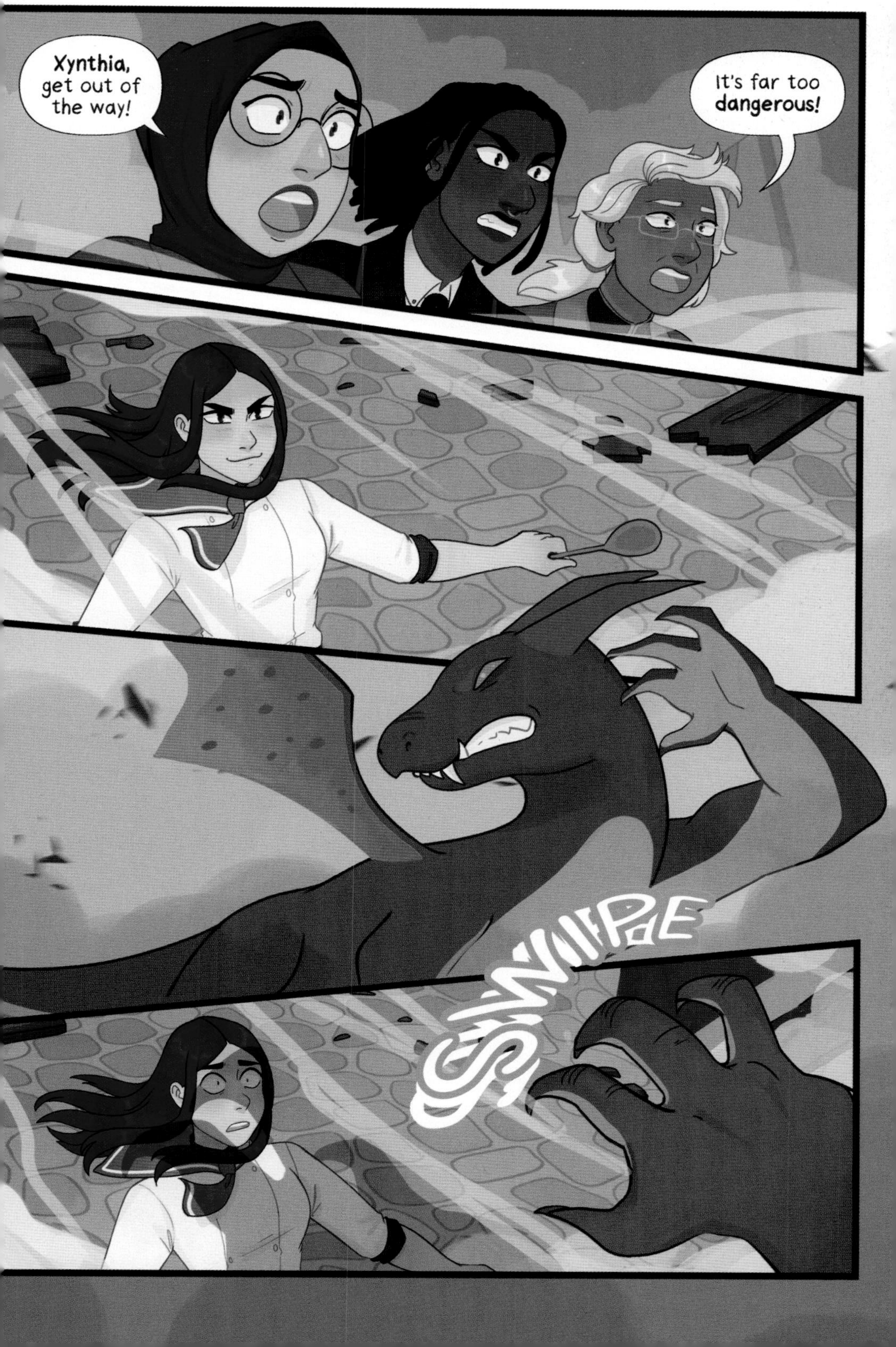
Xynthia, get out of the way!
It's far too dangerous!
SWIIPE

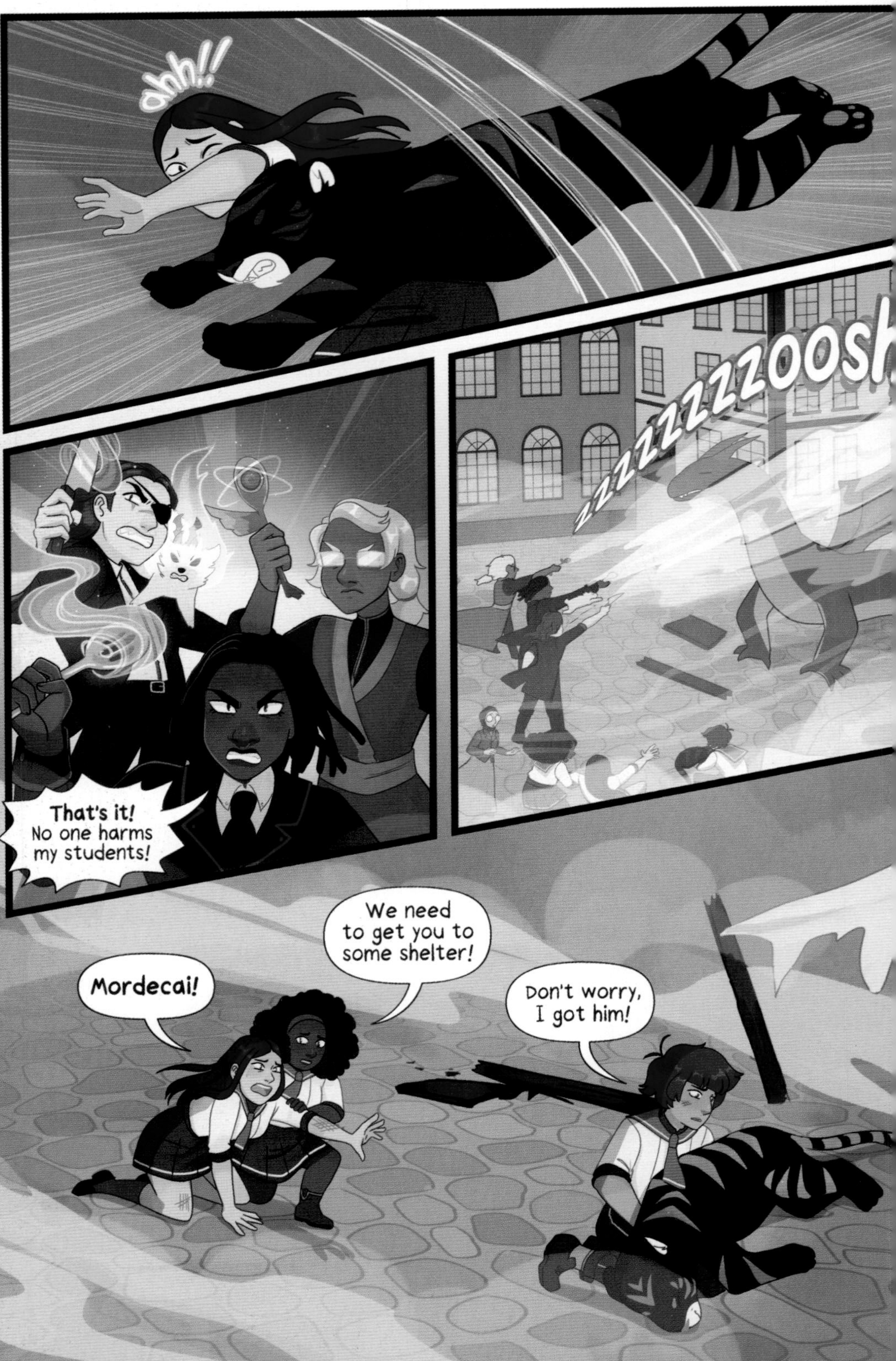
ahh!!
zzzzzzzzzZOOSH
That's it! No one harms my students!
Mordecai!
We need to get you to some shelter!
Don't worry, I got him!

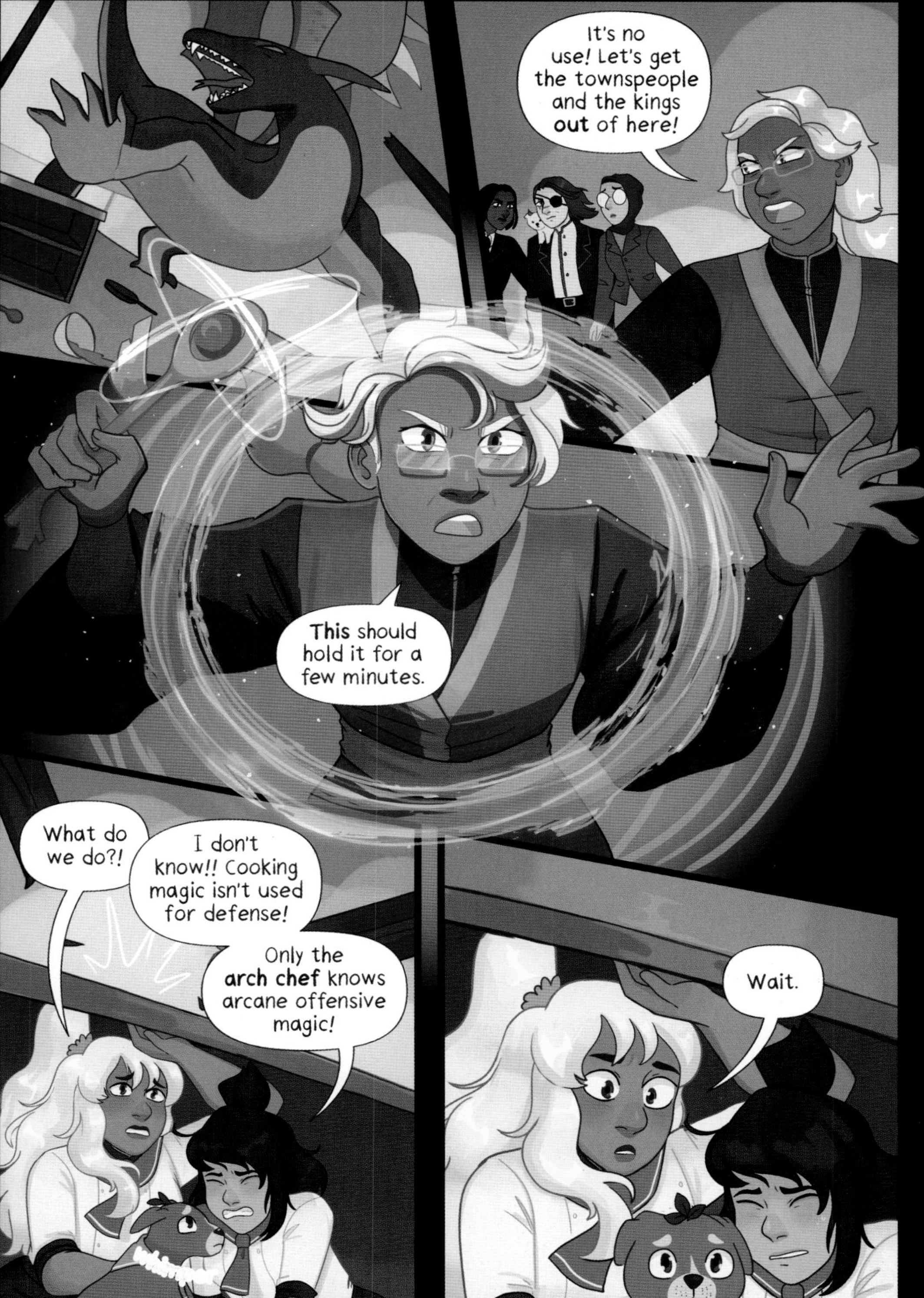

It's no use! Let's get the townspeople and the kings **out** of here!
This should hold it for a few minutes.
What do we do?!
I don't know!! Cooking magic isn't used for defense!
Only the **arch chef** knows arcane offensive magic!
Wait.

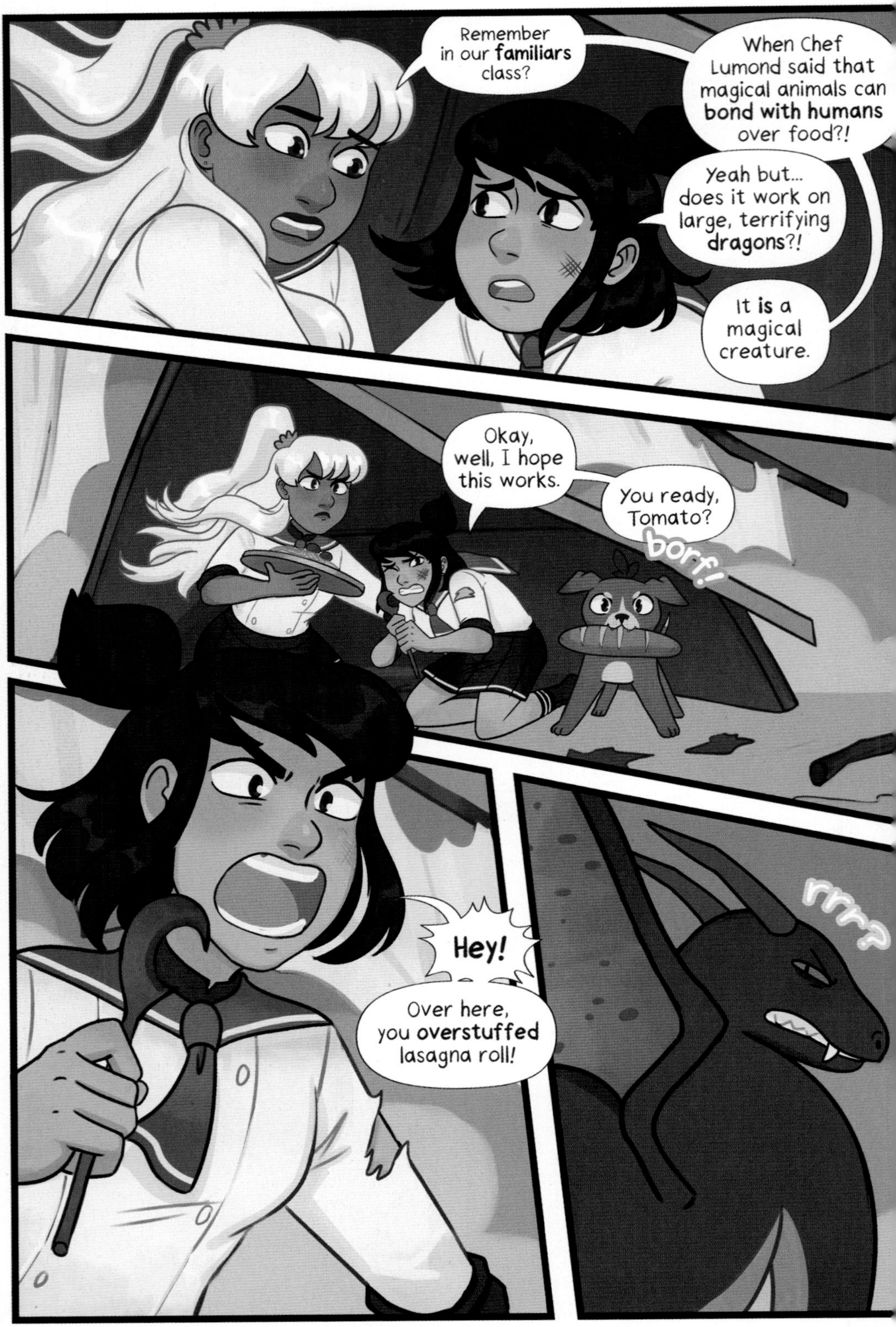
Remember in our **familiars** class?
When Chef Lumond said that magical animals can **bond with humans** over food?!
Yeah but... does it work on large, terrifying **dragons**?!
It **is** a magical creature.
Okay, well, I hope this works.
You ready, Tomato?
borf!
Hey!
Over here, you **overstuffed** lasagna roll!
rrr?

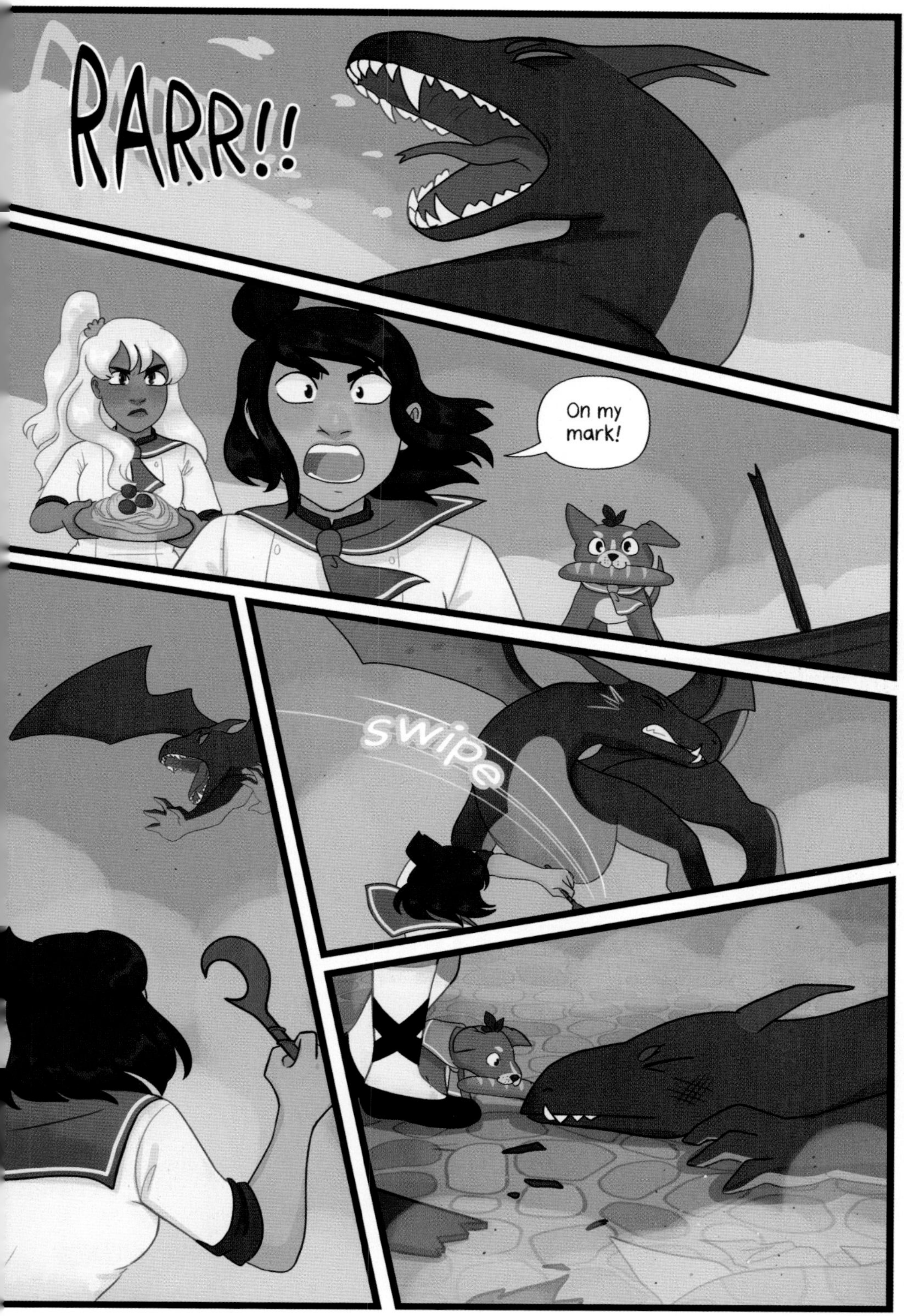
RARR!!
On my mark!
swipe

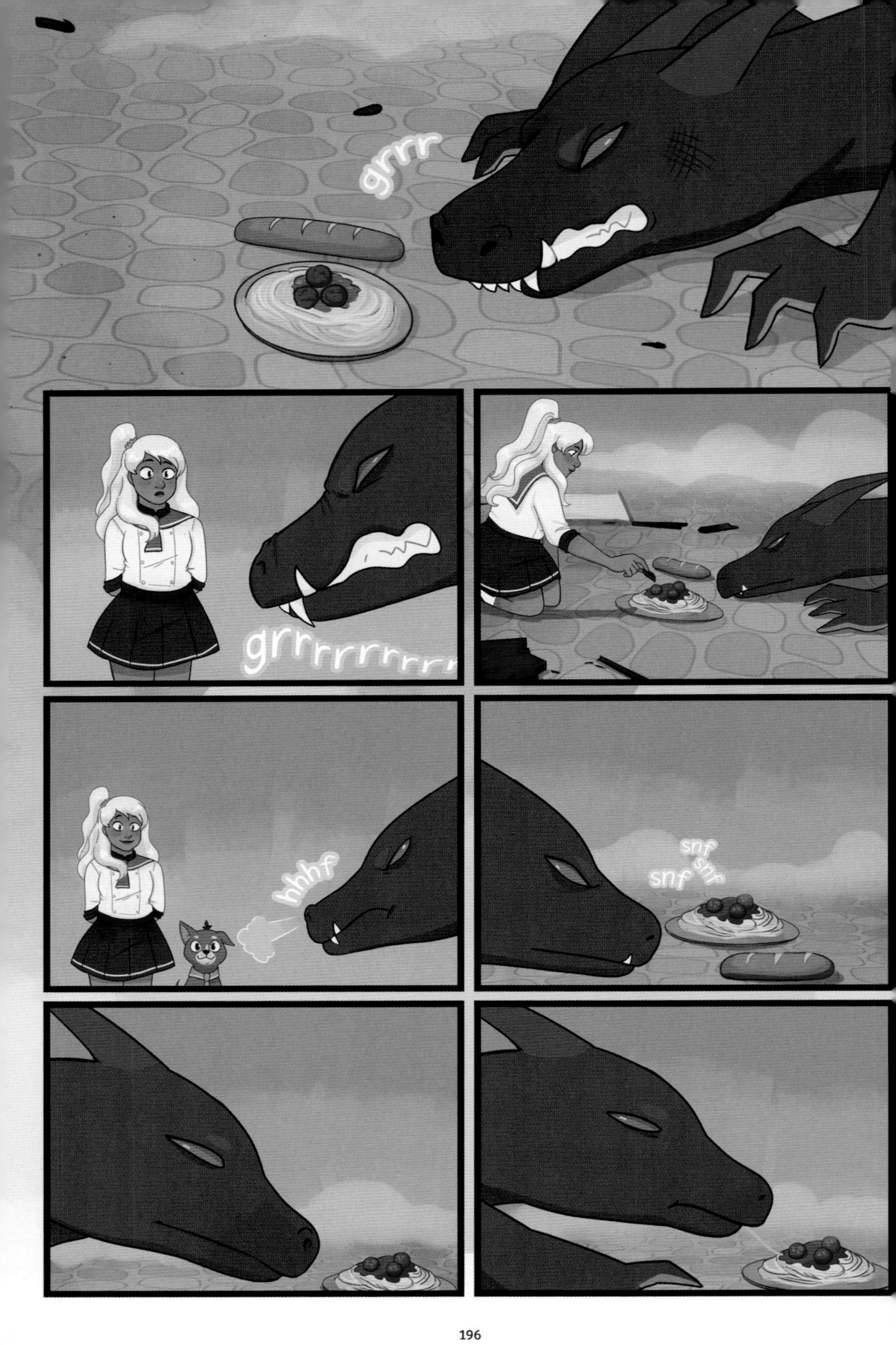
grrr
grrrrrrrrr
hhhf
snf
snf
snf

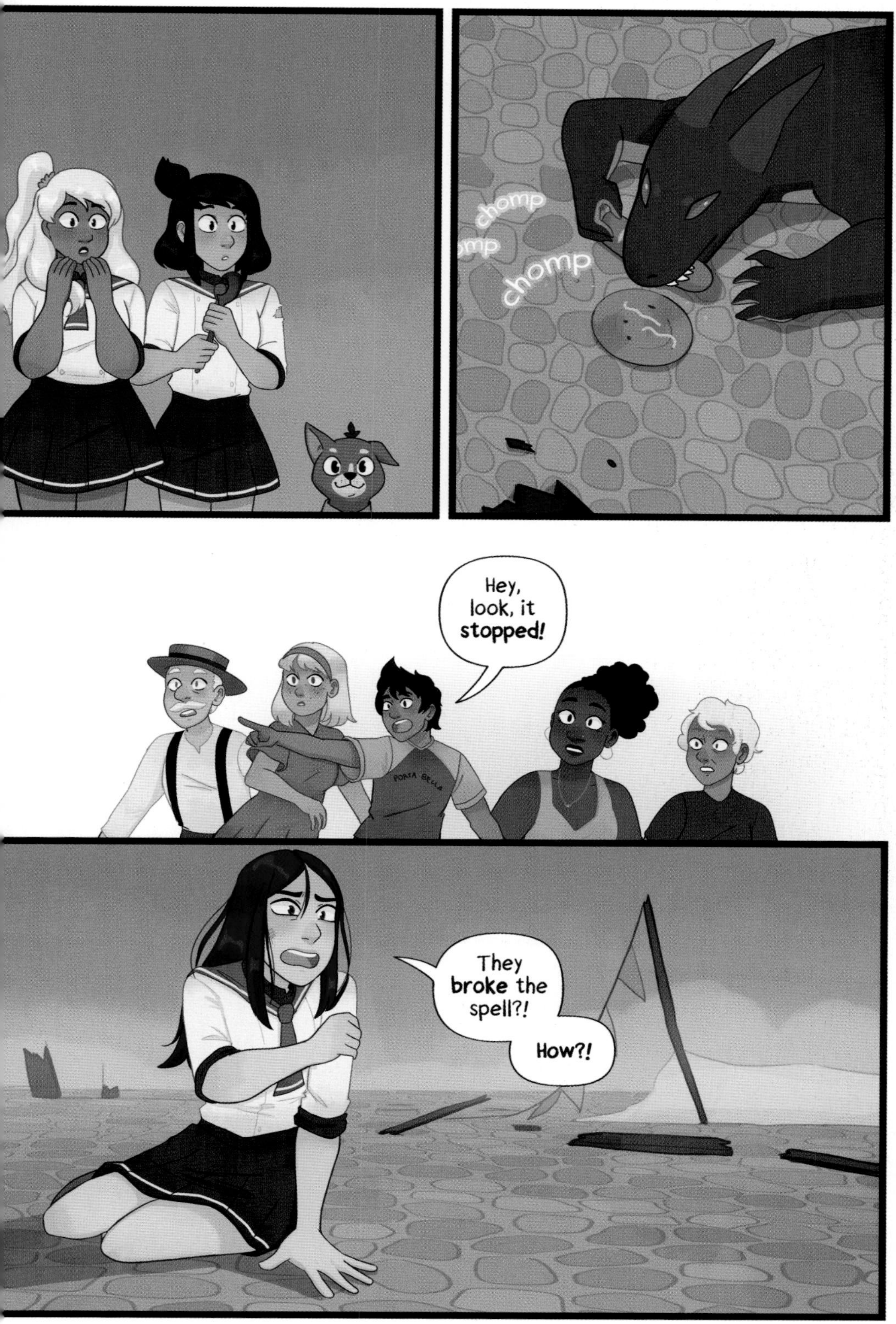
chomp
chomp
Hey, look, it **stopped!**
PORTA BELLA
They **broke** the spell?!
How?!

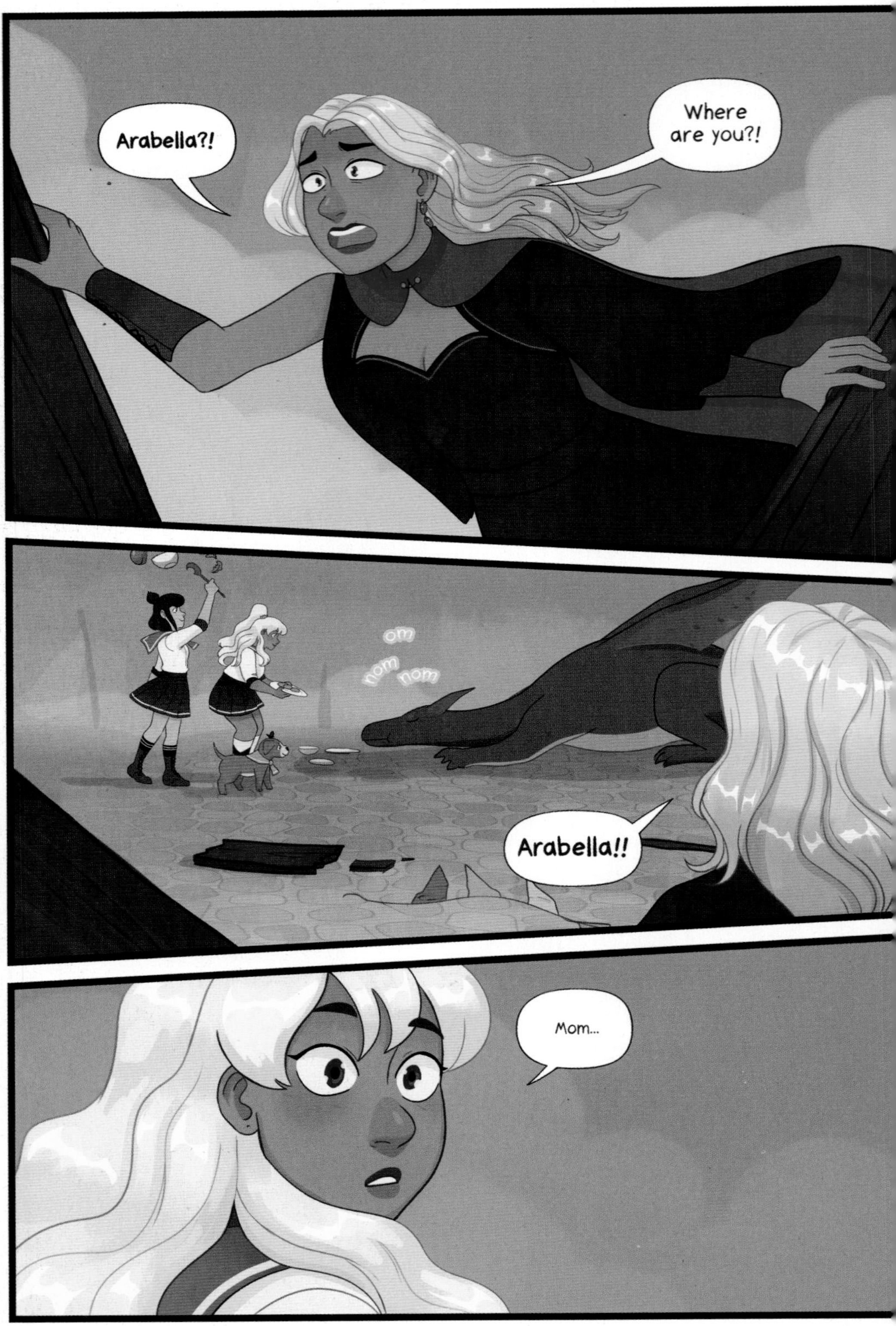
Arabella?!
Where are you?!
om
nom
nom
Arabella!!
Mom...

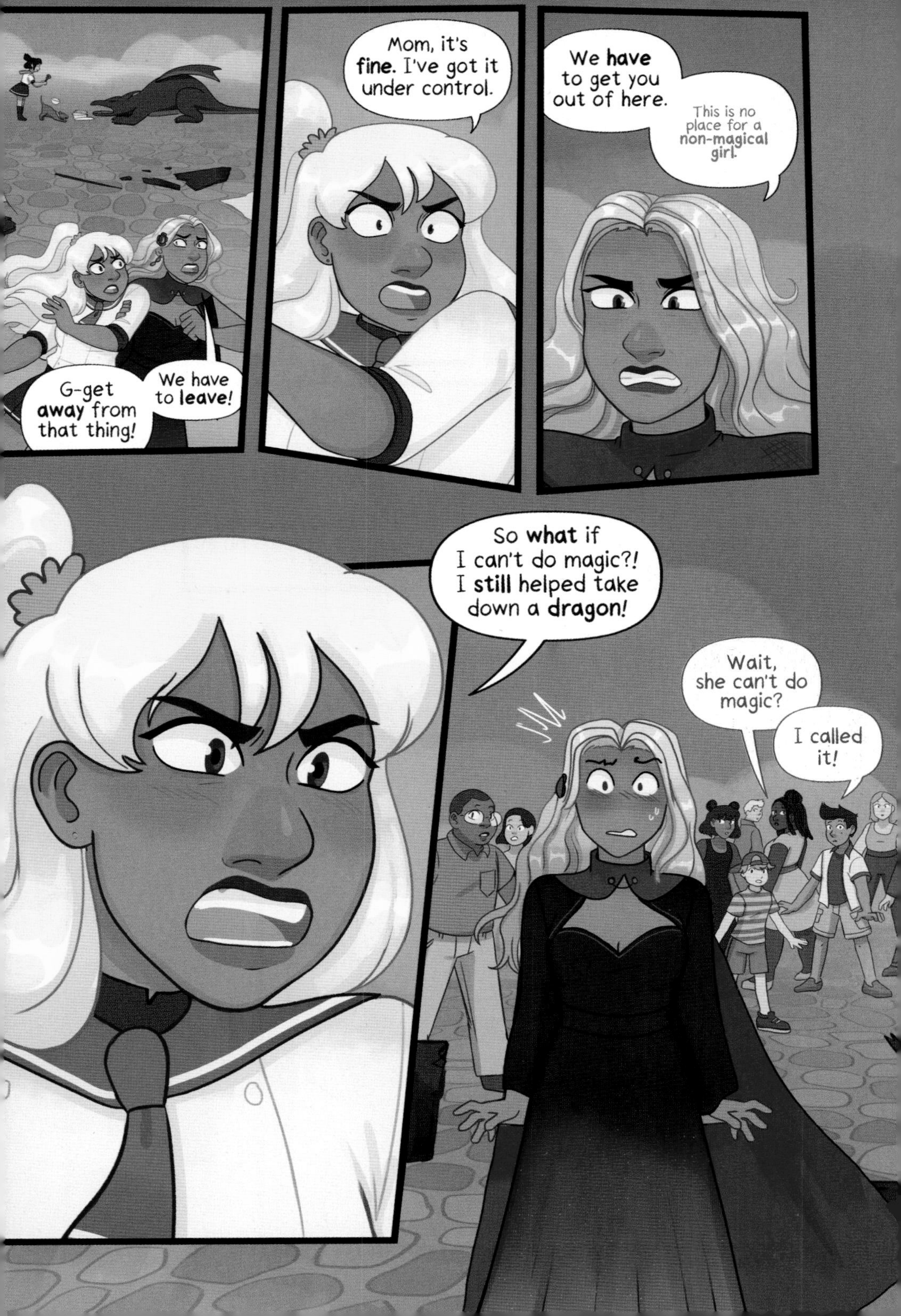
G-get **away** from that thing!
We have to **leave**!
Mom, it's **fine.** I've got it under control.
We **have** to get you out of here.
This is no place for a **non-magical girl.**
So **what** if I can't do magic?! I **still** helped take down a **dragon**!
Wait, she can't do magic?
I called it!

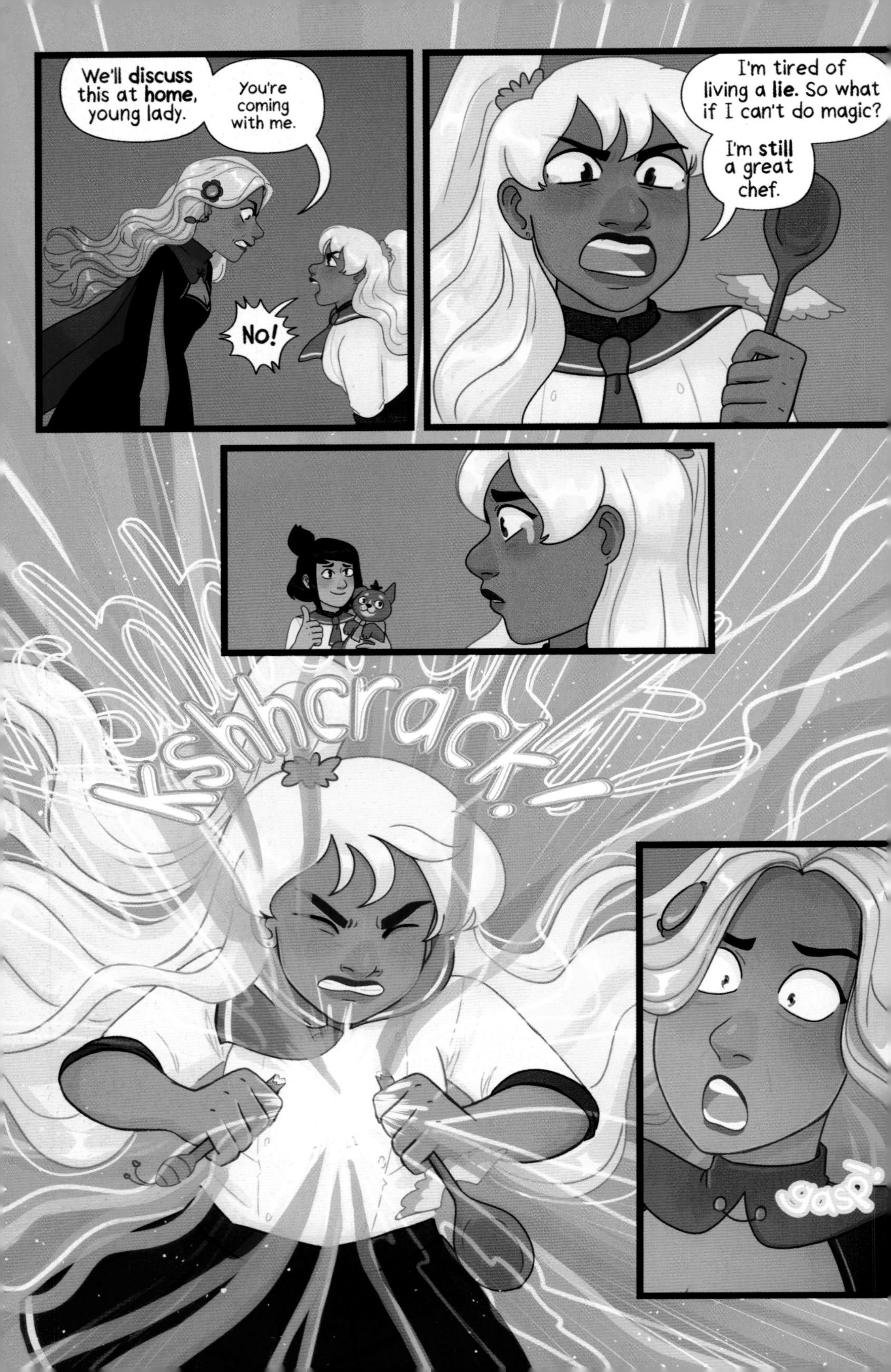
We'll **discuss** this at **home**, young lady.
You're coming with me.
No!
I'm tired of living a **lie.** So what if I can't do magic?
I'm **still** a great chef.
KSHHCRACK!
gasp!

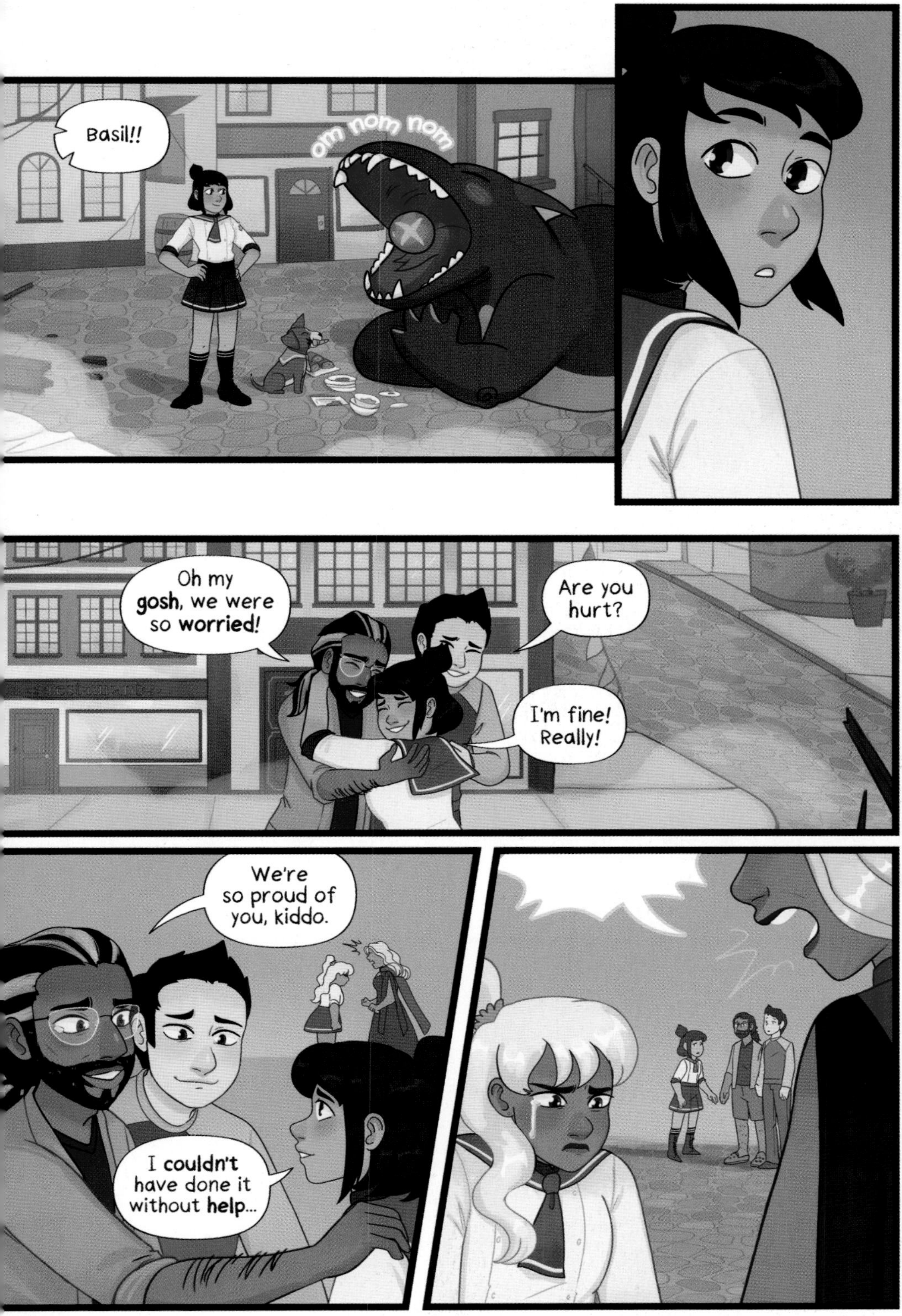
Basil!!
om nom nom
Oh my gosh, we were so worried!
Are you hurt?
I'm fine! Really!
We're so proud of you, kiddo.
I couldn't have done it without help...

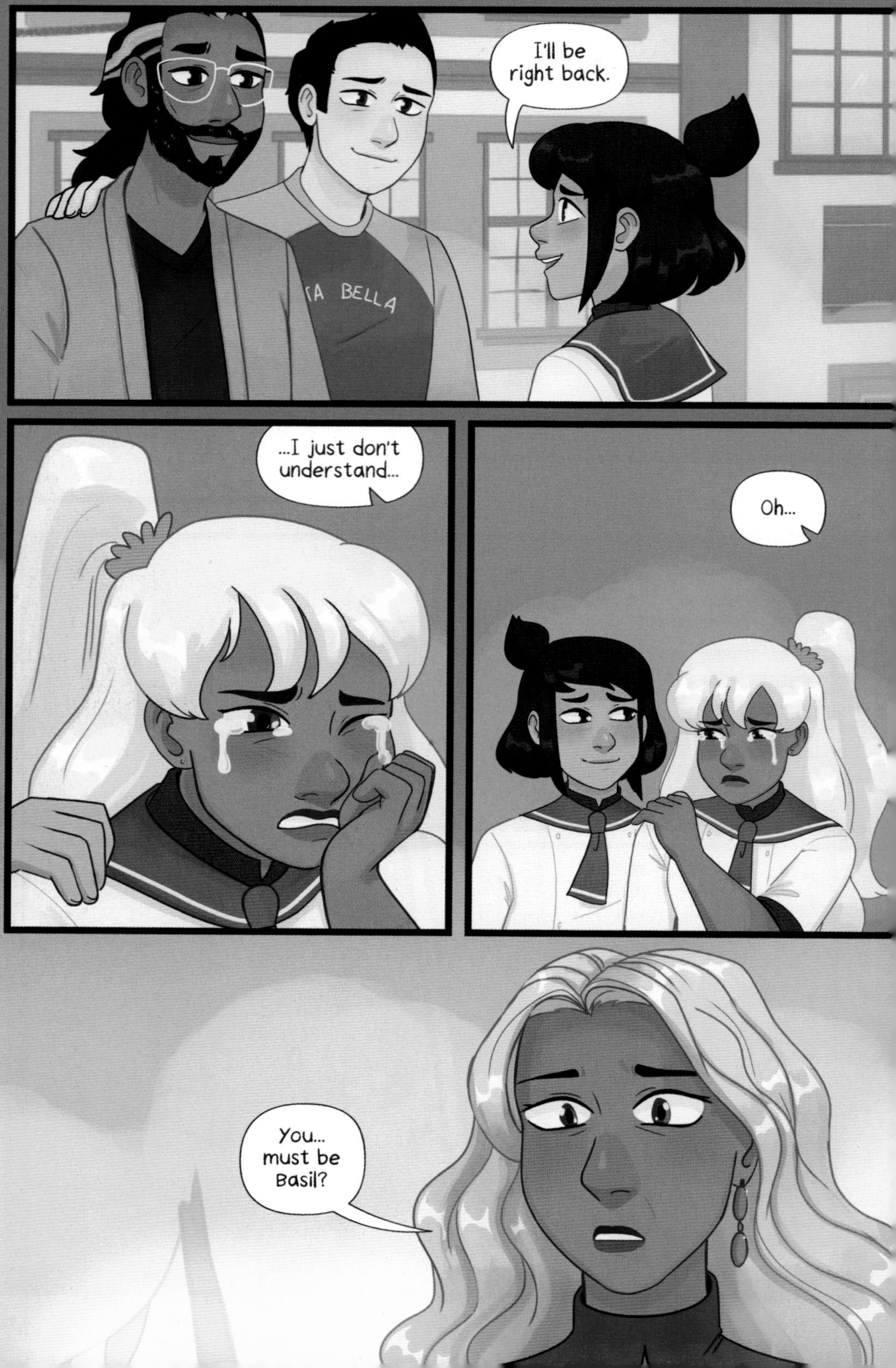
I'll be right back.
TA BELLA
...I just don't understand...
Oh...
You... must be Basil?

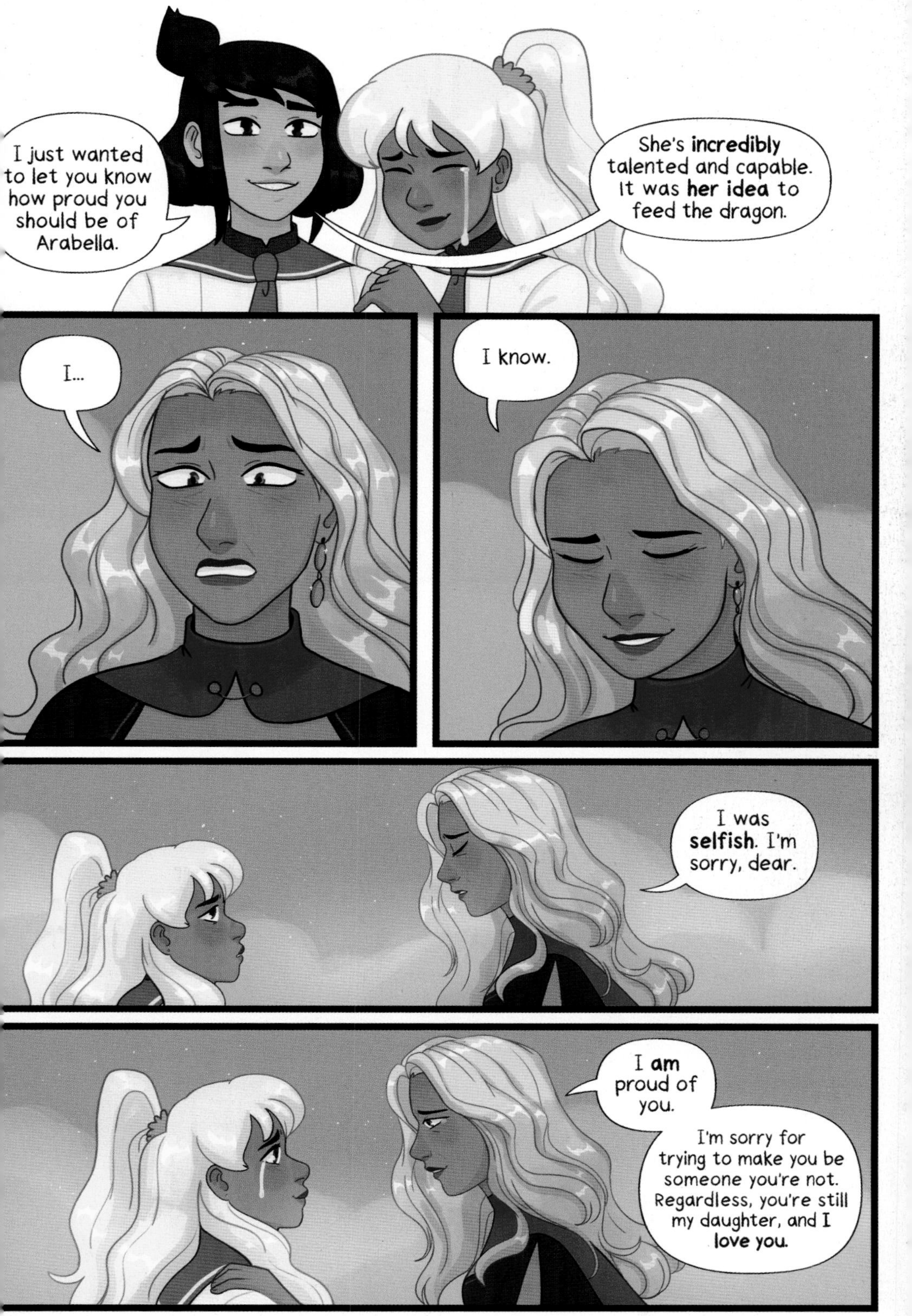
I just wanted to let you know how proud you should be of Arabella.
She's **incredibly** talented and capable. It was **her idea** to feed the dragon.
I...
I know.
I was **selfish**. I'm sorry, dear.
I **am** proud of you.
I'm sorry for trying to make you be someone you're not. Regardless, you're still my daughter, and I **love you.**

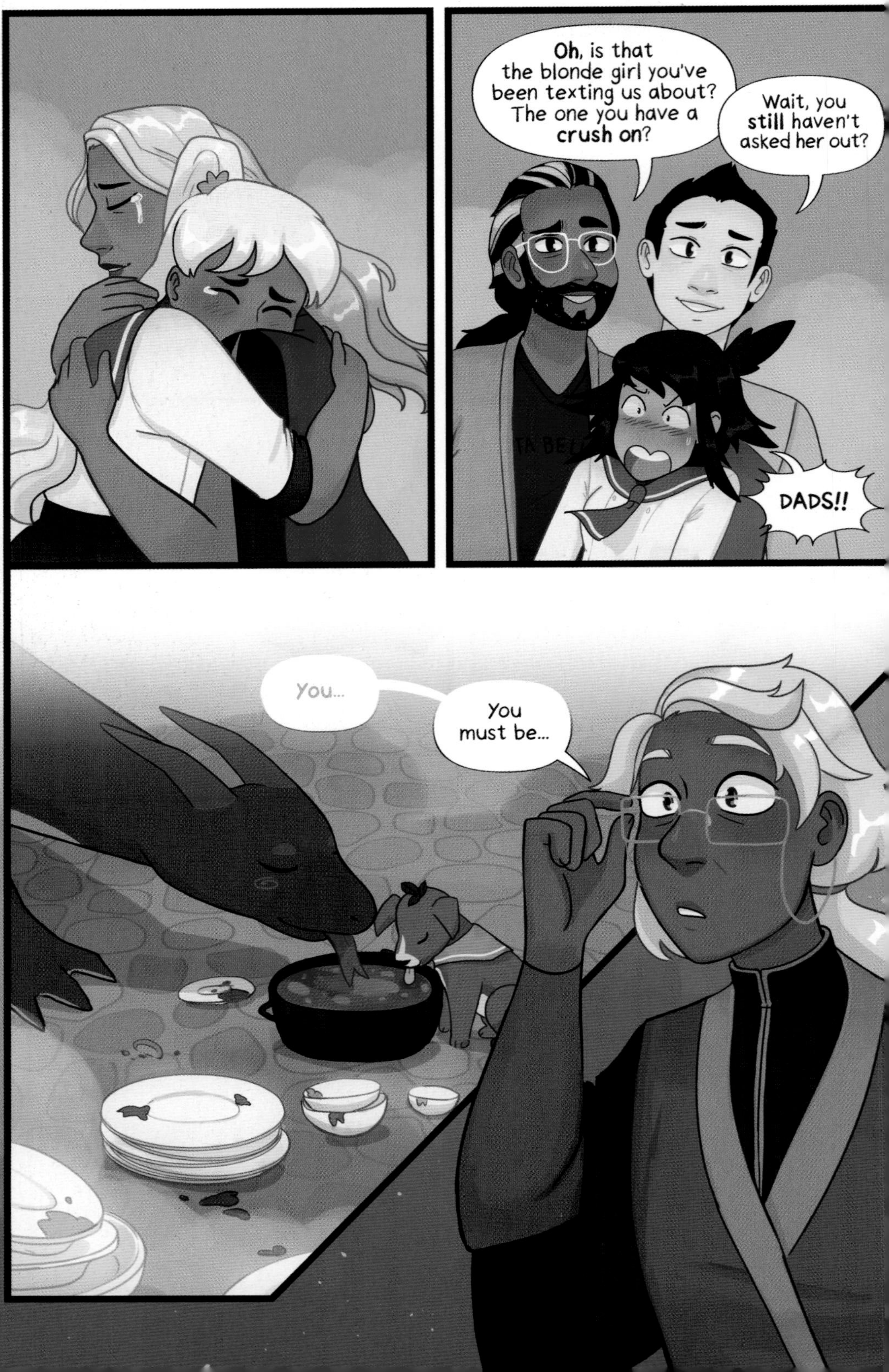
Oh, is that the blonde girl you've been texting us about? The one you have a crush on?
Wait, you still haven't asked her out?
DADS!!
You...
You must be...

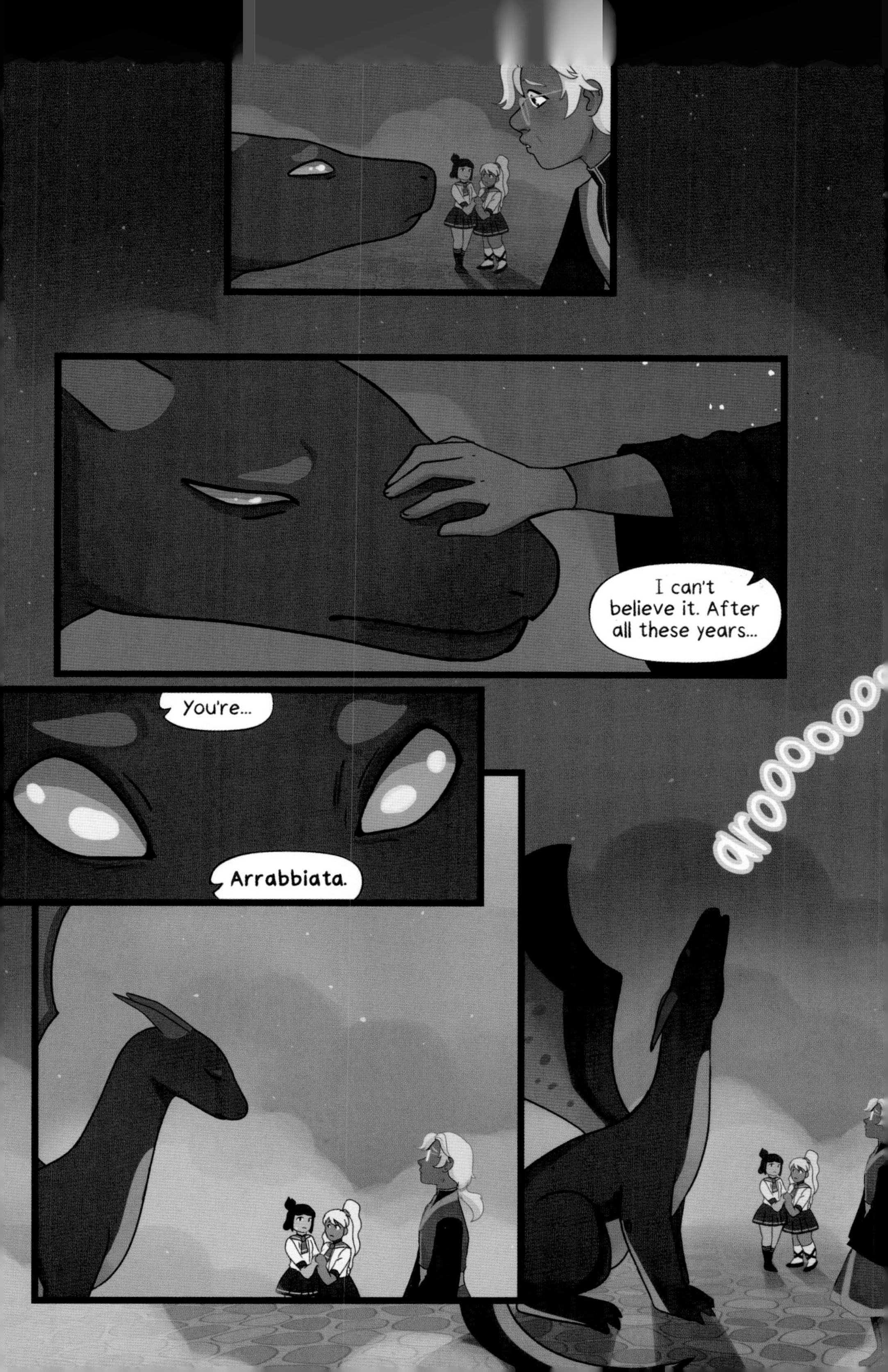
I can't believe it. After all these years...
You're...
Arrabbiata.
droooooo

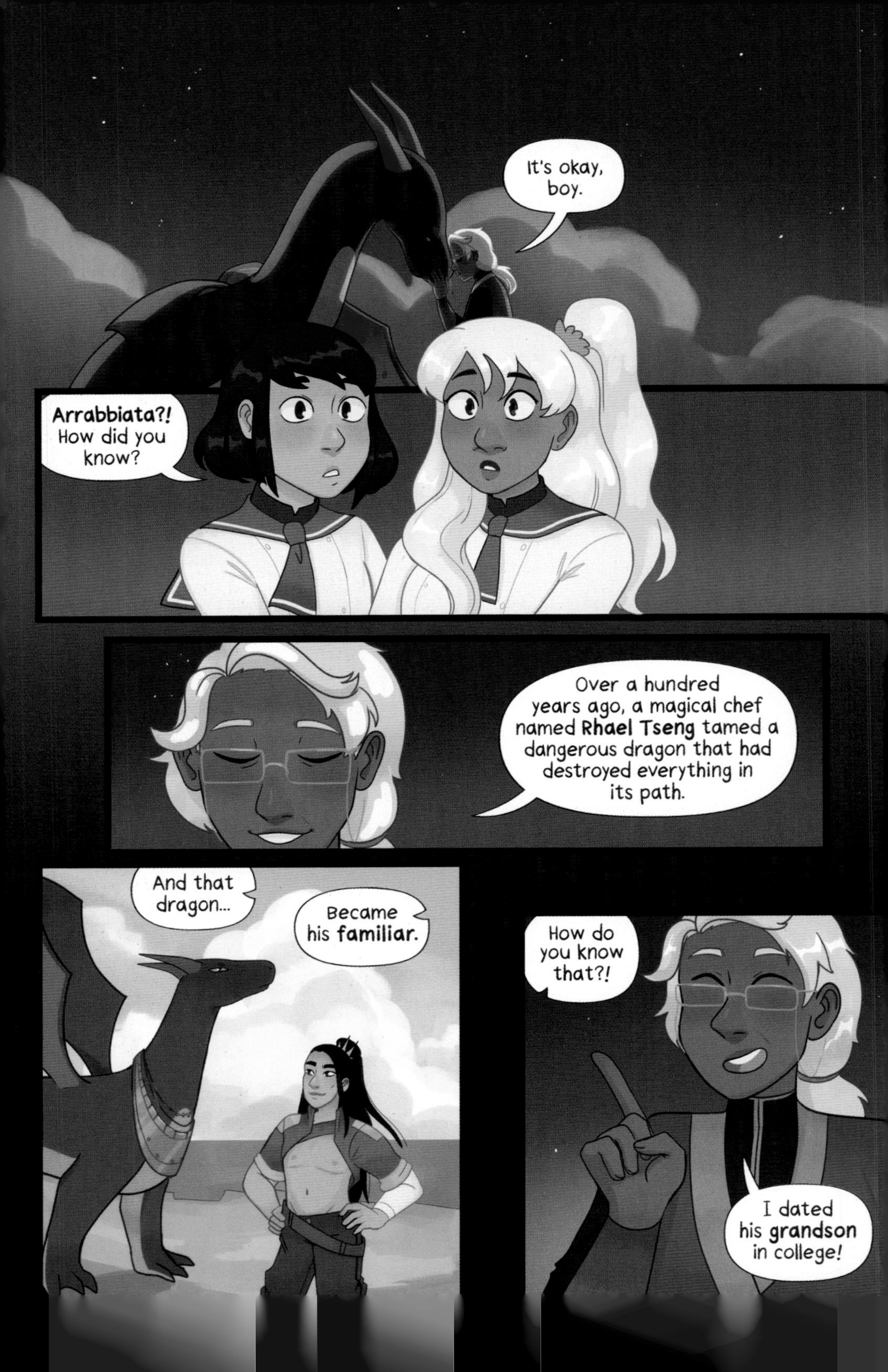
It's okay, boy.
Arrabbiata?! How did you know?
Over a hundred years ago, a magical chef named Rhael Tseng tamed a dangerous dragon that had destroyed everything in its path.
And that dragon...
Became his familiar.
How do you know that?!
I dated his grandson in college!

Unfortunately for dragons...
They always outlive their owners.
Poor thing.
You must have been so lonely and sad all those years.

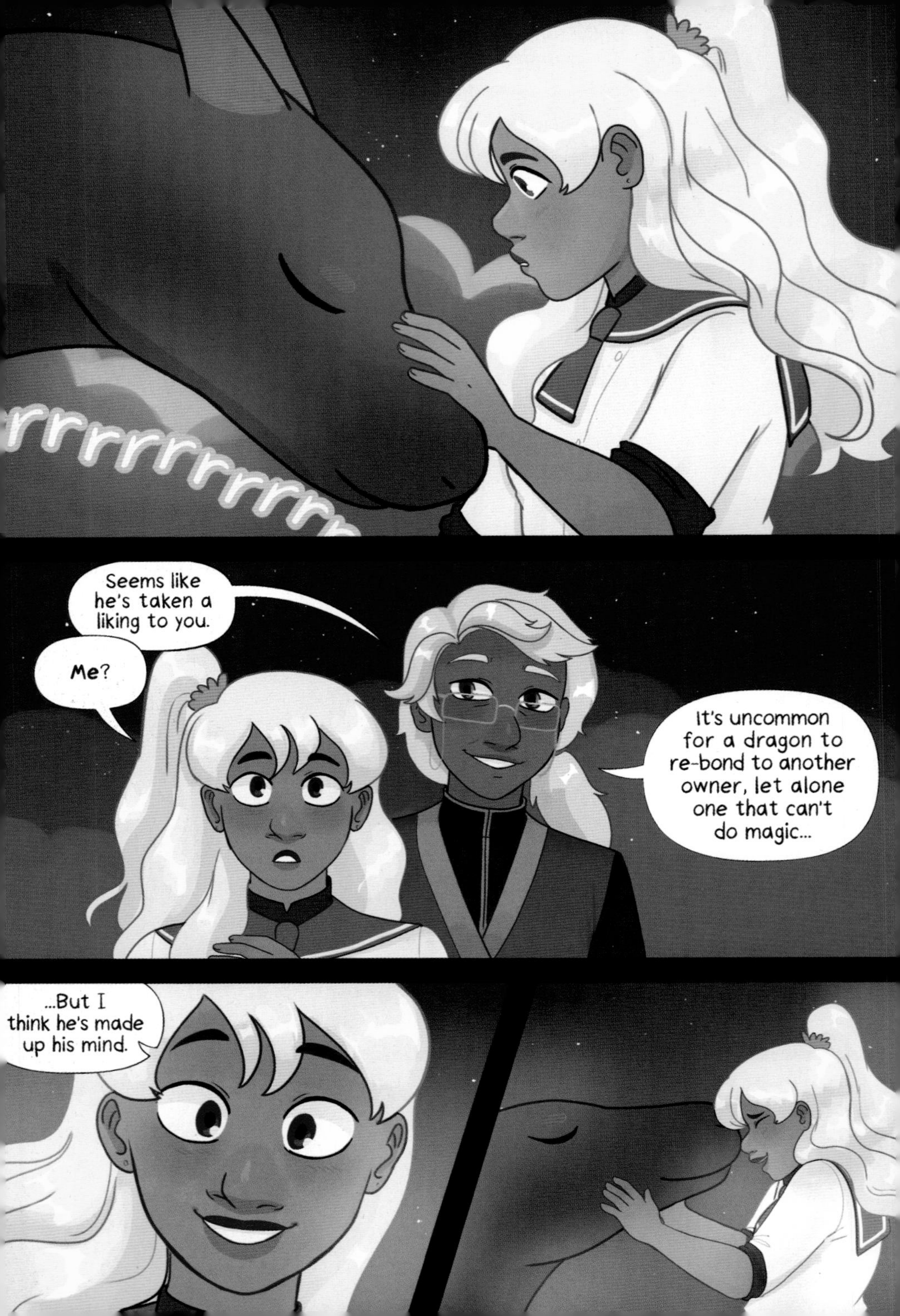
rrrrrrrrrrrrr
Seems like he's taken a liking to you.
Me?
It's uncommon for a dragon to re-bond to another owner, let alone one that can't do magic...
...But I think he's made up his mind.

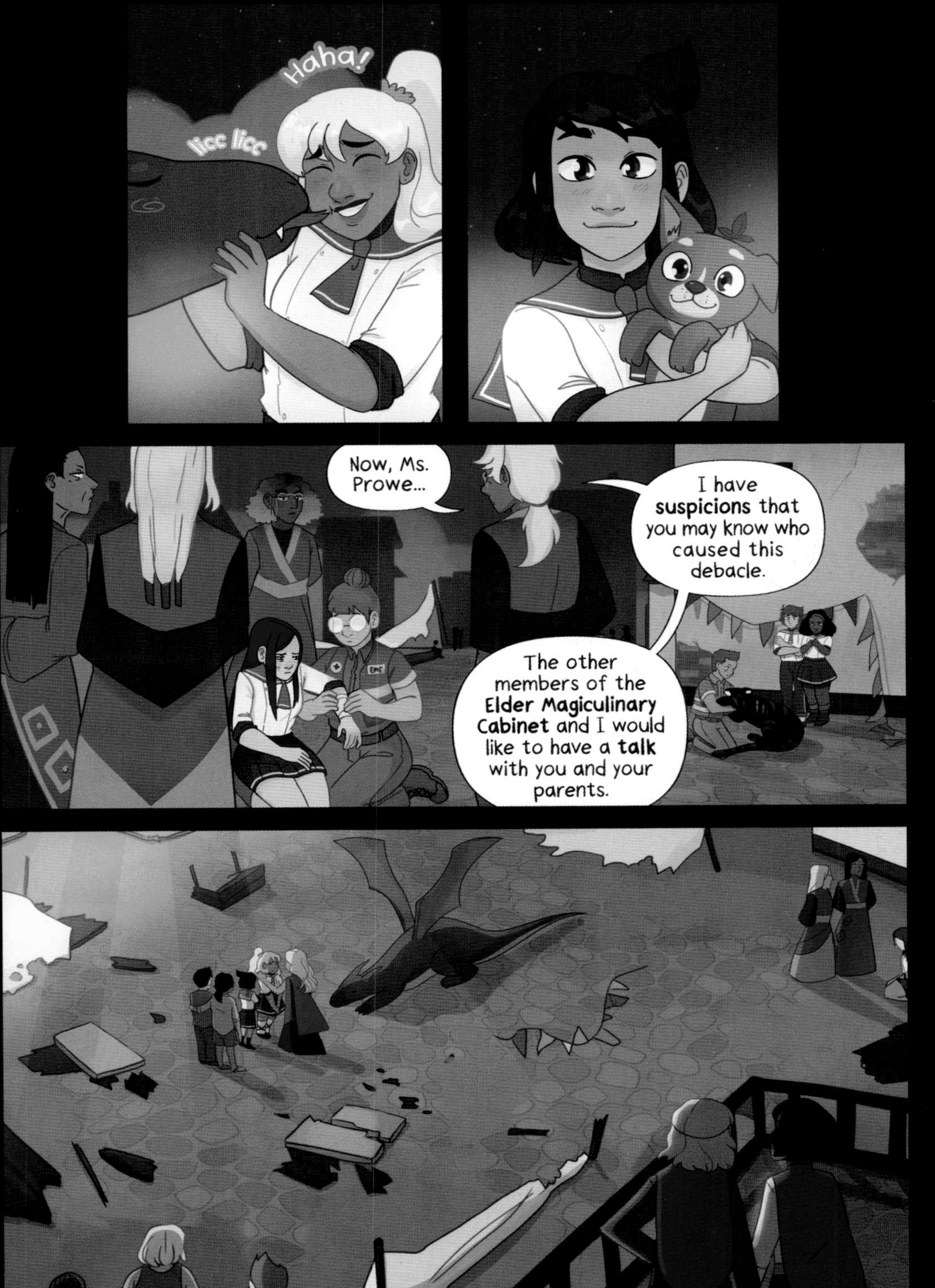

licc licc
Haha!
Now, Ms. Prowe...
I have **suspicions** that you may know who caused this debacle.
The other members of the **Elder Magiculinary Cabinet** and I would like to have a **talk** with you and your parents.

Chapter EIGHT

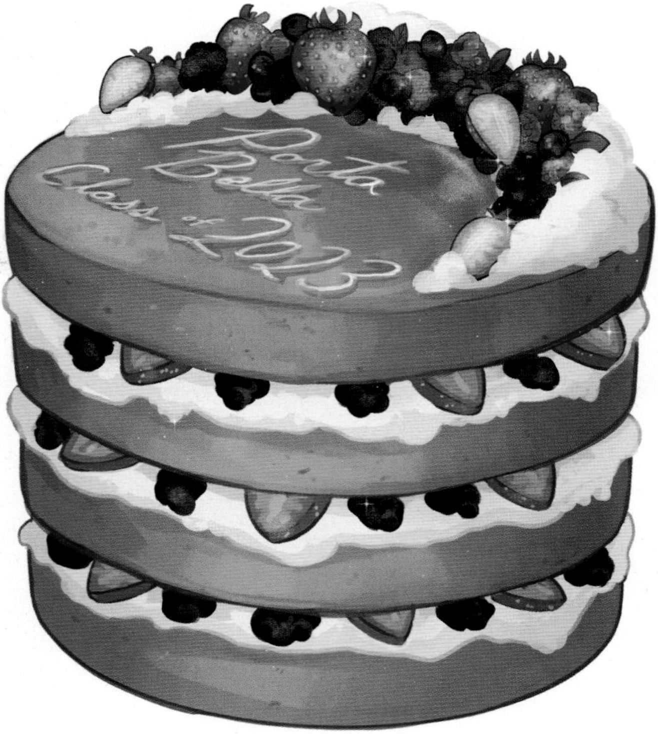
Ponta Bella
Class of 2023

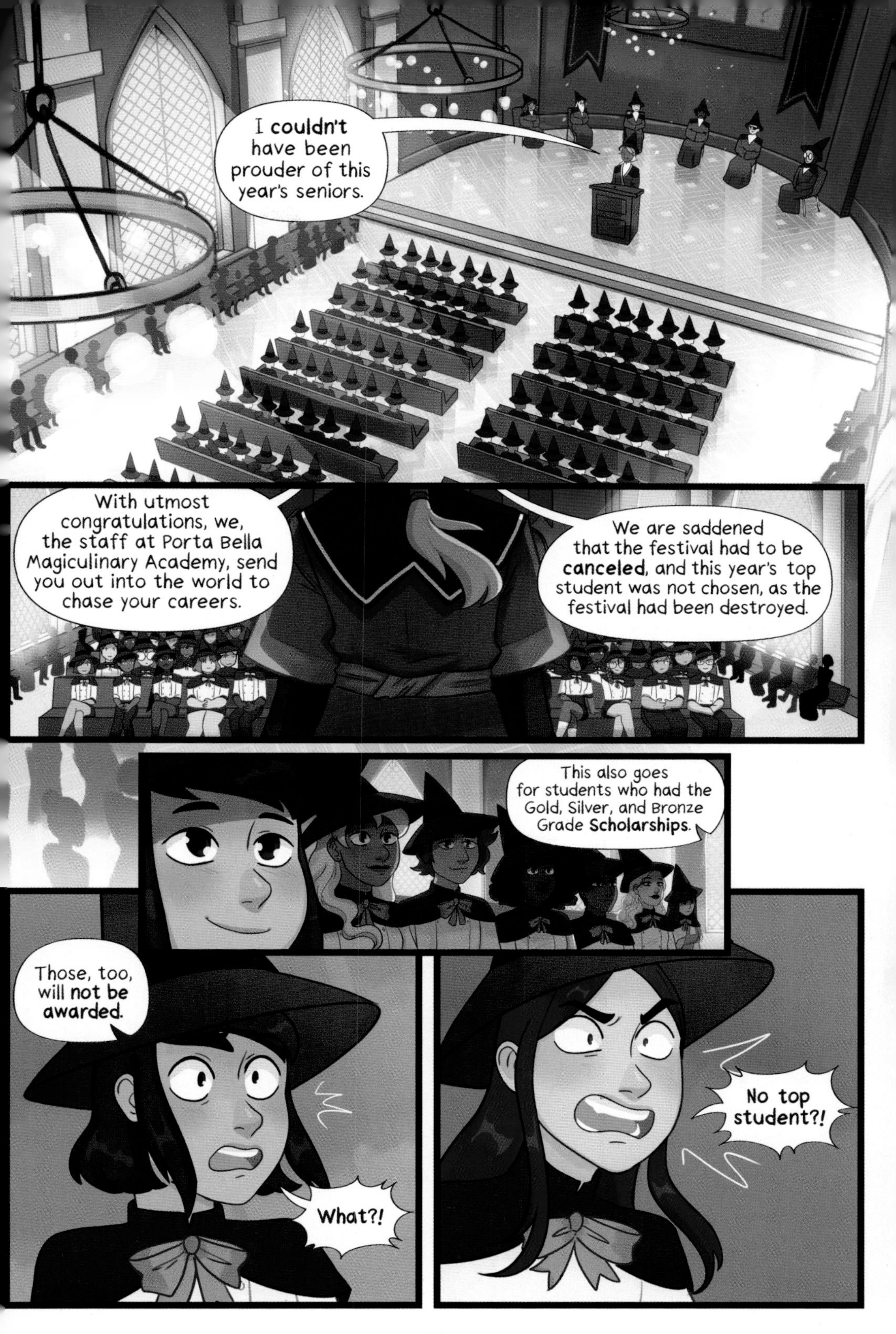

I **couldn't** have been prouder of this year's seniors.
With utmost congratulations, we, the staff at Porta Bella Magiculinary Academy, send you out into the world to chase your careers.
We are saddened that the festival had to be **canceled**, and this year's top student was not chosen, as the festival had been destroyed.
This also goes for students who had the Gold, Silver, and Bronze Grade **Scholarships**.
Those, too, will **not be awarded**.
What?!
No top student?!

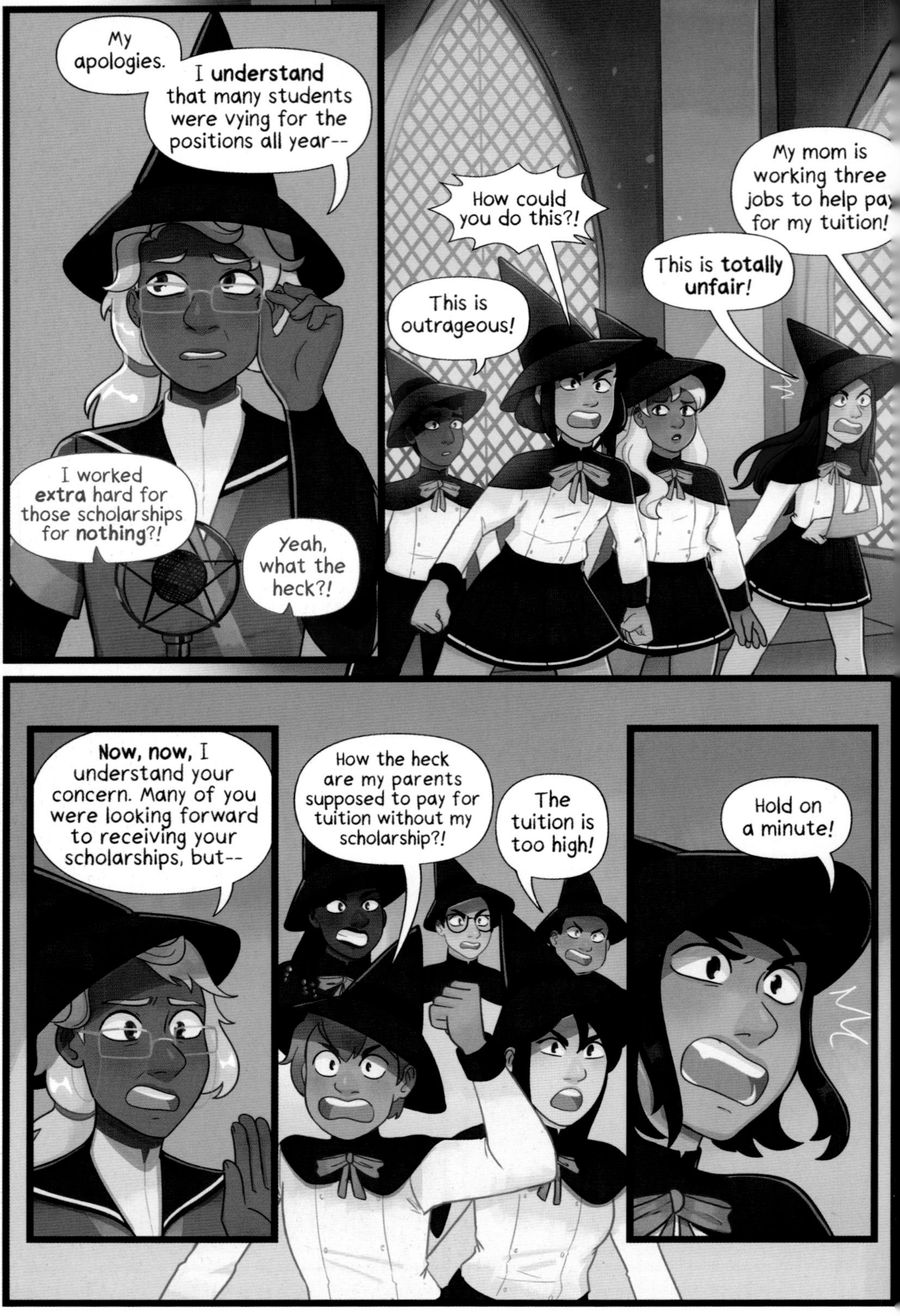

My apologies.
I understand that many students were vying for the positions all year--
I worked extra hard for those scholarships for nothing?!
Yeah, what the heck?!
This is outrageous!
How could you do this?!
This is totally unfair!
My mom is working three jobs to help pay for my tuition!
Now, now, I understand your concern. Many of you were looking forward to receiving your scholarships, but--
How the heck are my parents supposed to pay for tuition without my scholarship?!
The tuition is too high!
Hold on a minute!

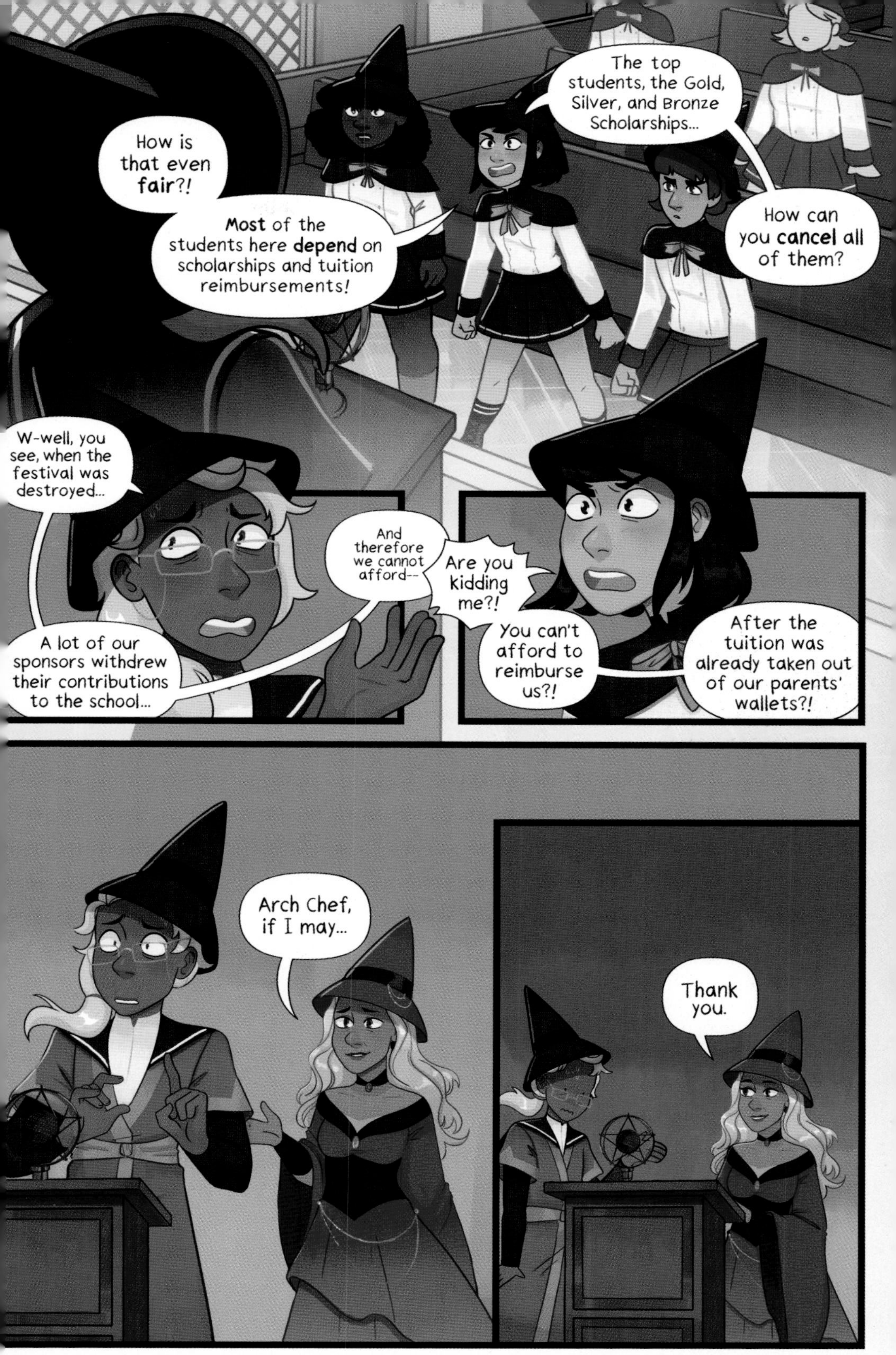
How is that even fair?!
Most of the students here depend on scholarships and tuition reimbursements!
The top students, the Gold, Silver, and Bronze Scholarships...
How can you cancel all of them?
W-well, you see, when the festival was destroyed...
A lot of our sponsors withdrew their contributions to the school...
And therefore we cannot afford--
Are you kidding me?!
You can't afford to reimburse us?!
After the tuition was already taken out of our parents' wallets?!
Arch Chef, if I may...
Thank you.

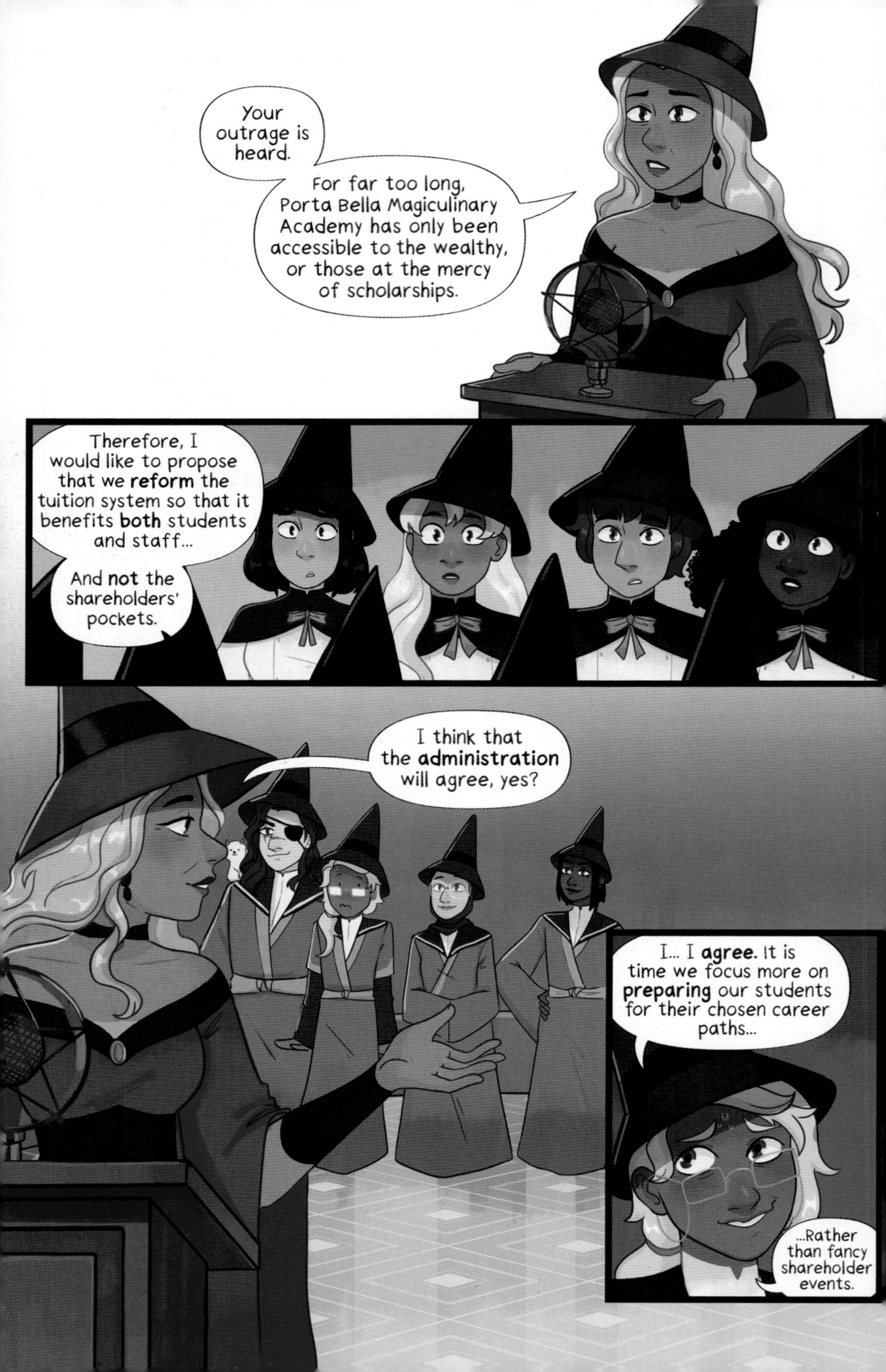
Your outrage is heard.
For far too long, Porta Bella Magiculinary Academy has only been accessible to the wealthy, or those at the mercy of scholarships.
Therefore, I would like to propose that we **reform** the tuition system so that it benefits **both** students and staff...
And **not** the shareholders' pockets.
I think that the **administration** will agree, yes?
I... I **agree.** It is time we focus more on **preparing** our students for their chosen career paths...
...Rather than fancy shareholder events.

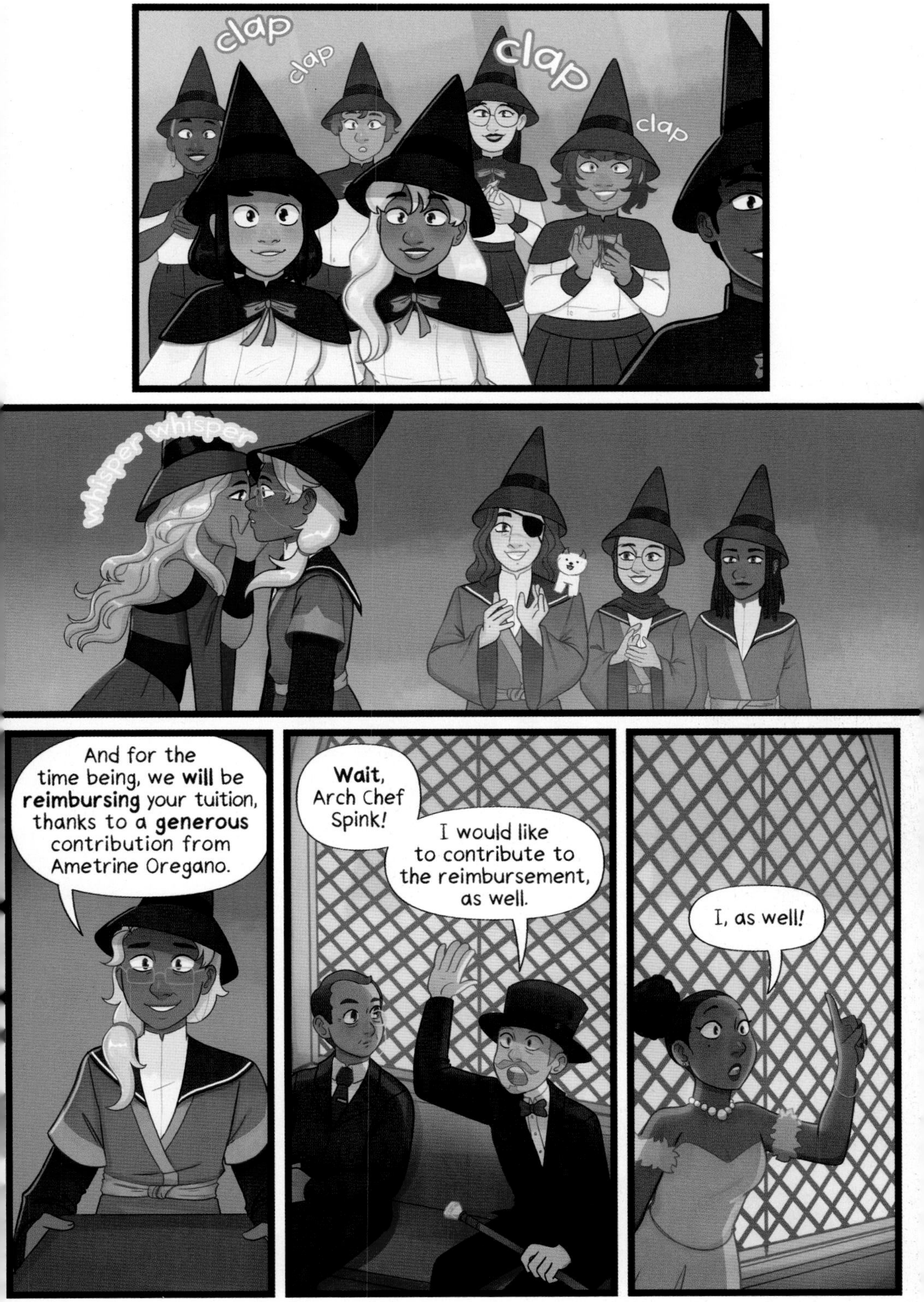
clap
clap
clap
clap
whisper whisper
And for the time being, we **will** be **reimbursing** your tuition, thanks to a **generous** contribution from Ametrine Oregano.
Wait, Arch Chef Spink!
I would like to contribute to the reimbursement, as well.
I, as well!

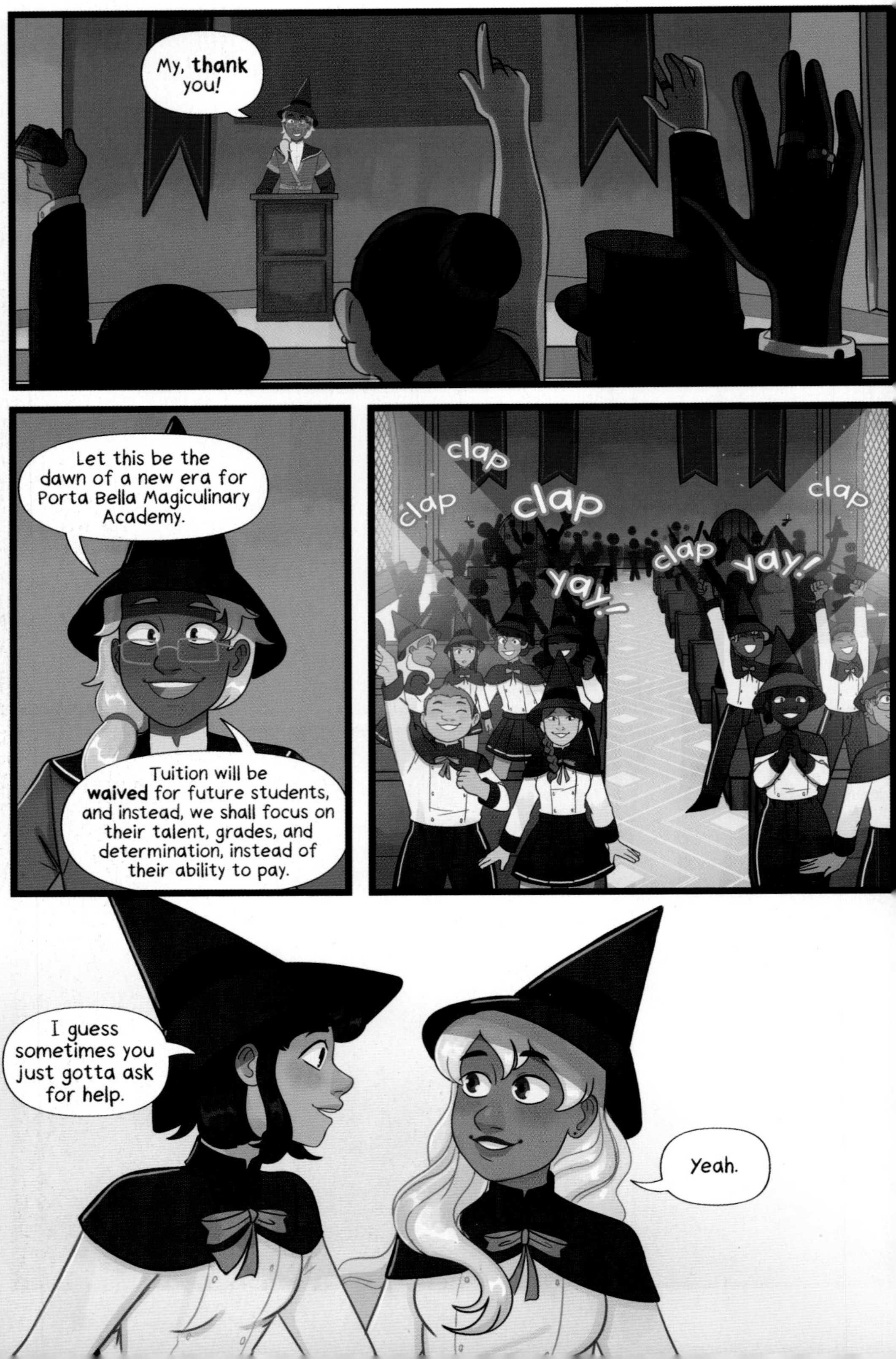

My, thank you!
Let this be the dawn of a new era for Porta Bella Magiculinary Academy.
Tuition will be waived for future students, and instead, we shall focus on their talent, grades, and determination, instead of their ability to pay.
clap
clap
clap
clap
clap
yay!
yay!
I guess sometimes you just gotta ask for help.
Yeah.

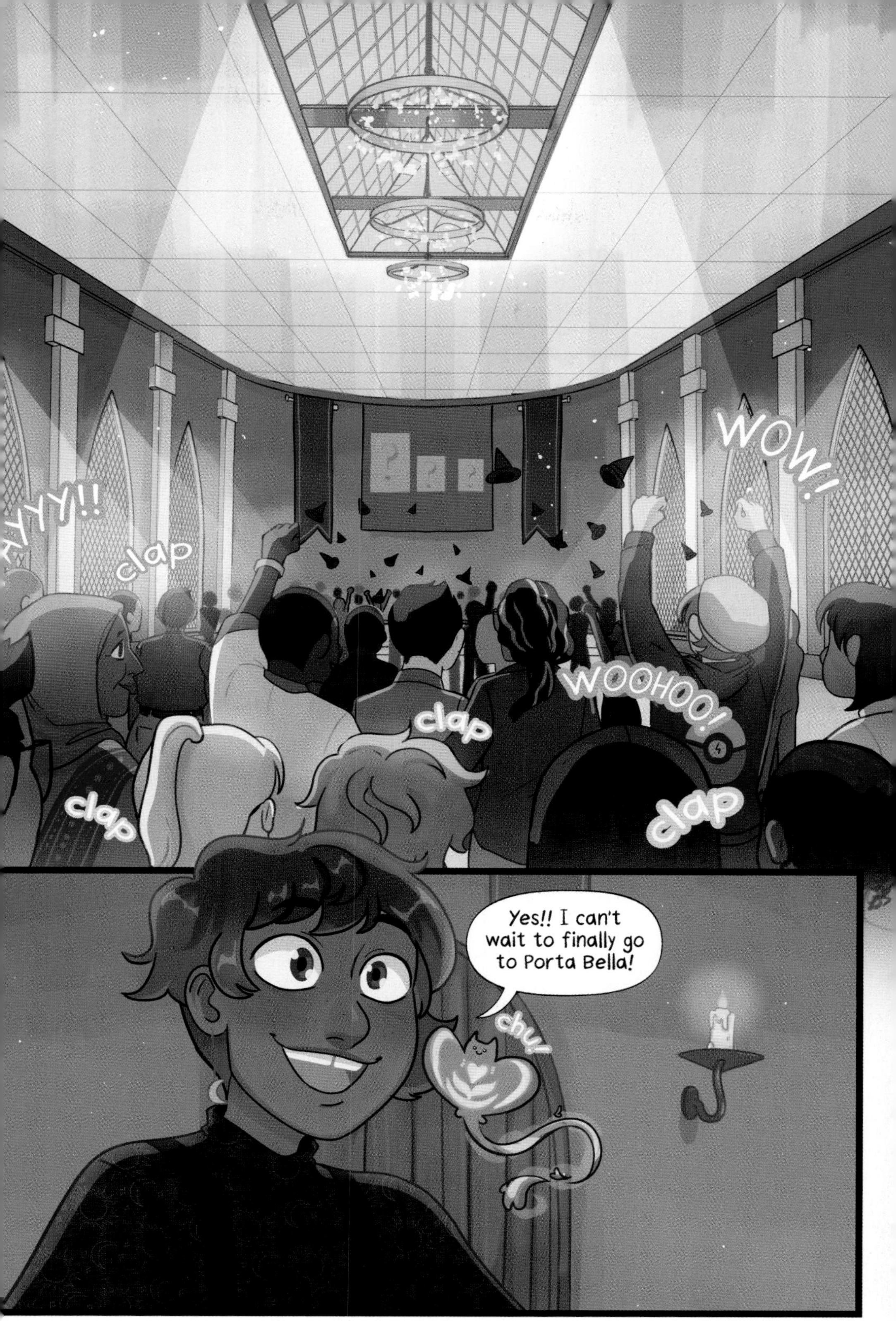
YYY!!
clap
WOW!
WOOHOO!
clap
clap
clap
Yes!! I can't wait to finally go to Porta Bella!
chu!

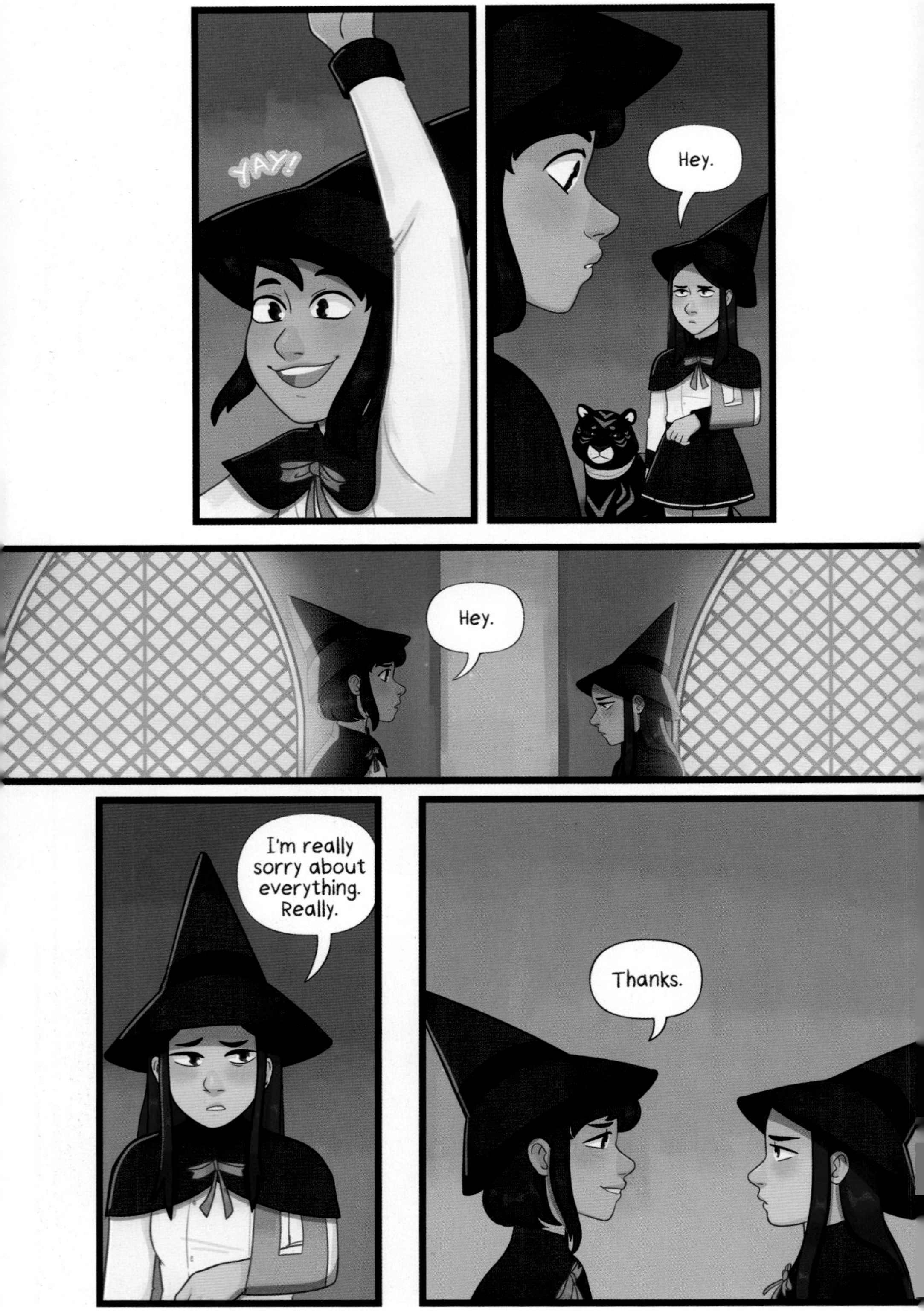
YAY!
Hey.
Hey.
I'm really sorry about everything. Really.
Thanks.

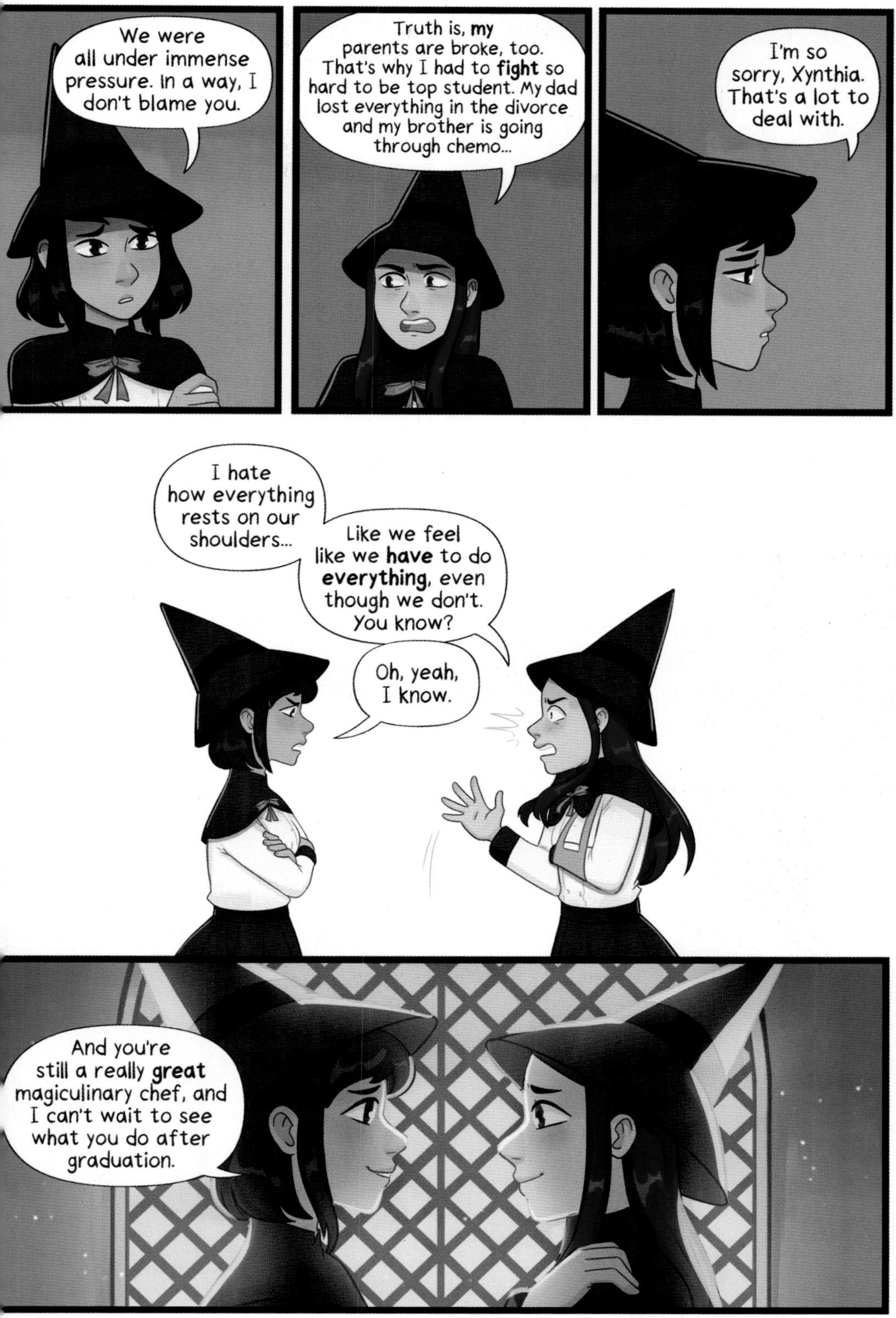
We were all under immense pressure. In a way, I don't blame you.
Truth is, **my** parents are broke, too. That's why I had to **fight** so hard to be top student. My dad lost everything in the divorce and my brother is going through chemo...
I'm so sorry, Xynthia. That's a lot to deal with.
I hate how everything rests on our shoulders...
Like we feel like we **have** to do **everything**, even though we don't. You know?
Oh, yeah, I know.
And you're still a really **great** magiculinary chef, and I can't wait to see what you do after graduation.

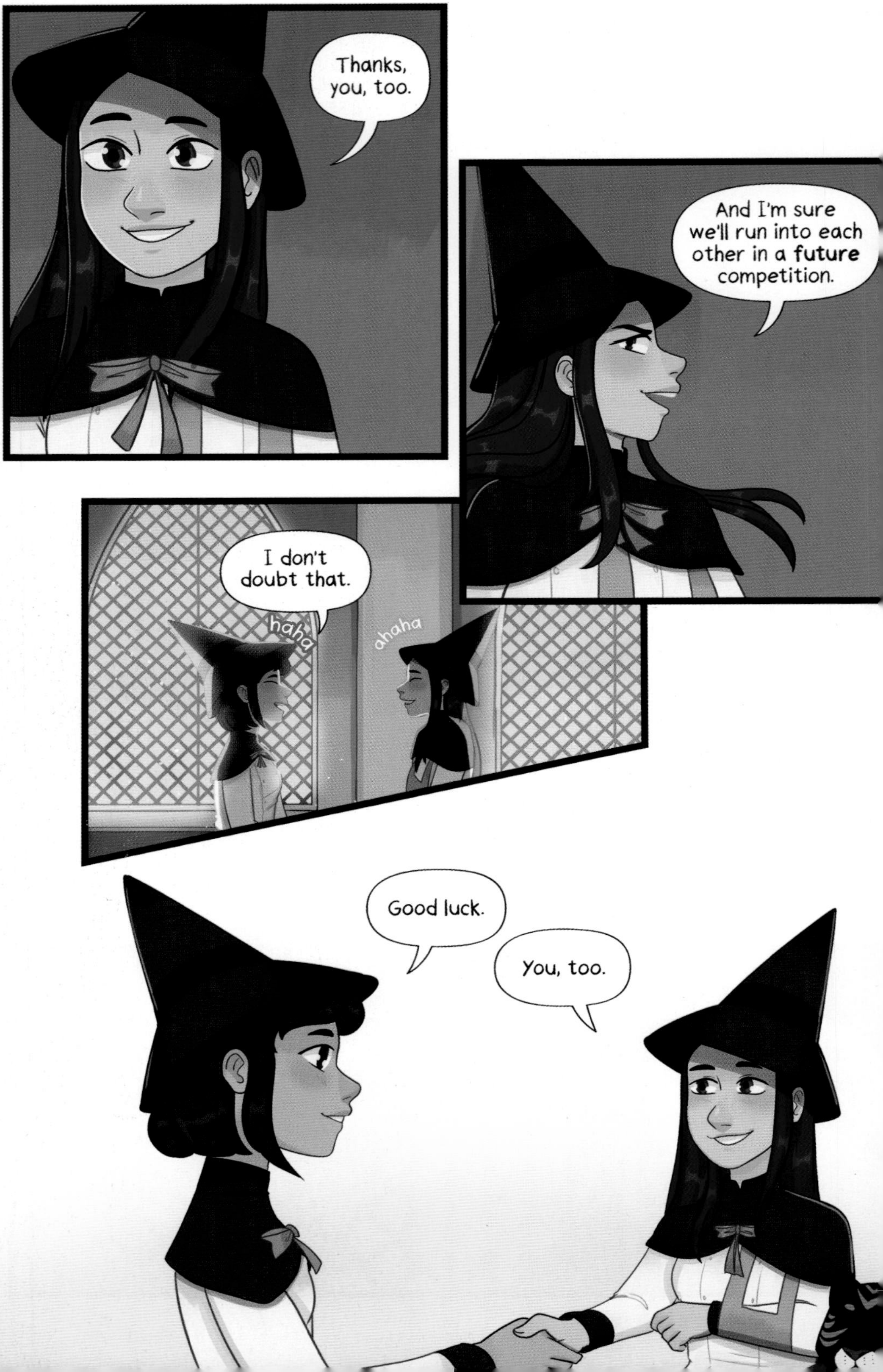
Thanks, you, too.
And I'm sure we'll run into each other in a **future** competition.
I don't doubt that.
haha
ahaha
Good luck.
You, too.

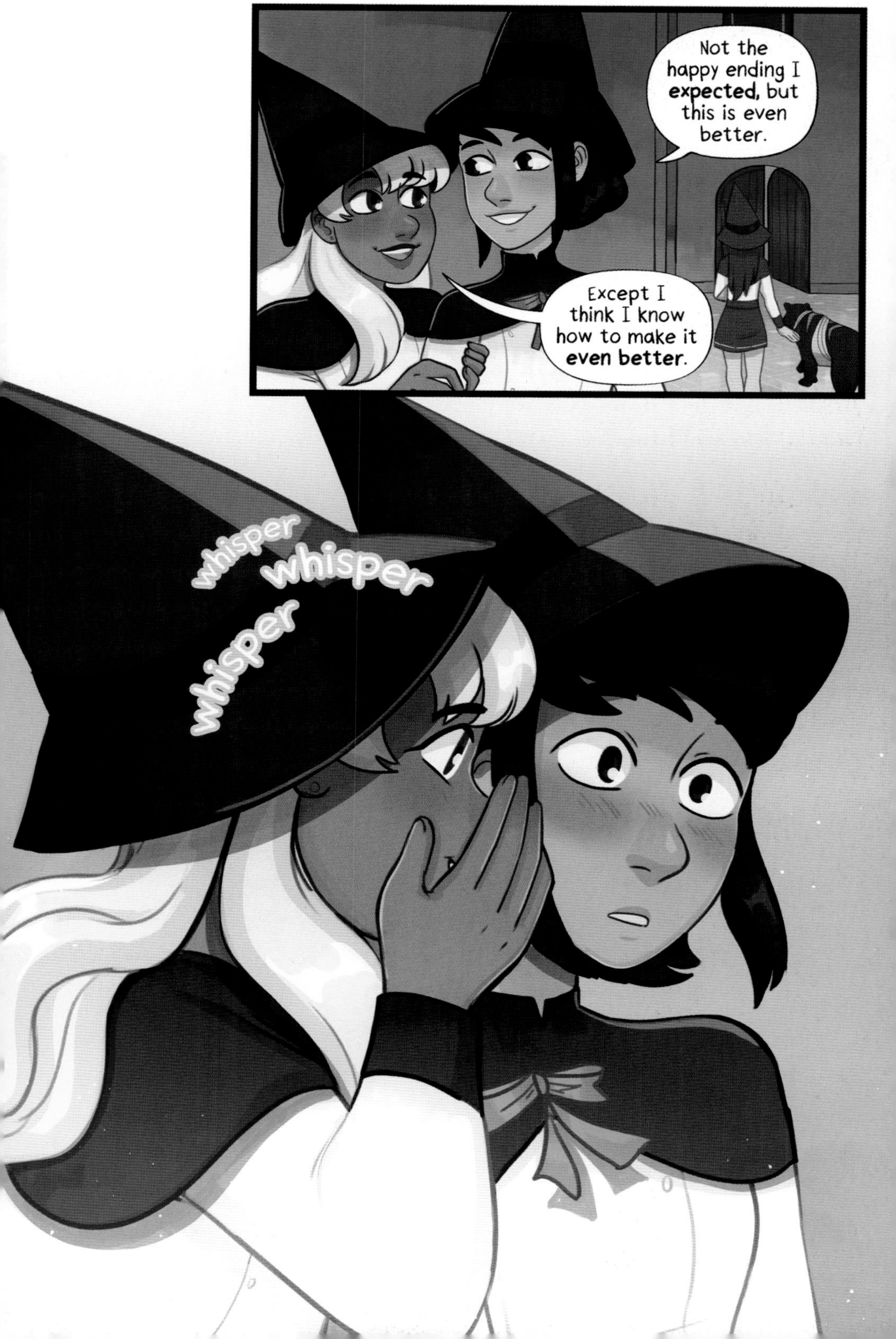

Not the happy ending I **expected,** but this is even better.
Except I think I know how to make it **even better**.
whisper whisper whisper

❧ EPILOGUE ❧

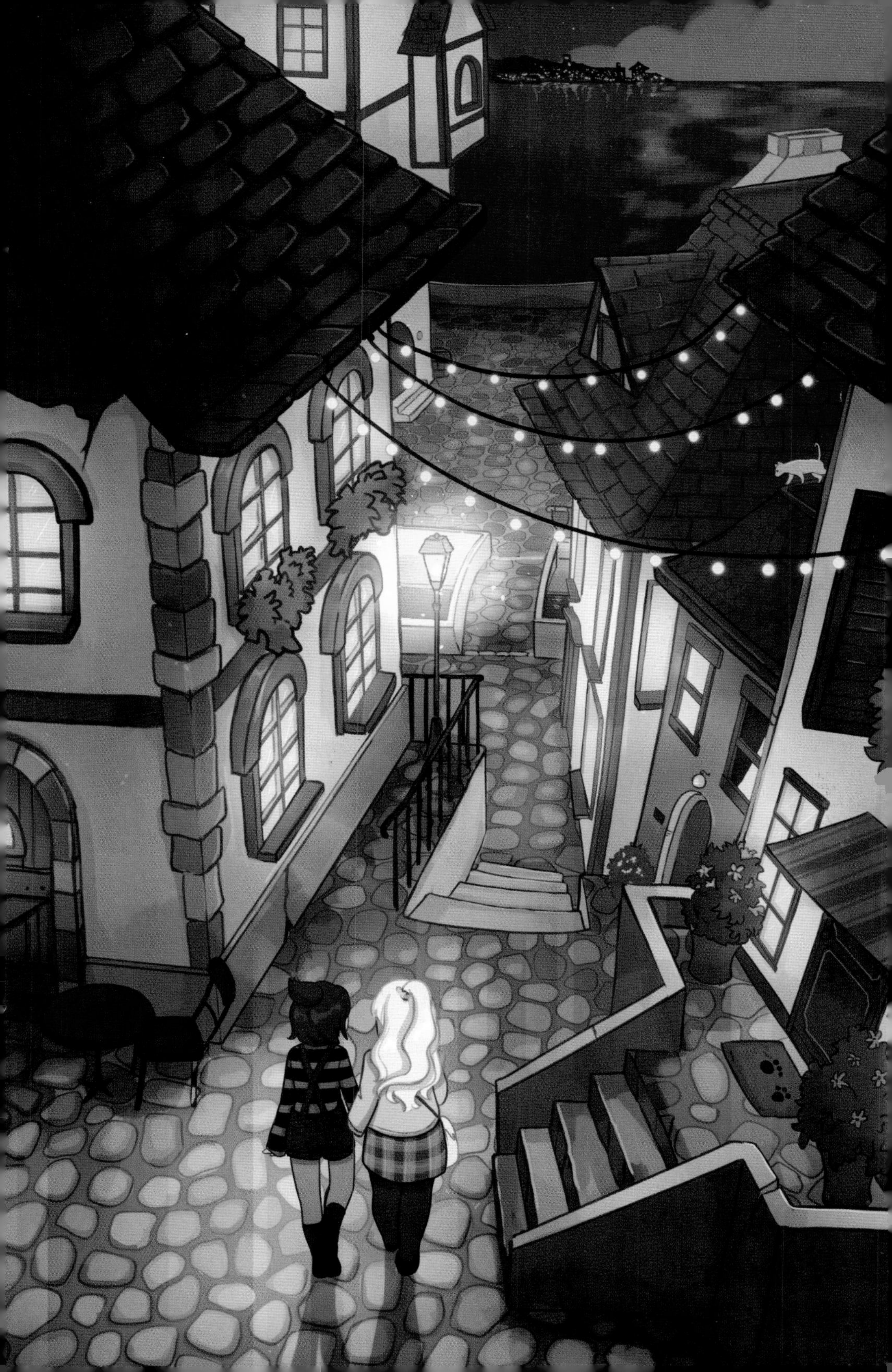

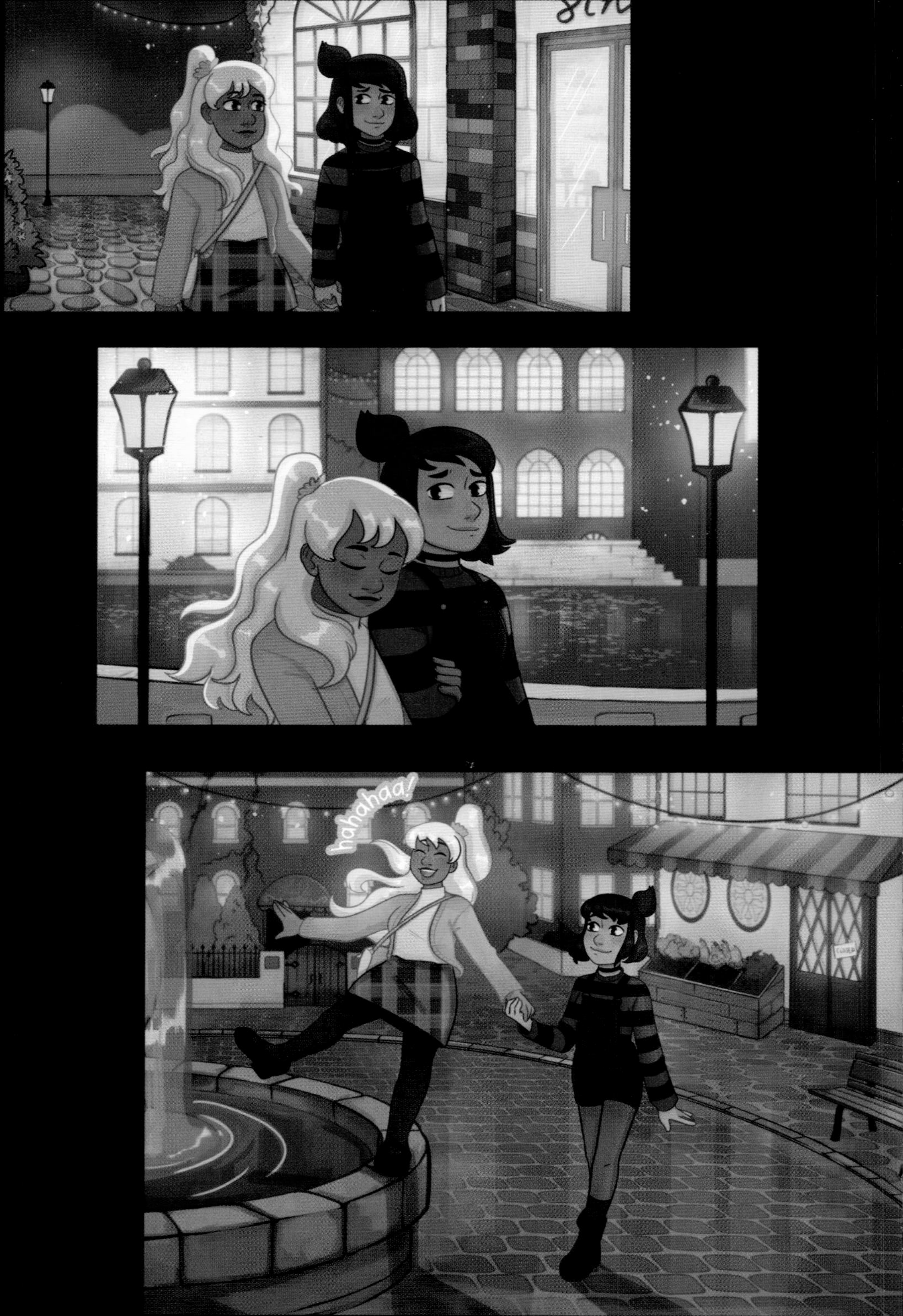
hahahaa!

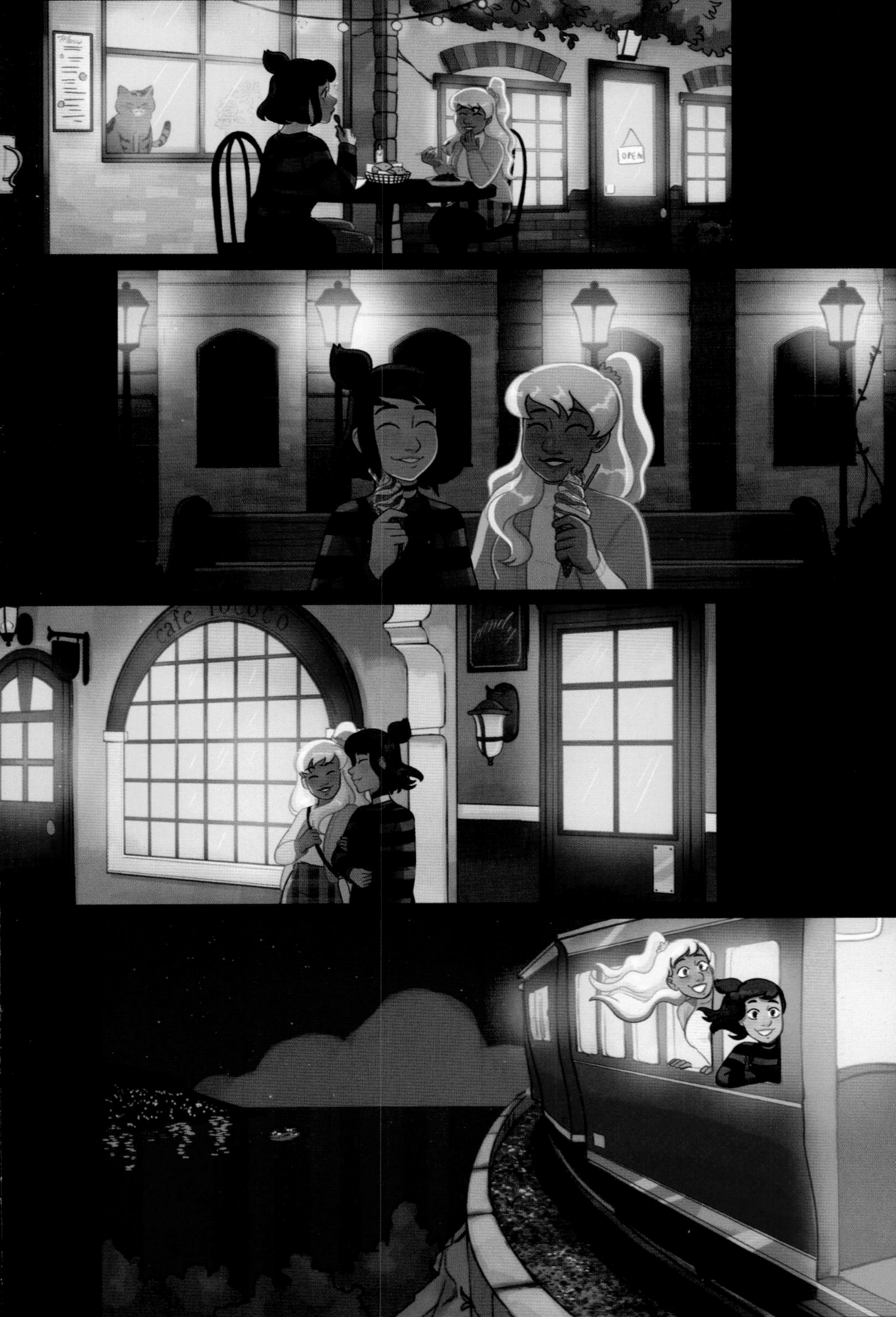
OPEN
cafe

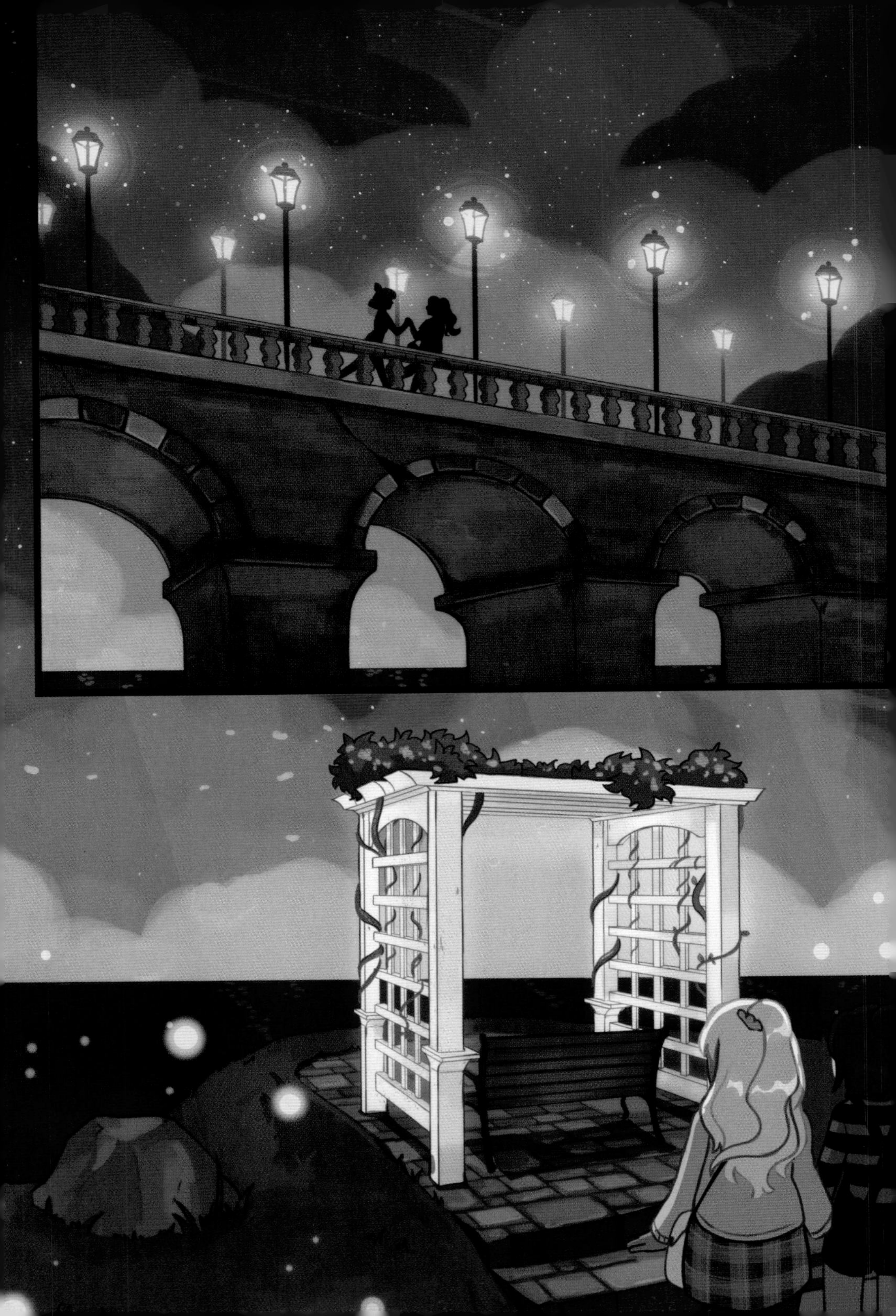

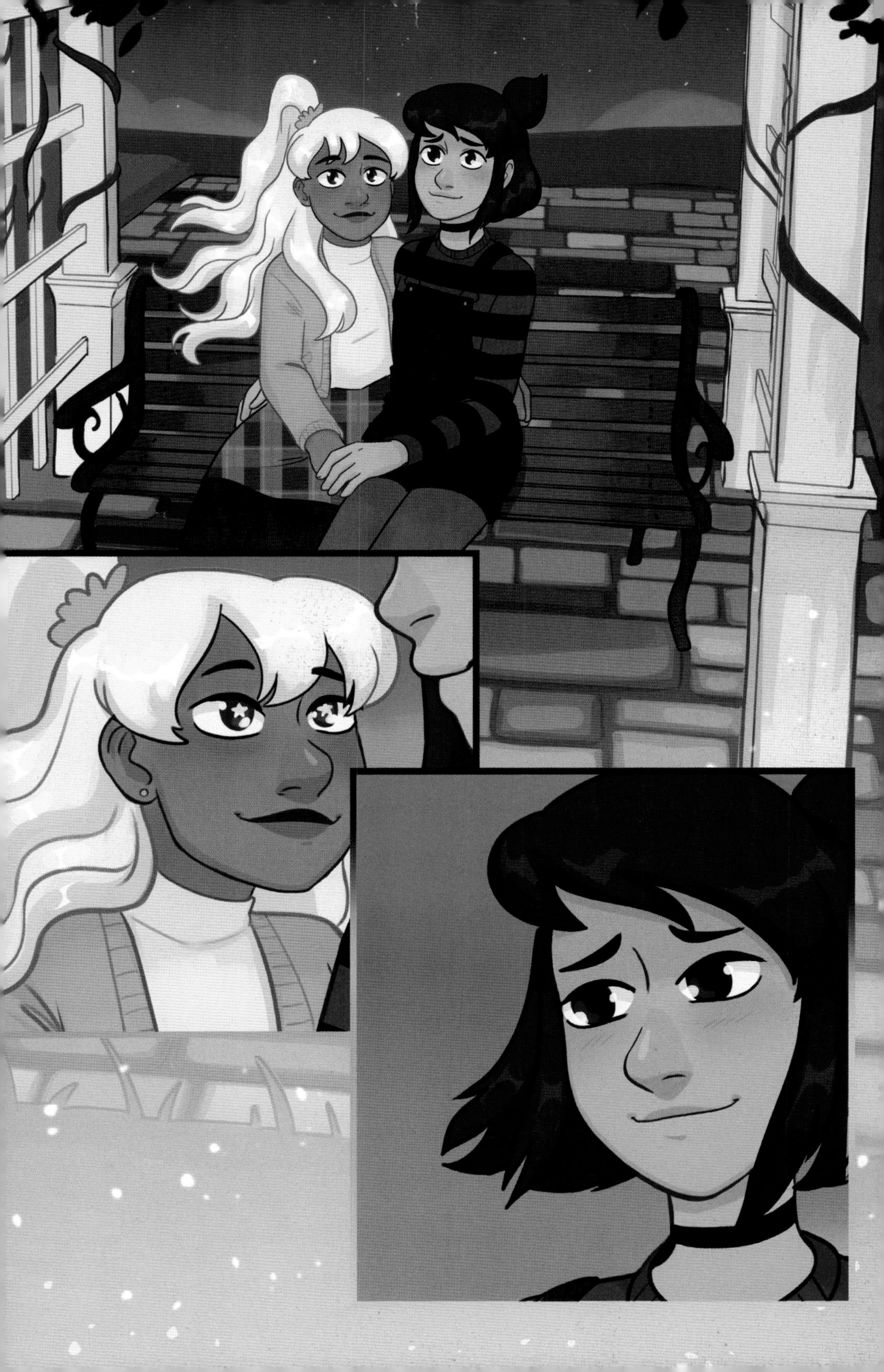

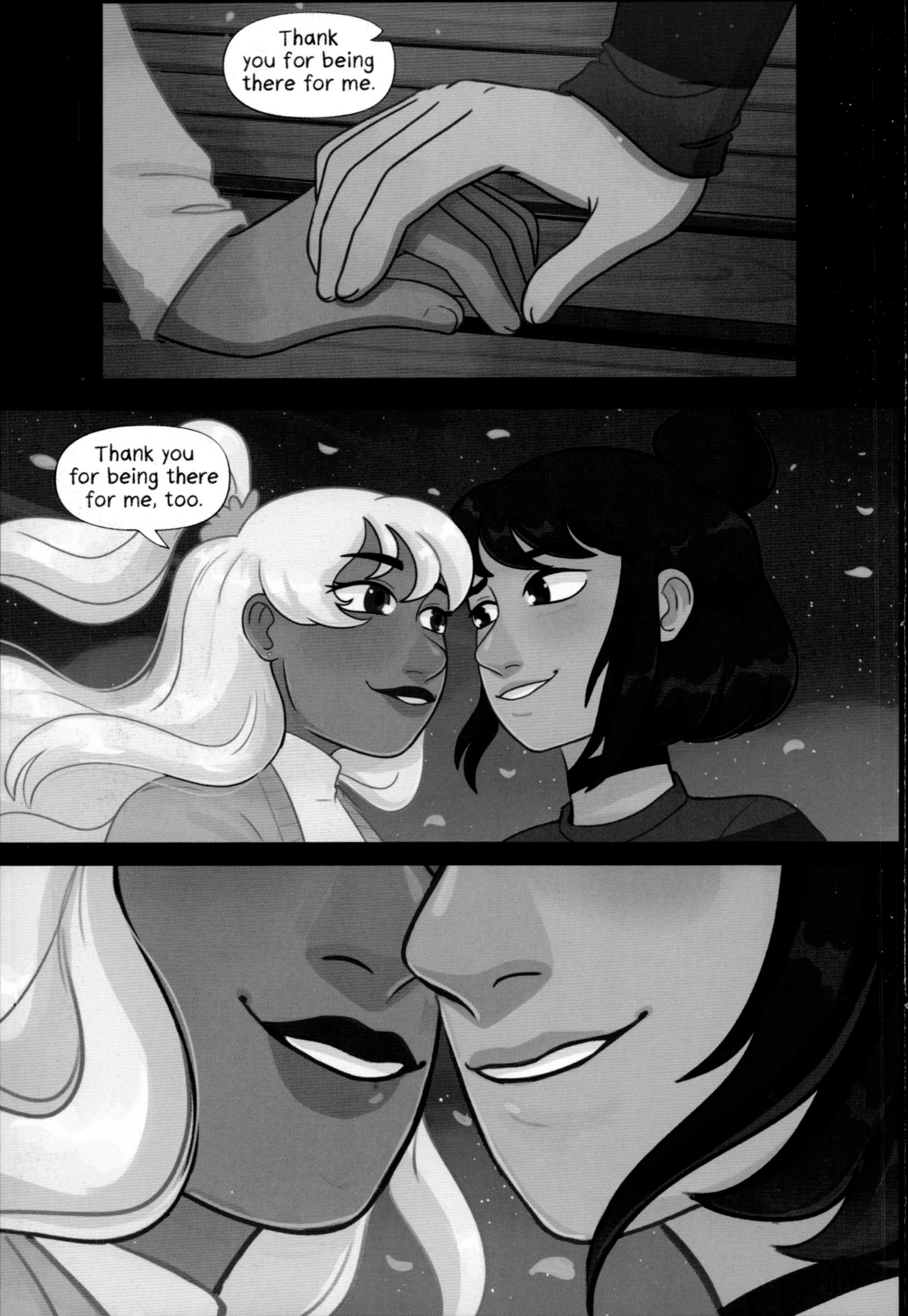
Thank you for being there for me.
Thank you for being there for me, too.